Praise for *Blueprints for Bu...*

"A hilarious, poignant achievement . . . Sch... bringing a vibrant, irresistible group of charac... ...ing *Blueprints* a positively addictive read."

—Meredith Maran, *People* (4 stars)

"Schappell is a diva of the encapsulating phrase, capable of conveying a Pandora's box of feeling in a single line. . . . Schappell's book crackles with the blunt, cynical humor wielded by people chronically on the defensive. Her women are caustic and witty, even in the face of sorrow."

—Jennifer B. McDonald, *The New York Times Book Review*

"What's best about these stories are the voices, electrifyingly alive, funny, and thrillingly honest. You know these women, right down to the way they like their coffee. Schappell is an effortless stylist, spinning prose so intimate, that you feel like these women are leaning over a table boldly telling you their deepest secrets. . . . Disarming, wickedly funny, and moving."

—Caroline Leavitt, *The Boston Globe*

"[A] raw and engaging collection . . . Schappell [creates] a bigger, more textured and complicated world than is usually found in collections. This, combined with the energy of the writing and the dark wit of these characters, will endear the book to Schappell's audience."

—*Publishers Weekly*

"Despite the talent for arch comedy that Schappell and her characters share, the tragic dimension of each story sears the heart."

—*Kirkus Reviews* (starred review)

"Schappell . . . creates wise, sexy, funny, and fathoms-deep tales of dire miscommunication."

—*Booklist*

"A memorable cast of female protagonists . . . with this seductive series of stories . . . Schappell agilely toggles between past events and the present day, providing an interesting dichotomy of how perspectives and attitudes shift with age, experience and parenthood. Taken altogether, an immediacy and intimacy are offered up in this generous collection."

—S. Kirk Walsh, *San Francisco Chronicle*

"The eight stories in Elissa Schappell's *Blueprints for Building Better Girls* connect in unexpected ways in exploring how contemporary women live."

—David L. Ulin, *Los Angeles Times*

"Schappell's sardonic, not-afraid-to-show-ugly voice quietly carries us along."

—*Elle*

"Incisive and bold . . . She writes with confidence about characters who dig deep and find confidence within—even if every choice is a double-edged sword. . . . The portraits are quietly realistic, funny and painful—and as rich as any characters in classical literature."

—Michelle Moriarty Witt, *The Charlotte Observer*

"Schappell's dark, funny, biting prose, gift for metaphor, and incredibly believable characters . . . ring with wit and truth. . . . Schappell evokes such masters as Lorrie Moore, Ann Beattie, and even Amy Hempel, with her mix of unbearable poignancy and wicked humor. . . . Her smart, flawed, strong, fascinating women are the stars of the show."

—Jill Owens, *The Oregonian*

"These are candid, deeply sardonic, very painfully funny stories that will remind some readers of the British satirist Helen Simpson, or a much darker, earlier version of Lorrie Moore."

—Juliet Waters, *Montreal Mirror*

"Winning . . . Schappell's complex, smart, brave, sad, and striving female characters . . . are much more than their labels. . . . vibrant and personal."

—Sarah Watson, PopMatters.com

"*Blueprints* is superior fiction, the work of a talented stylist with a cold eye. If there's any justice in the world, Ms. Schappell and her better girls will one day find a place among fiction's big boys."

—Emily Colette Wilkinson, *The Washington Times*

"The writing is vivid and often beautiful . . . a lot of the stories don't have a typical ending—they're more like snapshots of people's intimate, secret lives."

—*Rookie* magazine

"[*Blueprints for Building Better Girls* is] unsentimental, elegantly composed, and full of darkly funny one-liners and sucker-punch epiphanies that nail what it's like to swing back and forth between desire and regret, never able to relish the victory of snaring what you thought you wanted."

—*Whole Living*

"This is brave stuff. I learned things reading this book. Hilarious and heartbreaking at the very same time, these mothers, daughters, wives are all struggling to be honest with themselves—and we get the gift of Schappell being honest with us. These characters are poignant, searing, memorable."

—Elizabeth Strout, author of *Olive Kitteridge*

"Like many American women, Elissa Schappell's characters live in that zone where toughness and vulnerability overlap. In this remarkable, deeply engaging collection of stories, Schappell introduces us to a wide variety of female characters, from reckless teenagers to rueful middle-aged moms, and asks us to ponder the mystery of how those girls became these women."

—Tom Perrotta, author of *Little Children*

"Elissa Schappell writes earthquakes into existence—these stories will make you laugh until you're hoarse and sob, too, often within one perfectly rendered, unforgettable scene. Schappell reminds us that we don't have to look far afield for exotic, complex, hilarious and tragic stories—her rendering of women's inner lives is fresh and necessary. Her humor is the flashlight she shines into the deepest, darkest, truest aspects of her character's experiences."

—Karen Russell, author of *Swamplandia!*

"This is a wise, tough, and slyly funny book by a writer with a beautiful sense of detail and character. Schappell is a marvel when she gets in close with her people and brings them to moments of horrible, glorious revelation."

—Sam Lipsyte, author of *The Ask*

"Elissa Schappell's voice is so lively, smart, and honest—reading these stories is like sitting on a bench with a great friend and talking for hours about what's really going on; Schappell's such an incisive observer but she sees what she sees with big generosity and humor and warmth—what a pleasure to read these bursts of life!"

—Aimee Bender, author of *The Particular Sadness of Lemon Cake*

ALSO BY ELISSA SCHAPPELL

Use Me

Blueprints for Building Better Girls

Elissa Schappell

Simon & Schuster Paperbacks

New York   London   Toronto   Sydney   New Delhi

This book is for Connie Schappell and Andrea Deluca,
my adored mother and sister.

Simon & Schuster Paperbacks
A Division of Simon & Schuster, Inc.
1230 Avenue of the Americas
New York, NY 10020

"Elephant" originally appeared in *The Literarian*, The Center for Fiction's
online magazine.
"Monsters of the Deep" originally appeared in *Bomb*.
"Joy of Cooking" originally appeared in *One Story*.
"A Dog Story" originally appeared in *Anderbo*.
"Aren't You Dead Yet?" was adapted from a story that originally appeared in
the anthology *Lit Riffs* published by MTV Books, 2004.

First Simon & Schuster trade paperback edition July 2012

SIMON & SCHUSTER PAPERBACKS and colophon are registered
trademarks of Simon & Schuster, Inc.

For information about special discounts for bulk purchases,
please contact Simon & Schuster Special Sales at
1-866-506-1949 or business@simonandschuster.com.

The Simon & Schuster Speakers Bureau can bring authors
to your live event. For more information or to book an event,
contact the Simon & Schuster Speakers Bureau at
1-866-248-3049 or visit our website at www.simonspeakers.com.

Designed by Akasha Archer

Manufactured in the United States of America

10 9 8 7 6 5 4 3 2 1

The Library of Congress has cataloged the hardcover edition as follows:

Schappell, Elissa.
Blueprints for building better girls : fiction / Elissa Schappell.
p. cm
1. Girls—Fiction. 2. Young women—Fiction. 3. Women—Fiction. 4. United States—Social life and customs—20th century—Fiction. 5. Humorous fiction. I. Title.
PS3569.C474 B58 2011
813'.54—dc22
2011028068

ISBN 978-0-7432-7670-2
ISBN 978-0-7432-7671-9 (pbk)
ISBN 978-1-4516-0732-1 (ebook)

I will not become what I mean to you.

—BARBARA KRUGER

A lady never swears.

—LETITIA BALDRIDGE

CONTENTS

BLUEPRINTS FOR BUILDING BETTER GIRLS

Monsters of the Deep

I love you," Ross says.

I laugh, "You don't even know me," and he looks startled, like I've just exploded something in his face. He sinks back against the pillows, confused, like maybe he read the manual wrong. Aren't all girls supposed to want to hear this?

"I do so. I know you really well," Ross says, running his finger across the rainbow I've drawn arching over my hip bone, and down between my legs, hesitant but so eager it's pathetic, like even now, after all these months, he's worried that I'm going to stop him. I'm not going to stop him. If I stopped him, we'd have to talk. The last thing I want to do is talk.

"Hey." I pull away. "Why don't you put on the TV? *Monsters of the Deep* is about to start."

"But I'm so comfortable," he groans, but we both know he's so happy to be getting laid he'll do anything to keep me here. I could probably do the crossword puzzle, or knit while we're doing it. I'm sure I'm his first. Up until last year his mom was still making up his bed with *Star Wars* sheets. Luke Skywalker facing the Death Star with a giant lightsaber in hand, and a freakishly stacked Princess Leia, on her knees at his feet. *Lay-ya*. An adolescent nerd's wet dream.

"You're killing me," he says as his hand creeps toward my breast. I elbow it away.

"Dream on, mister."

"C'mon. This is so nice. Don't make me get out of bed now, Heather Feather," he says, knowing how much I hate nicknames. The fake casual way he drops them into conversation, to try them out, each one awkward and wrong in its own way (Heatherly because it sounds like *heavenly*), it's humiliating for both of us, even if he doesn't see it. For instance, last week, on our way home from the pool we stopped at the McDonald's drive-thru, and he slipped in, "What can I get you, *Lady Blue*? You wanna Filet-O-Fish or a 7-Up?" like it just came to him. He was proud of that, what a clever inside joke. Ha. Ha. Ha. You see, I like to have shows about the ocean on during sex, and I want to be a marine biologist when I'm older. I don't know why he's so desperate to name me.

I already have a nickname and he knows it.

I nudge Ross toward the edge of the bed with my hip. "I mean it. Turn on the idiot box. It's about to come on."

"Yeah, yeah, I get it," he grumbles. "I hope you're happy." He reaches over the side to find his underwear, then pulls them back on under the sheets. He's modest. Even after all this time, he can't walk the ten feet to the dresser with his bare butt hanging out. I avert my eyes because the sight of his boner is ridiculous trapped and straining against the cotton like it's trying to escape. I don't want to laugh.

Ross would never believe me if I told him I liked him best naked. It's funny how we're almost always naked, or half naked, together. It's easier, less complicated. Take away Ross's newly dry-cleaned varsity jacket, his white alligator shirt and pressed khaki shorts (that have been taken in and let out and taken in again), take away the Stevie Nicks–style gauzy blue halter dress I found at the Salvation Army, much to my mother's horror, and too-expensive white Bernardo leather sandals she insisted on buying me to counteract the dress (and which I've purposefully scuffed to hell), and we're just two sixteen-year-old Caucasian kids hanging out in your typical American boy habitat circa 1978. His bedroom is on the bottom floor, off the den. There are sliding glass doors, which make it easy for me to slip in and out, as I choose. The floor-length curtains, dark blue, are pulled shut for privacy. The walls papered with your typical boy posters—Farrah, Dr. J, the Boss, and a centerfold of a black metallic Corvette Sting Ray painstakingly extracted from some jerk-off magazine for gearheads. On the shag carpet are continually mounting piles of dirty clothes, T-shirts and jeans stiffening into various stages of laundry rigor mortis; the tube socks really appear to have suffered. Hanging over his dresser are two wrestling medals (neither gold) and in front of the mirror an arsenal of aftershaves. What woman could defend herself against Brut, English Leather, or Hai Karate?

Ross fidgets in front of the dresser, flipping through the channels so fast he passes our station twice. "Sonofabitch," he says, pounding the top of the TV. I know that I-love-you thing is bothering him. It could have been worse. I could have responded, "Don't say 'I love you' when you mean 'Thank you,'" which is what I said the first time.

"You know it's gonna be a rerun now." He looks at me over his shoulder. "You'll see."

"I don't care," I say, leaning back onto the pillows so the sheet falls away, pooling around my waist. I shake the clip out of my hair so it falls to my shoulders, almost covering my tits. On the top of my hand I've drawn a big smiley face; underneath it says, *Have a Nice Fuck You!* I bat my eyes at Ross.

From the beginning, he told me he liked my eyes. He said he'd never seen anyone with gray eyes before. He'd thought they were blue until he got up close. "I didn't know they even existed," he said, running his finger around my sockets, like he'd discovered something amazing.

He turns back to the TV. Ross knows better than to suggest reruns of some sitcom or a police drama, or a soap opera. And none of that *Mutual of Omaha's Wild Kingdom* crap either. It's not like I have a problem with the land animals, they just lack mystery. I mean there they are, in plain view, running around and rolling on their backs, hanging upside down, where anybody can see them.

Plus, everybody loves them.

My little sister, Cecile, tells me that when I grow up I should work with animals. She says that animals like me the way animals liked St. Francis of Assisi. Cecile comes out with that sort of thing sometimes. She's been saying that ever since we were little and we took a trip to the aquarium in D.C. and I was the only kid the mantra ray let touch it. It felt like wet velvet. From that point on I knew I wanted to be a marine biologist.

Cecile says she wants to be a nun, even though we're not Catholic. Every Sunday she walks to mass—good practice for being a nun, she says—and some Good Samaritan drives her home. My mom wants to go to church, she means to, she says, she loves all the singing, but every Sunday morning she seems to be coming down with the flu. Back in kindergarten, I drew my mother with an ice pack on her head.

My father, an electrical engineer, calls himself a man of science. He says, "Show me evidence of Jesus riding on the back of a brontosaurus and I'll believe in God." My father calls himself an atheist, but Cecile insists on calling him an agnostic because *atheist* sounds so final, and she is always hoping he'll change his mind. "He will be lonely in Hell," she says.

Ross and I used to go to the same school until he transferred last year. He was the fat kid. Even his friends gave him titty twisters and knocked his books out of his hands in the hall. The last day of school, someone hung him by his underwear in the janitor's closet. He told me he could hear the buses one by one pulling away. He says his parents *always* intended for him to go to private school junior and senior years, but I don't think that's true. Because he's a year older we didn't know each other, but we *knew of* each other, of course. He said he'd always thought I was pretty, but *you know*. I smirked at him. I was supposedly fucking bikers and college guys, what would I want with the Pillsbury Doughboy? The label was *slut*, not charity worker.

I get it, though. Everybody, regulars, pops, druggies, nerds, freaks, everybody—especially the hated ones—needs somebody to kick. We met at the pool last summer. For weeks Ross and I watched each other across the water, recognizing each other for what we were.

Ross always swam in a white T-shirt and long Birdwells. Like me, he had no interest in playing Marco Polo or Sharks and Minnows. In our first conversation we agreed that any game where people tried to drown each other was stupid and that, were we ever asked to play, we'd reject the invitation.

Most of the girls spent their time lying on top of the picnic tables. Basting themselves with coconut oil, tying and untying their bikini tops so they didn't get any lines, and passing around a homemade reflector, a *Frampton Comes Alive* double album covered in foil. They French-braided each other's hair, pretending not to notice the boys who circled them as they rubbed lotion on each other's hard-to-reach spots.

I set up my chaise longue in the shade, where the young mothers sat with their babies on blankets, and the older women played bridge and complained about their ungrateful daughter-in-laws and their varicose veins. At the end of the day the ground was littered with raisin boxes. I kept to myself, spending my hours swimming lengths underwater, and reading *National Geographics*, or one of my mom's paperbacks, like *Fear of Flying*. I made a pillow out of my folded-up clothes.

I'd learned never to leave my things in the ladies' changing room. If they were there at all, they'd be on the cement floor, sopping wet. One of my dad's striped button-down shirts, a pink batik wrap skirt, a white embroidered blouse from India, it didn't matter what it was. I learned to ignore it when a gang of girls cruised by, and started coughing *slut, slut, slut* into their hands. I know most girls would just stop going to the pool, but I'm never happier than when I'm underwater.

Ross was the same. He would have stayed in the water all day if it weren't for adult swim. When everybody had to get out so the moms in their skirted suits, which never really hid their cellulite-pitted thighs, could stand in the three feet and smoke, or swim sidestroke, heads above the water so they didn't mess up their hair. What is the point of swimming if you don't put your head underwater? It's like kissing with your mouth closed.

Ross dreaded getting out of the pool. You could tell by the way he walked back to grab his towel, as fast as he could without the asshole lifeguard blowing the whistle on him for running, arms crossed over his chest, the way he'd turn away when he pulled on his shirt, hoping no one was looking at his blubbery belly, or saw he had tits. The tits were the worst of it.

Even now, this summer, undeniably handsome, twenty-seven pounds shed, his chest smooth from bench pressing, every time he starts to pull off his T-shirt at the pool or in his bedroom, I sense there is still a moment of panic as he raises his arms up and the shirt sails over his head, the fat boy inside him hesitating.

Hesitating even though it's after five o'clock and all the teens have gone home, and it's just us, and some adults sitting around drinking gin and tonics and smoking, trying to get up a volleyball game. We are invisible to them.

"All you need is one friend," my mother tells me like it's the secret to life. "Remember when you used to go to sleepovers, all those birthday parties—don't you like those girls anymore?"

"I was in fifth grade, sixth grade."

"You had interests," she says, reeling off the evidence. "Pony club, ballet, swim team—"

"Mom."

"When I was your age—"

"Mom, please."

"All I'm trying to say is that it's not like there aren't any opportunities out there for you to be social. I heard that a bunch of kids had a bonfire at the pond last weekend. The police were called," she says, like this is a good thing. "I know. Why didn't I think of it before? Let's have a party—yes, a party . . ." I feel utterly helpless to stop her. "A boy-girl party. We'll invite all your old pals, get Cathy—"

"Stop."

"—Stacy and Belinda."

"No!" I shout. "No. No way."

I hate the fact that those girls' phone numbers are burned into my brain and probably will be until the day I die. My mother shuts her eyes tight, twisting her hands in her lap, in an effort to hold herself together. "Oh my god. I have one nerve left and you are working it. You wonder why no one calls?"

"Because they hate me, and I hate them."

"You don't hate anybody."

"Yes I do."

"I don't see why you can't at least try," my mother says, blinking over and over, like maybe if she keeps blinking she'll recognize me again. *Where is that girl I used to know?* Like I've tied her up and locked her in a closet.

What was I supposed to say?

Blame the leotard. I shouldn't have worn the leotard to school. Freshman year. No one was wearing leotards with skirts anymore. Was I trying to show off the fact that my boobs were suddenly bigger than theirs? Why didn't I wear the lipstick that changed with your mood, or the iridescent blue eye shadow that looked like it was made from the ground-up wings of endangered butterflies? Why didn't my mother ever tell me not to talk to other girls' boyfriends? How did I know I shouldn't have blushed when the head of the Pretty Committee's boyfriend pinned me against the locker and said, "Do you mind if I undress you with my eyes? If I told you you had a nice body, would you hold it against me?"

How did I know that one day kids whose names I didn't even know would begin talking about me behind my back— *Did you hear what that slut Heather Chase did?*—snickering about my *incredible school spirit. Hey, Header,* they say, *there's a party in your mouth and everybody's coming . . .*

The rumor was that after the basketball team made the playoffs, I gave the whole team—including the bench and the equipment manager—blow jobs. I don't know about the mascot. It's a giant owl. Can you blow an owl? Who would believe this? No one, least of all me, has that much school spirit.

I don't let that stuff get under my skin. The only one who is worth anything is the new girl. She's Indian. After only two weeks at our school, she gave up trying to get people to pronounce her name correctly and just told everybody to call her Lorraine. I've asked her to tell me her real name, because I want to call her that, but she won't. She says, "I'm Lorraine now." Because she's Indian, everyone expects her to be smart. Even when she tries to slack off, to turn in bad homework, the teachers give her A's anyway.

It's not like we're passing notes during study hall or gabbing on the phone at night, but we have an understanding. We sit at the same lunch table, and whenever we have to "buddy up" for a field trip or a fire drill, we're buddies. A single girl who needs nobody makes people uncomfortable, and my mom is right in this, appearance is everything, and appearing to have no one is like swimming alone in the middle of the ocean with a flesh wound.

Ross stands in front of the screen while the show's theme music starts, the camera floating just over the ocean floor as I squeeze my legs together.

"Ross."

"I want to see if it's a repeat," he says, knowing full well it doesn't matter. If he even thinks about changing it, or turning it off, I am so outta there.

The first time I asked him to turn on the TV before we had sex, he'd been happy to oblige, if perplexed. After all, no one was home that day to hear us.

"We're not watching it if it's the lobster one," he says, trying to sound all tough.

We both know he's full of shit.

The lobster episode explores the theory that lobsters are capable of love. Not parental love—they'll eat their young—but romantic love. The last shot is of a pair of lobsters walking claw in claw across the ocean floor. Maybe that's what makes them taste so good.

I stayed after school one afternoon last spring to help Ms. Sandburg, my biology teacher, clean the crayfish tanks. I was probably the one kid who didn't need the extra credit, but no one else volunteered. I like crayfish and I liked Ms. Sandburg.

When I raised my hand, someone made a crack. "Eww. It reeks like rotten fish in here. Looks like Heather-Straight-No-Chaser needs to napalm her twat."

I didn't know if Ms. Sandburg heard it, because then the bell rang. Later, though, as we were razoring the algae off the insides of the tanks, she said, "Don't listen to them, Heather. You know what Eleanor Roosevelt said?"

I have no clue what she's talking about.

"No one can make you feel inferior without your consent. People have always hated strong women. They fear we're one turkey-baster away from abolishing men."

What do you say to that?

"Listen, if you ever want to rap," Ms. Sandburg put her hand on my shoulder, "my door is always open."

She was cool like that. I felt bad that she had to keep reminding people to call her Ms., not Miss. In her bell-bottoms and aviator glasses, her macramé vest and her shag haircut, she made the other teachers look like fossils. I felt bad that everybody made fun of her car, a beat-up VW Bug, and her bumper sticker, A WOMAN WITHOUT A MAN IS LIKE A FISH WITH-OUT A BICYCLE. They said, "Shouldn't a science teacher know fish don't ride bicycles?"

It's ironic because that afternoon, leaving school, I was walking out to get my bike. The halls were freshly mopped and empty, the echo of my footsteps eerie but exciting. I sprinted down the hall. I jumped. The only evidence of human life was the smell of disinfectant.

I stopped outside the boys' bathroom. It was dumb, but I had to see. You know, for a second I had this idiotic thought: *What if there is nothing there? What would that be like?* It would be like my life hadn't even happened, like nobody even knew I existed.

But I was right. There I was on the wall, my name in Magic Marker, my phone number—*wrong*—in boy handwriting, like hieroglyphics in some cave, and me some ancient queen. It disappointed me to see that another girl's name was up there too.

Without even thinking I took a pencil from my book bag, yanked the eraser out with my teeth, and using the sharp metal part scraped her name off the wall. I scratched and scratched so hard the plaster underneath started to crumble.

I'm just glad that Cecile goes to St. Mary's now.

At the end of the school year, Ms. Sandburg got married and moved to Indianapolis.

When Ross comes back to the bed and starts to lick my stomach, I relax. He really is good looking now, the strong jaw, the ass that disappears when he wears Levi's. He's growing out his hair so you can see it's dark chestnut; it smells like the Johnson's baby shampoo his mom still buys him. He doesn't know how handsome he is yet. He works harder because of it. I know he expected that when he dropped all that weight everything would change immediately. All the starving would pay off. Chicks would line up to be his girlfriend, but it doesn't happen that way.

I run my hands through my hair, spread it out on the pillow, hold a long strand up to the light; it looks redder, less brown, when you separate it like that. My hands move over his arms and his shoulders, he flexes under my touch.

During the commercial I whisper in his ear, "You're so big, so strong, I can't *believe* how strong you are." That always makes him hard. He likes it when he can hold me down, overpower me. I let him. He lifts his head and moves up to kiss me. His bare skin against my bare skin feels amazing. Why can't we always be like this? I kiss his neck, lick the hollow of his collarbone. The first time I touched him there, just with my *finger*, he jumped a mile. Now, though, he trusts me; when I kiss his neck he lets his head fall back like a girl, and he sighs.

In the beginning, when we first started having sex, Ross was giddy. "I can't even believe this is happening," he'd say, palming my breast. "You're so beautiful. I can't believe you're real." He'd pulled a bobby pin out of my hair. "I'm keeping this," he said, waving it at me, "as proof."

"Believe it," I said.

Ross didn't want to believe the rumors. "I want to trust you," he said. "Honesty is important to me."

I told him, "No one knows me better than you, Ross," and it was sad but true.

• • •

The episode is called "Giant Squid: Myth, Mystery, or Reality?"—my favorite of all. Before Ross can say, like he always does, *How can it be a myth if we are looking at it?* I blow in his ear, and wrap my legs around his waist. On the screen, a giant squid is propelling itself underwater with its long tentacles, the motion somewhere between a rocket launch and a ballet dancer. The commentator's voice is deep and gentle like a hypnotist's; it pulls me in. He says, "Weighing more than a ton, Architeuthis is as long as a football field, and has the largest eyeball in the animal kingdom, as big as a dodgeball."

I shift and turn my head to stare at the screen. At the aquarium, you can stand right next to the glass and cup your hands around your eyes so nothing exists, and stare into the water until you forget what side of the glass you're even on.

The screen is deep green becoming black. Ross is moving inside me, eyes closed in concentration, like he's trying to find something with his cock. "Architeuthis is an elusive creature," the commentator murmurs as the squid disappears, pink into black, "inhabiting the deepest reaches of the sea, deeper, deeper than any man can go." Ross lifts my hips and I think how great it is that there are no footprints on the ocean floor. There are still places man can't go.

After he comes, Ross curls up like a shrimp and sleeps. I'm sorry to have missed the part where the science historian shows the old drawings sailors once made of giant squids, splintering ships, tossing men, little as French fries, overboard.

Ross is sleeping hard, his mouth open. While he sleeps, I pop a zit on his back. He's going to wrestling camp this summer. He's starving himself, running up and down the bleachers at school wearing a trash bag to sweat off the pounds. It's working too. He's dropped a weight class. Every day he is kicking ass. Pinning guys bigger than him. The coach tells him he's an animal. They can try to dodge him, scrabble out of his reach, but as he tells me, "I just go lower, put my head down and take out their legs."

"Their legs," I say, wishing he'd do this to me sometime. "Then what?"

"I throw them down, get on top of them, or flip them on their backs and pin them—there's the cradle," he says. "Where you get them behind the head and legs—"

"That doesn't sound very cradlelike."

"Or there's the fireman's carry. You're crouched, right? And you pick 'em up, hold them across the back of your shoulders, and then slam them down."

"That doesn't sound very firemanlike—"

"It's awesome," he says. "You have to be really strong . . ."

"I bet," I say. I think it odd that they've named these wrestling moves after actions that seem to be about comfort and rescue.

"They can struggle all they want, they can even escape, but I always get them back," he says excitedly. "I'm patient," he says. "I wait."

"But what about the guys who are bigger than you?"

He bites his lip. I can tell he's trying to decide whether to tell me something. He frowns.

"I just imagine them saying *fat boy, fat boy, fat boy.*"

I don't know what to say. I'm sick with embarrassment and tenderness for him at the same time.

"Once I had this dream where I was in an arena, wrestling, and all the people in the stands were cheering and screaming, foaming at the mouth like out for blood. A little light goes on, and I figure out—*Hey, wait, I'm wrestling my old self, that loser, the fat fuck,* and I was like, *yeah!* I fucking pounded him."

"Yourself?"

"It was hard-core."

"I don't dream."

"Everybody dreams."

"I know that," I say, annoyed. I'm smarter than him. "I mean, I don't remember my dreams."

"And I dream in color too," Ross says. "Most guys don't, you know."

Sometimes, at night, when we are in bed and he thinks I am sleeping, he gets up and lies on the floor beside the bed and does sit-ups—one hundred, two hundred, I count along with him. He does push-ups and jumping jacks and jogs in place in front of the mirror, then, exhausted and sweaty, he crawls back into bed. I roll over and put my arm around him, feel his heart beating.

"Aren't you going to ask what I am feeling?" Ross says when he wakes up, twining a piece of my hair around and around his finger, until it coils up in his hand.

Diaphanous pink and white jellyfish with tentacles thin and buoyant float over Ross's head on the screen. It had been so nice lying quietly side by side not touching, almost like strangers.

"You want me to ask you what you are feeling?"

"No, I didn't mean that . . ."

"I can . . ."

"No, it's a joke." He blushes. "You know most girls ask that—they always want to know, you know, *What are you thinking? Say something.* That's all."

"Most girls, huh? You have lots of girls do you, Mr. Casanova?" I poke him in the side, and he flinches. Every muscle in his body tightens. His hands automatically go into fists; he rolls onto his stomach. I hate how careless I can be.

"I'm sorry," I say. He acts like he didn't hear me.

I roll over too, and slide nearer to him so we are staring eye to eye.

"Wait. Don't I know you?" I say and kiss his sunburned shoulder. This is how a girl is supposed to behave. "Come here often?" I pick at his sunburn and hold the piece of dead skin up to the light like I'm playing the cloud game. No matter what kinds of clouds they are—nimbus, stratus, cumulus—my mother always sees Elvis, and my sister sees angels.

"Look, it's Jacques Cousteau." I adjust the angle slightly. "Look at that profile. See the nose?"

Ross doesn't like to be angry, but I know he is.

"I used to have a crush on Jacques Cousteau. When I was a kid, my dad and I used to watch *The Undersea World of Jacques Cousteau* together. Did you ever see that? It was our thing, just the two of us. It was great. We'd sit in the den in our bean bag chairs and drink ginger ale and speak in French accents, and any time my mother tried to horn in, which she always did, my father sent her out of the room."

I don't know where that memory came from, but it's embarrassing.

Ross nods. "Yeah. His boat was the *Calypso*." He kisses my temple, the place where my skin feels thinnest. It tingles. I don't think anyone has ever kissed me there before.

"So you gonna let me write on you, or what?" he asks with a smile, taking my arm and turning it over, searching for the perfect place.

When he notices the numbers on the inside of my arm, his fingers tighten on my wrist. He thinks it's some guy's phone number. He doesn't want to, but he does. If he'd just look, he'd see there are only six numbers. It's my mom's birthday. I was good about it when she forgot my birthday last year. She said, "You know I love you, baby. I'm just in denial that I am old enough to have a daughter who's sixteen years old!" I can assure you she wouldn't be okay if I forgot her birthday.

It falls to me because my dad forgot last year, and Cecile shouldn't be burdened with that responsibility.

I slide my arm out of Ross's grip and under the pillow.

"I don't think so." After all this, I'm not going to dignify his suspicion and I don't really feel like explaining. His mother still makes his bed and does his laundry. I'm sure she must wonder about the ink stains on his sheets.

"Aw, come on," he says. "Let me draw on you. Why not? What's the big deal?"

In a moment of weakness I agree. "Okay."

I reach over the side of the bed and grab my army bag. On the outside I've drawn, not very well, a whale.

"What's with the whale?" Ross laughs, pulling my bag away from me, holding it over his head so I'm forced to look at his armpits wisped with hair. It is never a good idea to look at a person's armpits. A bundle of Flair markers held together with a wiggie falls into the bedcovers.

"You're not one of those No Nukers, are you?" he says, removing the hair elastic.

"No. I'm all for nuking—just certain people, not animals."

"Right." He chuckles.

"Did you know that the whale is the only enemy of the giant squid?" I say, grabbing my bag back. "Did you know that?"

"Hmmm, that sounds familiar. I wonder why?" He sits up and leans back on his elbows. "Biggest eye in the animal kingdom," he says in the voice of the commentator.

"Architeuthis."

"Gesundheit," he says. "Come here."

"You know what," I say, twisting in his arms. "I don't feel like it now."

"Come on, quit joshing around, you promised," he says, holding on to me tight. I never promised him he could write on me, not really.

Even so, I offer him my arm, the one that isn't inked with stars. I always leave one pristine.

"Here," I say. "It's blank." Half my markers have disappeared in his sheets.

He examines my arm. "Nah," he says and lifts up the sheet. He looks me up and down, smiling at the lightning bolt on the inside of my left thigh, and while normally I wouldn't care, I am suddenly shy.

"Look at you," he says.

"Let's not and say we did."

"Roll over. C'mon, lemme see your back."

"Wouldn't you rather do something else?" I lift my head to kiss him, but he pulls back and with a deft wrestling move manages to flip me over onto my stomach. This is exciting.

He doesn't need to put his knee on my back. I'm lying still.

"Ah, perfecto," he says, pushing the sheet down to just above my ass.

"Ross."

I've drawn the whale on my bag floating head down. On

another show I'd seen an entire pod of whales sleeping just like that, suspended upside down. I wondered if animals dreamed, and if so what did they dream about. Being chased by bigger, faster animals? Interspecies mating? Food?

I fold my arms under my forehead and let my hair hang over my face.

He leans across the small of my back, his left arm resting on my butt, so I'm trapped. He takes his time.

"I don't do this, you know."

"Mmm."

"Never." No one ever asked.

"What are you doing?"

"Take a chill pill." He's really enjoying himself. "You know I can't draw, right?"

"Seriously, Ross, no disco sucks, or dumb sports stuff, or May the Force Be with You . . ."

"Hey, hey, take it easy," he says, "relax, artist at work—shhhh."

It was stupid to let Ross draw on me.

When I was little, my sister and mom and I used to play a game where our mother would soap us up in the tub and write the alphabet or make a drawing on our backs and we'd try to guess it. She always drew a star on Cecile, a peace sign on me. Even when I was older, she'd come in, sit on the edge of the tub, and ask if I wanted to play the game. I couldn't say no.

What good was saying no? It would only hurt her feelings. Hurt feelings put my mother in bed for weeks, face turned to the wall, no appetite, the way a flu bug might affect someone else.

My mother had written words too like *Smile, Mommy*, and of course, *I love you*. That was the easiest of all to figure out. But because the person in the tub couldn't actually see what the other wrote, you could lie and tell them it wasn't what they thought, or what they wanted it to be.

Once while we were showering in the ladies' locker room at the pool, she'd insisted I do it to her. "Try it on me, I want to see if I'm any good at it," she'd said in her girlish voice.

She'd guessed *stop* and *flower*, and then I wrote *I love you*.

"Oh, that's an easy one," my mother said, "I love you!"

"Nope," I said. "Try again."

"Oh," she said, sounding flustered. "Really, are you sure?"

"I'm sure. Sorry."

"I'm getting cold—can you hand me a towel?"

"You won't get good unless you do it a lot," I said, turning up the heat in the shower, soaping her back again. She stood dutifully with her face to the wall as I wrote on her back again, nonsense words. I don't know if she was really guessing from the way the words felt, or if she was just saying what she'd hoped I'd write.

"*Sunshine, happy, baby.*"

"You got it!" I said every time, even though she usually was wrong.

"That one I missed," she said, sounding confused, "that wasn't *I love you?*"

"No," I lied.

"What are you doing, writing your memoirs?" This was such a mistake.

"Okay," he says finally, and slaps my ass gently. "You're done. *Finito.*"

"It's about time," I say and roll onto my back.

"Serves you right, Heather," he says then hops off the

bed and heads for the bathroom down the hall. He always showers after sex. I wonder if his mom notices how much he showers?

I get out of bed and stand in front of his mirror naked. He's got a ticket stub from a Rush concert stuck in the side of the mirror. Who did he go with? I wonder. A girl? No. I don't wonder. I don't care. I'm just curious.

Like I'm curious about what he's done to me. What he wrote doesn't matter. In fact, I know that whatever it is it will just bother me. I find my dress hiding under the bed.

I saw a French movie once about a beautiful housewife who becomes a prostitute for kicks. There's a scene where she's in a hotel room with a man, and just as things start to heat up, she coolly stands up, removes her dress, and asks for a hanger. That stuck with me.

It's five o'clock. By this hour, anyone we know, or who would recognize us, has gone home. This is our time.

"You know, if you wanna go to the club, we oughta hustle," he says, his head finding its way through the neck hole of his "Born to Run" T-shirt. "Why don't you go hit the shower?"

"Why?" I say, surveying my arms, lifting up my dress to flash the ink on my legs.

He is looking at my arm, the numbers I have written on there.

It's gnawing at him. "What?"

"C'mon. Please." He gives me a strained smile. "It's been a shitty day. Practice sucked. I feel like—"

"What happened?"

"Forget it. It doesn't matter." I follow him as he walks outside and into the garage, where he's got a weight bench and free-weights setup. There's a refrigerator full of Gatorades and on top a pile of old *Playboys*, which I'm not supposed to see. He sits on the end of the bench, picks up a small barbell, and does some curls.

"Tell me."

"I don't want to talk about it," he says in this strangled voice. He pauses. Then: "I got pinned."

"What?"

"I got pinned," he says louder, like it just happened. "In front of everybody." He drops the barbell and jams his fists in his eyes. He sniffles and wipes his nose on the back of his hand.

I sit on the bench beside him. "So?" I'm not accustomed to seeing anyone outside of my mother cry. "Isn't that normal—isn't that the whole point?"

"No. You don't get it. Ross doesn't get pinned. Not anymore. Ross is a winner." Hearing him talk about himself in the third person is disconcerting. "Everybody saw it—my teammates, my coach, everybody. *That's not who I am.*"

I wonder how many times he'd had to repeat that line before it began to run like a loop in his head. *That's not who I am.*

"I can't do this. I'm like freaking out. This isn't happening."

"I know." I awkwardly put my arm around his waist. He drops his head on my shoulder. It's heavy. I breathe in through my nose, long and slow, hoping he'll naturally sync his breath with mine. He needed me.

We stay like that for a long time, not talking. Finally, I tell him I'm going to run to the bathroom, that'll I'll just be a minute. I want to give him some time to compose himself.

I wash myself over the sink. It's funny that Ross and I use

the same soap. You'd think he might be the manly English Leather soap-on-a-rope type of guy, but no. It's Ivory, *So pure it floats*. I scrub my arms and legs, my stomach, until it's all gone, the rainbow and stars, the fuck you, the smiley face, even my mom's birthday, gone. Finally, when I can't stand it anymore, I lift up my hair and turn my back to the mirror. Floating between my shoulder blades is a feather, and underneath it in balloon letters Ross has written R *loves* H. I'm embarrassed at the way relief washes over me like a wave.

When I come out to meet Ross at the car, I'm clean. I've let my hair down so he can't see that I've left his drawing—it's the only mark on me.

Ross is leaning against the hood of his car, a dark blue Corvette Sting Ray that he'd been saving for since he was thirteen. The car of his dreams. His dad told him if he won a gold medal at the state finals, he'd buy him a car. He got a silver and his dad gave him an advance on his allowance. The new car makes it official. The fat boy drove a brown Celica, the equivalent of dog shit. The thin boy drives a metallic blue Corvette, a two-thousand-horsepower yeah, baby, sex machine.

"Hey, sorry for flipping out like that," he says, reaching over for my hand. I don't say that it's the best thing that's happened to me in years. I can feel the heat coming off the car.

"You ready to split?" he asks as he unlocks my door. He always does this, unlocks my door first. I used to hate it. *I can open my own door*, I'd say, but I like it today. I don't feel repulsed, as I usually do, when he opens the door and I see trash on the floor, the sticky cups, burger wrappers, and empty pie boxes. I couldn't figure out why Ross, after taking such good care of that car, polishing each sleek curve, never seemed to clean out the inside.

On the way to the pool, Ross turns on the radio. For once, it's not Led Zeppelin or the Grateful Dead, but Blondie singing, "Rip Her to Shreds," my new favorite song. I know Ross is not a fan, but today he doesn't switch the station. I take his hand off the stick shift and kiss his fingers. I don't suck on them. I just kiss them. I'm happy.

He laces his fingers through mine, and drives one handed, not letting go even to shift gears.

"You know what I want, right now?" I say. I feel high. "Something sweet."

"What a coincidence"—he grins—"I was just thinking the same thing."

"I mean, candy."

"Then so be it. If my lady wants candy, then my lady shall have candy."

The old me would have said, "A lady is someone who doesn't have to work for a living," but I blush. His lady. Proper, respected, adored.

As we make the turn into the parking lot of the shopping center, I think I see something catch his eye in the mirror. He drives right past a space in front of the candy store, so we end up parking in the shade of a big row of gray Dumpsters at the end of the lot, near the tobacco store.

"You want to come with?"

"Um, no, you go ahead. I'll just hang out here with the car and wait. Check it out, that place has candy too, you know," he says, gesturing toward the doorway filled with stacks of newspapers, a few old lottery tickets on the sidewalk.

"No, I'll walk." I feel giddy, like a kid who can have anything her heart desires. "What are you in the mood for?"

"I don't know," he says, checking the mirror. "Surprise me."

I've never really been a candy person, but I want it today. I buy a handful of silver Hershey's Kisses for Ross, a bag of Swedish fish for Cecile, a roll of cherry Life Savers for me, and two bubble gum cigars, one pink—IT'S A GIRL!—one blue—IT'S A BOY! I'd forgotten you could slide the gold cigar band off and wear it like a ring.

By the time I get back to the car, Ross is nowhere. I scan across the highway thinking maybe he ran over to McDonald's for a hot apple pie and a shake, but I don't see him. I'm starting to worry when I spot him, at the other end of the lot, where a pack of kids are parked, car doors open, the sound of Styx's "The Best of Times" pounding out of the speakers. There he is. Leaning on the bumper of a maroon Camaro talking to some dudes. In the empty space between two cars, the girls, all of them in hot pants and tube tops, are giggling and shrieking, bouncing up and down, dancing the way girls do when they want a guy's attention. It takes a moment for me to realize who Ross is talking to. Kids from school, my school. I recognize those girls drinking Michelob Light and falling all over each other. I still remember Belinda's birthday.

The same kids who used to torture him, slam him into lockers, snap his ass with wet towels and call him lard-ass. The same kids who called me a slut, who carved my name in desktops, made rutting sounds when I bent over in front of my locker, crank-called my house breathing heavy in my sister's ear. Why is he standing there, talking to them? No, not talking, joking around, laughing like he's having the time of his life. Like nothing ever happened.

I'm confused. I don't know what to do. Should I wait, or walk over there? Let them see I am with Ross. That would change their opinion of me, wouldn't it?

Then he turns his head, stealing a look over his shoulder.

He must wonder where I am. His eyes track across the parking lot. Even from a distance, it's clear that the expression that moves across Ross's face is panic, fear. I want him to come back to me, or call out, wave. I want him to do something. Then he does; he turns his head away.

And I'm alone. In the open. Exposed. Quickly I move back behind the Dumpsters. Try to open the car door, but Ross has locked it. I think, *I'll walk home,* or I could hitchhike. Then I think, *No way am I walking home along the highway.* All those cars shooting past me. Adults shaking their heads—young women today—imagining I'm some stoned runaway, the guy from the aquarium who waves at you underwater when he feeds the fish, one of the Good Samaritans who drives Cecile home from church. Or worse, all those cars slowing down, people yelling out the window: "Yo baby, are you for sale?" "Did your father lose his license for that last DUI?" Hitch-hiking is stupid. It's a fantasy to imagine that a woman like Ms. Sandburg in her light blue Beetle with a HERSTORY NOT HISTORY sticker would coast up, roll down the window, Helen Reddy's "I Am Woman, Hear Me Roar" booming out of the eight-track, and yell, "Hop in, sister!"

No *fucking way,* I think. I'll wait for him. I lean against Ross's car. I run my hand over the warm swell of the bumper, my palm cupping the curve of the hood, the smooth blue paint job that sparkles. I reach down into my bag and pull out my key, and in one swift movement, I drag it hard and deep across my door.

I think about the part of the show where this marine biolo-gist with strangely moist eyes says that the best evidence they have of the giant squids' existence comes from the undigested pieces they find of them in the bellies of their mortal enemies: the sperm whales. I hated that. For all anybody knows, Architeuthis was the real winner here. It's just no one knows it yet. A few minutes later Ross appears, jogging toward the car.

"Oh, hey," he says like he didn't see me and ducks in on the driver's side. He unlocks my door from the inside. I'm barely in the car before he starts pulling out. "I didn't see you come out."

I can't look at him, and I won't say anything.

He drops his hand onto my knee. "So . . ."

"I want to go back."

"Back?"

"Back. Home. I want to go home."

We are driving along a road I have driven on my whole life. I still watch for the bends in the creek, checking to see how high the water comes up on the bank, I still hold my breath as we go around the blind turn, I can close my eyes and tell you where we are just by the way my stomach feels. I wonder if after I grow up and move away, if I came back would my body still remember this road, or would I have forgotten it?

"I'm sorry," he says.

"What were you doing?"

"Whoa, you don't have to jump down my throat. I didn't see you. I'm sorry," Ross says, his voice getting louder, "that I don't have eyes in the back of my head."

"Right."

"You know what? You're so fucking weird," he says, grabbing me by the wrist and shaking my arm like it's not attached to me. There's nothing even written there anymore.

"What do you think—I mean, what the fuck is that shit?"

"It's none of your business," I say, but I feel like screaming.

"Well, it's right the hell there, for everybody to see."

"You want to know? You really want to know?"

His eyes dart between me and the road.

"It's my mother's birthday. Are you happy?"

"Oh, yeah, right," he scoffs feebly. He knew my mom was crazy. He knew my dad wasn't around much. He's just not ready to admit he was wrong.

"I want you to take me home," I say, waiting for him to argue.

"Okay by me," he says, staring straight ahead. He knows the truth. He can't decide whether or not he'll choose to believe it. There's nothing I can do.

When we pull into the development, he passes my street and drives to his house.

"I said I want to go home."

He shrugs off my protest. When we reach the end of the drive, he jerks the emergency brake; the car lurches forward, then stops like a creature he's got on a leash. I get out of the car. My fingers find the gash in the door, deep and ragged like a bite.

There is a swagger in Ross's walk as he rounds the bumper, coming toward me with his arms wide open. "Aw, c'mon, babe," he says, like he knows he's been bad but expects to be forgiven. He tries to put his arm around me. "Let me make it up to you?"

"Get away," I say, wrapping my arms around myself.

He covers his face with his hands, and stands there, like he hopes when he takes his hands away I'll be gone. Does he expect me to feel sorry for him?

"Aw c'mon, you know how it is . . ."

"No, I don't."

He sighs like I'm being unreasonable.

"You don't even know me," I say.

"Yeah, right," he says sarcastically. "I never *knew* you—"

The feather on my back—R *loves* H. It now seems so trite.

"—and I don't *know* you now." He smirks at me.

"I know you," I say calmly. "I know you got pinned today, and you'll get pinned again."

His face begins redden. "The fuck I will."

"Sure you will," I say, punching him in the arm. "You know what. I bet I can pin you. Me."

"I said, shut up."

"Hey, hey, breathe. I'm just playing." I circle around him. "Guess someone can't take a joke today, can they, *big boy*?"

I bump him with my shoulder, then my hip.

"Come on, let's go in," I say, wrapping my hand around his waist, pulling him back toward the sliding glass door and the dark of his bedroom. "You know this was your idea. You wanted to come here. Get inside before somebody sees us."

"Wait. Not now," he says, pushing me away.

"Wait. You don't want to now? Or," I lower my voice to a whisper, "wait, you *can't* now?" When I stand up straight, I am as tall as him. "We can just *talk* if you want." I laugh. "Or, I can just go home," I say and start walking away.

He grabs me by the shoulder. "No," he says. He follows me in on his own. He slides the door closed. He stops to turn on the TV for me.

"Don't," I say. I push him onto the bed, take off my dress, peel off my panties. I kiss him the way I did when we first met, when I was learning how to kiss. When I made him wait because I'd never done any of this before either.

I licked my lips and unzipped him, pulled his underpants down, pushed his hand away when he tried to cover himself. I put him inside me and took him out, until he was panting. He begged me to let him keep his shirt on. He hugged himself, whining when I fondled his chest, about being cold, and when I took my eyes off him, he tried to dive under the sheets. He tries to stop me now, struggles, surprised at how strong I am. I move over his body with my mouth up and down his torso; inside his thighs I can see the shape the bruises are taking.

I breathe in his ear, "What kind of boy are you?"

A second later he has flipped me over, thrown me on my back, and is on top of me, pinning my arms above my head. He looks at me, the full length of me, then drops his head and kisses me. At first sort of roughly and then softly. After a while, he lets me back on top. Straddling him I lean down and whisper in his ear, "Fat fuck. You fat, fat fuck."

He rears up under me and roars.

I wonder, when we're done, what will be left of us.

A Dog Story

After a year of us trying to get pregnant, my doctor said, "Sometimes fate needs help." A former hippie who threw the *I Ching* every morning, she suggested that I cast my lot with the moon and gave me a small pink calendar. On the front was the silhouette of a woman with extraordinarily long hair, and the name of a prescription drug I'd never heard of.

"Female pattern baldness?"

"Just ignore that."

The calendar approach made sense to my very logical husband. He worked in the office of the city planner. His job was determining how many fire hydrants, water fountains, and stop signs were necessary in order to improve the quality of life in any given neighborhood. How many libraries, playgrounds, and schools, I wondered, did people need to be happy?

My mother, having given birth to four children, all of whom, except for me, had procreated, pressed the issue of my husband seeing a doctor. The clock was ticking.

"You know you can't have just one," my mother said, as though babies were peanuts.

According to tests, Douglas's sperm count was average, the

speed and motility of his swimmers normal, "if," his doctor said, "a little on the sluggish side."

Douglas said, "I prefer the term *laid-back.*"

Still, I could imagine his sperm, a file of pale balding men in Bermuda trunks and sunglasses, wading out to stand knee-deep in water, arms crossed, reluctant to go any further.

In truth, we had sex more than pandas, but less than dogs. And month after month, I got my period. And month after month, the plague of babies spread. Unstoppable, they slipped under the door and through the mail slot. Stork- and cabbage-leaf-embossed birth announcements fat with glossy photos of newborns, all wispy comb-overs and padded cheeks, watery eyes and pouts pearled with drool. With their looks of disgust, alarm, and defiant boredom, the photos felt like Wanted posters. Clearly, these potato-faced outlaws were itching for trouble, plotting to drive their parents to ruin and an early grave. We wanted one.

It seemed unfair. Friends who hadn't been trying, who wanted to wait before hatching number two, got pregnant. They threw up their hands in happy defeat. "What can you do?" they said, shrugging foolishly.

Worst of all, though, were the parents whose children were older. "Wait," they said. "Travel. Enjoy being a couple. Get a dog. At least a dog won't grow up to write a tell-all book about what lousy parents you were."

We wanted a dog, *of course.* No home was complete without one, curled up at your feet while you read the paper, barking at strangers, trotting alongside the kid as she flies her first kite. We just wanted a baby first.

Then, one day it just appeared. The plus sign. Plus one? A kiss?

We'd get the dog later.

The first time we heard the baby's heartbeat, my husband squeezed my hand. Tighter than on our wedding day, tighter than last summer at the Cape when I got pulled into the undertow. He squeezed my hand tighter than I'd ever imagined he'd dare squeeze anything. I liked that.

He shut his eyes to listen. "The syncopation—" Douglas said, grinning. He was imagining describing the musical nuances of Charlie Parker and Chet Baker, how he'd teach his child—no, his son—to snap its fingers. He let go of my hand and wiped his sweaty palm on his pants leg.

I said, "It's just a sea monkey now. What are you going to be like when it's real?"

"Don't say that," he said. "It is real."

Douglas told everybody—friends, family, neighbors, business associates, even the night doorman knew. *We are pregnant.*

When we went to our favorite place, an Italian restaurant around the corner, he told the waiter. The enthusiasm with which the man clapped my husband on the back and shook his hand, you'd have thought we were family. When he pulled out his billfold to show us his children's confirmation pictures, we beamed at each other. *We are pregnant!*

He told his mother he hoped it was a boy. She hoped it was a boy too.

My mother sounded overcome with relief. "Oh, Katie, this is wonderful news. I'm so happy for you. I knew you could do it," she said. The exact reaction I'd gotten when I'd told her I was engaged. "Douglas," she added, "must be beside himself."

I'd told only a few people. I'd told my best friend from college, because we'd gotten engaged and married at the same time and vowed to have babies together too. She was on her second. We hadn't spoken in nearly a year. When I told her I was *finally going to deliver* on my promise, she shrieked, "Hurray! Now we can take family vacations together!"

I hadn't planned on telling my friend Teddy; she'd guessed when I ordered a ginger ale at lunch, instead of my usual red wine. The fact that Teddy, who'd briefly slummed as a publicist at the ad agency where I worked, never wanted children ("I inherited that gene from my mother," she'd say) lent her an air of mystery and sophistication. "It's not that I don't adore children, I do. My clients are my children," she liked to say. "Plus, given all my darling nieces and nephews, I shall never want for potential organ donors."

She'd made a toast. "To Kate. You will be a fabulous mother."

I said I hoped so.

My assistant had been relieved. To a sweet Mormon girl whose chief pleasure seemed to be planning the office's birthday parties and showers, my mood swings and the nodding off at my desk, the donuts, meant I either was on drugs or had a brain tumor.

For the first time in his life, Douglas cooked. Dismaying heaps of kale, spinach, and turnips. Soups that smelled like compost. I told him, "It's your fault if this baby winds up looking like the bastard son of the Jolly Green Giant. And you know how people gossip."

He was good to me. He did things he'd never done before. Put his arm around me and walked on the side where the traffic raced by. In restaurants, he sent back food that suddenly seemed inedible; I'd feigned nausea a few times just so he'd do it. He wondered if the swelling in my feet was something we should worry about. While I napped, he did the dishes, necktie flipped over his shoulder. He danced. My husband, who never danced, not even at weddings, boogied around the apartment humming along to the radio. I joked, had I known he'd act like this I'd have gotten pregnant a long time ago. "I should always be pregnant," I said.

"Sounds good to me," he said.

I tried to do everything right. The moment the X (a kiss!) appeared, I'd stopped drinking and smoking pot. I swore off blue-veined cheeses, sushi, and all non-organic produce. I gave up coloring the gray in my hair, which with fairy-tale speed had grown thicker and shinier seemingly overnight. I was on the sofa searching the index of *What to Expect* to determine whether or not it was safe to paint my toenails when I felt the first signs of "quickening." I'd liked the term the moment I read it. It suggested that the baby was taking shape, setting up like clay, and quickly.

I wasn't sure, though. Maybe I was wrong. Maybe it was gas. Maybe I just wanted to feel it so badly I felt it. Then I felt it again. *No,* I told myself, *no. Maybe I shouldn't be happy. Maybe I should be panicking.* The third time—third time is the charm—I called to my husband.

He didn't dare get excited. "After all," he said, smiling nervously, "it could just be your imagination." I took his hand and pressed it low on my stomach. He shut his eyes. Then there it was, the sensation of bubbles, like laughter underwater.

First the baby, then him. It seemed for a moment like the two of them were laughing together. Already.

Before he could pull his hand away, I told him that if he moved his hand south, I'd really make his heart quicken. He blushed. It just came out. He said he knew it was stupid given how small the baby was, but he couldn't stop thinking about the soft spot. One unfortunate thrust and, at best, the baby would have a lisp or a lazy eye, or do just so-so on the SATs.

• • •

The fact that Douglas insisted on coming to my second-trimester appointment had come as a happy surprise, especially since it required him to cut out in the middle of his team's presentation to resurrect a Brooklyn playground that had become an open-air drug bazaar in an "underserved" neighborhood. The fact that my practical, notoriously thrifty husband was lobbying for the costly four-foot-tall elephant statues, hollowed out so children could crawl inside and hide—"What kid wouldn't like that?" he said—had taken everyone by surprise.

I didn't ask if he'd factored in the danger of a child crawling into the belly of an elephant and finding a crack pipe, or getting jabbed with an AIDS-infected needle. I didn't ask if he'd done the math on the possibility of junkies themselves moving into the beasts and making themselves at home.

Instead, ensconced in the examining room, the two of us giggled over the fact that the stirrups were sheathed with cloth booties advertising a birth control pill that also combatted teen acne. What would have once inspired indignation—the depths to which pharmaceutical companies would sink to sell their wares—now had us in stitches.

"Talk about your captive audience," I said.

"If it's a girl, I'm putting her in a bubble until she's eighteen," he said.

When the technician couldn't find the heartbeat, my husband asked her to keep looking, as if the baby were playing Marco Polo and had swum behind a kidney, or was curled up and holding its breath under my lungs. Until that moment we were a *we*; after, it was just *me*.

You know how it is, when the high school football team wins the championship, it's *we won!* When the team loses, *they lost.*

To be fair, Douglas never said *Kate lost the baby* with any blame or bitterness. Still, *Kate lost the baby*, especially when said to his mother, made it sound like I left it in a bowling alley, or drove off with it on the roof of our car. *Miscarried.* I hated that term too. It implied negligence on my part. It whispered maliciousness, irresponsibility, like I'd held the baby upside down, swung it by one foot, dropped it like a bag of eggs.

I didn't have to tell my mother, she heard it in my voice. "Oh, Kate," she said. Two days later, a spider plant arrived. It's impossible to kill a spider plant.

There were cards, and friends bearing the traditional dish of mourning, lasagna, appeared on our doorstep. Does every culture respond to loss with a variation on the easy-to-freeze, multilayered casserole? The bouquets of flowers went straight in the trash. I waited for someone, Teddy maybe, to say something like "The baby left? Just left? Fuck that lousy selfish blob. You've dodged a bullet. A bullet in a diaper." Instead they said: "You can always adopt. These things happen for a reason. You don't know, maybe it's for the best."

We had no real pictures to show, except the sonogram, which I'd tucked in my wallet like a first school picture. It was fuzzy and printed from a computer image. If you held it upside down, couldn't it be a jellyfish? Why keep a picture of a jellyfish? But I did.

My husband took time off work. The first time I called it *Oops, no paternity leave,* he'd smiled gamely. The second time he'd winced. "Please," he'd said.

At home, he ordered us takeout and brought me cups of weak tea. Rubbed my shoulders like a man with no feeling in his hands. He said what I needed him to say—even though it was the clip-on tie of clichés—*It will bring us closer together*—and it had. Here we were sitting on the sofa, closer than we ever did. He walked around the apartment turning on lights and electronics. It didn't matter if the room was empty. On went the stereo in the living room, the CD player in the kitchen, the clock radio in our bedroom, and the one in the shower. There wouldn't be even a minute of quiet when the Miles Davis *Kind of Blue* CD ended, because the voice of Terry Gross interviewing a ten-year-old oboe prodigy could be heard coming from the bathroom. You'd never have known that there were just the two of us in there.

After a week, I went back to work. My cover story, a virulent strain of flu, which, given how hollow-eyed and shaky I was, was believable. My assistant, who frowned on all stimulants, made an exception, bringing me a three-shot latte, the legal equivalent of crack cocaine. Then politely excused herself in case I wanted to cry.

Later, when she popped her head in my office to ask if there was anything she could do, I congratulated her on her new role as manager of health benefits for pregnant women and maternity leave. Then told her that, as of today, we had a new policy regarding in-office parties. I'd looked at our budget. All those cakes and balloons, they were bleeding us dry. I knew it wasn't going to make me popular, but I didn't care.

I'd never wanted this job. I'd taken the job as assistant to the head of human resources almost a decade ago, under the delusion that once I was in I could move over to the creative side. I'd fantasized that I wouldn't be operating copiers and faxes but rather, as my sinister-sounding title suggested, assisting my boss with the operation of heavy machinery, the jackhammers and drills, mining the most valuable parts out of an employee. Now I was trapped. It seemed ironic that, as the head of human resources, I couldn't produce a human.

At least the miscarriage gave me a Get-Out-of-Baby-

Showers-Free card. There'd be no more sucking mai tais out of baby bottles. No more games where you tried to diaper a Vaseline-greased watermelon, guess the guest of honor's weight, or identify the type of candy bar melted in a Pamper. All that paled in comparison to no longer having to listen to the wives' woeful bitching about how, despite their being thirty pounds overweight, unwashed, and covered in baby vomit, their husbands still couldn't keep their hands off them. They were *dying* to fuck them. Even with the baby in their bed. Even when the baby was nursing.

"You don't understand," a friend of mine had announced. "I told my husband as long as I can sleep through it and he doesn't wake the baby, he could do whatever he wanted to me."

She was right. I knew I'd get my sleep. My husband would see to that.

I didn't go, didn't even send gifts anymore. My gift was my absence. Free of me—in my invisible black veil and arm-band—the mothers could relax, swap baby pictures and tragic tales of cracked nipples and cradle cap.

Moving to Brooklyn wasn't a snap decision. We'd always said we might. Change is good, we said. So many couples get stuck in a rut. Brooklyn had excellent public schools and parks, easy access to all forms of transportation. The water taxi between downtown Manhattan and DUMBO would be fun. The fact that our once-adventurous friends demurred, saying they'd feel safer on the *Titanic*, was more evidence we needed a new life. In every way, Brooklyn seemed a better place to raise a child than Manhattan.

"Even the lesbians get pregnant in Park Slope," our real estate agent had joked as she led us down a leafy avenue.

A fleet of baby carriages seized the right-of-way like floats in a parade or a funeral procession. "All you have to do is touch a doorknob or sit on a toilet seat. I swear it's in the water."

It might as well have been true. There were pregnant women as far as the eye could see. Young and tattooed, graying and in clogs, fit and over thirty in T-shirts so tight you could see their belly buttons protruding like the stems of pumpkins. Only seconds after entering the room, they'd shuck off their coats and sweaters like strippers arriving late to a bachelor party, just in case you missed the fact that they were knocked up.

When we found a place after only a weekend of searching, it seemed like destiny. It was perfect. Our *pine box house*, we called it, because the only way we swore we'd ever leave it was in a coffin. We stood in the foyer, sunlight pouring through the windows, and gazed up at the high ceilings, the crown moldings, neither of us saying a word, like we were in a church. Standing in the kitchen, I imagined Douglas and the baby playing on the floor racing Matchbox cars while I tried to get a Thanksgiving turkey out of the oven.

There was a fireplace in the parlor. We'd sit in front of the fire and listen to music, play board games and let the baby cheat. When the baby got sleepy, it would put its head on the dog and use it as a pillow.

My husband stood in the bay window, gazing out like the captain of a ship plotting a new course. "We will put the piano here," he said. "We'll sit here together and I'll plink his, *its*, fingers on the keys. All the classics. 'Chopsticks.' We'll drive you nuts with 'Heart and Soul.'"

"Why not start now, Dougie?" I pulled up my shirt and offered him my belly. "Play a few bars."

He blushed. "Not here," he said, and moved to the hall to

admire the carved banister. In the hall was where I imagined teaching the baby to walk. Holding hands, I'd skate the baby down the hallway in socks.

I bought a new calendar. It seemed like bad luck to use the old one, so I'd thrown it out. I began taking my temperature and keeping track of the days. When it was time, I sidled up to my husband, who was hunched over a map of sewer lines with a ruler and pencil, and said, "Doctor's orders," in my best naughty-nurse voice. He blushed and kept his eyes fixed on the map. "Are you ready to explore Fertile Crescent?" I asked, wiggling my hips.

"Dear god, stop," he said, exasperated, as though I was some sort of dim-witted sexual predator. Mortified, I dropped the act. "It's time," I said. He sighed, put down his pen—his fingers so blue with ink the tips looked frostbitten—and trudged into the bedroom.

"I'm sorry it's such a chore," I said, trying not to notice how he recoiled when I reached to unbutton his shirt.

"I'm tired, Kate. I'm sorry. This playground is one headache after another. Can't you understand? I'm tired."

Occasionally I'd try to trick Douglas into making love to me when I wasn't ovulating. I was lonely. Sometimes it worked, other times he was less trusting. "Are you sure? Let me see the calendar."

Adopting the dog wasn't my idea. I always crossed the street when I saw the animal shelter people camped out on the sidewalk. The moment the grim-faced volunteer opened the cage, the fluffy dog burst out like a showgirl, like she'd been waiting her whole life for Douglas to show up and save her. He was smitten.

The woman, whose tan, heavily lined face suggested a lifetime spent in the sun smoking cigarettes, smiled knowingly. "Ah, that one," she said, lighting a cigarette, "has a lot of love to give."

My husband held the dog in front of him, making faces like he was trying to get it to laugh. He was undone. What a little cutie-pie. He couldn't understand how anybody could abandon a dog like this.

He asked if she'd been abused. He'd heard stories of dogs adopted from the pound who one day are model dogs, then the next snap and bite the face off the baby.

"Well, do you have a child, sir?" she asked, like she was setting a trap. "Do you?"

He looked at the ground.

"Not yet," my husband said, "but someday. Soon, hopefully." He reached for my hand and squeezed it. He wanted that dog. The dog anyone would want. The one that would be the easiest to give away.

"Then no question. You picked the winner," she said, exhaling smoke out her nose. "She's the best one we've got." The dog reclined in my husband's arms, offering up her belly.

In order to give Douglas and the dog a moment alone, she turned to adjust the shelter's banner. MEET YOUR NEW BEST FRIEND, it said, and underneath it in a handwritten scrawl, *The life you save may be your own!*

The cages on the bottom represented the bargain basement rack. In a corner cage was a reddish brown dog sitting with his back to the street. I didn't walk around the cage because I was curious to see his face or wanted to look in his eyes. I didn't. I was just stalling. Even so, as much as I fought it, I couldn't help myself. He was an older dog, with a long, wedge-shaped head that made him look regal, proud. It made me mad that he wasn't even trying to save himself.

"Go ahead. Pet him if you want. He won't bite," offered another volunteer, whose expression, despite her earnest smile, telegraphed a perpetual disappointment in the human race. She stared at me, then picked up a large plastic bottle filled with donated change and began shaking it like a melancholy maraca.

She was testing me. Daring me to prove that I wasn't scared, or heartless. Which left me with no choice but to stick my hand in the cage. The moment I touched the dog he closed his eyes. Did closing his eyes mean he was happy, or that he didn't want to get attached? All I knew was that suddenly adopting a dog—*today! A dog! A dog off the street!*— seemed the thing to do. It wasn't crazy. People fell in love on the street all the time.

I gazed over at Douglas, who gave me a pleading look. You would have thought from the terrible expression of pain on his face when he handed the little dog back that the two had been physically attached.

"We'll have to talk it over," he said quietly.

"Don't take too long. It's August. Vacation time." The overly tan woman snorted, exhaling smoke through her nose. "You'd be sick to your stomach if you knew how many people abandon their pets just so they can go to Disneyland or the Jersey Shore for two weeks without having to pay for a kennel. Let them out in the morning like it's any normal day—then lock up the house and go. Dump them in a parking lot behind the supermarket. Drive twenty miles out of town and leave them in a field by the side of the road."

"Don't some of those dogs find their way back home?" I said. "You always hear stories—"

"Ha!" the smiling volunteer snapped. "I'd like to wring the neck of the bastard that made *The Incredible Journey*. That idea that if a pet is really loyal—"

"Let's just say," the raisin-faced woman interrupted, "that where we usually provide a two-week *stay*, we're now offering a more *limited* time engagement."

My husband rubbed my shoulders. He whispered in my ear that a dog would be good for us. It would take our minds off of things. We wanted a dog. We were dog people. We'd get pregnant again, and everybody knew it was bad to bring a baby into a house with a new dog, or vice versa. And didn't we want two kids? If we were ever to have a dog, now would be the time to get it. And, he said, "we'd be saving a life."

He said he didn't care which dog we got. He just wanted one.

I looked in the cages. The red dog had turned around again. Like he'd gone back to his book. He was the one who wouldn't beg, the one who thought his fate was sealed.

For days after, both my husband and the dog wore a look of surprise.

He'd never have had any life without us.

I wanted to name him Mojo. "That way," I said, "if he ever gets lost, or runs away, we can say, *We've lost our Mojo.*"

Douglas looked baffled. "Why would we lose him? Why would he run away?"

We compromised. *Thelonious* Mojo sounded soulful. It suited him. As did the red-and-black watch plaid dog bed I'd insisted we buy.

The evening we brought Thelonious home, Douglas took

a picture of him curled up in his bed, a squeaky toy in the shape of a rolled-up newspaper at his feet, and e-mailed it to our parents and friends.

"Put down the date we adopted him and his weight," I said, half joking. "Which one of us do you think he resembles most?"

He ignored me and hit Send. "I think I should probably take him out for a walk," Douglas said. I could tell he liked the sound of that.

"We'll go together. As a *family*," I said. "Baby's first walk."

Douglas clipped on the leash he'd spent more time shopping for than his last suit. In the park, he'd yielded the leash reluctantly. "I want a turn too, you know," I said, tugging on it.

"It's just the traffic," he said, not letting go. "There is too much traffic. I'm concerned, that's all. It's hazardous. There should be another stoplight at the intersection." Tomorrow at work he'd pull out the highway plans, run the statistics for vehicular manslaughter.

"Fine." I let go. "You realize how silly this looks, us fighting over who gets to hold his leash?"

Douglas wrapped the leash around his wrist. If the dog took off, he'd amputate his hand. "I'm only thinking of his safety." He frowned. "I'm a first-time father. Nervous."

That night and every night afterward, the dog slept in the bed between us. If the dog wasn't already on the bed, Douglas would go get him and put him right there. At first, I liked the novelty of the two of us getting into bed together at night. That hadn't happened since the first years of our marriage. Even back then there were times when, five minutes after him, I'd slide between the sheets and he'd already be asleep, or faking it. When I'd started getting into bed before him, showered and perfumed, Douglas had started working late in front of the TV. Passing out on the couch, fully dressed, covered by a blanket of work sheets and building plans, like a homeless architect. Now we were getting into bed at the same time, but my husband was bringing his work, as well as the dog.

This would bother any wife. Since we were supposed to be trying to get pregnant, it really bothered me. Any time I sighed or rolled my eyes, he'd shoot me a look. "Is something wrong?" he'd ask, like he was calling my love for our dog into question.

"Does he have to lay right here between us?" I'd say. "I can't even see you."

"I can see you," he'd say, scarcely looking up from the proposal he was drafting, most recently to build a dog run, complete with doggie water fountains, in Bed-Stuy. Who knew there was a woeful lack of places for the underserved canines of Bed-Stuy to exercise?

"You act like I'm not the one who chose him," I'd remind him. "I picked him. You forget it was me who saved him from the gas chamber. If you'd had your way there'd be some floozy trophy dog in a sweater and rain boots in his place."

He'd put his hand protectively on Thelonious. "I'll turn out the light."

There were times we'd be petting him together like concubines in a harem, our fingers would touch, and a charge would pass through me.

My mother called from Florida, where she was visiting my sister and her three children, to check in. "You sound depressed. I hope you're not depressed. You know that there's depression on your father's side of the family," my mother said, "and alcoholism. Are you taking vitamins?"

"Gee, thanks," I said. "You always know what to say."

Douglas didn't have to tell me Thelonious hated it when we fought. In the beginning, as soon as he heard raised voices, he'd trot into the room, stare at us reproachfully, and my husband would start looking for the leash. "Thelonious has to pee," he'd say, or "I didn't walk him long enough earlier." Then he'd head for the hills.

After a while, at the sound of yelling, the crash of a dish thrown on the floor, Thelonious would crawl under the sofa, or our bed, and hide. "Look what you did," Douglas would say. "Are you happy now?" Then the dog wouldn't come out until he gave him the all-clear sign.

After a fight, to make it up to him, I'd buy Thelonious a bone, some rawhide. I'd give him a full can of wet food and let him lick the inside of the bathtub after I got out of the shower.

My husband worried. If I behaved like this with a dog, how would I be with a baby? Being allowed to lick the inside of the bathtub wouldn't comfort a baby.

We hadn't been back to that Italian restaurant since the night we'd gone there to celebrate. It was an hour on the train from Brooklyn, but it was our anniversary, and we didn't have a restaurant in Brooklyn that felt special yet. Douglas had been resistant until a friend of his from the dog run (father of Rudy, a Jack Russell Terrier and Thelonious's supposed "best dog friend") offered to take him for a few hours. According to Douglas, the two had hit it off immediately and now needed nothing more than a "There Goes a Squirrel" video and a box of Milk Bones to entertain themselves.

I'd been tempted to get stoned before dinner. The topper on an already stressful day was trying to calm my assistant, who—having discovered a picture of a Fudgie the Whale cake with his eyes blacked out and a slash through him in the break room—was certain her life was in danger.

I'd wanted to smoke, but I hadn't because Douglas, who hadn't gotten high since we started trying to get pregnant, wouldn't have approved, and it was our anniversary.

I know neither of us imagined we'd see that waiter—the one who'd toasted our future, who'd shown us his kids—again. Douglas was poring over the wine list when I saw him across the room, waiting on another table. He recognized us. His face lit up, and he waved. *Perhaps*, his expression said, *we had pictures?* He mimed rocking a baby. I shook my head no. He was perplexed. Perhaps we'd left the baby at home? I made an exaggerated frowny face. He looked at me blankly. I gave him the thumbs-down. He still didn't get it. I drew my finger across my throat. This time I saw it register in his eyes just before he turned away.

Another waiter came to take our order. I hadn't imagined Douglas would mention we were celebrating, but I dared to hope that when the wine arrived we would make a toast to our anniversary. I was tired of always being the one to have to acknowledge such occasions.

"I'm sorry," I said, cupping my hand around my ear. "Were you about to say something?"

"I don't think so," he said. "Is it cold in here?"

"No." I vowed not to pick up my fork until he raised his glass.

He cut into his veal, took a sip of his wine.

I couldn't stand it. "Shouldn't we drink to us? It *is* our anniversary."

"Yes. Of course," he said courteously, touching the lip of his glass to mine.

Then: "How is work?"

"Work is fine," I answered.

Then he asked me if I enjoyed my meal. No. He did not like the wine. The conversation went on this way throughout dinner. It was as if neither of us was speaking in our native tongue, and lacking fluency in the language we shared, we'd resorted to talking about the weather, about food, about what time it was.

"Next time," he said, signing the bill, "we'll give that place on Fifth Avenue a shot. You know, there's much better Italian in Brooklyn."

"But," I said, "this is our place." He shrugged. My words echoing, like my husband was a large empty room.

I'd waited outside on the stoop while my husband went inside to get the dog. He hadn't suggested I go with him and meet this new friend, and I wasn't in the mood. I thought about the cuff links I'd given him as an anniversary gift. Each had a real piece of a New York City subway map preserved under glass. They were one of a kind. I thought about how he'd apologized for not having time to wrap the book of flower photographs he pulled out of the bag from the chain store he'd ducked into after work.

It was a small thing, small like a sliver of glass.

Thelonious, off the leash, trotted alongside Douglas the whole way home. Their strides were so perfectly synced— they could have been one organism. They always walked faster together than they did separately, and it annoyed me. I didn't try to keep up with them. Soon they were half a block ahead of me, then a block. If Douglas and I got divorced,

I'd want equal custody. He was insane if he thought I'd give him the dog.

In the way animals can sense when a storm is approaching, five minutes after we got home Thelonious took refuge under our bed. I said we should talk in the kitchen. I yelled at Douglas for not raising his glass first, never making the toast, ever. He didn't love me. He couldn't love me.

"You're drunk," he said disdainfully, frowning as I lit a joint off the gas burner of the stove. "Oh, that's lovely, Kate. No, really. How perfect." Wasn't I supposed to be getting healthy, maximizing my chances—*my* chances, not *our* chances—of getting pregnant?

I imagined fetuses on a real estate tour trooping through prospective wombs, our potential baby knocking on my uterine wall, testing the foundation, gauging the ambience. The quality of life factor.

I took an extra-large hit and held my smoke.

The next morning, feeling lonelier than usual, I decided to ignore the invisible his/hers sign on our headboard, and nudging Thelonious out of bed, crossed over to my husband's side. I examined the curve of his neck, the fine hair on his arms, his fingerprints. If the shape of a man's fingers mimicked the shape of his penis, then did all piano players have long, rectangular penises? I couldn't remember what Douglas's penis looked like. Half asleep, I kissed him. He didn't look worried or flinch. Half asleep, he kissed me back. I wondered if he was kissing in his dream, if he was turned on, and who my husband might be dreaming of. If only we were, both of us, always half asleep, I thought, we could grow old together.

That night all the lights, even Douglas's reading lamp, were off when I got into bed. I'd assumed he was asleep or playing dead until he rolled toward me and put his hand on my waist. Thelonious jumped off the bed and left the bedroom.

See, his touch said, *there's no problem*. Then, as though he'd been rehearsing, he said, "I want to make love to you."

I was glad for the dark. We were awkward with each other. It was hard to find our rhythm. Apologies were exchanged. In the middle of it I thought, *I wonder if this is the last time we'll ever have sex*.

After he came, he kissed me. The way gamblers kiss a poker chip for luck.

The next day he called me at work. "I have an idea," he said. "I think we should get away. Go to the Cape. This weekend."

"Now?" It would be Easter weekend.

"I know the plan wasn't to go back until that second week in July, but"—he hesitated—"that doesn't mean we can't go now, right?"

"Sure," I said. It would be better to go now anyway. Because you never knew with the beach. A hurricane could come and rip up the shoreline, flatten the clam bar, wipe out the cottages. Everything could get washed into the sea by the time July rolled around. Plus, we agreed, it was high time we took Thelonious to see the ocean. He'd love it. He'd romp in the waves, roll in the sand.

For three days we walked on the beach, watching like proud parents as Thelonious retrieved the tennis balls Douglas threw in the water and ate an old corn dog he found in the sand. All things a baby couldn't do. He sat perfectly still and stared at the sea. He was such a dreamer, that dog. He trotted back to the blanket and lay down right beside the two of us.

We ate lobster rolls at our favorite shack along the beach

highway. Knee to knee at one of the communal picnic tables, we listened to a lovesick cricket answer the chirp of a man's cell phone—chirp, chirp, chirp. Our neighbors laughed.

At night in our cottage, in the dark, we had sex in a narrow bed and held each other. We wanted a baby. We were on vacation. This was what you did. We were following the instructions, checking off boxes.

We got up early while the sun was fighting to rise above the sea and walked the beach. I wished I had my camera to take a picture of the two of them, my boys, standing side by side looking out at the horizon, both so serious, like they were actually seeing something. They were looking at the future.

"What do you see out there?"

Douglas sighed. "I think I can see the coast of England."

On the last morning, we all slept in. The weather had changed. By eleven o'clock, it was clear that the sun wasn't going to make it out of bed and that, instead of warming up, it was getting colder. It looked like rain, and I was grateful. Bad weather always made ending a vacation a little easier. Even so, my husband suggested we take a walk. One last walk, he said. He clapped his hands for Thelonious to come, but the dog stayed put on the rug like he wanted us to have a private moment.

So the two of us set off alone. For some reason, Douglas took my hand, and so we walked that way, holding hands, going slowly, leaning into each other, the way people do when they've gotten bad news.

We didn't talk at all. I laid my head on his shoulder. I thought, *Is he thinking this is the last time we'll come here? The last time I'll look at this part of the ocean?*

When we got back, Thelonious was asleep. He could

barely bring himself to open his eyes. He had no interest in catching a Frisbee. He was ready to go.

While I was packing up the car, they took a last turn around the cottage to make sure we didn't leave any CDs or sandals or dog toys behind. While I finished arranging the suitcases, Douglas gave Thelonious a pre-car-ride drink. Kneeling beside the dog, he rubbed his ears and stomach while Thelonious tried to drink from his bowl.

"Does he seem a little off to you?" he asked.

"Maybe he's homesick," I said, "or, no, just a little tired."

My husband kissed him on the head. "You're the best boy in the world," he said, refilling the water dish. "You know that? I love you. The best."

Thelonious hadn't shaken the bug he'd gotten at the Cape. However, like a child who doesn't want to bother or worry his parents, he didn't fuss. I should have known something was wrong when he started curling up at my feet at night, when he came over to me during dinner and put his head on my knee, right in front of Douglas. I should have known by the way he looked up at me like I'd understand.

I'd insisted on taking him to the vet.

"Why? He's just a bit under the weather," my husband said. "Maybe you two have the same thing."

In the waiting room of the clinic, the shy dogs hid behind their owners' legs, while the others, despite their owners' begging, frisked about, jumping on strangers and wrestling like little kids. Thelonious sat patiently by my side. He was such a good boy. I couldn't help feeling proud and a bit superior. I put my hand on his shoulder and felt it. The same thing I'd felt the first time I saw him. He was mine. I'd saved him.

The vet was an older man with an Irish accent, who wore his white doctor's coat loosely over a country-doctor-style corduroy jacket and a thick fisherman's sweater, as though he wished he were James Herriot delivering calves in the middle of the night.

The vet listened to Thelonious's heart and lungs.

"He's been a little listless lately," I offered.

"How long now?"

"Just a few days." I couldn't be sure.

"Any other symptoms?"

"Not that I know of." He shined a flashlight in Thelonious's eyes. I watched the dog's pupils enlarge.

"Got any blood in the stool?" he asked, sticking the tongue depressor into Thelonious's mouth. Both of us gagged.

"No blood," I said.

The vet's best guess was anemia. "You'll be wanting to crush up the pills and hide them in his wet food," he said. I hated wet food, the smell, the sluice of it as it slid out of the can, it made me retch, but I'd try. Still, I told the vet, "Thelonious is too smart for that old trick. He'd never fall for it."

The vet shook his head and assured me, "Canines are genetically wired to please their owners. It's in their nature. If a dog trusts you, you can get away with *anything*."

This was exactly why my husband had insisted I be the one to dose Thelonious's Alpo.

"I'm sorry, but I could never do that to him." Douglas winced and wrung his hands. "He'd know."

It was just understood that I could betray that trust. I was the only one of us with a strong enough will to do what was needed. Thelonious would also need medication three times a day. Douglas left earlier and came home later from work than

I did. Consistency was important. He wouldn't want to inadvertently give Thelonious too much or too little. He wished he could work from home like I could, but he couldn't. I was more than happy to stay home with him for a day or two. "Just until he's back on his paws."

While my husband was at work, Thelonious and I lay in bed spooning and watching reruns of cop shows from the days when they wore trench coats, smoked cigars, and had no time for dames. I'd gotten hooked on one where the murder victims narrate the bumbling attempts of detectives to solve their cases. They'd shout: *Right there! The knife my wife is using to cut the kids' peanut butter sandwiches! That's the murder weapon!* Or whisper: *That lying, scheming bitch!* There was something about having seen the victim's body Swiss-cheesed by bullets, or blue in a bathtub with a toaster, that made the justice sweeter than usual.

Occasionally I'd get up to check the computer; I ignored the e-mails from work. The first time I vomited, Thelonious got out of bed and came to sit in the doorway of the bathroom like he was worried.

"It's okay," I said. "I'm just pregnant."

I'd taken the test the night we'd come home from the vet. I knew even without the test, before I realized the similarity between a plus sign and crosshairs.

"But it's a secret," I said. "You can't tell anyone."

When Douglas came home early from work and saw us together in bed, it was his turn to look jealous. However, when Thelonious seemed too tuckered to lift his head for Douglas to scratch behind his ears, he looked worried.

"Has he been drinking, Kate? Have you been monitoring his hydration? Did you give him his pills? On schedule? Has he eaten anything? He has to eat, Kate. It's imperative. If he doesn't eat he can't ingest the medication." He got down on his haunches and looked into our dog's eyes. "Does he look thin to you, Kate? He looks thin to me," he said. "I'm worried."

I heard him on the phone. "He doesn't have the same pep. He's an older dog—not old—but his energy . . . He's a little thinner than usual, but he's a thin dog . . ."

The vet was talking.

"Really?" He sounded surprised. "No. Morning is good."

This vet was younger with a ponytail and a sunburned nose. She wore pearls. "Thelonious, that's a pretty name," she said, looking in his ears. "What do they call you, Thelonious?"

"Thelonious," my husband said.

She would have to take blood, and then X-rays.

"He looks better, doesn't he?" my husband asked as she disappeared into the back room to take the picture. I wished I could lie on that table alongside my dog. Crawl under that lead blanket.

Minutes later she returned with the results. She could tell we were the sort of people who would demand proof. This time, though, I didn't need to look. My husband examined the X-rays blindly, nodding, even as the vet used the term "like hamburger," as though the news—good or bad—depended on his reaction.

"I'm sorry," the vet said, wiping at her eyes. "I'm new."

"Are you sure?" my husband asked. She had a ponytail, for god's sake. How could you take her seriously?

"It's very clear," the vet said, composing herself.

Douglas turned to me, helpless. "How could we have missed it?"

I wondered whether if we'd come sooner Thelonious might have been cured.

I said we'd take him home. We'd wrap him up in his plaid blanket, take him home and make him comfortable.

"I can't tell you what to do," the vet said, "but you should know, he's in a lot of pain."

"I want to take him home," my husband said. He couldn't stand to let go.

Then the vet told us she'd never seen a dog as stoic as ours. "How did you do it, Thelonious?" she said, rubbing between his ears. "How long have you been walking around like this, huh?" Thelonious looked tiredly from me to my husband.

"It's your choice. You can take him home," she said. "He might live this way for weeks, a month perhaps, but . . ."

"He was a rescue dog," I said.

"Take your time."

For the second time ever I saw my husband cry. I took his hand, and we held each other for a long time before he hoisted himself to sit on the examination table. Gently, he lifted Thelonious's head into his lap, stroking it while the vet readied the needles. They broke my heart. The first shot relaxed him. The second put him to sleep.

While he was still warm, I kissed my dog, and closed his eyes.

Are You Comfortable?

A ll I'm asking is that you please take your grandpa out to
lunch," Charlotte's mother said, struggling to zip the overstuffed suitcase in the middle of her bedroom floor without
ruining her nails.

Charlotte, lying in the middle of her mother's newly made
bed, yawned. "Yes, ma'am. I'm looking forward to it."

Charlotte wondered if her mother was simply ignoring the
leg of nude panty hose dangling over the edge of her bag. A
good daughter would haul herself up off the bed and tuck that
forlorn-looking leg inside the case before the zipper caught it,
but Charlotte was too exhausted to move. She was a bad person. She chewed on her thumbnail.

"Your daddy and I will be back Monday night, sooner if I
have my way. You hear?"

It was early. Were she back at school right now, she'd be
in the front row of her European history class, but Charlotte
didn't want to think about that.

It wasn't her idea to come home. There had been an accident. It was a small thing. No one was hurt but her. Just a
bump on the head, although the doctor had said she could

expect more bruising and tenderness. She could have walked away—it was that sort of thing—but she was sick. That explained why she'd crashed her car. According to her mother, when she and Charlotte's father came to get her, she was out of her mind with fever. She had said crazy things.

For the last three weeks Charlotte had been sleeping until noon, or until she heard her mother's white BMW pull out of the drive to visit her grandfather at the Golden Oaks. After ramming his Cadillac into the large yellow and orange sign that welcomed you to the retirement village, he'd been declared unfit to drive. The revoking of his driver's license was an injustice her mother had protested vehemently and had yet to recover from. Since then she'd gone over every day to tidy up her father's room, and spring him for lunch.

When Charlotte asked her if she didn't miss playing tennis with her foursome, DAR meetings, having even one afternoon to herself, she'd acted surprised that Charlotte could even think such a thing. *Heavens no. He's my father.* If Charlotte considered the sacrifices her mother had borne happily and without complaint as martyrdom, then her mother was afraid she'd failed to raise her right.

Charlotte's mother sat back on her heels for a moment to catch her breath and frowned. She hated the look of an overpacked suitcase, but one never knew what sorts of attire the other businessmen's wives might bring—skirts and blouses, cocktail dresses, evening gowns—and her mother didn't want to be caught out. Her white silk shirt stuck to the middle of her mother's back. *Men and horses sweat, ladies perspire.*

"I'm so glad you're feeling up to it. I'd be at a complete loss otherwise," she said, pinning the suitcase under her full weight. "You're a good girl."

"I'm happy to go, Mama." How could Charlotte's mother not see that leg of hose? *A lady always crosses her legs at the ankle, never at the knee.*

"That's so nice," her mother said gaily. "You know, he didn't say it outright—your grandfather never would, and being a businessman, he'd understand—but I could tell he was disappointed when I told him I had to go out of town with your father, but then when I said *you'd* be coming to take him out"—she paused—"he was so elated."

"I'm happy to go, Mama." The sound of her own voice, as perky and mechanical as that of a talking doll she'd had as a girl, caught her off guard. That doll had been her favorite until the string you pulled to make it talk broke.

"Well, I know what a treat it'll be for the two of you to spend some time together."

Watching her mother wrestling with her bag, rear end bobbing up and down, skirt riding up, made Charlotte queasy.

Charlotte smiled at her mother. "I can't wait." Her mother swore that the simple act of smiling made a person happier. She also swore that you could say just about anything, insult a person, lie right to their face, if you did so with a smile.

It wasn't that Charlotte didn't love her grandfather. What kind of girl doesn't love her grandfather? It was just—what would they talk about? They had nothing in common save their alma mater (and they'd both gotten in on his genius), but since she'd left school—just two months before her graduation—they couldn't talk about that.

Her grandfather's motto was *Knowledge is the key that unlocks life's riches.*

"And if he asks why you aren't at school, why, you simply tell him the truth, sugar," Charlotte's mother said. "You have *mononucleosis.*" Her mother insisted on using the scientific term as though repeating an official diagnosis.

Charlotte was certain that if her mother knew the nickname for mono was "the kissing disease," Charlotte would be suffering now from scarlet fever. "Right, mono. I'm sorry, Mama, I forgot."

"Charlotte Anne," her mother snapped, "I'm just trying to help you here." She looked like she was about an inch from crying. "I'll tell you what you do. You simply tell your grandfather you've been sick, and came home to rest and let your mama take care of you."

What was wrong with Charlotte? Hadn't her mother moved a TV into her room, brought her ginger ale, and peanut butter and honey sandwiches arranged in the shape of a smiley face with a banana for a nose, just like when she was little? She'd brought her magazines, *Vogue, People,* and *Seventeen.* "I know you're not seventeen anymore," she said, "but it used to be your favorite.

"Are you listening to me, Charlotte?"

Wasn't her mother always checking on her? Kissing her forehead, especially when she thought she was asleep, letting her lips linger on her skin like she was taking her temperature? Who else does that?

"You haven't been well," her mother stated firmly. "It's true. That's the god's honest truth."

That's the truth, Charlotte said to herself. She was unwell. So unwell she wasn't even supposed to answer the door for the mailman, or take out the garbage. *And, yet,* Charlotte thought, eyes fixed on the sheer leg meandering out of the suitcase, *you're leaving me here all alone for four days. All alone in this house.*

Charlotte picked at her cuticles with impunity, tearing at

a hangnail knowing her mother wasn't about to start harping on her about ragged cuticles making a girl look cheap. At least she'd lost weight. Ten pounds in three weeks. What did her mother always say? *You have such a pretty face.*

"You simply tell your grandpa your professors are allowing you to finish your course work over the summer. He'll understand that. You were raised right. You've always been a good student, haven't you? You're very conscientious, you always have been. You've never been in any kind of trouble." *Girls who look for trouble find trouble.* "All you have to do is finish a few papers." Charlotte watched her mother's knuckles go from pink to white. "And for heaven's sake," she said, forcing levity into her voice, "it's not like you dropped out. You're a nice girl."

Wasn't that what the parents of boys said they wished for their sons? Charlotte thought. What they themselves wanted most? For their son to meet and marry *a nice girl*?

There'd been no point in telling her mother she had no intention of ever going back to college. Telling her now would just upset her more. Later on, she might pretend to fuss, but she herself had dropped out junior year to get married. She said that in her time it was fashionable for a girl to go for an M.R.S. degree. Making it sound like a girl could declare husband hunting as her major. Her father—well, he wouldn't care. His big dream had never been more than to get his little girl married off right out of college to some boy he could go fishing with, and set her on grandbaby duty.

The only one who would care, the only one who wouldn't understand about her dropping out of school, was her grandpa. Leaving school would be unfathomable to him.

"I know it's hard sometimes to put the needs of others before your own. But charity begins at home." Her mother sighed dramatically. "Do you honestly think I want to go on this business trip with your daddy? I don't, not one bit. I have no choice. All the other wives are going, and how would it look if I wasn't there?" she said in a huff. "*Your* daddy says I deserve a break. He says I need to *get away*. Well, that's just patently false."

Charlotte didn't need her father to explain to her why he needed to get away. Ever since she'd come home, any time they accidentally bumped into each other in the kitchen or the hallway, he nearly jumped out of his skin, like she'd given him an electric shock.

"I'm so sorry," he'd stammer, all red in the face and overly polite.

"No, it was my fault," she'd say. "I'm sorry."

Then he'd fumble around in his pockets for candy and press it into her hand. Root beer barrels, Lemon Heads, Tootsie Rolls, always some candy from her childhood. His new taste for candy was, her mother complained, making him fat.

"I hope you're not fretting about the driving," her mother said, and with a swipe of her hand the stocking leg disappeared inside her bag. An act which, for some reason, filled Charlotte with a sense of defeat. "You just remember how well you did going around the block. Each time you got better and better. You're a better driver than me now, I think," she said, laughing self-consciously. "You've simply got to remind yourself *that* was an accident, remember? It won't happen again," her mother said, and with this she yanked the zipper closed.

Charlotte smiled at her mother. "I know. I'm fine. I can drive. I'll go this afternoon, even. You want me to take your car or Daddy's?"

Her car's name had been Baby, and it'd been a present.

The morning of her high school graduation, her father had woken her up, told her to close her eyes, and led her out to the garage. And there she was, a brand-new baby blue Volvo tied up with a giant yellow bow. Where did car dealerships get bows that big? How would you tie a ribbon so big?

She'd screamed. She'd thrown her arms around her dad and kissed that wide, smooth cheek. He'd hugged her so her feet left the ground. "You deserve it," he'd said and kissed her back. Back then he could kiss her back.

"Safest car on the road," her father had said, dropping the keys into her hand. She'd felt the weight of his promise. She'd always be his little girl. He'd never stop trying to protect her.

She'd had Baby all four years of college. She'd driven everywhere and everybody. She and her friends drove places they could have easily walked to, like the supermarket and the liquor store, and places like Burger King at midnight, and a bar out in the sticks that didn't even open until three in the morning. She was a good driver. Responsible. Even after a few cocktails, people gave her their keys.

Sometimes she'd take a drive all by herself, pop a mix tape in the stereo, and turn the volume up loud enough so she could sing along with the Supremes, *You can't hurry love, no you just got to wait*, without hearing her own voice.

"Now, you know you'll be fine if you simply take your time," Charlotte's mother said, still kneeling on top of the suitcase. "A cautious driver is a safe driver."

"I can drive," Charlotte said. "I'm a great driver."

It wasn't like Charlotte had planned it. She'd only known when she got into her car that, as long as she kept driving, moving invisible and untouchable as wind, she was safe.

She didn't know how long it was before she realized at some point she'd run out of gas. When she noticed, the trees seemed to be coming closer and closer to the road, darting suddenly out of the shadows, inches from her bumper, then back into the woods, and waving their branches at her. *Me, me, me*, they cried, demanding her attention. Like they'd been waiting for her. Known she was coming. *Me, me, me! Pick me!*

She'd chosen a big tree on purpose, one that could take it, not a little one.

"I know you're fine, honey, but are you certain?" her mother said, pausing to right the hem of her skirt over her knees. "You've got to tell me if you're feeling at all unwell, sugar. I just want you to be comfortable."

"I said I'm fine."

Charlotte had begun to notice that in times of stress her mother spoke in a singsong that made everything she said sound like a nursery rhyme. It made Charlotte want to scream. Instead she coughed, loud and hard so it made her throat hurt and her mother wince.

"I have to tell you," her mother said, standing up stiffly and coming over to the bed. "You look so much better." She kissed Charlotte on the forehead. "You must feel better."

This wasn't a question. It was a command. *You must feel better.* Charlotte wasn't such an idiot she'd argue with her. It was pointless.

The first day Charlotte was home she'd slept all day long and didn't eat. The second day she'd slept less, eaten two saltines, but wouldn't change her clothes. On the third day, when she refused to eat, change, or bathe, her mother, who had until this point seen no reason to bring in a doctor, had called the family practitioner. Whom, despite the fact that he was quite elderly and his examinations were limited to the use of instruments found in a children's medical kit—stethoscope, hammer, tongue depressor—her mother trusted implicitly.

His diagnosis was simple. "She's just run down."

Run down. Charlotte wondered whether the doctor meant *run down* like a clock or *run down* like chased and caught.

"You be glad it's nothing serious," he said, patting her knee.

It was the first time Charlotte had ever seen her mother really cry. She'd taken Charlotte's face in her hands and wept. "You know I'd just die if it was something serious. Something worse. I'd just die and go straight to heaven, baby."

"You know what I bet would put a smile on your face? Talking to your girlfriends," her mother said like she hadn't mentioned it ten times before. "I just know Teddy and Deb would love to hear from you, honey. It's been a while."

It had been, and that was fine with Charlotte.

Two days after Charlotte left school, her four best girl-friends had all gotten together and called her on the same line, passing the phone back and forth between them. It was very sweet and thoughtful, but despite Deb trying to corral everyone, everybody was talking at once and laughing and then Bender told a terrible joke—*What do you call a boy hiding in a bush? Answer: Russell*—and Charlotte had begun to feel claustrophobic, like they were all stuffed in a telephone booth together and she was at the bottom, and she'd thought she'd die if she didn't hang up that instant. Only Bender had persisted in calling her in the face of no response. Three sheets to the wind, and she was leaving a message on Charlotte's parents' machine: "Are you okay? It's okay if you're not. You know you can talk to me, right?" In the background Charlotte could hear Neil Young singing about a hurricane.

Charlotte yawned loudly and without covering her mouth, but her mother ignored it.

"I forgot to mention one thing," her mother said, turning away. "When you see Grandpa you need to make certain things are tidy. You understand? You know he likes it nice and tidy—throw out any crackers, any little packets of stuff . . ."

Six months earlier Charlotte's mother had been alerted by a social worker that her father was hoarding packets of ketchup, nondairy creamers, and Sweet'n Low. The social worker said this was worrisome. Charlotte's mother said she never realized it was a crime for a man to enjoy condiments in the privacy of his own room.

"And toothpicks," she said now. "There may be lots of toothpicks. And plastic knives." She tossed this off as though collecting plastic knives had been a lifelong hobby of her father's.

"Of course," Charlotte said, like there was nothing oddball about it. "I'll be on the lookout for knives."

"And you won't forget his laundry, will you?" Her mother had saved the best for last. "Be discreet; take a plastic bag and put it inside one of those Tiffany shopping bags."

"Yes, ma'am."

"You simply need to get his trousers, underwear—use your best judgment—you know, anything else that—" She hesitated; she wasn't going to say "anything that reeks of urine."

Charlotte knew her grandfather had cut the toes out of his socks and soaked his undershirts in bleach for so long they'd almost completely disintegrated. She assumed he'd lifted the bleach off the cleaning cart, or found a supply closet and taken it for himself. Hiding a bottle of bleach would be just as easy as hiding the pint bottles of bourbon snuck in for him by her mother. ("My father is a gentleman. I refuse to deprive him of his right to enjoy an occasional nightcap. It's just civilized.")

Charlotte wondered if perhaps her mother was worried that in the absence of liquor he might accidentally drink bleach. Or paint thinner. Again. ("You know men," her mother reported that she'd told the social worker, who despite being a woman and divorced wasn't having any of it. "A simple accident," she said. "It wasn't like he mixed it with tonic, and garnished it with a twist of lime. He hadn't drunk but a tiny bit. A taste.")

The paint thinner was what had gotten her grandpa moved out of his cottage at the retirement home, where he'd lived alone for three years after her grandmother died, into an apartment in the assisted-living wing.

Charlotte couldn't understand why her mom had so resisted her grandfather's move, but she had. All it meant was someone checked in on you every day, did your laundry, and made sure you turned up for meals—albeit no longer in the formal dining room, where the other residents dined. Still, she'd fought the decision tooth and nail. She said he was being railroaded into moving into the main building so they could sell his cottage at a premium.

It was the dining room bit that bothered her mother most. The snub. There'd be no more eating off nice china, no more talking about the stock market with former captains of industry and reminiscing about the glory days of their careers. From here on out it would be plastic plates and dining companions who couldn't remember the names of their children, let alone the name of the country club they once belonged to. Nobody ever came back from Assisted Living. Her mother thought it might just as well be called Assisted Dying.

But in the end he signed the papers. He hadn't even told Charlotte's mother until after it was done. He was always a good businessman. It was his decision, and because he was supposedly of sound mind and body—after all, that was the point her mother had been arguing—she had to abide by it.

"So you won't forget?" her mother asked, finally meeting Charlotte's eyes. "Get his laundry."

The laundry was key. If the staff found out her grandpa was having *issues*, they'd have just cause to move him into the health center, and it was bad enough he was in Assisted Living.

"I won't forget."

"And you'll go today?"

"I said I would."

"I just don't want him to be lonely."

Lonely. She was just being dramatic. How could a person be lonely at the Golden Oaks Retirement Village? Why, just the phrase: *retirement village.* It sounded like a bunch of elderly Eskimos had pulled up stakes and gone off to start their own exclusively geriatric, all-cotton-top town.

They'd spend their time making beaded belts and napping in deerskin hammocks and telling stories from the old days. And it wouldn't matter if you told the story of how you courted your wife or broke into business a hundred times, because after a while these memories took on the weight of legends.

You wouldn't be allowed to be lonely. *It would be against the rules.* If you got lonely, they'd give you a pill. If that didn't snap you out of it, you'd get taken out back and shot.

• • •

The entire way there Charlotte had the feeling her mother's car was driving itself, her faithful steed doing her bidding. All Charlotte had to do was keep her speed steady, and when the broken yellow lines on the highway started flying by the window like snips of ribbon, hold on tight to the wheel so she wouldn't drift into the other lane, or off the road.

Me, me, me, the trees had called to her. *Me, me, me.*

In the parking lot she sat in the car panting, windows up, waiting for her heart to settle down. Her grandfather wasn't going to care if she showed up or not. He was too busy whittling birch-bark canoes and tanning animal hides, scanning the skies for bald eagles. He might even be relieved Charlotte hadn't shown up. Maybe all this time what he wanted was peace.

She didn't think about how last night she'd fallen asleep wondering if her grandfather, ten miles away lying in his own bed, was still awake. Did he read in bed at night, did they let him watch that TV? Did they give him something to help him sleep?

She bet those nurses stood in the doorway and watched him brush his teeth and get ready for bed. She bet he did what they told him to do. She bet he was good. She hoped they appreciated that.

Charlotte had come late with full knowledge her grandpa would already have eaten lunch, and that, as it was well past 1:00, she had an excuse for keeping their visit short. She could make polite conversation for an hour or so. As her friend Bender used to say, *I can do anything for ten minutes.*

As she approached the building she realized she'd forgotten to park around back, like her mother always did. Which meant she'd have to walk through the health center to get to Assisted Living.

Today it seemed everyone had been carted into the hall for an airing out, meaning there was a whole gauntlet of geriatrics to be run. A woman strapped in a chair was howling, beating the air, fighting an invisible swarm of bees. A pair of twins, each with a Raggedy Ann doll in her lap, stared up at the fluorescent tubes in the ceiling, blinking their eyes like moles unaccustomed to the light. The rest of the elderly had been arranged in a line against the wall, those who weren't completely collapsed leaning hard out of their chairs, clutching the armrests, like the wind had blown them into these positions and they'd petrified, mouths hanging open so wide you could throw in a penny and make a wish.

But still, given the way the pianist, a tiny violet-haired lady whose sneakered feet scarcely brushed the pedals, was swaying and thumping on the keys, she and her audience would both have been surprised to find she wasn't actually playing.

Charlotte spotted her grandfather, natty in a seersucker jacket and green corduroy pants, from behind. He was sitting over by the picture window at a table with some other men playing cards. One man was in a gray jogging suit and a West Point baseball cap. Fastened to his walker was a bike basket decorated with a plastic rose and military ribbons. The other man was wearing a sweatshirt, NUMBER ONE GRANDPA. Charlotte felt a little bad about having never given her grandfather such a gift. Then again, she'd never seen her grandfather in a sweatshirt.

Even without that jacket on, without seeing his face, she'd have known him straightaway. It had though occurred to her that he might not recognize her at first. She'd cut her hair off. She'd done it herself, and without looking in the mirror until the end. Her mother had nearly fainted when she first saw her. Charlotte stood behind, gathering herself. She wondered how it must look, a girl, his granddaughter no less, hovering behind him like a strangler.

She touched his shoulder. "Grandpa," she said.

"Well, hello!" he said, turning to greet her, reaching out to shake her hand. It took her a second. It was her grandfather, but not him. His hair wasn't neatly combed back but parted low on the side, and he wasn't wearing his lovely gold glasses but what looked like a pair of brown plastic safety goggles he would have worn in his shop. The oversize lenses magnified his eyes. He looked simple. It got Charlotte in the back of her knees.

"Grandpa," she said, shaking his hand, then leaned down to kiss his cheek. That's what granddaughters do.

"Well, hello there," he said, as flustered and pleased as if she'd been Marilyn Monroe.

Despite the fact that she'd just seen her grandfather at Christmas, he looked much older. Her mother might have mentioned that.

"So, how are you doing today, Grandpa?" she said, trying not to look at his eyes behind those terrible glasses. They were perched crooked on his nose like a cartoon character who had taken a punch.

"Far as I know, I'm fit as a fiddle." He stretched out his arms, patted his chest.

"I'm so happy to hear that. That's real good."

Charlotte had walked with what she hoped looked like breezy confidence to the nurses' station. Along the front of the desk was a collection of teddy bears dressed up like doctors and nurses, a patient with a thermometer sticking out of its mouth, as well as a garish, oversize arrangement of red and yellow gladiolus. Coffin flowers. Charlotte wondered where they came from. Every time her mother attended a wedding, dinner dance, or funeral, she'd always bring the leftover flowers to the nurses, anything to butter them up so they'd be nice to Charlotte's grandfather.

"Excuse me, ma'am," Charlotte said to an aide who was tossing pills into paper cups like jelly beans into an Easter basket. "But there's— Mr. Halliday, my grandfather, his glasses seem to be missing. Is it possible—"

The aide peered at her through bright blue contacts, then at her grandfather, sitting across the room, flipping over cards like he was playing solitaire. "He's got glasses on," she said matter-of-factly. "As far as I know, those are his."

Charlotte smiled politely. How could the aide not see something was wrong? What did she think? That Charlotte's grandfather was in the middle of a welding project? He looked retarded.

She noticed her hands starting to make fists, so she took hold of the counter. *Good manners cost you nothing. The lack of them cost you dearly.* "Forgive me, ma'am," Charlotte smiled harder, "but I know for a fact his glasses are gold, and oval. My whole life, he's always worn the same ones—"

"You're saying those don't belong to him?" The nurse studied her grandfather with suspicion, then barked, "Whose glasses did you take, Mr. Halliday?" Charlotte jumped.

At the sound of his name, her grandfather smiled and as if summoned, pushed himself away from the table, and got up.

"Maybe I made a mistake," Charlotte stammered. Now she'd gotten him into trouble. Getting him out of there—right now—seemed the only answer. "Maybe they're new. My mother may have told me, and I forgot. It's truly of no concern."

At that moment a familiar-looking nurse appeared behind the counter. "Why, look at you, honeybunch!" she said, rather too energetically. "Haven't you just grown into the spitting image of your mama." She leaned in close to stare at Charlotte's face, her eyes like chocolate chips pushed into dough. "And how's your mama doing today? Is she here with you?" she asked hopefully, looking past Charlotte like maybe her mother was right around the corner.

"No."

"I sure pray nothing's wrong. It's not like her—"

"Oh no. She's wonderful. On vacation actually," Charlotte heard herself say, knowing full well her mother would have dearly wanted her to say she'd been dragged kicking and screaming from her daughterly duties, or lied and said she'd been walloped by some virus and didn't dare risk infecting the Golden Oaks community.

Charlotte smiled. "She's on a pleasure cruise."

Her grandfather was hanging back behind her, like she was his chauffeur. He didn't seem to be listening, which was good. It certainly wouldn't do for him to ask her mom when she got back, "How did you enjoy your cruise?"

"Well, good for her," the nurse said, smiling stiffly. "You know your mother is such a good lady. What a dear, always got a little something for us—fudge, lemon squares . . ."

"Yes, ma'am."

"Bundt cake." The nurse looked at Charlotte in a meaningful way with those chocolate-chip eyes, like she was thinking, *Where is my damn Bundt cake?*

"I was just visiting with my grandfather. I thought I could take him out for a drive. Not far."

"Well, aren't you a lamb to come help out."

She was a lamb, wasn't she?

"Taking time off school too?" the nurse asked, rearranging the line of teddy bears on the counter, fluffing the dress of a teddy with a tiara.

"Oh, the time," Charlotte said. She wondered if that nurse had any children. If they were in trouble, or ungrateful for all she did for them. Charlotte couldn't imagine a nurse being a bad mother.

"Don't you forget to sign him out," the nurse said, pulling out a dark leather-bound book, so big she needed both hands to lift it up onto the counter. "And when you bring him back, sign him back in. You hear? Gotta keep a log. Everybody present and accounted for."

The nurse pushed the ominous-looking book toward her, stuck a pen in her hand, and waited. Charlotte's vision blurred at the sight of so many names and dates, like reading the guest book on a ship cruising the river Styx.

Then, out of the corner of her eye, she saw her grandfather making for the door and blue sky.

"Hold on, let me shut off the alarm till y'all are out the door," the nurse said, pointing toward Charlotte's grandfather's ankle, around which was an electronic band, like one of those shock collars people put on dogs to keep them on the property.

"Is that really necessary?"

"You never know," the nurse said. "God forbid somebody wanders off and gets lost, or run over by a car. Everybody thinks they want to get out," she said, "until they actually do. They get out there and they panic. Totally confused. They can't remember where they live, or their name . . ."

Charlotte wondered which was worse, not remembering the terrible things that had happened to you—which meant one day you'd make the same mistake again—or remembering the bad things over and over again.

"Well," she said cheerily, "thank god we're not there yet."

As soon as she got into the car, Charlotte started to panic. She couldn't just drive her grandfather around for an hour. And he hadn't put on his seat belt. She wasn't about to tell her grandfather, a grown man, that he had to wear a seat belt.

"All right, then," her grandfather said with great enthusiasm. "What's on the agenda? Lunch?" Charlotte almost said, *You've already eaten*, but what else was there to do anyway?

The Pig and Barrel was a dinky little restaurant in a strip mall near the railroad tracks. The train made an appearance every hour on the hour. Her mom always took her grandfather there. Charlotte would rather have gone where they could sit outside, eat something fresh and light, quiche or salad. Nothing that had ever had hair on it, nothing that had ever had eyes. But she had no idea where to find a place like that.

Her grandfather spotted the men working on the telephone lines before she did. "My lands, will you take a look at that," he said, leaning forward in his seat, craning his neck to gaze up at a man in a hard hat standing in a metal basket, near the top of the telephone pole. If Charlotte were a good granddaughter, she'd have pulled off the road and let him watch. After all, this was his idea of a good time. He wasn't one of those old coots, content to sit in the parlor singing ragtime songs and stringing macaroni necklaces.

"Would you look at all those wires?" He shook his head in wonder. "Where do you think they go?" It sounded odd coming out of his mouth. Heavens, the man had helped build the first television set, and before that his own shortwave radio right in his garage.

"It's a great big world out there," he'd said to her once, headphones on. "China, India, Russia." You could tell even though he'd built the radio years ago, had tuned in hundreds of times, it still amazed him. When he'd put those earphones on her, she could hardly believe it herself, like voices from outer space. She didn't know what language they were speaking, but she knew he was a genius. The smartest man she would ever know. It was hard to believe they were related.

She wondered what had happened to that radio. She wanted it.

"My, my, this is awfully pretty countryside," he said as they drove past the golf course. "What is the proper name of this fine town?"

"Turner," she said. He had lived here for fifty years. How many times had he written his address down in that time?

"Turner," he said. "Turner." He made a little grunting sound in the back of his throat and pushed the button to roll down his window, then pushed the button again and rolled the window up, and then down, up and down, up and down.

"So tell me," he said, "are you from this town?"

"What?"

"This town—" he said irritably, like a judge whose patience is being exhausted by a dim-witted witness.

"Turner."

"Of course, Turner, I'm well aware. I'll remind you, young lady, I'm a resident of Turner. I live here." He hesitated, waiting a beat, like he expected her to correct him.

"Yes sir, you do indeed. Fifty years or more now." Her

shoulders and knuckles had started to ache from holding the wheel so tight.

"Yes indeed." He sighed and settled back into the seat. "I think one can consider that home." Again he made the sound in his throat. A strange spidery feeling started building in Charlotte's chest. If he didn't recognize the place where he'd lived for half a century, wasn't it possible he didn't recognize her either? That he could just forget he had a granddaughter?

"Do you remember," Charlotte said, "how you taught me to drive?"

"Me?" he said, sounding surprised.

"Yes, you. We'd be going down a hill, and you'd suddenly take your hands off the wheel and say, 'Somebody steer, somebody steer, we're out of control!'"

He chuckled. "I did that? Why, I can't believe that!"

"All the time," she said, tightening her grip on the wheel. Maybe that didn't really count as teaching her to drive, but she wanted it to be true.

"Really?"

"Yes, you did that." She'd never told anyone. Her parents would never have let her drive with him again. "You were steering with your knees, but I didn't know that then."

"Well, no, I suppose you wouldn't," he said, pausing. "What a good trick."

The Pig and Barrel still retained the feel of the insurance office it had once been. The tinted windows and faux dark mahogany paneling gave it a shady trust-us-we're-doing-the-best-we-can-for-you-given-what-you're-paying ambience.

The hostess was a big, trashy-looking blond girl, her face

round like a corn muffin and puffy with acne scars. Charlotte would have bet the hostess was her age, but she looked older the way poor people do sometimes.

"Well, hey, Mr. Halliday," she said, making like he was John D. Rockefeller. "How're you doing? You're looking spiffy. Your regular table okay for you today?"

Charlotte cleared her throat. "I'm his granddaughter," she said, resenting the familiarity.

"That's so nice," the hostess said. "Now follow me." Picking up menus, she strutted in front of them, swinging her hips like she was special, like those menus made her special. That and her long yellow hair that stopped just above her butt. Charlotte touched her own hair. *A lady never touches her hair in public.* That girl's hair was so long you could have grabbed her and swung her around, sent her flying right into the wall.

Charlotte's hair used to be past her shoulders, but hair as long as the hostess's was just tacky. With that skanky hair and the big old crucifix around her neck, big as a beer key, she looked like one of those evangelicals. The kind that give all Christians a bad name.

They followed her past the salad bar, which had a double-wide sneeze guard, to the table. "I see you got you some new glasses, Mr. Halliday," she said fawningly.

"Well," her grandfather said, like she'd just paid him some swell compliment. "Well, yes, I suppose I did."

She led them to a booth near a window and, with a grand gesture, bade Charlotte's grandfather to sit. Charlotte's mood lifted. She should've guessed her mother would insist on a booth; a common table wouldn't do. It felt more private.

She picked up her menu, and then immediately put it down. It was sticky. What was the point of laminating something if you didn't sponge it off? It made her sick.

"I already know what you want, Mr. Halliday—don't I? The regular, right? A burger medium . . ." Charlotte guessed they were supposed to feel special that the hostess herself was waiting on them, and that she remembered what her grandfather always ordered when Charlotte's mother brought him to lunch.

"No," Charlotte said, louder than she meant to.

"I think I'd like a beer," he said matter-of-factly.

"Make it two beers," she said, "and a chocolate milk shake."

"Beer and shake," the woman said, pursing her lips. "Nothing to eat? No lunch today?"

Charlotte shrugged. "You heard Mr. Halliday. The man said he wanted a beer."

The hostess was clearly taken aback by her rudeness, but Charlotte didn't care. Her grandfather hadn't noticed. He was casually loading packets of sugar and grape jam into the pocket of his suit coat. *Damnit.* She'd forgotten to search his room for condiments. She'd have to remember to do it when she dropped him off. That and his dirty laundry, she couldn't forget that.

Even though her grandfather had always been a bourbon man, he downed his beer in three impressive gulps. "Chugalug, Grandpa!" she said without thinking, but he didn't take offense. When he belched—obviously amused, like this was a trick he'd just learned—Charlotte didn't take offense either. She took a big swallow of her beer. She'd forgotten how much she liked beer.

"Liquid lunch," she said, raising her beer in one hand and the frosted milk shake glass in the other. She took a sip of the shake, then put it in front of him. For a second he just stared at the old-fashioned soda fountain glass, then took a draw on the straw. "That is the best thing I think I have ever tasted," he said, grinning like a boy.

"I know. It's heaven, isn't it?"

She felt proud and happy. She'd done the right thing getting him out of there and coming here. They sat there not talking, but that was okay. Charlotte was like her mother in that silences usually made her uncomfortable. Her mother said being a good conversationalist is like driving a car. Your job is to keep the conversation moving, steer people toward appropriate topics and points of common interest, be ready to put on the brakes if an unsavory topic arises, like *Why did your daughter leave school? How is your father's dementia?* Otherwise the conversation goes into a ditch.

Right now their conversational car was safely parked. Her grandpa looked lost in thought. And happy, like he was picking up radio signals from the other side of the globe, Budapest, Australia, Tokyo. Then, it took just a second, the dial in his brain switched to another frequency. He frowned.

"You look pale," he said.

"Come again?"

"Pale. Peaked . . ." He examined her face with the same level of concentration he'd once applied to locating the crossed wire, the bad fuse that prevented the radio from picking up or sending signals.

She held her breath.

"Don't be silly. It's just the light in here. It's very unflattering."

He folded his napkin and laid it beside his plate.

"If you will pardon me," he said, pushing himself up from the table, and headed for the restroom. There were smudges on the lenses of his glasses, fingerprints. When they got back to the Golden Oaks, she'd clean them for him really well.

When they got back to the Golden Oaks. Charlotte stopped, suddenly realizing she'd forgotten to bring a bag to sneak her grandfather's sodden clothes out of the building. She could ask the hostess for a plastic bag, she supposed, or better, order something to go to avoid any questions. *A lady never in dress nor manner attracts undue attention to herself.*

Charlotte finished her beer and signaled the waitress for two more. When had she become a girl who signaled a waitress for beers? She was sorry her grandfather was still in the men's room when the train, bright red and gold, like a giant toy, came roaring up the track for its 2:30 appearance. For a second she felt the urge to wave. As the train passed, whistle shrieking, she remembered that she'd sworn to never drink again, but here she was, on her second beer.

She was halfway through it when the hostess appeared. Her grandfather, the hostess said, had been in the men's room a good twenty minutes now. People were waiting. Charlotte thought, *Why don't you go get him, you know him so well? Isn't your job to make us feel welcome? Hosted?*

Charlotte told the hostess that maybe she didn't notice but the train had shook the ground when it passed. The silverware had jumped on the table. Her grandfather probably thought they were having an earthquake.

The hostess repeated that people were complaining. Given the amount of makeup she wore, she was clearly prone to exaggeration. Still, Charlotte stood up and walked over to the restroom. She was a good granddaughter. She knocked hard enough so he could hear her, and put her face right up next to the door. "Grandpa," she said. "Grandpa. Come in, Grandpa . . ."

"Hello?" he answered. He sounded confused and surprised and very far away, like he was lost in a cave and had given up any hope of being rescued.

"Hello. Hello," she said, so relieved she laughed, shooting a look at the hostess. Everything was just fine. She waited for him to say, "Just wait one more minute please . . ." But he didn't say anything.

She put her hand on the knob, half wanting it to be locked, half relieved when it wasn't. When had her grandfather become so trusting he didn't lock the door of a public bathroom? No, he must've unlocked it for her.

"I'm coming in," she said and counted to ten, then another ten. She wished to God her mother were here.

Please, God, Charlotte prayed as she opened the door; *sweet Jesus, please don't let anything be wrong—don't let him be lying on the floor, or bleeding—just let him be washing his hands.* And there he was, standing, one hand on the wall as if he were bracing himself because the rumble of the train *had* really alarmed him. Then she saw his pants were down. He didn't seem to notice. She looked away immediately and shut the door behind her. She cleared her throat.

"You almost ready to go?" she said, trying to mimic her mother's voice.

All he had to do was pull up his underwear, pull up his pants, and zip. Everything would be fine. Over. She'd forget it ever happened. It never happened. "Grandpa," she said. "Charles."

Two seconds, he could just pull his shirt over the top of his pants. No one would see. Charlotte would put her arm around him—and hold his pants up by the waistband as best she could and get him out of there. Get him to the car. Let the restaurant people think he was sick. It was that milk shake. Hostess probably spit in it. They'd walk straight out. Charlotte would run him back to the Golden Oaks. Have a nurse do up his pants. That was their job, wasn't it?

It would serve her mother right, wouldn't it? Let everybody

whisper about how she abandoned her father. What about her daughter?

It wasn't fair, though. She couldn't do it. She had no choice. Maybe he wouldn't even know she was doing it if she was really careful. "It's okay," she said.

Touching his shoulder, praying he'd stop making the grunting sound in his throat. "I've done this a million times. I'm a pro."

Of course, nothing was further from the truth. She couldn't do it. Her hands were shaking. Just the thought of touching the skin sagging over his kneecaps, the blue squiggles of vein inside his thighs, the gray spiderwebs of pubic hair, made her want to pass out.

She kept her head down. She just wouldn't look. She told herself: *It's not a dick, it's a chicken neck, a hot dog, an old garden hose. Chicken neck, hot dog, garden hose.* She reached out and pulled up the waistband of his briefs. The loose elastic slid up, and she imagined his penis slipping down inside his underwear like an old walrus diving underwater.

She could have left his fly undone, but that would be wrong. Like a sad, dirty old man. *It's almost over,* she told herself as she crouched down. She thought, *One day I might do this for a child, mightn't I?* And he was zipped.

"There we are," she said. Her voice was shaking all over the place. "Good as new."

Her grandfather didn't say anything. He let her take his hand. She didn't remember ever holding his hand before. Neither of them looked at anybody as they left the restaurant. Charlotte dropped a pile of money on the table. They kept on straight ahead, out that door.

She got the car onto the road and kept her eyes on the yellow lines. *Zip, zip, zip.* Fast. Stayed on her side of the road.

Zip, zip, zip. She didn't know how much time passed before she noticed she was headed away from the Golden Oaks, back toward home.

Her grandfather hadn't said a word since the bathroom. Hadn't made a noise.

Then, as they were turning in to the development, gravel flying everywhere, he said very clearly, "So, tell me, is there anyone special in your life at this time?"

"Excuse me?" She straightened out the wheel.

"A gentleman," he said, looking at Charlotte hopefully. "A beau."

"You mean—"

He nodded. "A boyfriend."

The word knocked the air out of her. "No. There's no boy-friend."

She felt the dog before she saw it, felt it smack against the side of the car by the front wheel, felt the car hump up over it as the car skidded hard to the right, crashing into a mailbox, which stood for a second, then fell.

I hit it. I hit it. I hit it. I hit it.

She waited for someone to come running out of the house screaming and waving their arms, but nobody came. It was so quiet you could hear birds. She'd tell them she was sorry. She wanted someone to notice. Come over. She wasn't the kind of girl who'd hit and run. But no one came. And nothing changed.

She couldn't move. Her mother would kill her. That's all. Just kill her, for the car, for her grandfather, for lying, for not getting better. She watched as her grandfather's hand appeared by her side, took hold of the gearshift, and put it into reverse.

"Back it up now, darling." His hand was now on the steering wheel.

"What about the dog?" She imagined it in the street, bleeding and scared and barely breathing. It belonged to someone.

"I didn't see any dog."

Was there not a dog? There was a dog. She was sure. "I didn't mean to."

"Let's get you out of here."

"I can't do it."

"Yes, you can," he said matter-of-factly. "Just follow my instructions. Place both hands on the steering wheel. Remove your foot from the brake pedal. Place it firmly on the accelerator and steadily—"

"Where is it? What happened to the dog?"

Was that it in the woods behind the house? Or there behind that swing set? Heading for the trees, was that it, limping? That shadow?

"Do you hear me? Focus," he said, then he leaned over, took the wheel, and started to turn it. "Time is of the essence. Now, give it a little gas."

Like that the car leaped backward, away from the mailbox, off the curb, and back into the street, like magic. He took his hands off the wheel.

"Now drive." He pointed toward the road. "Go."

"We know these people," she said, pointing to the Millers' ruined mailbox. Her mother would die of shame.

"Keep your foot on the accelerator until I tell you to stop," he said firmly. "Go. We'll think about it later—all things in good time."

● ● ●

While Charlotte struggled to unlock the side door of the house (she didn't want to go in through the front, where anybody could see), her grandfather admired the yard. It was like nothing had happened at all. Maybe nothing had happened. It was, however, far past the time she was supposed to have returned him.

"This is all rather lovely," he said, nodding appreciatively at the rhododendrons and azalea bushes he used to trim, the flower beds he'd once weeded on the weekends for her father. His face was as blank and pleasant as that of a man on a garden tour. His blue eyes were magnified through those thick, murky lenses.

"You ought to admire it," Charlotte said. "You must have spent hundreds of hours out here in this yard. Remember?"

"I'm fully aware of that," he snapped, in a voice unfamiliar to Charlotte. "And I'll thank you not to condescend to me, young lady. Might I remind you that I am your elder? I demand your respect."

"Yes sir. My apologies," she stammered. "I never meant to imply—"

"Accepted," he said.

She wouldn't tell him that he was responsible for completely rewiring all the house's circuits, that if it weren't for him, they'd have always had to go to bed at dusk. That he'd installed the burglar alarm. Her mother made her promise to set it while they were gone, but she wouldn't because it felt like setting the timer on a bomb.

"Why don't we go inside now," Charlotte said, trying to sound calm and sweet, while holding the door open for him, willing him to hurry up before the neighbors spotted him. *Come on, old man, come on, one more step . . .*

Just as she was about to scream, he finally walked through

the door. "Do you know the people who own this fine estab-
lishment?" he said, striding through the foyer with pleasure,
pride. "I do. Indeed, they are old friends of mine, from—
Lands sake, we go back a long way. Yes, a long way."

Charlotte headed into the kitchen. Her head was buzzing.
"Can I get you a drink?"

He followed. "My, my," he said, glancing out the window.
"Is it the cocktail hour already?" He checked his wrist for the
time, but he wasn't wearing a watch.

"It's that time, Grandpa. Isn't it always that time? Somewhere in the world?"

He took out his comb, brushing his hair straight back, just
as she had wanted to do when she first saw him this afternoon.
He was fine. She felt better already.

"What can I get you from the bar?"

The light on the answering machine flickered on and
off—three messages. Three messages. Three messages. All
from her mother, no doubt. Maybe Bender.

I ought to just cut that cord, she thought. First thing bur-
glars do when they find people at home during a robbery is
cut the phone cord. Then they say, *Don't do anything stupid,*
and tie everybody up.

"Sit down." Charlotte pointed to a kitchen chair. He sat.
"Good. Now that you're comfortable, wouldn't you like a liba-
tion? A li-li-libation?"

For the first time she thought maybe she was a little drunk
from lunch.

"A julep would be refreshing," her grandfather said in a
voice that sounded like it was traveling light-years to reach
her. Across a string connecting two tin cans. He lowered his
voice. "If you think the folks here can manage a decent julep."

Years ago at a Derby party he'd taught her how to make a

julep. He'd showed her how to muddle the mint, sift the fine sugar into the bourbon, then fit the screen over the pitcher and pour slowly. The secret was to double-filter it. Charlotte thought he liked making the juleps more than drinking them. She was sure hers had been terrible, but he'd drunk them, or made it look like he had. He was a clever man.

They actually didn't have fixings for juleps, but she'd promised. She took down a tall glass, threw in a handful of ice, then the bourbon—even though he'd taught her you always put the liquor in first, as that was the only way to get a precise measurement. He said if you didn't measure, the cocktail was invariably too potent. She shook some sugar out of the bowl— no teaspoon—and squeezed a whole lime into the glass. Maybe the green of the lime would pass for mint.

He took the drink and, after a long sip, licked his lips. "This is very refreshing indeed," he said. "What do you call it?"

"It's a julep, Grandpa. You taught me how to make them years ago."

He tasted it again. "Fine and dandy," he said, nodding his approval. Then a serious look came over his face. "You know, we are concerned about you," he said. "Your grandmother and I both—she called me today from the airplane and asked me to give you her love and best wishes."

For a second Charlotte thought he was talking about her mother. "Who?"

"Your grandmother."

"Forgive me," she said, then "I understand." Her voice sounded like a recording of a recording. The refrigerator hummed like it was getting ready to launch into song. She sat down beside it on the floor and felt the warm air puffing out from the vents—an island breeze. She lay down and closed her eyes.

"Frankly," he said, "we're concerned. Is it school? Have your grades slipped?"

"Concerned?"

"Yes. I'm concerned. Has something happened?"

"I can't take you back to your place, Grandpa. Not tonight. You have to stay here tonight. With me."

He shifted nervously in his chair. Checked his invisible wristwatch. "Your grandmother should be on her way," he said, the low grunting sound building in his throat again. Charlotte ground her teeth. It was unbearable. She wanted nothing more than to hit him. Shut him up. Why was he doing this?

"Don't worry," Charlotte said. "I promise. I'll take care of you."

To prove it she got up off the floor and made him another drink, this time skipping the sugar and lime. He took it from her like a child.

"But," he said in a small voice, "where will I sleep?"

"Did Mom tell you I dropped out of school?" Charlotte said.

"Oh," he said, smiling blankly. "Is that so?"

"I was in an accident." How many times had she said just this?

"An accident?"

He crossed his legs, and then uncrossed them.

"Are you comfortable? I mean there in that chair?"

He nodded. Still, he couldn't have looked more like a hostage if she'd bound him hand and foot with rope.

"I'm glad. Because that's just part of the story."

Her grandfather folded his hands in his lap. Did it even matter anymore if he knew who she was?

"I haven't told anybody the whole story. Nobody. I just

couldn't. I didn't want to. I can't. I won't. But"—she forced herself to slow down—"I need to tell someone, and I trust you. I know you'll—"

She was about to say, "I know you'll understand," but that wasn't it.

"I had an accident," she said, then stopped. "No, let me start over. I met a boy at a party. It was a beach party. They'd carted in all this sand. I'd gone with my girlfriends. We were having a ball. Then I met this boy. I'd seen him before, but I'd never really noticed him. Not in that way. I wondered why, because he was cute. Then I thought, *Well, Charlotte, it's not like people are noticing you left and right either.* Right? I thought, *Maybe we were meant to find each other.*

"We started talking. He told me about where he was from. He told me he and his mom were really close—he'd just gotten a care package from her. I liked that. You know I'm close with my mom too. He asked if he could get me a drink from the bar—it was just a crush of people. Plus, it was his house. He asked me, would I like a mixed drink, or a beer? I said a beer, unless the line for the keg is too long. I didn't want him to have to wait in line for me. The minute he left I was struck by this fear he wasn't coming back. That he'd forget. But he did come back, with my drink, actually two drinks, two gin and tonics, because he said he didn't want to have to return to the bar any sooner than he had to.

"All night my friends kept flashing me the thumbs-up. In the first few hours I had dreamed our whole future together—all of it, first kiss, the nicknames we'd have for each other; my friends saying how jealous they were of how in love we were, and how lucky I was—*The way he looks at you.* You see, I'd never been that girl. I imagined his friends becoming my friends, and how they'd say to me, *Wow, I've never seen a guy so whipped.* Telling him I was one in a million. The kind of girl you marry. I had just about planned the whole wedding in my head. Where we'd live, how many kids, the kind of dog we'd have.

"Then, you know, suddenly, everybody seems to have gone home, and the lights come on. You could see keys, and change, an earring buried in the sand. It really was like being at the beach. It seemed magical. I didn't want the night to end.

"You don't know how happy I was, so relieved when he offered to walk me home. He said he had to go upstairs to his room and get his keys. He asked me if I wanted to wait for him downstairs, or come up and see his room. *A gentleman never leaves a lady unattended without permission.* I thought, *Why not?* When he took my hand and we walked together upstairs, I thought, *First holding hands.* Next would be, *First walk home.* Then, *First look at the moon . . .*

"The first kiss was sweet. *First kiss!* Is it wrong to admit that I liked being wanted?

"Then everything started happening so fast. I asked him to *slow down.* I told him, *Let's kiss some more.* But he didn't want to kiss. He said, *I want you so bad it hurts.* I said, *Come on, please. Stop it. You're going to rip my shirt.*

"He laughed. *So, why don't you stop fighting and try and enjoy yourself?*

"I said, *No.* I did. I said, *Stop. Not like this.*

"Then time slowed to a crawl. He said, *Are you crying? Why are you crying?* I begged him. *You're hurting me,* I said. *Stop it. You're scaring me.*

"He said, *You don't want to leave, do you? I hope not, because you're not going anywhere.*

"After he was done he said, *Do you still want me to walk you home?*

"I just ran. My friends said, *You have to go to the hospital, to the police, you have to tell somebody.* But how? Who? I didn't want them to know. I didn't want to talk about it. Ever. I wanted it to go away. To die. You know, these things don't just happen . . . See why I had to leave?

"What was I thinking, wearing that skirt? I know you're disappointed. I can tell. I know it and I'm sorry. But you have to know I tried. I did, I swear to you I tried.

"You want to know the worst part? I thought he might apologize. I hoped. How much easier it would be if he apologized. Even a week, no, two weeks later I thought if he called and told me he was sorry, really sorry—that it was a mistake, a miscommunication, he was drunk, that he really did like me, he really did think I was pretty, and he really did want to date me—I thought that if he really liked me, I'd call what happened *bad sex*, saying *bad sex* the way you'd say *bad oyster*. I'd never even think the word *rape* again." Charlotte paused. "I've never said that word out loud.

"Rape."

Her grandfather was sitting perfectly still. He hadn't moved at all. He reached for his empty glass and, rattling the ice cubes, brought it to his lips.

"Are you comfortable there?" Charlotte asked. "I'm almost through, I promise. I totaled my car—do you remember my car? Baby? Everybody thought it was an accident, but it wasn't an accident. Can you believe anybody would believe that lie? I've never had an accident in my life. I'm a very careful person. I obey the law. I'm a good girl."

Her grandfather listened, his face grave. "How god-awful. I'm sorry to hear it."

He put his glass on the table and gazed around the kitchen admiringly—taking in the curtains, the refrigerator—like it was someplace exciting and special. "Are you well acquainted with this place?"

"And I'm still scared," Charlotte said. "Who am I? Minute to minute I don't recognize myself. Can you understand that?"

"I can." He nodded sympathetically.

She thought so. He knew. He reached into his coat pocket and drew out his comb, examining it like an artifact. Then, turning it over in his hands, not looking her in the eye, he asked again, "Where will I sleep?"

"And I'm so tired," she said, taking the comb out of his hand. "Please, look at me."

He shifted uncomfortably in his chair, then stood up and walked over to the kitchen window. Peering out at the woods, hands pressed against the glass, he watched as the sun, red and round as a rubber ball, dropped behind the trees.

Elephant

Paige sat on the edge of the sandbox waiting for Charlotte to show up. She was surprised at how much she'd missed her. Across the playground, her four-year-old daughter, Allegra, was lying on her stomach across a swing, pigtails dragging in the dirt. Paige checked her watch. In her pocket was a little Lucite ring carved into the shape of a rose. She'd seen it at a street fair and immediately thought of Charlotte. Despite the fact that they'd only been friends since the beginning of summer, it felt longer. Before Charlotte left to visit her family in Virginia, she had given Paige a leather change purse embossed with a pigeon (an inside joke). Paige had never expected her to write, but a few days ago an antique postcard with the image of Vita Sackville-West in her white garden — *Look, Mom, no rats! Thinking of You* — had arrived.

That morning it had taken Charlotte twice as many Oreos as usual to bribe her daughter, Lucy, tired and cranky from last night's flight, into putting on her pink jelly sandals, and twice as long to wrangle her, bucking and thrashing like a rodeo bull, into her stroller. After which she felt done in, and close to tears. Now she'd be late. A lack of punctuality, her grandmother said, suggested you thought your time was more precious than other people's. It also, she had added, gave people time to ponder what other faults you might have.

Charlotte had begun looking forward to her reunion with Paige from almost the minute she set foot in her mother's house two weeks before. The feeling had only intensified when her husband, Ronnie, was called back to New York after only three days to deal with some disaster at the brokerage firm where he worked.

Charlotte was fretting about seeing her friend—what if something *had* changed?—when she saw her standing by the sandbox and was overcome by that thrilling feeling of ownership she'd once experienced when she saw Ronnie on the street, her heart expanding. *There she was.*

Paige and Charlotte had first met at the playground. Without a word, each had recognized the other as a sister in the bonds of chronic sleep deprivation. It wasn't anything so obvious as dark circles, dirty hair, or the word *diapers* scrawled on the back of a hand. Or even the fact that they both were wearing their husbands' oversize sweaters. It was seeing the identical expression, the haunted, bewildered look of the POW on the other woman's face. How did this happen?

This moment of recognition had caused each of them to look away. Return to staring dully through the playground fence, which as far as they were concerned, might as well have been electrified and laced with razor wire. The playground had been a big selling point for both families. It was nearly brand-new. At the very heart of the playground stood a herd of elephants, four bronzelike sculptures that ranged in size from toddler to child height to the biggest, which stood over five feet tall. All of them except the smallest were hollow inside so kids could climb in and hide.

Before it became fashionable, the neighborhood had supported a lively drug trade; tribes of squatters occupied the abandoned warehouses while the homeless slept in cardboard boxes near the bridge and beat their clothes on the banks of the East River. Paige and Jack, filled with pioneer spirit, had moved in when the park was still impressively seedy. Charlotte and her husband had come later, after *The New York Times* anointed it and rents began to escalate along with the appearance of organic produce, yoga studios, and boutiques displaying sweaters and shoes like museum pieces with prices to match.

The fact that each woman had chosen not to congregate with the other parents and caregivers over by the benches had not been lost on either of them. It seemed significant that both had turned away from the social groupings that spring up naturally in places like playgrounds and prisons. Still, despite these promising signs, they were cautious. Other mothers had presented themselves as potential lifelong friends but had ultimately been drawn back to work, had given in to the siren song of the suburbs, or despite their initial bonding, had proved incompatible once you discovered they spanked, voted Republican, or when you were over for a playdate made you put a nickel in their "swearing jar" every time you cursed. Allegra never swore ever, but Paige did. Paige's quip as she stuck a dollar in the jar *just in case*—that the swearing jar might more accurately be renamed "the therapy jar"—was not appreciated. As a result, the potential friend pool became shallower, the pickings slim. In that way, the playground wasn't unlike a singles bar. As time passed, standards fell, until they found themselves being seduced by a copy of *Swann's Way* in a *New Yorker* tote bag, a woman in Ray-Bans wearing an R.E.M. T-shirt with pearls.

Now as the mothers watched their daughters digging a

hole together in the sandbox beside the elephants, each held her breath hoping the other little girl wasn't a hair puller or a bucket stealer, a Band-Aid eater or a baby talker. As time passed and their daughters remained bent over their plastic shovels, laboring as tirelessly as gravediggers, they relaxed.

Finally, Charlotte, who could never bear a silence, said, "You girls are doing such a great job there. Working together."

Paige nodded. "They are indeed."

"Are you digging to China, Lucy?" Charlotte said. "I liked doing that when I was a little girl. Why, I could dig for hours."

Truth was, her mother would no more let her dig in the yard than fly to the moon. In wintertime, while the other kids were romping in their front yards and building snowmen with wide aphasic grins to stand sentinel, Charlotte was relegated to playing in her backyard. The snowmen behind her house looked like they were stealing a smoke.

It wasn't meanness on her mother's part. It was simply that the sight of an unspoiled, perfectly white blanket of snow stretched across her mother's front lawn made her happy. She had said that if Charlotte and her father ever came up with something creative, like their neighbor who'd started a trend by making a lawn jockey snowman, they had her blessing.

Watching Lucy jabbing at the sand with her shovel, Charlotte resolved she'd let her daughter dig wherever, and whenever she wanted.

"Oh yes, I loved to dig as a girl," Charlotte said.

"Looks like fun," Paige agreed.

The girls, seemingly mesmerized by their task, ignored their mothers. "Is it a pit?" Charlotte asked. "Or a swimming pool?"

"From here it looks like a tunnel," Paige said, though her first thought was *trench*.

"You two aren't planning to escape, are you?" Charlotte laughed nervously. Why had she said that? She couldn't count how many times Lucy had torn out of the playground, barreling through the gate and onto the sidewalk, only to be intercepted by a stranger. Invariably a mother, her baby strapped into the stroller like a sleepy test pilot, would collar Lucy the way you would a hyperactive dog. Charlotte would, as ever, lie. *She never does this.* Only to get a smug, pitying look in return.

Charlotte kept on. "Are you playing family? Are you making a cake?"

"Or," Paige grinned, "are you pretending to be witches?"

At this, the girls stopped and turned, each giving her mother a look of disdain. A preview of what they could expect when their daughters became teens.

"I guess it's a secret, then," Paige said.

"Oh, a secret," Charlotte said in that aren't-they-so-cute-you-could-just-die voice. "You two have a secret!"

Aha, Paige thought, there was the catch. The woman was one of those imbeciles who let their children record the outgoing messages on their answering machines. The stammering and giggling, the sound of parents feeding their child the lines. *It's message not massage, pumpkin!* Where did these people think they lived, over the rainbow? In a hollow tree?

They sat in silence for a moment, and then Charlotte yawned extravagantly. Paige yawned in solidarity. When she was still premed she'd known exactly how many muscles it took to yawn, at least a hundred. For as long as she could remember, she'd believed that being able to take care of people, having the power to fix people, was the greatest, most noble thing a person could do.

She liked hospitals. When she was growing up, her older sister, Emily, had been anorexic and had, since the age of sixteen, checked in and out of hospitals and psych wings as though they were hotels and she was an heiress with money to burn. The doctors and nurses complimented Paige's lack of squeamishness when they took her sister's blood; other parents made note of how strong and supportive she was of her mother and sister. *What a trouper.* She didn't know whether it was her or her mother or father who began telling people Paige wanted to be a doctor, but it stuck.

Then in the spring of her junior year of college, while reading Goethe on the commons lawn, she realized she just didn't feel that way anymore. It was far more pleasurable to puzzle out the meanings of words, chase the solution to how to say *She was consumed with ennui* through the pages of a dictionary (which wasn't easy, not every culture had a word for ennui), than to try to figure out why someone had a sore throat and could no longer swallow. A book got published. A throat just got sore again. If you misconjugated a verb, no one sued you for malpractice. You stopped swallowing, you died.

Paige couldn't help wondering if Charlotte worked. She knew it was wrong to judge women who didn't work, to view them as witless and pathetic. After all, feminism was all about equality, and giving women the power to make their own choices. She couldn't help it, though. She wanted to ask, but because she thought she might really like Charlotte, she didn't. It was better to wait. You never knew. The reactions to her expressed desire to go back to work had ranged from looks of pity more on par with admitting one could no longer afford meat (*not even pigs' feet*) to such horror you'd have thought she'd announced, "I can't wait to get back to my job kidnapping babies and selling their organs on the black market."

Charlotte yawned again. "Goodness grape juice, forgive

me," she said, wiping her eyes. "I'm simply exhausted. I didn't sleep a wink last night."

"Ah, sleep," Paige said. "You know what they say—sleep is the mother's drug of choice, but like heroin, only the very rich and the very poor can afford it."

Charlotte wasn't sure what that meant, but she laughed anyway. "I've heard that one before," she said, and made a mental note to remember it so she could tell Ronnie. He'd like it. He could use it on clients. Ever since they'd moved to New York City, he had spent at least two nights a week taking clients out and showing them a good time. He'd gone to all the trendiest restaurants and bars. Like the retro-cool bar in Chinatown she'd read about in *New York* magazine. Once a dive and a big artist hangout in the 1980s, it now served dim sum in addition to its signature pineapple boat cocktail. The jukebox, Ronnie said, was *out of control*. Like being back in college. Motown, the Police, U2. She felt a pang. She should have known when she suggested a "date night" (they hadn't had one in at least six months) at a new restaurant called Home, which specialized in traditional American comfort food—fried chicken, biscuits, key lime pie, all their favorites—that Ronnie had already been, and *the food sucked*. Which was good really, since Charlotte was starting to fear the only way she'd ever lose weight was to be in a coma for six months with nothing but a Slim-Fast IV.

"My husband, Ronnie, says let her cry it out. It worked with the other two. We, um, have an older boy and girl, R.J. and Mandy . . ." Charlotte waited for the raised eyebrow. The only people in New York City to have three children were either on welfare, rich, or too selfish to consider how they were overpopulating the earth. However, Paige's face conveyed no judgment at all, only interest.

" . . . but I can't just let her cry. Lucy is different. Not different *different*, just—"

Paige laughed, but nicely. "I get it." Her husband, Jack, would never let Allegra cry.

"Don't get me wrong. Ronnie really is a great father, and husband. He is. Every weekend he tells me, *You sleep in, honey. I'll take the kids.* Which is nice, especially considering how hard he works."

Ronnie hadn't been planning on a third child. Charlotte was the one who'd wanted it, who chose to let her diaphragm languish in a drawer and gather dust. Ronnie's first response to the news had been incredulity—*"How is that possible?"*—followed by disappointment—*"Well, there's another nail in the coffin"*—but Charlotte knew he loved Lucy.

"Of course they offer to let you sleep," Paige said, "but it's like being starved for a week, then being told you can eat a whole rib roast and cheesecake on Sunday. You can't live like that."

"You're right," Charlotte agreed, watching nervously as Lucy kicked sand into the hole, praying that in her enthusiasm she wouldn't inadvertently blind Allegra, or make her cry. "Now, Lucy," she said in a warning tone, but as usual her daughter showed no signs of obeying her. Ronnie was right. She could be a pistol. Although Charlotte hated it when he called her that, *a pistol.* All she could think of was a gun pointed at her head.

Without thinking Charlotte blurted out, "I think Lucy is trying to kill her mother," instantly horrified that she'd said it out loud. "No, I'm just kidding," she said, regretting ever opening her mouth. Sometimes she felt unfit for human company. Like she'd just been let out of a cage.

● ● ●

The next day on her way to the playground, Paige, recognizing another mother she used to know crossing the street, stopped the stroller so abruptly that, had Allegra not dutifully remembered to buckle herself in, she'd have been catapulted into the bushes.

"Are we hiding?" Allegra whispered, hands over her mouth. Another child, so delighted by the fact that she and her mother were in cahoots, crouched behind some shrubbery, would likely have blown their cover, but not Allegra.

"No," Paige whispered. "Not really, we're just waiting." Watching as the woman, all in black, one of those twenty-dollar art magazines tucked under her arm, slipped into a café that sold five-dollar cups of coffee. Alone. Without children. That *bitch*.

Evie was an artist, and they'd met at a Music for Aardvarks sing-along in a local coffee bar that sold vegan baked goods and welcomed nursing. Evie had a little boy, and a daughter Allegra's age. She was easy to spot in her black jeans and punk rock T-shirts, like IGGY POP, I WANNA BE YOUR DOG. Her black motorcycle boots and a line of five gold hoops riding the curve of her ear as though her wardrobe could disguise the fact she was someone's mother. *Two people's* mother. Within an hour of their meeting, Evie had told Paige she was getting a tattoo. A heart, like your classic sailor tattoo, but instead of "Mom," it would say "Dad." She'd told Paige she was an artist, and that she'd recently started painting again—it was shit, all of it shit—but it was all that was saving her. Paige told her she was jealous. That she was a translator who hadn't been able to work or even read a book in English let alone Italian since her daughter was born, and it was killing her.

"All it took to light a fire under my creative ass was my

father dying," Evie offered blithely. "Although I don't recom-
mend it for everybody."

Paige hadn't known how to respond to that, but Evie didn't
seem to notice. The fact that this black-clad hipster mom had
chosen to share the story of her father's long, slow death from
cancer, and their relationship—*Call me Electra*, she'd joked,
how after he died she'd cut off a lock of his hair—had made
Paige instantly feel close to her. Made her wish she and her
father were closer.

After a while, though, she began to suspect that Evie would
tell anyone who'd listen about her dead father. She didn't know
if Evie had always been emotionally promiscuous or if it was
the grief talking. It was like she was infected by sadness, and as
a carrier she made everyone around her sad. Which seemed
reckless and a little selfish to Paige. When you're contagious
you quarantine yourself. Evie should stay inside until the grief
ran its course. Stay away from other people, children, anyone
whose psychological immune system might be compromised.

The final straw was the day they were in a new café that
specialized in cupcakes when a song came on the radio and
Evie started to cry. In front of her kids. That her children
hadn't seemed bothered at this loss of control, but accustomed
to their mother's tears, made Paige profoundly uncomfortable.
It was selfish. Unfair. She'd never cry in front of her daughter
if she could help it. Allegra, being Allegra, had wordlessly
pushed her cupcake toward Evie.

All it had taken was one unreturned phone call to lose
Evie. Even so, Paige had no desire to reconnect with her.
Moreover, she didn't want to introduce her to Charlotte. It
would be awkward. She didn't imagine the two of them becoming best friends, but it could happen. It was also possible
that Charlotte, having met Evie, would question Paige's taste

in friends. *You are known by the company you keep.* Who knew what she might say? So Paige hung back until she was sure Evie was out of sight. Then she quickly made her way into the playground.

Charlotte, hoping that Paige might naturally gravitate to the place they'd met the day before, lingered at the sandbox, waiting. In order to get Lucy to stay put, she'd had to let her bat rocks over the fence with a naked Barbie doll she'd found in the street. Had her mother seen this, she'd have asked, "Doesn't Lucy have any little playmates who are girls?"

Paige had shown up shortly after, with her darling daughter in tow. That was the afternoon, sitting on a bench near the sandbox, that they cemented their bond. Each agreed that nursing a child old enough to have teeth and work the buttons on his mother's blouse was disgusting; agreed, watching their daughters run through the spray of the fountains, that the mothers who encouraged their children to cavort naked in the water, haute hippies who looked like they belonged on an Eileen Fisher commune, should be prosecuted for child abuse. In the few awkward moments of quiet, they yawned.

"I could never understand how anybody could join a cult, but I do now," Charlotte announced. "I'm halfway into the brainwash cycle right now."

"What makes you think you haven't joined a cult?" Paige said. "You just slept through the paperwork."

"That explains a lot," Charlotte said, both of their gazes drawn to a red-tailed hawk that had, with missilelike speed and efficiency, snatched a fledgling from the top of the fence. "Good lord," Charlotte said. "I hope the girls didn't see that. Did they?"

Paige shook her head reassuringly. If *they* had witnessed this colorful circle-of-life moment, it hadn't fazed them at all. "Do you remember Patty Hearst?" she said. "She claimed to have been brainwashed into robbing banks by the SLA. They locked her up in a closet, deprived her of sleep."

"I do," Charlotte said, recalling how that photo of the striking heiress dressed in military fatigues and a beret, holding a huge gun, had unnerved her. "I don't remember exactly what happened, though. No surprise." She laughed. "Did her parents pay the ransom?"

"Ha, this is the best part—the deal was that if Patty's parents fed all the poor people in California, the SLA would let her go. It was crazy, impossible. So the Hearst family donated millions to soup kitchens all over California to get their daughter back. And guess what? After all that, she chose to stay with her kidnappers. Not only *that*, she had the nerve to say *they could have done better.*"

Paige could imagine her parents trying to come up with the ransom. Her mother cashing out her IRA and lugging a coffee can of quarters to the Coinstar. Her father would request that the kidnappers wait a few days before cashing his check, which would likely bounce.

"She did come back to them, though, didn't she? At some point she came back, *right?*"

"Well, she got arrested," Paige said. "She claimed she was suffering from— Oh, fuck, what's the syndrome that makes you identify with your kidnappers?"

"Can you imagine that conversation?" Charlotte wondered aloud. "She must have thrown herself on their mercy. My mother would just die. I mean, truly."

"Fuck me." Paige hated that she wasn't as quick-witted or smart as she used to be. "You know that syndrome—I know you know it—the one where a hostage becomes attached to her captors?"

Charlotte hesitated. "You mean motherhood?"

Paige burst out laughing, felt something in her chest, like a knot, come untied.

Charlotte blushed. She hadn't meant to say it, but she had and Paige had laughed. Charlotte wasn't used to people laughing at her jokes. She wasn't used to making them. She smiled. She was on a roll. Or, as her mother used to say, "on a *role*," meaning Charlotte was acting like someone she was not. But this *was* her, wasn't it?

"Wait," Charlotte said, suddenly serious. "What pray tell are the girls up to?" The two mothers watched as Allegra and Lucy went charging toward the herd of giant elephants in the center of the park.

Charlotte had forbidden Lucy to play on the elephants. Every day some child, pretending to be an Indian prince trekking across the desert or a dancing girl in the circus, fell off, smacking his or her head on the meager carpet of foam padding underneath, or losing a tooth. What really worried Charlotte, though, was that Lucy would crawl up inside one of those hollow animals. Dark and smelly. It was scary. There could be a snake, or a nest of rats, in there right now, and she'd never know it.

"They're fine," Paige said. "Don't worry." There was no reason for Charlotte to worry about Lucy, she was a natural tomboy and big for her age. Although at some point she might want to start caring about her weight. "Sit," Paige said soothingly. "They're together. Allegra will keep an eye on Lucy. She is actually very responsible. She picks up other children's trash. It's a bit embarrassing. Let's hope it's not any indicator of her future career path."

"I think that's nice, very civic minded," Charlotte said, watching uneasily as Lucy jumped off the back of an elephant, picked up a stick, and whacked a tree with it. At least she wasn't pulling up flowers, though usually when she did that it was to make a bouquet for her mother, so how could Charlotte complain?

"Uh-oh, I almost forgot," Paige cried. "When the police booked Patty Hearst, she listed her occupation as *Urban Guerrilla*."

"There's a job title," Charlotte said. "Maybe once the kids are out of the house I'll pick it up as a second career."

Paige laughed. A second career? Maybe there *was* hope.

Charlotte relaxed. Maybe she *was* funny.

When minutes later Allegra fell out of the belly of the biggest elephant statue, Charlotte screamed. Paige, however, just sighed, strolled over to her daughter, collapsed on the ground, and began rubbing her back. "Look at the baby!" she cooed. "Look at the beautiful newborn baby!" until Allegra began to slowly wiggle her arms and legs and blink open her eyes, and with Paige's help stand up unsteadily to take her first steps, and then, in a flash, she bolted back into the herd and disappeared.

Paige turned to Charlotte and rolled her eyes. "Sorry about that. She can do that for hours. It's the baby thing, I guess. *Girls will be girls.* Sometimes, though, she gets in there and then decides she doesn't want to come out, and I have to do an emergency C-section."

"No. I was just afraid she'd hurt herself." Charlotte said nothing about the rats.

"Not likely. Allegra is her father's child. Fearless, coordinated, resilient." An image of her sexy husband, Jack— Handsome Jack his college friends still called him (much to his embarrassment)—with his shirt off, playing squash, his beautifully muscled back, appeared in her head. It made her tired.

"I was about to ask you what you did when my daughter—"

"I'm freelance. Computer design."

Freelance *computer* design. Charlotte had practiced saying this until it felt natural. You couldn't spend five minutes with a New Yorker without being asked what you did. What was your purpose? In California, it had been exercise, and the environment. Thank heavens it was just a year. She didn't know her rising sign, or engage in any activity requiring you to chant or wear a leotard. She'd lied about using cloth diapers.

At least New York and Richmond were in the same time zone. Her mother said she could never get used to the West Coast time difference. She'd apologize for calling so early— what was it, 4:45? 5:00? "Your daddy just left for work, so I thought I'd call to check in." It didn't matter. Lucy was usually up, so Charlotte was up, and anyway Ronnie was sleeping. It was always the same, both of them in their dressing gowns, drinking coffee at the kitchen table, no husbands around. They talked. The weather changed, what they were making for dinner changed, but the rest stayed the same. Charlotte's father was good, her mother's garden was thriving, her tennis elbow was getting better. Ronnie was great; work was going well; the kids were growing, happy; she was good, great, happy, well, meeting some friends for lunch. It was an old song, but they both knew it, and there was something to be said for that.

"So," Paige asked, "are you working now?"

"Well, no. Up until Lucy was born—before I got into design—I was working in the publicity department of an ad agency in Chelsea. Four days a week. Before I went on maternity leave, the head of human resources promised me my job would be waiting for me whenever I chose to come back, but then—"

In truth, Kate had offered her reduced hours, and she'd declined. Ronnie would die and go straight to heaven if he knew. He'd been pressuring her to go back to work. Even if it just covered the cost of a nanny.

"But then there wasn't a job, right?" Paige jumped in. "How typical. You know that's illegal. You could sue them to get your job back." *You're lucky*, she thought.

"The worst part," Charlotte lied, "was I trusted her. I felt so betrayed. We weren't best friends, but we were friendly. It was only later that I realized she was the only person in the entire office who never once asked to see a picture of my kids."

That part was true. Charlotte could understand a man's not asking, or caring, but another woman? There was something unnatural about that. Even gay women wanted babies. A girl she knew in college, who to her surprise turned out to be a lesbian (maybe it was that year abroad) had gone to China to adopt a baby. China!

What did a woman who didn't want children want? Or, what did she want more than children? It was creepy.

"Anyhow, freelance is the way to go," Charlotte continued. "And I get to spend time with Lucy—she really is a lot of fun—and I'm free to pick up my other daughter and son from school. These are the most important years, after all, right? Children do need two parents, but right now the mother is most important."

"That's true," Paige said, though Jack was more of the mothering type than she was. Everyone said so. He was more patient, more eager to take Allegra to the park, to read her a bedtime story, more willing to let her sleep in their bed. It was hard seeing what a great father Jack was, for Paige not to won-der what it would have been like if her parents hadn't divorced. If she'd seen more of her dad. If it hadn't just been weekends and there hadn't been a stepmother then stepbrothers.

Paige wished Charlotte had stopped at "freelance is the way to go."

"So, what do you do?" Charlotte asked, secretly hoping Paige was just like her.

"I'm a translator," Paige said, feeling at once proud and a fraud.

"Oh, how interesting. What do you translate?"

"Books."

"Really? What have you translated lately?"

Paige winced. At least Charlotte hadn't said, as so many people did, *Have you translated anything I'd know?*

"Well," she began, "before Allegra was born I'd been work-ing on this manuscript, an absurdist Italian novelist some Hollywood actor had cited as his greatest influence during an interview, and so suddenly everybody was dying for this book. It was a rush. Then, three weeks before my due date, I go into labor.

"Long story short, Allegra isn't much of a sleeper, Jack—my husband—was traveling a lot for business—he's a furniture importer—and so time passed. It wasn't as if I wasn't thinking about it. I was. I was. You have no idea how much I wanted to get back inside that book, into a foreign language I could actu-ally decipher. Not *goo goo ga ga*. I just didn't have time. Then I hear from a friend of mine, a fellow translator, that the house had reassigned it."

"That doesn't sound like a very good friend."

"And my editor didn't even have the decency to call and tell me. So, I call him, and he tells me I missed my deadline.

Which I suspected, I'm not a fool, but they *usually* call you when you're late. So I asked him, 'Why didn't you call me?' And he says, 'I know you just had a baby, so I just *assumed*, when we didn't hear from you, that as *a new mother* you were *too busy* to complete the job.'"

"He should have called you," Charlotte said, full of righteous indignation. "It's unfair, not to mention very rude."

"He didn't respect me enough to call me." That was the bitter truth.

He'd clearly felt he was being a big man, generous, when he let Paige keep her advance despite the fact she hadn't produced a manuscript—but it wasn't about the money. As Jack, in an attempt to comfort her, had pointed out, they didn't need it. True, *they* didn't need it. *She* needed it. Before Allegra was born, before Jack's concerns about his daughter's happiness and welfare eclipsed hers, he'd have understood that.

"Well," Charlotte huffed, "people have babies all the time. Heavens, the world doesn't stop."

But it had, in a way, for Paige. Everyone seemed against the idea of her continuing to work. Even her mother, a single, working mom who had always preached about how she and her older sister could be whatever they wanted to be (her sister, the craziest person she knew, was currently training to be a therapist), had urged Paige not to go back to work if she didn't have to. "Don't go yet. Wait. Be a mom. Savor every single moment of your daughter's life. It goes by so quickly. Too quickly," she said, her voice filling with emotion. "Your work will always be there."

But it wasn't there anymore. Her mother couldn't possibly understand what it was like to have your life taken away like that. Her mother had never wanted to be anything but a mother. She'd never even remarried. She couldn't understand how difficult it was to balance marriage and children, forget having a job. Her mother could say she'd wanted to be a concert pianist, but that was a hundred years ago. If she'd really wanted to be a musician, she'd have stuck with it. No, she wanted to be a mother. She loved being needed. Paige didn't.

For the last two years Paige had passed on every book party invitation she received. Two minutes in a room full of male authors whose wives stayed home with their children or, worse, women just thirty who'd opted to have books before babies or, worst of fucking all, women who had managed to have babies yet somehow continue working, filled her with six months' worth of despair. The looks on her peers' faces as they rifled through their minds' Rolodexes searching for her name. *Oh, wait, I know who you are; you used to work in publishing, didn't you? You're an editor? A writer? No, right, a translator.* It was unbearable.

Of course, now, now that she felt ready, more than ready to return to that world, there were no more invitations. Editors she'd worked with had moved on, or out. The competition, the new young guns, were able to do twice the work in half the time, and were willing to do so for half as much.

A few weeks ago, while Allegra was napping, she'd drafted some letters, trying to strike the right balance between eager and desperate. Thinking about Evie had strengthened her resolve to send them.

Paige yawned. Charlotte yawned too.

"Hey, here's a fact for you," Paige said. "Did you know that the symptoms of sleep deprivation mimic those of Alzheimer's?"

"Where did you hear that?"

"Are you kidding me? I can't remember, but it's true, isn't

it? Forgetfulness, confusion, inability to distinguish reality from fantasy?"

"I get it." Charlotte smiled.

"So," Paige said, "any chance you're free tomorrow?"

Over the next few weeks, Charlotte and Paige shared everything. They confessed dalliances with bulimia, premarriage infidelities, lost weekends in college with Johnnie Walker and his brother Jack Daniel's, and professed to being more than acquainted with various drugs. Paige boasted of smoking Thai stick in high school, and spending the nineties doing rails in dance clubs with her gay best friend—who, Charlotte was secretly pleased to hear, Paige barely saw now that she had a kid. Charlotte told her about how she and this wild friend of hers named Bender (Paige could swear she'd heard of this girl; after all, it was a small world) used to go to this bar in the middle of nowhere at three in the morning to party with the farmers. Paige told of hiding in the bathroom at a five-year-old's birthday party, chasing a Klonopin with a margarita the hostess had thoughtfully provided for the grown-ups, and how after the violent clubbing of a Dora the Explorer piñata— candy sprayed obscenely around the room—Paige had been so eager to flee she'd unwittingly crammed another child's shoes on Allegra's feet. Even though they were a size too small, Allegra hadn't complained or even mentioned it, and Paige hadn't noticed she'd taken the wrong shoes until a day later.

Charlotte gasped with delight. "What did you do?"

"At that point, I couldn't very well call the kid's mother and tell her about the mix-up. What would I say? Mind you, even if you leave out the foot binding and hobbling of my daughter's feet, I'm still a drunken thief. No, I threw the shoes away."

Charlotte shared the horror of having to attend a parents' dinner at her older kids' school by herself because Ronnie was working. She was nervous and so had begun to drink, which she really didn't do anymore. She was sure she'd made a fool of herself. The next morning, after barely managing to drop the twins off at school, she'd been forced to dash into the bathroom at Starbucks, with Lucy strapped in the stroller, to vomit. When she came out, there was an impeccably dressed woman, head to toe white cashmere, staring at her aghast.

"You're kidding. You poor baby," Paige said. "What did you do?"

"I told her I was pregnant."

"You didn't. You did not!" Paige jumped up to go knock wood on the side of a tree. "What did she say?"

"She congratulated me."

Charlotte wished it were true; however, it was hard to get pregnant if the only times your husband wanted to go to bed with you were when he was knee-walking drunk or if it was a major holiday, like Christmas or the Fourth of July.

"You couldn't pay me to go through that again!" Paige howled with laughter.

Since Allegra was born, Jack had started calling her Hot Mom, which he said he meant as a compliment, of course, but Paige didn't want to be the hot mom in yoga pants flush from a Baby Om class, exhausted from her husband letting their child sleep in their bed the night before. Paige wanted to be Jack's hot wife, in a black cocktail dress, talking dirty in ten different languages, ready to make love until she collapsed from exhaustion.

He didn't see her that way anymore.

They'd been having sex in the shower when he whis-pered naughtily in her ear. "You're my MILF. Mother I Like to Fuck," he said, like she didn't already know what that meant. As a wife, she was owed sex as much as he was, yet increasingly it felt like an obligation, June Cleaver flat on her back making a shopping list in her head. That wasn't like her.

She'd always scorned those wives who treated sex like a chore they should be paid for, the same as shoveling snow or feeding the dog. Who relied on maintenance sex, blow jobs, the erotic equivalents of an oil change, to keep their marriages running smoothly. Yet here she was. It scared her.

"I think women would have more desire for their husbands if they paid them for it," Paige said. "Laid a fifty on the dresser, and the wife could spend it on whatever she wanted. Nothing for the children."

"I'd make more money with a paper route," Charlotte re-plied.

She wanted a cookie, an Oreo maybe. Just a few weeks ago Ronnie had walked in on her with a tube of slice-and-bake Toll House cookie dough, eating it like it was cheese. She'd rather he'd seen her on the toilet.

"On the sunny side, at least we have husbands," Charlotte said, rummaging more frantically in the net bag on the back of the stroller. "Good ones too. Not like those fathers you see prowling round the teeter-totter at ten o'clock on a Sunday morning—"

"Strutting around like that Snugli is an extension of their penis. All hail the Great Sperminator!" At that moment, a hawk circled overhead. "What do you think he's hunting?" Paige asked, pointing at the sky.

Charlotte didn't look up. "Not even watching their children. You can always pick them out—no coats, no socks, half the time the boys are still in their pajamas, grimy faces, roaming the park like a pack of savages. The girls, hair in knots, half dressed in some whorish getup, high heels, half Disney Princess, half pole dancer. They might as well be orphans."

Paige chuckled. Charlotte was looking past her, not at the bird of prey, which sadly was becoming just a blot on the sky, but into the middle distance. Her cheeks were flushed.

"And what is Dad—how-good-of-him-to-take-them-to-the-park Dad—doing? Flirting with some little Dutch au pair who barely speaks English, or gabbing on his g-d BlackBerry like 'Look at me, I'm a captain of industry. If I put down this phone, planes will explode in midflight, the stock market plummet, illegal aliens pour in over our borders. All that is keeping you safe from certain destruction is this phone and me.'

"Meanwhile, he's probably on some phone sex line. And I feel like shouting, 'How could you, how dare you even think of leaving your wife? Your children, your children, aren't even grown yet!'"

Charlotte was panting slightly. "Oh my," she said, visibly shaken, as though she'd been speaking in tongues.

Paige didn't have to meet Ronnie to know she'd dislike him. She reached over and squeezed her hand. It was sweaty.

"Is everything okay?"

Charlotte laid her hand across her forehead. "Don't listen to me."

"No, *really*. What's going on?"

"I'm fine," Charlotte said, waving her off. "I'm just tired. You know. It's a good thing we're going to visit my parents next week. Not Disney World, but we'll all be together as a family. That is what matters."

"When do you leave?"

"I can't remember the date, exactly." Charlotte yawned, suddenly exhausted. "I think I have a mental block against it."

"Did you know that the symptoms of sleep deprivation mimic those of Alzheimer's?"

Paige had made this joke the second time they met.

"I know. You're right." Charlotte laughed halfheartedly, remembering how her grandfather in his fleeting moments of clarity had gone through his photographs, writing the names of his family and friends below their images. Wife, daughter, father. Still, there were some—a portrait of his sister and his mother holding hands, himself as a boy in a coonskin cap— over whose heads he'd put only question marks.

The day before Charlotte left to visit her parents, Paige brought a bottle of wine disguised in a Hello Kitty thermos to the park, and they sat on a bench drinking it out of Dixie cups.

"We're such bad girls," Paige said, raising her glass.

"To us," Charlotte said.

They drank. "A lady drinking in public. It's a scandal. My mother would just die," Charlotte said and grinned, satisfaction spreading as the wine began to relax her.

"To our mothers," Paige said, grateful Charlotte's mother wasn't her own.

Through the fence, they watched a pack of gangly black teenagers in parkas with big fur collars and Moon Boot–size sneakers circling the park on bikes that were clearly far too small for them.

Paige, liberated by the knowledge that her friend would never think she was being racist, said, "Do you bet they stole those bikes? I mean, look at them."

"Probably," Charlotte said, then without missing a beat, "Do you bet they're selling drugs?"

"We could ask," Paige said jokingly. "Do you want to buy some weed? Acapulco Gold? Maybe some crack? A speedball?"

They'd both gotten a kick out of that, and both were relieved when the boys didn't circle round again but began pedaling away, no doubt home for dinner.

Watching the boys shrinking to dots, Charlotte cried, "You missed a sale!" She felt so exhilarated. It was almost like they'd done it, but better than that, because they hadn't.

"Nope, no hope in dope." Paige shook her head, grinning.

Charlotte chimed in, "Hugs not drugs. Coke, don't blow it."

"Crack. It's what's for dinner."

"Just Say No."

"It was a million years ago, wasn't it?" Paige sighed. "Just Say No. I'd do some coke right now if someone came up and gave it to me."

"Me too," Charlotte said. She might with Paige.

A pair of teenage girls in matching halter dresses, hair shiny and past their shoulders, glided into the park arm in arm, and stood just inside the fence like they were contemplating a shortcut across the park, then thought better of it. College students, Charlotte thought. Paige guessed fifteen, maybe sixteen.

"So, girl talk. How old were you?"

Charlotte looked confused. She knew what Paige was asking.

"When you lost your cherry, and where? I was fifteen, in my bedroom at home, while my mother and sister were in the living room watching A Star Is Born, for the tenth time, weeping hysterically."

Charlotte was dumbfounded.

"And he spent the night. In my canopy bed with my whole collection of Beanie Babies and stuffed animals piled around him. Lions and tigers and bears, oh my." What Paige remembered best was that when she woke up, the guy was sleeping beside her with a unicorn clutched to his chest.

"Your mother knew?"

"My mother didn't care," she said, wondering if this was in fact true. "You think I'm joking? When I came home from college, I ran my vibrator through the dishwasher. She treated it like it was any other home appliance."

Charlotte paled.

"Don't be shy now. I just told you my story—"

It wasn't as though Charlotte had never talked about it. She had. She'd talked to a therapist. She told Charlotte rape wasn't sex, it was violence. It wasn't as if she hadn't been with other men in the seven years before she met Ronnie; she had and he knew that. She hadn't had sex, though. Wouldn't. Couldn't. Didn't want to. Not until Ronnie. She'd read that after seven years of not having sex you could consider yourself a virgin. She liked that. Even so, she'd felt a moral obligation to tell Ronnie before they married, even though she feared, silly or not, he'd ask for the ring back.

Charlotte didn't have to ask her mother to explain what she meant when, in the middle of shopping for her trousseau, she'd offered, "You realize, I hope, that a lady doesn't need to tell her husband all her secrets. That's silly, honey. A little mystery is a good thing." Then she'd laughed, the sound a high, ringing chime. *What fun we're having!* "Why, the first ten years of my marriage I went to bed with a full face of makeup on." Her mother had paused, rubbing the silk of a nightgown pale as moonlight between her fingers. "You don't have to talk about everything."

Charlotte looked at Paige. Then at the ground. The grass was matted with food crumbs and gum. She could tell her, couldn't she? She wanted to.

"It wasn't my choice," she said, and now couldn't take it back.

"Oh—" Paige looked pained.

"You know, I don't like to talk about it. I've *never*—" Charlotte wished she could stop herself.

"I'm sorry. I'm so, so sorry."

"No, no. It's just me." Charlotte wiped her eyes and smiled. "Forgive me? Just pretend—"

"Stop it. I know. Every woman I know has had something like this happen to them."

"I shouldn't have told you that . . ."

"Why? I understand." Paige moved closer to Charlotte on the bench and reached for her hand. "And if not me, who?"

So, Charlotte told her. From a distance, only another mother could have told that she was crying. She was crying the way mothers learn to do. Her body betrayed nothing. There was no wiping her eyes, or heaving shoulders, no sound at all. Until she put her head on Paige's shoulder and began to wail.

Charlotte was gone for only two weeks, but it felt longer. During her absence, the rats had come back in force. Maybe it was the heat of late August, the trash cans overflowing with spoiled lunches, swollen diapers, and sticky ice cream wrappers. Maybe it was because the red-tailed hawks had vanished. You could hear the rats scrabbling under the shrubbery, catch sight of a length of tail, bald and pink as it slipped behind the water fountain. When the sun started to dip toward the horizon, they'd become even bolder, parading across the pavement and in between the feet of the elephants.

The neighborhood civic association had begun putting up posters: STOP BABIES GETTING RABIES! with the image of a crying baby and a defiantly evil rat with a slash through it. Paige couldn't understand why others didn't find the posters and the asides people had scrawled on them (STOP BABIES WITH RABIES BEFORE THEY KILL AGAIN!) as hilarious as she did. Even the suggestion of amusement at the image of foam pouring out of a rabid infant's mouth and the tagline NANNIE GET YOUR GUN! elicited nothing but dirty looks from other parents. It was too hot for sex, Jack said. He was excited about going back to India. He wished she could accompany him, but there was Allegra, and leaving her with Paige's mother wasn't really an option. Maybe she and Allegra ought to visit his mom in the country. Maybe when he got back they should go look at some houses in Pelham? Just look. She reacted badly. Her life was here. Her friends were here. Her work was here. Jack didn't call her on it, but she knew what he was thinking. It was easy to forget.

It had been weeks since she'd written those editors asking for work. She'd have taken anything really, it didn't have to be literary. An Italian bodice ripper. She hadn't honestly expected they'd respond quickly; after all, it was summer. People fled the city in the summertime. Still, she'd hoped. Even though she knew, in her heart of hearts, that they wouldn't respond at all.

The entire way to the park Lucy had carried on, kicking and screaming like she was being kidnapped. Charlotte couldn't stand it anymore. At the top of the hill, with the playground in sight, Charlotte stopped. She crouched down beside her daughter and in the calmest voice she could muster said, "Are you excited? Won't it be nice to see your friend Allegra again?"

The girl howled in her face. "I hate Allegra!"

Charlotte grabbed Lucy by the arm. "How can you say that? That is no way for a young lady to talk. You love her. You're best friends."

"Noooo. I hate her!" Lucy shrieked.

Charlotte dropped her voice. "I swear, if you don't behave yourself, I will just die." She tightened her grip. "Do you hear me? I will just die."

"Hate," Lucy said, less defiant now.

"I mean it. I will smack you silly, I will," Charlotte said, ready to do it. As if speaking to her daughter that way (she'd never spoken to anyone like that) wasn't bad enough. She wanted to hit her.

That silenced Lucy.

Mercifully, while Charlotte was hugging Paige, and Paige was hugging her back, Lucy let Allegra hug her. Lucy didn't say a word. She didn't follow her over to the swings or take Allegra's hand but headed off alone for the bouncy bridge. Neither woman noticed, and even if they had, they wouldn't have cared.

They were eager to exchange their gifts. Each cried, "You didn't have to!" Each was happy the other had.

"I love my little rose ring," Charlotte said as she worked it down her pinkie. Was there ever a more beautiful ring?

"I love my lavender sachets," Paige said. They were made of violet silk, heavy with lavender. She'd put them in her underwear drawer. Scented panties. That might turn Jack on.

They were perfect gifts.

"So," Charlotte said brightly, "what did I miss?"

"Here? Nothing. The rats, of course. How was home? Tell me everything."

Charlotte took a deep breath. "Well, we're a bit like a traveling circus, aren't we?" she said. Her southern accent always got stronger after time at home. "Poor Ronnie got called back after three days. Unavoidable, of course. It put a bee in my mother's bonnet. She'd ask me two, three times a day if I'd talked to him. How was he getting by without me? It was eleven o'clock at night and he wasn't home? Had I tried him on his cell phone? How could the children possibly fall asleep without saying good night to their daddy? She said, 'I always knew where your father was, *especially* when he was traveling.' What does that mean? Then she says, 'Won't it be nice,' she said, 'when the kids are in college, you can accompany him?'" Charlotte loved that idea, but she wasn't so sure how Ronnie would feel about it. "You notice though she doesn't offer to babysit."

"Count your blessings," Paige said. "Last weekend my mother and sister invited Allegra over for some grandma, auntie time. They had tea while I went shopping, got a bikini wax. When I picked her up, she was wearing hot-pink nail polish, mascara, and red lipstick, and was singing, "Hey Big Spender," which my sister had taught her."

"You're kidding."

"And she had a rash, so she was in our bed all night long." Paige yawned. So much for the wax. Jack had gotten up in the middle of the night to sleep on the sofa. He'd never done that before, ever.

"Well, honey, I barely saw Ronnie last night." Charlotte's voice was strained with forced cheerfulness. "I don't know if I got the arrival time wrong or he did, but he didn't have his phone on, so he was nearly two hours late."

"You're not serious?" It sounded like something her father would do.

"And when he did finally show up, there we were, the four of us, all dirty and tired, at the curb sitting on our suitcases like a bunch of gypsies. His sweet little family."

Ronnie had looked great. He was a different man. You'd have thought he was the one on vacation. Well rested and thin. All that time in the gym was paying off. He looked ten years younger. He'd picked up the kids and, hugging each one, said, "Look at you. Look how much you've grown. Next thing you know, you'll be off to college," like it was his fondest wish. He had kissed her too.

"Honey, you should have called me," Paige said, imagining how ragged poor Charlotte must have been. Ronnie was an asshole. "Next time you call me."

"We weren't home five minutes before he looked like his dearest wish was to get back in the car and hightail it outta there."

Ronnie had apologized for how he'd *let the place go*. There was no food, the fridge was empty, the garbage can full of take-out containers, and at the bottom, she found the bright blue foil of a condom wrapper. While Ronnie was falling asleep, watching the end of the Yankees game in bed, Charlotte had put the children to bed. R.J., who hadn't let his mother tuck him in for a year now, wanted a story, so she read while braiding Mandy's hair. Lucy, who'd wanted to sleep on her brother's floor like a dog, had woken when her mother picked her up, so Charlotte had lain with her until she fell back asleep.

From the bench Charlotte watched her daughter scale the front of the slide like a mountain climber, much to the unhappiness of the children in line on the ladder, who were yelling at her. Lucy, if she noticed at all, didn't care. Allegra wasn't there. She was off with another girl, both of them lying across the swings, arms outstretched, pretending they could fly.

"You must be ruined," Paige said, sounding worried.

"I am hot," Charlotte said, running her hand across her brow. "You know what they say, *Men and horses sweat, ladies perspire.*"

"Really?"

"I'm just tired." Charlotte yawned so wide tears came into her eyes. "A few nights of sleep in my own bed and I'll be right as rain." Why was Paige looking at her that way? "It's fine, really. It'll take some time, but once we get back into our routine . . ." Charlotte's voice trailed off.

"If you knew what motherhood was going to be like, really knew," Paige began, "would you do it again? I don't mean the pain, the childbirth part, that's nothing. . . . I mean the rest of it."

"It can be hard." The fence was higher than Charlotte remembered. Someone had found a child's sun hat and put it on top of a parking meter.

Paige couldn't look at Allegra. "I love her," she said, "but if I'd known how hard it was going to be—what it would do to my marriage, what I'd have to give up, my career, my sense of self," Paige's voice trembled, "I'm not sure I'd have done it."

"How can you say that?" Charlotte was frightened. "You don't mean it."

"Is this what you planned on?" Paige asked. "Is this what you wanted?" Charlotte closed her eyes and said nothing.

The sun was setting, and each woman shivered. It was getting cooler, almost dark now. The girls were just shadows. They stayed like that, not moving at all, until the streetlights began to come on.

The Joy of Cooking

I was halfway out the door when the phone rang. Another person would have let the machine pick up, but you know how it is when you're a mother.

"Thank God you're there," my daughter Emily said, sounding out of breath.

"I am, but sweetie," I said, "I'm in a bit of a rush . . ."

"No, no, wait! Don't go," she cried. "Please, *Mommy*? I'm begging you. I just need one thing, I promise."

I looked at the clock: 4:00. Yoga started at 4:30. My doctor had recommended it for stress reduction, and the pain I'd been having in my hips. After yoga, provided I wasn't bleeding or paralyzed, I was planning to pop into the drugstore and buy new lipstick. Something youthful but sophisticated with shimmer. My mother always said that a woman should have a signature lipstick the way a man had a signature cocktail. I'd married and divorced Emily's father, Terry, in Cherries in the Snow. After that, I was going to treat myself to an overdue haircut at Sheer Delight. Something new, possibly even a little racy. I'd been toying with the idea of bangs. Then, at 6:30, I was meeting Hugo, the new man shelving the philosophy section at the bookstore, where for the last fifteen years

I'd been working as a cashier and bookkeeper. It was just coffee, but let's just say it had been a long time between cups of coffee: 1,825 days to be exact. Five years. Not that I was counting.

It isn't easy to meet men, let alone carry on a relationship when, for all practical purposes, you're a single mother. Even though Terry was around, it wasn't like Emily and Paige lived with their father, or he ever took care of them. Not that I'm complaining. My daughters have always come first. I have no regrets.

The girl who'd picked up my shift for the afternoon was named Bea. Last month, she and her boyfriend had decided, on a whim, to drive to Arizona and back over the long weekend, but his car broke down in the desert. She'd called the store collect from a payphone. I'd accepted the charges without thinking. I'm lucky that, of all the things I have to worry about, my girls running off with a man, is not one them. Bea's trip didn't sound at all romantic, but I understood. I'd have gone anywhere with Terry when I was twenty-two. It took me back—which might explain why I'd been flirting with Hugo. Why I had shaved my legs.

Emily cleared her throat theatrically. "Well, you'll just have to wait a minute, as I have an announcement to make. Today," she paused, "I became a woman."

Emily was twenty-four.

"I bought a chicken. I did. With legs and everything."

"Really?"

Emily didn't cook. She chopped salads, sliced fruit, and poured brewer's yeast on popcorn. She went to restaurants where she tortured the waiters with special orders, everything steamed or boiled, sauce on the side, then ultimately returned half of it. Emily had been anorexic for almost half her life.

I assumed she meant a dead chicken.

"I have a suitor!"

It sounded like she said: *suture.* Slap a steak on a black eye, a chicken breast on stitches. I wish I didn't think this way.

"A *suitor*, Mommy. A gentleman caller." She sighed as if she might faint from the mere pleasure of saying the word. Emily had often lectured her sister, Paige, and me on the subject of love, saying, "When Percy Shelley, the *poet*, drowned, Mary Shelley carried his burnt-up heart in her handbag for the rest of her life. *In her handbag!* That's real love. That's what I'm waiting for."

I wondered, *How long before that heart started to stink?*

"You mean, a boyfriend?" Emily had admirers, mostly older men she'd met through the art museum where she worked. Elderly patrons who enjoyed the company of a slight, pale-skinned girl with long dark pre-Raphaelite hair, able to converse about romantic poetry, renaissance art, and classical music through drinks and intermission. But she never had boyfriends. It was understood that she didn't like to be touched.

She had always told me everything. Kissing was sublime, but the rest of it—she'd shudder—reliving the feel of a man's hot hairy hands on her body, his breath on her neck—was disgusting. After her freshman year in the dorms at Sarah Lawrence (zero privacy, a roommate who look like a dairy maid and whistled in her sleep, boys loitering in the halls night and day like pimps on street corners), she'd come back home to live with me. Or she had, until last year when her therapist insisted that in order for her to *separate* she had to move out. It was ridiculous. Now she was in a snug fourth-floor walk-up that I could afford, three blocks away. She didn't mind the stairs. She liked stairs. All that mattered, she said, was that it was close to me. Close enough to run over in her pajamas to borrow a cup of sugar.

"He's been wooing me for a few weeks now, and I thought it was time I made him dinner, because that's what you're supposed to do, right? Cook?" She took a breath. "Which is why I called. I need you to give me the family recipe."

I could tell that she was biting her nails. Biting them down to the pink. She'd eat her nails, chew the skin off her fingers. But you couldn't get her to eat a hot dog.

"Mommy? Is there something wrong?"

"No. I'm just surprised." A few weeks? We spoke every day, two sometimes three times a day, and she never once mentioned she was dating someone.

"You promise? Otherwise, I'd have to throw myself under a train, or walk into a river with stones in my pockets, or something." *Or something.*

"I promise. I'm your mother. You just caught me with one foot out the door. And I'm meeting *someone* tonight for a drink." I waited for an interrogation. *Someone Who?* Emily had a gift for zeroing in on the shortcomings in men I'd normally turn a blind eye to. Imitating the strut of the attorney who, despite being round and balding, retained the arrogance of a once-beautiful person; mimicking the nervous throat clearing habit of the accountant; pointing out the receding chin and mustache of the college professor. "Only stagecoach robbers, rednecks, and the cop in the Village People should have mustaches," she said. "I just could never trust a man with a mustache." But I wasn't twenty-four anymore. And he was separated from his wife.

"So, can you give it to me? Now?"

"I don't know what you're talking about."

"Seriously, Mother. Are you claiming there *is* no family recipe? Because Paige told me there was," Emily said, as though she'd caught me in a lie. "Paige told me that the other night when the two of you were having dinner alone together"—she paused meaningfully, jealousy lurking in her voice like a maniac with a hammer—"*she* said you gave it to her."

It was true Paige and I had dinner alone. She wanted to stop by and pick up some books—poetry books I'd owned in college. Back then I always had a copy of Dante or Rilke in my bag and a pack of cigarettes. I was surprised that Paige, who was pre-med (a fact I was very proud of) even wanted them. She seemed surprised to find I owned them.

She'd discovered them on the bottom shelf of the bookcase in my bedroom. When I found her, sitting on my bed, running her finger down their spines like she was checking for scoliosis, she demanded to know, *Whose are these? Where did they come from?*

"My old piano teacher used to say that you don't know a culture until you read their poetry. . . . It sounds silly now, but when I was your age I'd wanted to be a classical pianist, playing concerts all across Europe . . ."

"I believe that too," Paige said, a hungry look in her eye.

When she called the next day to ask if she could borrow them, I told her she could have them. They were gibberish to me now. "Come," I said, "and you can stay for dinner."

The chicken I'd made for Paige wasn't from a family recipe, or even out of a cookbook—just something I'd seen a friend's mother do years ago. I was surprised I remembered it. The closest I had come to inheriting a recipe from my mother was rescuing her copy of the *Joy of Cooking* out of a box she'd packed up to donate to the church after my father died. "Ha," my mother said, "they ought to call that one *No Joy of Cooking*."

It had been the only cookbook my mother ever needed while my father was alive. All of the dishes he required—beef stroganoff, pork chops, and Hawaiian chicken, even the vanilla ice box cake, which my mother made for my birthday year after year, insisting that it was *my* favorite—all four had come from that book.

"Is this recipe something grandma used to make?" Paige asked, as she helped herself to seconds of chicken and stuffing.

"My *mother*? No. Your grandmother wasn't really the homemaking type." I topped off our wineglasses. "Cooking, cleaning, children. She felt it was a kind of servitude, I think."

"I can totally see that." Paige nodded, as though her grandmother's chafing at motherhood was a point of pride. "Who can blame her?" She licked her fingers. "She wanted more."

It wasn't like I didn't want more, too. I'd always planned to go back to piano. I thought I could wait until the girls went to school, until they didn't need me so much. But then they kept on needing me. Well, one of them, anyway.

After dinner, and deep into a second bottle of wine, Paige asked if she could smoke. I had no idea she smoked, and didn't know whether to scold her or, because we were having such fun, ask if I could bum one. It had been years, but I did neither.

She told me about a friend of hers who'd purposefully had sex with a man in order to contract crabs.

"Although, because she was pre-med," Paige said, "she preferred the term 'pubic lice' or in Latin, *phthirus pubis*."

These crabs, Paige explained, weren't ordinary civilian crabs, but rock 'n' roll royalty crabs, having been passed, via groupies, from the Rolling Stones to Aerosmith to Guns N' Roses, for decades. It made her feel connected to something larger, a part of history.

"Like those sourdough starters that were so popular in the seventies," I said. "Mine was supposedly a direct descendant of one that Alice Waters started in Berkeley.

"Or what about herpes?" Paige winced. "Herpes is the worst—like an old rock star, herpes never really dies, it just fades away."

The recipe for the chicken I made Paige was so simple I could have just told it to her. In her first year of pre-med she'd memorized all 206 bones in the human body, including the ones babies are born with that then disappear. Still, I'd written it out on a recipe card carefully, in my very best *keep-this-for-posterity* script.

Secret: Puncture a lemon several times with a fork and insert it inside the bird—this will keep it moist. Paige wouldn't know about the lemon. That was something I could give my daughter who didn't need me. A *lemon*.

She looked pleased. "Thanks," she said, then careful not to bend it slid the recipe carefully into her handbag.

"Do you even have a roasting pan?"

If she didn't I'd get her one for Christmas.

"I'm sure I can manage," she patted the pocket where she'd put the recipe for safekeeping. "Don't worry."

"I practically had to stalk Paige to get the recipe," Emily complained. "I literally had to call her ten times, god knows where she was. Finally, at seven in the morning, she picked up. Even so, she said all she could remember were the ingredients, not the proportions. So you see, Mommy, you have to help me."

I shrugged off my coat and put my keys on the kitchen counter.

"Did you get the lemon?"

"What lemon?" Emily said, sounding dismayed. "She left out the lemon. That is *so* like her."

"It's just a silly lemon. It's not important." If Paige forgot, it was most likely tiredness, although it could have been spite.

"No. It has to be good—just as good as the recipe you gave Paige. No, better."

"It will be. I promise." For Emily it would always have to be better.

"You are the best mommy in the world, you know that?"

"I'll make it easy."

"Good, because remember, I'm no good with numbers."

This, I knew, was a lie. Emily was obsessed with numbers. The lower the better. For years the goal was to keep herself under 200 calories a day. She'd tried to stop counting, but it was hard. Old habits don't die with sudden-aneurysm efficiency. They go in and out of comas, existing on life-support for years.

"Why don't I just come over?"

"No. I can do it," she said firmly. Then she shrieked. "Eek! It's slimy. Its legs won't stay closed—I'm putting on rubber gloves—bad chicken, slutty chicken. Oh god, it's disgusting. I can't even look at it. I think I'm going to be sick."

My Emily, who loved horror movies, who giggled through the shower scene in *Psycho*, was horrified at the sight of a raw chicken.

"Hold it steady in the sink," I said. "Turn on the water, not too hot, just lukewarm, and wash it. Gently. There's no need to scrub."

"Soap?"

"No soap. Just pat it dry." I could have been teaching her how to wash a baby. Then there was a loud thud and the sound of the phone being dropped.

"Oh no, oh no, I dropped it! It squirted right out of my hands."

"Just pick it up and start over." Good thing it wasn't a baby.

There was the thump of the chicken being dumped into the sink.

Her voice broke, "I can't do this."

"Yes, you can." I wanted her to do it herself. It was time. She ought to be able to make a damn chicken. "You'll need to preheat the oven, 350 degrees." I stopped, it was my call waiting, loud and insistent. I knew Emily could hear it too.

"Did you ever cook for Daddy? When you were courting?" she pressed on, ignoring the sound, as she always did.

I checked my caller ID. It was Paige.

"Of course," I said. "We did that sort of thing back then."

"You think chicken is good, right?"

"Chicken is good." The phone beeped once more, then stopped. I poured myself some wine.

"Good, I thought so." Emily's voice eased.

"*Coq au vin*," I said. "That was the first meal I ever made your father." He'd come to my apartment. It was tiny, with a galley kitchen not even big enough for two people to stand. "I made it from a recipe in a women's magazine. The pearl onions, the red wine, the French name—it all seemed so sophisticated. Until the chicken turned purple."

Emily groaned. "Well, that's completely and utterly disgusting."

"I misread the directions, and poured in three times the amount of Cabernet," I said. "Your father and I got drunk on that meat."

"I'm sorry, Mother, but that's not exactly romantic."

It was, though. Terry was the most charming, handsomest man who ever wanted me. He played guitar and dreamed of sailing around the world. He kissed my ears. He called me baby. He was rich with million-dollar ideas.

We married at twenty-three. It was the seventies; even then it seemed young. The marriage lasted thirteen years. Thirteen is the lace anniversary. My husband gave me a divorce. My mother and father were married at twenty-three, it was the forties, so it would have seemed old. The marriage lasted forty years. Forty is the ruby anniversary. Forty trumps thirteen. My mother got a gold necklace with a ruby drop, a bead of blood at her throat.

For forty years my mother ignored my father tooting his horn and whistling at women on the street, endured him placing his hand on the behinds of hundreds of waitresses and shop girls. Forty years she held her tongue, twisted her napkin in her lap, glaring murderously at me when I dared to look at her with anything close to pity.

I am forty-eight and I can still fit into my old wedding dress. Every year, I try it on to gauge how my body has changed. It's a little tight around the middle, but if I gave up my nightly glass or two of wine, started running again, or did yoga, it would fit.

At twenty-four, Emily is one year older than I was when I had her. Paige is two years younger than Emily. Paige kayaks and sails and ran a marathon for fun. I never worry about her. Emily boasts of her great eating habits, attention to nutrition, she walks everywhere. I worry about her breaking a bone.

Estimated number of times a week Emily calls me? Twenty. Exact number of times a week she calls her father? One. On Sunday—long-distance from my house. Zero is the number of times Emily has, to my knowledge, entertained a man in her apartment. The number of times Emily has cooked for me? Also zero.

I do the math. It all adds up.

"Okey, dokey," Emily says, "step one of the stuffing completed. I'm done with the carrots and celery." Celery is a staple of Emily's diet. It has six calories, and chewing burns ten. If you stop eating sugar, carrots taste like candy.

"So now the onion," I say. I hear her blade, cutting fast, like she thinks if she chops fast, she can out-distance the tears. I'm afraid she's going to cut herself.

"Gee, this is such fun," Emily says with a happy sniffle, "or maybe it only feels that way because I'm in love."

"Love?" It stuck in my throat like a bone.

"I despise the word *stuffing*. Don't you, Mommy? Why would anyone eat anything that promised to stuff you?" I sensed her shiver. "So, now I'm just supposed to pack this mess into that hole?"

"Don't over fill it—it expands."

She laughed. "Will it explode?"

I almost wished that would happen. What would Prince Charming do? Laugh it off, take her in his arms and tell her not to worry? Would he insist they salvage the bird, and then, afterward, tell her: *Baby, it was delicious.* Or would he judge her? Scowl as he made a mental note: *Not wife material. Can't have poultry blowing up left and right! Someone could lose an eye!*

"Emily," I said, fighting my annoyance, "maybe I could just tell the recipe to you and you could just write it down . . ."

"Oh pardon me. I just thought, in light of these *extraordinary* circumstances, you might want to help."

"I do want to. I'm sorry. The phone. It's just hard this way."

"Forget it, Mother. I'm letting it go." She took a deep breath. "Because," she said, "did I mention that I'm in love?"

Fifty was the estimated number of lovers Terry had during our marriage. He didn't offer this number with remorse, or grief, or pride, more like a seasoned tax attorney. He delivered the information to me because, he said, "It's been weighing on my conscience for too long." As though his conscience were a beach chair, groaning under the fat ass of his indiscretion.

Every year for a decade after we split, I got an AIDS test.

Did I mention that I'm in love?

Terry's second wife is thirty-five. Thirteen years younger than me. They have two boys. Emily, Paige, and I, we call them the Toxic Test Tube Twins. They are in grade school and, Emily says, "blond as Nazis." Terry told the girls the divorce was my idea. I was inflexible, demanding. No fun. I told them zero about his screwing around. I was ashamed to admit that, no matter how much and how good I gave, it wasn't enough. Two hours was the amount of time the lifeguard at the YMCA estimated Emily had been swimming before she passed out last year and nearly drowned. Five minutes was the amount of time Emily estimated she was unconscious. One second is how far away Emily swears she was from going into the light.

Because Emily wasn't living with me, and had long ago stopped recording her gains and losses on a piece of graph paper taped on the bathroom wall, I didn't know until then that she'd dropped below seventy-five pounds. Seventy-five pounds was the magic number. It meant she could be checked into the eating disorders wing of the Melrose Institute—that made two times in six years.

Sixteen days after she was released she moved into her own apartment. She'd bought her own scale, light and high tech that measured with digital precision, down to the ounce, as well as calculated your body fat. In comparison, my own scale, a large gray slab with a needle that wavered uncertainly, seemed out of the Stone Age, as precise as using a sundial for a stopwatch.

The hospital is one hour and forty-five minutes away. I bought the complete works of Stephen King on CD for the car ride back and forth. Vampires, witches, ghosts; tales of the undead dead terrorizing the innocent. Each day another monster claimed another victim and the hero got closer to slaying it.

The hospital where my mother is bedridden is twenty minutes from my home. She sleeps a lot. Some days all she will eat is a gallon of vanilla Häagen Dazs. She has a sweet tooth. When I visit we sit outside the hospital on a bench so she can smoke, three cigarettes an hour—her tank of oxygen, which she drags everywhere, sitting just inside the door, like a chaperone past caring.

When I told my mother that Emily was in the hospital too, she sighed. "It's such a shame you weren't able to keep that husband of yours. He was so dashing. He made a mean Old Fashioned too," she said, shaking her head with grave disappointment. "Those poor, poor girls. But, you know, you did spoil them. I told you, if you pick up a baby every time it cries, it will grow up thinking every time it cries someone will pick them up." She put her hand on my leg. "Now, look at you. Look how well you turned out."

I know she's old. Sick, too. Still, it wouldn't be the worst thing to never see my mother again. Amount of money I'd inherit: zero. Amount of money Emily's ninety-day stay cost me: $40,000. Amount my insurance company would pay: $10,000.

Five was the number of group therapy sessions Emily took part in each week. Four the number of one-on-one sessions with a psychiatrist. Three meetings with a nutritionist. The number of times she was tied to her bed during her stay? One.

Given her medical history, Emily's chances of ever being able to have a baby are one in one hundred. The internist at Melrose was the first of three doctors to tell me that. I wanted to cry. How could Emily not have a daughter someday? It was like hearing your child would never be happy. The age of the unmarried doctor who so glibly gave us this news? Maybe twenty-six. Number of children? You can bet zero.

Emily might have dated him. It happened all the time. Pretty girl, cute doctor. I liked the idea. A doctor-husband, one who could perform CPR, set broken bones, prescribe painkillers. Someone I could trust to take care of her. At twenty-three, she was one of the older girls in the program — a seasoned pro among teenagers. During group therapy, the mothers and daughters sat in a circle. You could tell that the mothers had made an effort to look nice. No sweats or sneakers. The mothers wear lipstick. We do our hair. We don't look like the parents visiting children in other parts of the hospital. The daughters, dressed in regulation blue gowns that hit just below the knee, stared icily at us, like gang members cracking their knuckles, shivs made from melted-down toothbrushes hidden in their thick wooly socks. Their matching hospital bands like friendship bracelets.

For us, the girls recalled—in poetic detail—their inaugural purge. They did so with the nostalgia of a first kiss. Masters now, some boasted that the simple act of kneeling and bringing two fingers toward their mouths could trigger their gag reflex. One said she could make herself vomit by just thinking the word *meatball*.

They talked shop: Amphetamines. Ipecac. Enemas. Emily flashed her scars. Showed off the tooth she'd chipped bingeing on frozen éclairs. Even here—especially here—it was a competition. A race. Simple math. The one who'd lost the most weight won. The thing is, to win was to die. You didn't even get the trophy.

We weren't allowed to cry. Just witness. "This isn't about you right now," the group leader would remind us. How was it not about us?

Did I mention that I'm in love?

"Now we're ready to butter the skin."

"Excuse me? No, *we're* not. The skin? You've got to be kidding me. I was just starting to pull it off."

"Stop. Stop now. If you remove the skin, the meat will dry out."

"But it's disgusting."

"It's flavor."

"It's fat."

It had always been like this. She'd ask for my advice, listen intently, nod her head, and then ignore it.

I heard my call waiting, again. I checked the number. Paige. She'd have to wait. "Well," I said, "you have to weigh the two evils against each other. If you don't follow the recipe, you can't control the outcome. You don't know what could happen. It could be a disaster. Now get the butter. Use a whole stick. Cover the bird—in around the legs—don't be shy."

"Ugh. I can't believe I am doing this. It's making me gag. What is the exact amount of butter the recipe calls for?" Emily asked, suspicious.

I was getting tired. I wasn't going to offer to go over there again. If she wanted me, she'd have to ask me. Beg.

"Does every recipe require you to crayon disgusting fat all over the bird?"

"So, tell me about this boy," I said. "I mean *man*." Maybe if I distracted her, she'd butter the entire chicken without noticing.

"Well," she said, excited. "He's terribly handsome—"

I knew the type. Vain. The kind of man who can't resist catching sight of his own reflection, admiring his profile in the back of a spoon.

"—and an actor."

He was poor. I knew it, poor, and short, probably a dwarf.

"How did the two of you meet?"

"Ah," Emily said, as though she imagined one day she'd be telling this story to their children. "It was at the Social Security office. I lost my card."

"Really?"

"I'd been trapped in that circle of hell for what felt like eternity, literally, clinging to Jane Austen for life, waiting and waiting for my number to be called, when out of nowhere this gentlemen appears before me—"

I could picture him—square chin, arrogant.

"—and begins to mime picking roses."

"How romantic," I said.

It was easy to see Emily feeding off all that attention. The good-looking man, all those people. Her cheeks flushed, hands clasped at her chest, her eyes wide and sparkling. Intoxicated.

"It was! He even pricked his finger on a thorn. It was so sweet. Then he presented me with this bouquet and the whole place positively erupted in applause. It was so—"

"He's a mime?" I said, fighting laughter. I poured myself two more inches of wine.

"He's an actor," she countered, suddenly irritable. "Extraordinarily gifted too. Wait until I show you the review of the last play he was in. It was a small role, off-off Broadway, but the critic singled him out, he called him a *promising young thespian.*"

"*Sounds* promising," I said. "Have you finished buttering the skin?"

"And Mommy, he's got the face of a poet. *Byronic.* It's beautiful. You've got to see us. Everyone says how fantastic we look together."

I chew on the inside of my lip. Everyone? *Who are these people you've shown him to, before introducing him to your mother?*

"And he does magic."

"That's a plus."

"After filling my arms with these enchanting roses, he made a silver dollar appear from behind my ear. Right there in the middle of the Social Security office. It was glorious. He swore he'd stand there all day long pulling silver pieces out of my ear until I agreed to have coffee with him. He said, *I'll lose my job, go broke, fall into poverty, and it will be all your fault . . .* "

"Did he really?"

Falling into poverty made it sound like an accident, a slip off a bridge into a sinkhole of threadbare coats, government cheese, and wonder bread wrappers that did double duty as galoshes. I wanted to say, *People don't fall into poverty—they're pushed.* I'd peered over that precipice when the hospital bills started mounting and Terry stopped sending us checks. I protected my girls, because that is what a mother does. I made sure they still had designer jeans, department store makeup, expensive haircuts. I didn't, but they did.

"I hope you got to keep the silver dollar," I said.

"I knew it!" Emily snapped. "Oh, I just knew it. I knew you'd act like this. I should never have told you! Why do you insist on criticizing me all the time?"

"I'm not criticizing you," I said. "What do you mean?"

Then, just like that, she hung up on me.

Emily celebrated her Sweet 16 with lime Jell-O, in bed, on the children's wing at Mercy General. She was so small, and the hospital mattress, in comparison, so thick it reminded me of the fairy tale *The Princess and the Pea.* Paige and I stuck a candle in a low-fat iced carrot muffin, even though we weren't allowed to light it, and sang to her. She wouldn't eat either the Jell-O or the muffin.

The year she turned fifteen, Emily insisted she didn't want to celebrate, then was disappointed we hadn't had thrown her a surprise party. She licked her fingers and ate her cake— angel food, raspberry sauce on the side—crumb by crumb by crumb. In a joking voice she sang, "It's My Party and I'll Cry if I Want To." When Terry came to pick the girls up to take them to his place for the weekend, I asked him if he didn't think Emily looked a little thin. Her periods had stopped. A fact which filled her with glee.

"I'm a little concerned," I said.

"Nah," he said, "she looks great. You're just jealous."

Fifteen was the year Emily started complaining about not being able to find clothes that fit. "Why don't they make double 0 sizes?" she'd ask saleswomen, whose expressions of barely disguised jealousy made them look bloated with envy.

00Emily, license to purge.

In her size 0 jeans Emily sat on the floor with Paige playing slapjack, trying to teach her how to eat an M&M by first cracking the shell with her teeth.

"You can't eat just one," she said, digging her hand into the pocket of her sweater, where she'd dumped half the bowl of candy. When she stood the pocket hung down like a teat.

Her own breasts had disappeared.

At fourteen Emily said she wanted butterfly cupcakes, just like when she was 11. Exactly the same. So I'd dug through my cookbooks, my recipe box, and the kitchen drawers until I found it.

She'd insisted on a new party dress, a manicure, an arrangement of pink roses, a lace tablecloth, my wedding china, and silver. "Everything," she kept saying, "has to be perfect." She was so excited, she couldn't stop running in circles. She must have kissed me ten times.

One hour before the guests arrived, she was in tears. The balloons looked stupid, the dress made her look fat. Paige stroked her hair trying to comfort her. Even though it was just three girls for pizza, cupcakes, and a scary movie, *An American Werewolf in London*—Emily said it was too much. But when they showed up, presents in hand, she was suddenly all smiles. In her bedroom, the girls giggled and danced to the Bee Gees' "Staying Alive," striking poses in the mirror. That night Emily complained of a stomachache—too much junk food—and asked to save her cupcake for the next day.

On her thirteenth birthday, faced with a vanilla cake with white icing and fresh daisies, she stood over me as I cut and warned, "Not too much." I felt a pang. Here she was, like a grown woman demurring, "Just a sliver for me."

While Emily and ten of her best friends sat in a circle on the floor playing Telephone, Terry sat beside me on the sofa. As the girls whispered into each other's ears, passing along the message, I murmured, "You smell like perfume."

He didn't miss a beat.

"I stopped at Macy's on the way over, thinking that perfume might be appropriate for the occasion—you realize she's not a baby anymore, but you know what it's like—the beauty department. It's a jungle out there. It's dangerous. I tell you it's no place for a man. The saleswomen popping up from behind every counter like the Viet Cong, shooting eau de toilette like tear gas."

"Did you get her something?"

"Are you kidding me?"

I laughed, relieved. Later, I'd think, *booby-traps left and right.*

At twelve Emily requested yellow layer cake with rainbow sprinkles in the batter. This was the cake all the popular girls were having at their parties. The slice was a four-inch wedge and she ate it with a fork. Terry's phone had rung in the middle of singing "Happy Birthday," the sound of a funky jazz trumpet coming from his pants pocket. Before Emily had even blown out her candles, he'd stepped out into the hall to take the call.

Twelve was the year of counting calories. Sit-ups. It didn't seem that abnormal. It didn't make me happy, but I thought it was just a stage, like drinking Long Island Ice teas and smoking clove cigarettes. Anyway, Kate Moss–thin was in and Terry was right: Emily was a little pudgy.

The year Emily turned ten I made her chocolate devil's food with chocolate icing, in the shape of an Arabian stallion. I used black licorice whips for the mane. Emily ate two pieces in record time, and got frosting on her nose. Terry laughed, "Hey, whoa Bessie! No one's going to take it way from you!"

By accident, Paige swallowed three pennies. Terry joked, "These too shall pass."

At five it didn't really matter what flavor her cake was. What mattered was that Terry made a precious miniature merry-go-round to go on top. It actually moved, the girls took turns spinning it. Paige tried to eat one of the carousel horses. Terry and I kissed. We whispered to each other that we were the luckiest people alive.

On her first birthday I made my baby girl a carrot cake and she fed herself with her fist. She squealed with delight. I thought: *So, this is love.*

How many hundreds of times had I thought about that cake?

"Did you just hang up on me? Did you really just—" I was furious.

"Oh my gosh, Mommy, I'm so sorry, I got another call," Emily said, unfazed by my anger, and not sounding sorry at all.

"Don't do that ever again. I mean it," I said, but she wasn't listening.

"You'll never guess who that was. Jenny. And guess what?

She's actually thinking of moving here in a couple of weeks—isn't that fantastic? It is. I promise you if she doesn't escape the clutches of her evil mother, someone will die. I told her she *had* to stay with me until she finds a place, it'll be like a sleepover. Oh my gosh. *Jenny.* We'll make s'mores and stay up late watching scary movies, and do facials. I've never had a real roommate."

Emily and I had done all these things, countless times. Snuggled in my bed, a bowl of popcorn between us, we watched the Terminator cut a murderous swath through humanity, with typical cyborg savoir-faire. It became a joke between us, whenever one of us left the room, we'd say, mimicking that Bavarian monotone, *I'll be back.*

"I don't know who that is."

I hoped she wasn't one of those girls whose arms and legs were covered with thin white scars, like they'd taken some shrapnel. Or one who stuck out her boney chest proudly like she expected someone to pin a medal on her.

"*Jenny,* I can't believe you. She was one of my best friends at Melrose, Mother. She was dear to me. You must remember her. Tennis player? I took her under my wing."

There might have been a girl named Jenny who talked into her lap so softly that you had to lean in to hear her, whose mother kept reaching over to adjust her gown, and touch her hair to fix her up.

"The one who was in the car accident?"

"No. You're thinking of Charlotte—the one who got raped," she said. I confess I felt a flicker of jealousy. As terrible as that was, at least there was an answer to *why.*

"She didn't belong there. She was a wannarexic, a lowly Thanksgiving bulimic, not committed at all. And suiciding on aspirin? Please. How J.V. Her mother was a piece of work, wasn't she? With her Stage 4 tan and Nancy Reagan helmet hair. Anytime her daughter opened her mouth to speak, she'd start shaking her head. Did she think no one noticed?"

I winced.

"I'm sorry, I don't remember her," I said.

"Honestly?"

I knew exactly who she meant. I wasn't going to pick at her bones.

I never spoke to that mother. We had waited for the elevator together, however, the tacit understanding that we were undercover demanded we only acknowledge each other with a nearly imperceptible nod. She always waited until she got off the elevator to remove her sunglasses. I remembered the mother, but not their story. But it was always the same. The daughter battled her anorexia on her own. She was, everybody said it, a survivor. It was such an inspiration to see how she'd grown, like a pink flowering cherry tree, out of the cold barren soil of her childhood. She'd flourished. She'd blossomed. While in the eyes of the world, her *mother*, the poisonous root of all this evil would stay just that—a stone-hard immutable root buried in dirt. No one saw how much the mother hurt. No one knew, or cared, what she'd lost.

"Have you got salt?" I asked.

"Salt is bad for you," Emily said.

"Everyone needs salt. You'd die without it."

"It causes bloating."

"It tenderizes the meat, and brings out the flavor. You need it."

"Fine, fine," she said.

"Pour the salt in your hand," I said. "You'll need more than you think."

"Ouch." She whimpered.

"More," I said. "You'll want to salt the inside too."

"But it stings. It's burning my fingers." I knew how raw the skin around her cuticles must have been. "I mean it, Mommy. It really hurts.

Did I mention that I'm in love.

"Your grandmother always cut out the wishbone before roasting a bird. Your grandfather thought it made it easier to carve."

Emily gasped. "That doesn't seem right. The wishbone? How could she? That's terrible. Did she just throw it away?"

I couldn't remember ever breaking a wishbone with anyone until I met Terry.

"Most likely. Do your fingers still hurt?"

It's the wrists that give the girls away, one of first things the mothers always mentioned. They'd say: *I had no idea. She hid it. She always wore baggy pants and sweatshirts, you know, it's the style, and then one day she pushed up her sleeves to dry the dishes and I saw her wrists . . .*

Even in summertime Emily wore long-sleeved shirts and layered sweaters, pulling the sleeves down over her hands because she was cold. Always cold, even in July. She'd grab my hands to prove it. "Feel how cold I am."

I'd say, "Cold hands, warm heart." But I was thinking: *I bet I could break Emily's wrists if I wanted to.* Later, at the coffee urn that had been set up down the hall away from the meeting room so we couldn't hear our daughters, we talked about their spines, and the way their clavicles stood out like Victorian ruffed collars, and how we counted their ribs. What poor protection they seemed for their heart and lungs. We called our daughters skeletal. Skeletal. A word that, when spoken, felt like eating something soft with bones. One mother described the sight of her daughter in a bathing suit as Auschwitz on the Jersey Shore. Out of courtesy, I laughed, though no one else did.

Standing at the table, we dumped creamers flavored with vanilla, hazelnut, and Irish crème into the weak coffee so it tasted like hot melted ice cream. Sweet and thick and disgusting. Some days there were powdered sugar donuts.

One donut has 270 calories.

"So you've salted the skin, and stuffed it?"

"Yes, Mommy—it's completely, disgustingly stuffed."

"You buttered the bird? Around the legs."

"Um, yes."

"Did you *really* get in there?"

"Yes. Enough."

"Do you have your string ready?"

"String?"

"A needle would be best. You don't want the stuffing to fall out, do you?"

She groaned.

"I'm just trying to help you. If you can't sew it up, you can just tie the legs together."

"This dinner has to be perfect, mother. Do you understand me? Perfect."

"It will be."

"So, I'll do it the right way. Properly. I don't have string, but I've got lots of yarn, and yarn is prettier anyway."

At Melrose they taught the girls to knit. Cast on twenty, knit, knit, knit, purl, purl, purl. It kept their hands busy and their minds off food. Over the years, Emily had knit Paige and me sweaters. We'd open them with trepidation, admire the stitchery, try to resist her pleas for us to model them, but she wouldn't let up. It was always the same. In her mind we were gargantuan, and the sweaters resembled woolen sleeping bags. Humiliated, she'd tearfully demand them back, promising to fix them. Every time, I assured her they'd be perfect if we just washed them and threw them in the dryer. They were so pretty, and we wanted them so badly, but it didn't matter.

"Do you have a needle with a big enough eye for yarn?"

"Mother, I have more stuff like that here than you can imagine. Hold on." I waited for several minutes before Emily came back on the line. "All right," she said, sounding nervous. "I'm threaded and ready."

"Then start sewing the hole closed."

There was no sound.

"No, no I can't. I can't. It's too scary."

You don't know scary, I thought. For ten years I'd kept a pair of slip-on sneakers in the coat closet by the front door, and a twenty-dollar bill in the inside pocket of my car coat just in case of emergencies.

"Stop talking, Emily, and start making stitches."

She was twenty-one when I'd found her in the tub. I just knew. Like the cliché: *A mother knows.*

In the waiting room of the E.R., Emily sat with her arms wrapped in white bath towels, moving between belligerence— *Why did you save me?*—and begging me to forgive her. *I'm so sorry. I didn't mean it. I love you. I never want to leave you.* When other sick or injured people came staggering into the waiting room and fell into seats beside us, she looked embarrassed at not being dead.

"Don't tell Dad," she said. Then, "Have you called Dad yet?"

Three hours later, Emily and I were behind a blue cloth curtain. She was lying down and I was sitting beside her bed, focusing on the green and white tiles behind her head, the perfect squares like a map of Manhattan. I decided I'd take Emily to New York City on her birthday to go shopping. Because it's a grid of numbered streets, running east and west, we could always figure out where we were. If she got lost, I could find her.

It occurred to me thousands of people would come through this hospital, lie on this bed, hundreds of mothers would sit in this chair, and some of the people they loved would die. But that couldn't happen to us.

Emily lifted her head. Her hair looked matted. "Mommy, are you there?"

"Always," I said.

She was groggy from the Valium they'd given her so she'd stay still while they stitched up her wrists. The thread looked black and stiff as hair. I counted the stitches. 10 in each wrist. People always remembered how many stitches.

"Thankfully," the doctor had said, "she cut across the veins, not up and down. Beginner's luck."

"Voilà!" Emily shouted. "I did it. Triumph is mine! I really did it and it's a masterpiece. Aren't you proud of me?"

"I am. That was fast. How many stitches did you do?"

"Three."

"Three? That's all?"

"Well, that's all there is room for. But I do have enough thread left to embroider hearts and flowers on the breast."

Calmly I asked her, "How many pounds is the chicken, sweetheart?"

"I don't know. I didn't weigh it, mother. Two or three."

It wasn't a chicken—it was a Cornish game hen.

"What? What's wrong?" Her voice was climbing, scrabbling like an animal with tiny toenails. "Tell me, tell me now. Oh no. It's too small, isn't it?"

"Don't worry," I said. "It'll be enough."

I could see this tiny, pitiful bird lying bound on the plate between my daughter and the man she loved, each of them eyeing it, trying to figure their meager share. I could almost laugh.

"It doesn't matter," she said quickly. "I wasn't going to eat that much anyway."

She'd been a fat baby, eight pounds ten ounces. I remember the picture Terry had taken of newborn Emily and me outside the hospital with his new camera. I don't know if it was the flash or sunlight bouncing off the windows, but the bundle in my arms was brilliant white, like it had just exploded. I'm squinting down at her, temporarily blinded perhaps, but not surprised.

Twenty-two years later, seventy-seven pounds heavier, I brought my baby home again. On the way back, we sang along to Carole King's "I Feel the Earth Move" and she talked nonstop. "I can't wait to sleep in my own bed with my comforter, see my books, and take a bath." I flinched. Her lip trembled, "Oh but I'm going to miss my friends so unbearably much. You can't even begin to imagine. I miss them already and it hasn't even been one hour—the pain is exquisite." She threw her head back against the seat and closed her eyes like she was fighting tears.

"Oh baby," I said reaching out to squeeze her shoulder, but before I could, she turned away.

"You can't possibly understand. They're like family to me. Family I've chosen in *my heart*," she gasped. "I don't want to cry anymore. I can't. I'm spent." She sniffled. "How is Paige?"

"Good. I haven't seen her in a while. She's so busy with schoolwork. She's got a new boyfriend, he's in law, and very tall she says."

"Have you been in touch with Dad? Did you tell him I was coming home today?"

"He knows."

"It doesn't matter," Emily said, "No one in the world gets it—gets *me*—like *they* do," she said. "They accept me for who I am, and love me unconditionally."

"I love you," I said. "You can't begin to know how much I love you. You can't." After I parked, before I got out, she'd grabbed my arm.

"I promise that will never happen again. I promise," she said, then leaned over and rested her head on my shoulder, rubbing her nose against my neck. She smelled like vanilla, Vaseline, and rubbing alcohol.

"Am I still your baby?" she asked in a small voice.

"You're always my baby."

"Your *first*," she said, as though this were an accomplishment.

"Always the first."

"But," she sighed, "not the only."

"No," I said touching her cheek. "But first. First always."

"You did a great job, Em," I said, knowing how dismayed she must be about the chicken. "You're home-free now. When are you expecting him?"

I had no idea how much time had passed. When was the last time I'd eaten?

"He's supposed to arrive at six, and he's very punctual, which you know I appreciate. I despise rude people."

"So put it in a half an hour before you think you want to eat, and just check on it."

"Do you think it's going to be good? Really good? It is, right? It's going to be wonderful. No, it doesn't matter, right? It doesn't matter."

I thought again of the purple chicken I'd made for Terry. How excited I'd been to cook for him. To show him how worthy I was of his love. The memory of how young and romantic I'd been—unforgivably romantic—had grown less painful over the years. Lately, I'd become nostalgic for the days when I felt hopeful.

"I just want everything to be perfect," she said. "Did I tell you I bought these beautiful linen napkins and—"

"You won't forget to set the timer, will you?"

"Mommy . . ." I could hear her beginning to chew her cuticles again. "Mommy, no matter what, *no matter what,* you'll always love me, right? You'll always be there? You'll always help me? Like this."

"Of course. I'm your mother."

"Promise me. Even if I ran off to Fez to be a belly dancer, or moved to California, you'd still—" she spat out a piece of finger skin.

I laughed. "You'd hate California. No one reads. And there are earthquakes," I said, aware of a sour taste in the back of my throat, the pressure of a headache from drinking wine on an empty stomach gathering behind my eyes.

"Don't say that, don't be silly," Emily squeaked. "Oh, Mommy . . . I don't know how to tell you this, but we've been talking about moving to Los Angeles. Running away together. Isn't that divine? Not this week, of course, but soon. Can you even believe it?"

California was more two thousand miles away.

"There are, of course, so many more opportunities for thespians on the coast."

"You can't possibly be serious."

I heard her inhale sharply. "Oh my god, I forgot candles! How could I possibly forget candles? What am I going to do? Oh no, no, no. This is horrendous! I had it all planned out— crimson tapers. I set the table this morning, lovely lace tablecloth, wineglasses. How could I be so stupid? I'm not ready at all. I've got to hang up, Mommy, right this instant!"

"Don't forget the bird!" I cried. "You have to tend to it, Emily. Watch it. Baste it. It's a small bird."

"Oh god," she wailed, "this is a colossal mistake, isn't it?"

"No. It's good. It's normal. It's right."

"I really ought to say good-bye now."

The phone felt warm and heavy in my palm. I stared at my ringless fingers. Hands get thinner with age. My mother's hands seemed smaller every time I saw her.

"So," I said, trying to sound casual, "when will I see you again?"

"I'm not really sure. I'm pretty busy." She sounded distracted. Was she thinking about what she was going to wear, or gazing at her pretty table, wondering if she could do without candles?

"I'm free in the afternoon on Saturday, or—"

"Mommy, I'd love to keep talking, but I really have to go. Why don't you call Paige?"

"I said I can't tonight, I have *a date*."

There was a long silence, as though Emily had only just

realized she had no idea who I was going out with, or where I was going.

"Wow," she said. "I did it, didn't I?"

"You did," I said. "I'm glad." Was it terrible that some part of me wanted her evening to fail?

One day she'll cook for me, I thought, *and we'll eat again together.* I knew it. I knew it the way I knew I'd always be hungry. Like Emily, only different.

Aren't You Dead Yet?

I

Ray never paid taxes. He pirated cable, and stole paint from the store where Rothko and Schnabel had bought theirs. He'd dropped out of art school after six months, to wash dishes in a diner in Alabama, and before heading to New York City on his motorcycle in 1988 destroyed all the paintings he'd ever made, except those his mother refused to give up.

These were some of the details Ray and I used to say that future generations would learn about him in their art history books. Facts that would inspire them to throw a girl in the car and drive all night to Niagara Falls just to see the expression on her face the first time she saw them, the way Ray did to me. Give them permission to commit whatever acts of thievery necessary to make their art. "The artist exists in a class outside the rules that govern common man," Ray said. "Society owes the artist who fires men's souls, shows him what he himself cannot or refuses to see, a debt—yet it's a debt society never pays back. Thus, the artist must take what he needs, whatever he needs, if he is to make art. And no artist," Ray said, "worth a damn can afford to pay fifty dollars for a tube of cad-mium red."

The truth was Ray could afford paint, and cable too. It was principle not poverty that drove Ray to steal. I was one of the few people who knew the truth. That Ray had grown up with two parents and a little sister, in this upper-middle-class suburb of Detroit, in a neat ranch house with a crew-cut green lawn, lace curtains, and dark pine paneling. His mother called herself a homemaker, and his dad the man of the house. He'd played football in high school—although, he was quick to add, Kerouac had too.

I was also cursed with a happy childhood. No food stamps, or beatings, or even interesting childhood diseases to draw on for writing plays, outside of a lingering, low-grade sense of uneasiness that I wasn't normal. However, it would never have occurred to me, nor would I have dared, to take off like Ray had or drop out of school. It wasn't like me. My parents would have worried, worse, been disappointed. Even now they were helping me pay my rent.

"Face it," I said. "We're damned."

"Yeah." Ray grinned. "That works. Man, when we walk down the street and people ask who the hell we are, we'll say, 'We're The Damned.'"

"Hello," I chirped, extending my hand in introduction. "We're Beth and Ray, but you can call us The Damned."

Nobody would care about our childhoods, Ray insisted. "It's your death that matters."

The first time he told me this we were in his studio with a futon on the floor, this crappy sofa he'd pulled off the street, and his art, charcoal sketches of industrial landscapes slashed with rain, on the walls. We were sitting on a Navajo blanket listening to The Velvet Underground "White Light/

White Heat" with a jug of red wine and a block of government cheese that had been in his mini fridge for weeks. He'd picked up this Swiss Army knife we'd been using and flipped the knife away from him in a perfect arc so it landed tip down in the floor.

"I've always known that I'm going to die young," Ray said, pulling the blade out of the floor. He said this with such conviction that to question him would have been akin to calling him a liar. "I've made peace with the knowledge that my genius won't be recognized until after I am dead. Look at Van Gogh; he only sold one painting before he died. He never got what he deserved."

"Rarely," I said, "do people get what they deserve."

Ray nodded, rubbing his hands over his cheeks, shadowed with stubble. "I'm living proof, right? Look at you. You put up with me. When they write about me, they'll have to write about you too, you know. You're my muse.

"We'll be famous together. What do you think? Ray and Beth." He stopped dead. "Nah. Not Beth. Come on. *Beth*, it just lays there—no offense, sweetheart, but you know what I mean? Dead on the doorstep. You've been Beth long enough. You're too good for *Beth*."

"I agree, I've never liked that name." The idea of renaming myself thrilled me.

I hadn't minded my name, really, until freshman year of high school, in 1976, the year that lame Kiss song was number one everywhere. If it wasn't on the radio or coming out of somebody's eight-track, then some joker was serenading me, *Beth, I hear you calling, but I can't come home right now.* I was Beth. Beth of Ohio. In a Snoopy T-shirt and a jean skirt, aviator-rimmed glasses and a retainer. I was Beth waiting by the phone, waiting for my life to show up.

I didn't want to be Beth anymore.

"You could be—Elizabeth, Lee, Lou—that's cool—Liz, Lizzie . . ."

"Lizzie. That's catchy—a little subversive. I like it. *Lizzie Borden took an ax, gave her mother forty whacks . . .*"

"What's your middle name?"

"Diane." There was Diane di Prima.

"Diane?" He made a face, like how in the world could two such disasters have befallen one girl? "Elizabeth Diane?" The shackles of normalcy, oh, how they bind.

"Wait, wait, I'm thinking," he muttered, running his hands through his thick black hair, which appeared more like fur to me than hair, as if it would help. "Ah! I got it. What about B?"

"Buzz, buzz. I like that. It's edgy, lethal to some. I dig stripes."

"Nah. B. Just the initial B. Miss B. Like Madame X."

"Or Lizzie? Ray and Lizzie sounds prettier than Ray and Miss B."

"You're right, it should just be, initial B. It's much cooler. Christ, I'll call you whatever you want. Lizzie, or Lee, or Lou-lou—"

I liked Loulou.

"—but trust me, B is perfect. *B is Ray Lovett's muse.* B. It's fucking brilliant. Mysterious. An enigma. Let them wonder about you."

"B is only B on the page. It sounds like Bee. I'd get to be both."

He answered, *"There is no Ray without B,"* with unsuspected tenderness. "No me without you."

"No me without you," I said, trembling with the knowledge. "What can I make you for dinner?"

I count the moment Ray walked into the Soho art book-

store where I was working (flipping through the postcards—
Cocteau, Genet, Mayakovski—like flash cards), to-go cup of
coffee in hand, his jeans splattered with paint, a toothpick laz-
ing out of the corner of his mouth, as the moment my life, my
real life, began. It was Ray who first told me I was meant to be
a writer, on the basis of reading a one-act play I'd written during a summer writing course I'd taken at NYU, a course taken
just for the credits I needed to graduate from my podunk university back in Cincinnati.

When Ray declared, with enough conviction for both of
us, "You're a writer. You know it," I did. "All you need is for
the truth to wake up in you so you can see it. For Christ's sake,
B"—his eyes were burning—"you don't need anybody's goddamn permission to be a writer," he said like I'd be getting
away with something. "So write."

He gave me that.

Ray had this uncanny gift for giving me things I never
knew I needed or wanted. I'd spent my life following the
trends, borrowing clothes from friends, searching for my
look, and Ray found it—or maybe he'd always had it. He
made me, me. Every week there was some new treasure he'd
found for me at a flea market, a resale shop, a sidewalk sale.
Things so perfectly me I might have owned them in another
life. I had no idea sixties-era vintage dresses, faux fur coats,
and rhinestone-encrusted cat's-eye sunglasses were me. I
was suddenly crazy about collecting the hands of old man-
nequins, and vintage etiquette books, like the 1963 edition
of *Blueprints for Building Better Girls*! Ray and I'd take turns
reading it aloud to each other. It was hilarious how clueless
these women, teetering in heels, on the cusp of the sexual
revolution, were.

In these trying times, it is more important than ever that we take a firm hand in shaping the lives and characters of our young women, not only through instruction but by exhibiting, in our own manner and dress, all the finest qualities of woman-hood, on which future generations should model their behavior.

When I added, "Uh-oh, the burning bra is about to hit the fan," Ray shot me *the look*. This was the sort of thing I should write down. I should be writing everything down.

"Don't you get it?" Ray would say. "Ideas are like moths, drawn to the artist's light. You gotta capture them before they fly away or die."

The first real thing that Ray ever gave me was this black leather-bound journal with a band around it. He must have stolen it because it was really nice. "What kind of writer doesn't keep a journal?" he said. "You want to be real? You gotta write shit down. Write it all down like you expect people to one day read it."

Up until then I'd been using spiral-bound stenographers' notebooks, which had suited me just fine. Ray often spoke as though he were dictating. He'd say something like, "The power of art," then pause so I could grab my journal. "The power of art, B," he'd begin again with gusto, "is that it transcends the boundaries of space and time. Art spits in the eye of death."

When Ray discovered I wasn't using the book he'd given me, he was pissed. I tried to explain that I hadn't written in it because I loved it so much and I didn't want to ruin it. The pages were so nice, and sewn in, you couldn't just rip them out. Whatever stupid thing I wrote down would be in there permanently.

"I can't tell you what to do," he said, "but don't be an idiot. I don't care if you use it or not, but you want the truth? Here it is: Nobody gives a shit if you write, or not. Nobody is ever going to say, *Oh, B, share your thoughts with us,* until you become somebody. Then"—he laughed—"then, they'll buy the paper you wipe your ass with."

The art history book might say that while Ray's unsentimental representations of classic American themes such as the road and the American West were nothing new, his energy, his bold, muscular brushwork, and the enormous scale of his paintings were distinctive. They would quote his reaction to the criticism that he refused to create gallery-friendly works: "Here's how it is—I don't bow to anybody. My work is in proportion to my vision. I piss on minimalism."

They'd write that he'd welded his hulking frames out of metal salvaged from junked cars. The first being a silver 1962 Ford Galaxie he'd totaled himself. Totaled and walked away from without a scratch.

It had taken less than two weeks for me to see I had to move out of this sublet I was sharing with two other girls on the Upper East Side. Girls I hadn't realized until I met Ray were tedious, bourgeois poseurs, who knew nothing about art, or music—Madonna, really? I could have dealt with having to initial all my food—from cantaloupes to quarts of milk and white wine—the chore rotation chart, the smoking, even though my own clothes had begun to smell like Salem menthols, even their opinion that anyone who didn't attend an Ivy deserved to be pushing a broom (and here they were always quick to add, "present company excepted"), I could have stuck it out, but they didn't get Ray. That wouldn't fly. They said he was weird and rude, and laughed at the wrong times. He looked at them funny. He drank beer that didn't belong to him. They didn't get me anymore either. I'd changed. What had Ray done to me? They appreciated the whole arty writer thing, it was why they loved me, but really, I was just going to blow off the Cantor Fitzgerald booze cruise? And what was up with the leopard coat, and why on earth would you dye your hair black? Was I now some kind of Bohemian? What was next, poetry readings?

I'd reported all this to Ray, laying my broken friendships at his feet as a sign of my mounting fidelity and devotion, and he'd praised me. They didn't get it. They were no different from his old friends, who'd all sold out, or turned into squares, or just burned out.

"Friends come in and out of your life like busboys in a restaurant," he'd tell me. "Except for us, right? We are *The Damned*. Nobody leaves."

"In order to create, the artist must be on the outside," he told me the night we came upon this crappy little tiki bar in Chinatown with Christmas lights in the window, Dean Martin and Don Ho on the jukebox. There was nobody in the joint, and no sign, so we called it Lucky's.

It had a purity and naïveté that spoke to us. It hadn't been fucked with yet. The murals on the walls—childish representations of a family of tiki gods posed in front of a smoking volcano, and a raging sunset, tangerine, violet, and pink, so vivid as to be radioactive—they were real. The drinks were real cheap—half a week's paycheck easily covered a bender—and special.

The house specialty was this orange and mango rum cocktail served in half a pineapple. We'd sit at the bar and drink, watching the bartender, a slim, serious man, carve pineapples into boats and, using only cocktail straws, napkins, and a few toothpicks, construct intricate sails and riggings.

"You know," Ray would say, "the longer I sit here, the clearer it all becomes."

• • •

Before signing the lease, I'd called Ray to come and look at this studio apartment I'd found on Tenth Street and First Avenue, right above an Italian bakery. It was only the second floor, and I was afraid of being burglarized, and worried it would be too noisy with all the cars. Ray disagreed.

"Ah, B, no one is going to rob you." He grinned. After all, what did I have that anyone wanted?

"And fuck the traffic, you'll get used to it. After a while, B, it'll sound like crashing waves." He inhaled. "Smell. Fresh bread. Christ. We could live off that air, right? You could grow fat on that air."

He said *we*. As it was, Ray would spend as much time in my place as his own, even though it was just blocks away. I'd cook for him. Cheap stuff. Eggs with potatoes and green peppers. Rice and beans. I'd make him pie. He loved cherry pie. Because of this the biographer might suggest we'd been lovers. We had been twice. Both times Ray was drunk and it was dark. It felt more accidental than anything else. A momentary loss of control. Like hitting a patch of black ice—he slid into me, and then it was over. Ray told me, "Jackson Pollock was a bad lay." I didn't care if Ray was a bad lay, that wasn't what we were about anyway. It was deeper than that.

There would be no photograph to accompany Ray's textbook entry. He refused to have his picture taken. "They never look like me," he said, which was true. I'd made the mistake of trying to sneak a few candid shots. But he'd hear the shutter the way a deer hears the trigger. He told me the Navajo believed the camera stole your soul.

The editors could reproduce one of his self-portraits, though. Ray insisted all artists had to make self-portraits. Van Gogh's were among his most famous works. In the paintings, with the dark squint of his gaze, and pugilistic set of his jaw, the fact he'd chosen to depict his nose as more prominently broken than it was in real life, his dark hair defiantly untamed, he looked like the quintessential tortured romantic.

There is this one pencil drawing, where his nose is straighter, his lips fuller, almost feminine, his expression unfocused and uncertain; it was like he'd drawn himself without him knowing it. If you look closely, you can see all the eraser marks.

All of the self-portraits he gave to me as soon as they were done.

He told me, "If you don't take them, I'm just going to destroy them." We couldn't risk that.

If I got to choose the image that accompanied Ray's entry, it would be a painting of the two of us at a gas station in North Dakota he made after our first road trip. It's called *Number 28* because the trip took place over his twenty-eighth birthday. He'd wanted to see the Badlands because those surreal rock formations looked like the lunar surface, he said, because he'd never live to see thirty—or the day when people traveled to the moon the same way they did to Miami. "That high desert," he said, "is the closest I'll ever get to walking on the moon."

The entry would note that the painting was from the private collection of Elizabeth Stark, a.k.a. Beth, Lizzie, Bee, or B, Ray Lovett's muse, great American playwright, and majority owner of Ray Lovett's work.

The paintings and drawings were gifts, repayment of loans, apologies—for punching out my kitchen window, for forgetting my birthday. Not that I minded any. We weren't like normal people. We were special. Artists. No one had ever looked at the world the way we did. No one had ever compared the stars in the night sky to burrs stuck on the sleeve of God's coat, or felt like we felt—moved to tears by the haunting intensity of Goya's black paintings. *He painted them on the walls of his house! He'd never intended to show them to anyone!* No one had ever driven a hundred miles an hour on a Kansas straightaway screaming out the windows, *"We are The Damned!"*

I'd never felt more alive than when I was dead tired in the front seat of Ray's car. Never. In the beginning I'd offer to drive, but Ray said he couldn't relax if someone else was driving. Even me.

I was his copilot. It was my job to keep us in sandwiches and black coffee, navigate, switch out mix tapes—Sonic Youth, X, the Pixies, according to Ray's mood—and man the radio. Ray would cry out, "Oh, baby, I need to be saved! Deliver me from Top 40 and I need me some Christian rock," and I'd find it. *Dropkick me, Jesus, through the goalposts of life.*

Sometimes we just talked. There are conversations that you'll have in a car you'd otherwise never have. If no one else could hear you, if you weren't sitting so close, if the driver didn't have to look at you, if there wasn't always the possibility you could crash and die. Ray told me stuff I'd never tell anybody.

Every time we got out of the car for food or gas, or to sleep, Ray would slap a kiss on the side of his car and I'd get out the postcards I'd lifted from the bookstore and we'd leave a message on the gas pumps—*I Drive Therefore I Am*—or in the bathroom—*For a good time call Jean-Paul Sartre.* For the freckled and slightly cross-eyed teenage waitress at IHOP in Goodland, Kansas, who'd brought Ray four refills, he wrote, *You won't always feel this way.*

In the painting *Number 28*, we're at a gas station. I'm sitting in the passenger seat of his pristine '62 Galaxie, one bare foot stuck out the window. Behind me a figure in dark work pants and a white T-shirt, desert boots and aviators, stands by the road with his back to me, staring at the horizon. You can see half of my face in the passenger's side mirror. Part of the painting's appeal, the book might say, is the question of whether the woman is gazing at her reflection or at the man behind her.

II

I'd quit the bookstore in Soho before they could fire me. I told them I was leaving so I could devote more time to my writing, which was true, but it was also true that for six months Ray had been lifting fifty-dollar coffee table books and selling them at the Strand, to supplement his income as a bike messenger. The money was lousy, but they paid cash, so no taxes, no "paper trail," and he only worked when he wanted. It had to be that way so he could paint whenever inspiration hit him. I knew that. He said he hated me paying for everything—cooking him dinner, buying the beer—but I didn't mind.

"We're The Damned," I said. "This is what you do. You'd do it for me."

The same week I quit I'd scored a job at another bookstore— big like a city—I started taking this playwriting class. It was my instructor, a Kate Millett devotee, who encouraged me to write *Food Fight,* which was about three young women—one fat, one thin, one average—in a diner, each struggling with her relationship to food and each other. The drama builds as the girls become more and more anxious over what to eat, and who will eat what, or not eat. There's all this shame, and anger, and regret. I didn't see it at first. At the end the waitress brings out a brownie sundae with three spoons and violence erupts. I'd never written anything like that, nothing expressly female. Nothing that felt true like that. I mean, nobody cared about that stuff.

Ray wanted me to read it to him. He insisted. I'd always read my stuff to him, you know, but this time was different. I was nervous, you know it wasn't *serious*—give me a break, right—Beckett didn't write about women and food, but I did it. Afterward he said, "It's satire, right? You might want to draw that out more."

I won't lie, that stung, but I knew he was right.

"I have trouble telling when something is finished. How do you know?"

"You just know," Ray said. "Or I know. When it's done, it's done. I never go back."

When I got the call that there was a theater downtown that wanted to do a reading of *Food Fight*, I'd asked the guy to repeat himself three times. Still, it wouldn't feel real, it wouldn't matter, until I told Ray.

I couldn't help myself. He wasn't halfway in the room before I ambushed him.

He didn't react at first. What did I expect? He just shook his head like maybe he was hearing voices.

"I know, I know," I said, "it's crazy. It is. I made the guy repeat himself so I could write it down." I showed him the notes I'd made on the back of the envelope containing my second turn-off notice from the phone company. "I knew if I didn't write it down, I might think I'd made it up."

"Wow," Ray said, the word dropping, with his bike messenger bag, onto the floor. He leaned back hard against the counter like I'd just poked him in the chest. "Wow. I'm sorry. I meant congratulations. This is great, B."

I told him, "I could never have done it without you."

"Don't be stupid," he said. "You did it."

I explained to him how the theater was kind of a joke—they made their name with erotic puppet shows featuring political figures, like Margaret Thatcher screwing Ronald Reagan up the ass, Jesse Helms in blackface singing "Old Man River."

I told him the guy curating the reading series was a friend of a friend of mine from my writing workshop.

"This is exactly what's wrong with the art world. It's all about who you know," Ray said. He waited a second. "But you deserve it, B. You deserve it. All of it."

"You know it doesn't pay anything, of course," I said. "I can still write 'starving artist' on my tax return."

"You don't have to say yes, either. You can decline. Politely *decline*."

"No. I want it."

"Then the money shouldn't matter to you," Ray said, jerking open the refrigerator door to get a beer. There was none. "Your name is on it. You know what they say. All that matters is they spell it right."

It never occurred to me that Ray would be jealous. I wanted nothing more than for him to get a show. That was why I'd pushed him to submit his slides to a bunch of galleries downtown putting up group shows. I'd convinced him. He hadn't wanted to. It wasn't his bag. "The art world is nothing but a corrupt clusterfuck of imbeciles," he declared. Finally, though, he'd given in, consented to sending his work to three places. The only places he had any respect for. Places where he'd be proud to show.

Even though it just proved his point, Ray didn't tell me they rejected him. He left the slit-open envelopes propped up on the kitchen table for me to find.

When he showed up at my place later smelling like whiskey, I was sitting at the table reading. The evidence of my crime still right there in front of me. I tried to apologize.

He was furious. "I don't want to talk about it. You know I don't give a shit about those assholes. What I *am*, what I am is disgusted with myself. Disappointed and disgusted that I let you talk me into doing something I never wanted to do. I should have stuck to my guns."

"You're right. I was wrong, but hey, think of this, my friend—*you* sold a painting not a month ago. How many of those wannabe Keith Harings can say that?"

As soon as I said it, I knew how wrong it was.

The painting he'd sold was to my parents. He needed the money. My parents had met Ray. They'd been impressed. When he wanted, he could be very charming. Very formal, he opened doors, pulled out my mom's chair, called my father sir. He'd brought dessert, a pie from downstairs I bet he'd lifted. He made coffee. When my parents left, he shook my father's hand, and kissed my mother on the cheek.

I'd told them he was going to be big, how these days art was more of a sound investment than real estate. I'd picked out a good one—not the best, Ray had to save the best. Even with the "family discount," he'd cleared two hundred bucks.

He said nothing. I might as well have punched him in the stomach. "So . . ." He rubbed his palms together like he was itching to grab the wheel. "Where should this celebration happen, girlie? Atlantic City? San Fran? Name it. I don't care. Let's blow this pop stand. Let's go. Let's get outta here."

I didn't want to say it. "Oh, Ray . . ."

"Ah, right."

"No. You know I want to. I'm sorry. I'm out of sick days.

Last time—remember—when the alternator crapped out, and
I had to call the store collect—"

"Forget it."

"Next weekend?"

"Nah. Whatever. I get it, doll. It's nothing. *De nada. Que
se* fucking *ra*. It's ladies' choice tonight. My treat."

"Are you sure?" This was a surprise.

"Why the hell not. Where you wanna go?"

Over the last year, Lucky's had begun to get popular. It was
still off the beaten path, tucked down a side street away from
the tourists and novelty shops peddling paper dragons, the
fish stores selling eels and frogs on ice and live turtles in plastic bags ("Pets or meat?" Ray'd say)—but they'd raised their
prices and redecorated. They'd also touched up the mural
of the tiki gods, now in front of an erupting volcano and, it
seemed, covered in third-degree lava burns, and painted over
the sunset.

As long as we could sit at the bar, I figured Ray would be
okay.

Even at nine o'clock, the sidewalks of Chinatown were
mobbed. Ray hated crowds. He became very protective of me.
He'd hold on to my hand, or tight to my arm so we wouldn't
get separated, messenger bag slung over his shoulder, cursing
the tourist hordes and mindless slowpokes who'd stop dead
in front of you and look up to *ooh* and *aah* over how tall the
buildings were. *You know what's wrong with you people?"*
Ray'd say. *You have no consideration for other people at all. No
manners. You're uncivilized. You don't give a damn about anybody but yourself,* allowing his bag to smack into anyone fool
enough not to get out of his way.

• • •

I knew before we even reached the bar it would be crowded. I couldn't have imagined how crowded it would be, or that they'd installed a faux thatched roof over the bar.

Ray stopped at the door. "What did I tell you? I knew it. Didn't I predict this?"

"It's crowded."

"Nah." He spit on the sidewalk. "It's over."

"No it's not." I thought once we got inside, he'd be cool.

They'd washed the windows. Inside I saw a guy with muttonchop sideburns and a goatee just like Ray's holding court by the bar, a guy with a flattop, wearing a bowling shirt with LUCILLE embroidered on the pocket and prescription Wayfarers. I was pretty sure I recognized him from one of those twenty-dollar art magazines Ray flipped through at Gem Spa when he thought I wasn't looking.

"We're out of here," he said, turning around.

"No, come on, Ray," I pleaded.

I knew he couldn't say no. "Okay, but this is for you."

By some divine providence the minute we closed in on the bar two seats opened up. Ray dropped his shoulder like a tackle, muscling past two girls who could have been my old roommates to claim them for us.

"My apologies, ladies," Ray said, waving me into one of the seats, "but don't you know who this is?"

Ray paid for the first round. "Worth, every, penny," he said, making a point of counting out the bills. When our pineapple boats arrived, Ray lifted his up and studied it from all sides. "You're a true artist, my man," Ray announced, his voice carrying throughout the bar. "*You*, my friend, *you* ought to be in the fucking Whitney Biennial." The barman, uncomfortable with the attention, bobbed his head.

I took a sip. It was sweeter than usual.

Then Ray raised his drink. Before he even said a word, I'd started to blush. I didn't want to gloat, but I was happy.

"To you, B. I mean it. This is big," Ray said, touching the stern of his boat to mine. He then turned to the lovely Asian waitress standing at the end of the bar folding napkins into the shape of water lilies.

"B's about to have her first play produced."

I corrected him. "It's just a reading."

"This girl, right here. Remember the face." He pinched my cheek.

"Dee?" she said.

"No, B," Ray repeated. "Just B."

"Or Beth, Elizabeth," I added.

I knew it was coming. "*Beth?* Or *Elizabeth.* I get it. I see how it is. The truth comes out. What good is success if all those assholes from your past don't know it? Right?"

"Very funny," I said. He was right, though. All those jerks growing up who thought I was just Beth, plain old, goofy Beth, future substitute teacher, soccer mom, bank teller, I wanted them to know. "What, I can't be B *and* Elizabeth?"

"Suit yourself," he said.

When I finished my drink, Ray set both our boats on the bar and with a good shove sent them back down to the barman for a refill, calling out, "My man, did you hear the news? What do you say to a couple drinks on the house? For the lady. It's a big night for her, don'tcha think?"

The bartender, pretending not to hear, busied himself with the cherries. The waitress averted her eyes.

I elbowed Ray in the side. I was so embarrassed. "Stop it," I hissed. "I don't want any free drinks. Don't be silly. We'll pay."

"No, no. You'd think, since we've only been coming here

since the fucking birth of this place—back when we were the *only* customers," Ray said, his voice getting louder, "they'd have the decency to spring for one free drink. Not for me, I don't fucking care. I don't need it, but for you, B. For you."

"I don't care," I said. I just wanted to change the subject. "Tell me about the new painting—the pier. I want to hear all about it."

His face brightened. Ray hadn't worked for weeks after his slides came back. He said he was working, but he didn't smell of turpentine, and there was no tape on his fingertips the way there was when he was working. When he'd surprised me by picking me up after work in the car, he was buzzing, happier than I'd seen him in months. He'd driven me to see the source of his inspiration. Right off the West Side Highway, sunk in the Hudson River at Fifty-ninth Street, was a dilapidated pier, a hulk of rotting wood, its twisted iron beams sticking out like bones.

"It's going to be epic. Man, I mean huge. Fucking beautiful—a poem—a tragic fucking poem. People are going to sit up and take notice. Think about it, it was nothing before, but now, man, it's gorgeous. You see it, right?"

What I saw was a pier, collapsed on its pilings, rusting, half submerged, and sliding into the river like a creature that had been brought to its knees. "Amazing," I said.

After the third round, our boats began to leak. "Somewhere around Cap d'Antibes," I said, "we started to take on rum . . ."

"We're surrounded by water, you know that?" Ray was getting drunk. "You forget. Everybody gets so damn caught up in their meaningless little lives they forget they live on a fucking island."

I started to say something.

"A toast to B," Ray bellowed. "Or whatever the hell name

she decides to call herself. Pick one! Let the record show I always knew she was going to be the darling of the New York *theater* world, that it was just a matter of time before the *mainstream*" — he pushed his boat back down the bar — "get it, wink, wink, main*stream* claimed her. Promise me, darlin', you won't forget the little people."

"Aw, cut it out."

"What?" His tone had turned to mocking. "All you've ever wanted was to be famous. Right? That's always been your dream."

"I don't care about being famous," I said defensively, watching as Ray tore apart a handful of sugar packets and emptied them out over the top of his boat. "There is only past suffering," he said, staring at the flame, "present suffering, and future suffering."

I was thinking, *You're wrong, I'm happy,* when Ray flipped open his Zippo and set the boat on fire. There was a gasp as the liquor and sugar ignited into a burst of blue, spitting flame. The bartender looked up. What if the thatched roof caught on fire?

"The boats are burning! The boats are burning on the shore!" Ray sang out in a stentorian voice. "And I set sail in a ship of flames . . ."

"Ray. . . . We should go," I said, pulling on his arm. "Come on. Before they throw us out."

"What's the matter? Afraid of a little fire, scarecrow." He cackled. "Aw, man, it'll burn out," he said. "Look . . ." The flames were out. There was the smell of burnt sugar. He looked disappointed. "You didn't like that? I'd think you'd appreciate it."

"We should go."

"We'll go when I'm ready to go," Ray growled, then lunged for my purse, fisting around the bottom for money, snatching up the few loose bills.

"Here you go," he shouted, waving the dollars at the barman like pom-poms. "To a true artist!" he cried, stuffing the wad into the man's tip jar.

It seemed a good idea, once we were outside, to cross the street immediately.

"I'm so tired I can barely stand," I said, adding a yawn for good measure. "Let's get home. I'll make us some grilled cheese. You know there's got to be a Godzilla or kung fu movie on." I didn't want the night to end like this.

"You gotta be kidding me," Ray said. "The night is young— look." He pointed at the sky washed gray by the city lights, the stars drained away. "You can't even see the stars yet."

"Ray."

"C'mon. It'll be fun, for Christ's sake. A nightcap. You deserve it," he said, taking my hand.

I was always a sucker for that.

The man in the windbreaker appeared out of nowhere, out of the dark, cutting across the street toward us, fast, pulling something out of his pocket. We both knew what was happening. Then Ray let go of my hand.

I stopped. He kept walking.

I saw the knife. I saw it glint, although Ray would say it was just the zipper of his coat. I saw Ray too. I watched him walk away, as did the man, his mouth falling open in disbelief.

"You! You! You left your woman?" the man yelled at him. Ray ducked his head, fists punched down in his pockets. He wasn't running away, but he hadn't stopped.

"You just going to run away and leave your woman here?"

the man hooted and leered at me, but Ray wasn't watching, and he wasn't coming back. I just stood there, unsure of what to do, whether I was allowed to move or not.

"Hey, you, I see you!" the man yelled. "You a pussy!" Then louder, "Pussy, pussy, pussy!" the force of the blast, *Pussy, pussy, pussy*, echoing and echoing in the street. Ray didn't stop. The man looked back at me and spit on the ground. Shaking his head like he felt sorry for me. And then he was gone.

III

I did all the things you do when someone disappears. I called. I wrote. I staked out his place. Nothing.

The week after Ray left me in the street, he'd come to the apartment while I was at the bookstore, and taken everything that was his. I'd known something was off as soon as I opened the door, but there was the TV, the stereo. It was like somebody had rearranged the room just slightly. Were the Fiestaware plates in the dishwasher? No. I glanced at the sofa. Where was the dark blue Navajo blanket he'd brought over when they cut off the heat? Gone. In the bedroom, the fifties mohair sweater on my dresser, the beat-up wristwatch he'd been letting me borrow since mine broke. How was I supposed to know what time it was? What the fuck?

What else had he taken? What had he taken of mine?

For days, I'd searched the apartment and found nothing missing. Nothing. He hadn't taken the small china mannequin hand where he left his keys, or what he'd claim was his greatest vintage score—a leopard muff. If he were a woman, he said, he'd carry it everywhere. I'd been on the verge of sleep when I realized I hadn't seen that Niagara Falls souvenir spoon in the drawer. Only to discover later, sadly, it had fallen behind the sink. Ray hadn't taken a comb, or a record or a tube of toothpaste. This was why I couldn't believe he was gone. If he'd really left, he'd have taken something of mine, wouldn't he?

The only thing of his he had overlooked was this dirty white T-shirt stained with tomato sauce I'd pitched in my hamper. I'd almost washed it. I'd kept it in there with my dirty stuff, like he'd just taken it off. The day I'd found it in with the rest of my laundry in the dryer, I'd cried. Now he was really gone.

On the one-year anniversary of Ray leaving, I'd gotten drunk on cheap white wine and taken down all his paintings, crying so hard the junkies next door turned down their stereo to listen. The walls, despite my cleaning efforts, would bear the ghostly outlines where the paintings had hung until I was forced to repaint them. It would have made Ray laugh.

In the morning, when the light hit them right, they reminded me of footprints. I hated Ray but I hadn't thrown the paintings out. I resisted cutting them up. Resisted burning them like a woman from work who'd gone through a bitter divorce suggested. I'd pried out the staples cleaving the canvas from the stretchers. I'd slit the drawings out of their frames. Then I'd rolled them up like maps and stashed them in a box in the back of my closet. Maybe Ray was right—maybe one day he would be famous and I could sell them. Maybe one day he'd come back for them, and I'd be waiting here for him with a big empty box.

Or not. The reality was that the traffic below my window didn't sound like the pounding surf. Car horns weren't the calls of seagulls.

A friend sublet me her apartment on the Upper West Side. It was bright with windows, quiet, and a good place to write.

Emboldened by the fact that an actress seeking indie cred wanted to star in *Food Fight*, I quit my job at the bookstore. I started going out with theater people, and home with men, and a few boys who, when I was drunk, looked older.

For a few years, I saw Ray in train stations and at art museums. I chased him through an airport, where the Last Supper was being played out in a T.G.I. Friday's. All the disciples hunkered over plates of nachos and atomic chicken wings, and Jesus bathed in the golden neon of a Bud Light sign waved me over to join them. I gave up sharing an onion flower with the Son of God in the hope of grabbing the hem of Ray's coat. I'd wake up in tears but grateful for even a glimpse of him.

I was pissed off when, after five years, Ray began invading my dreams while I was in bed with the man starring in my new play, a reimagining of *The Odyssey* set in the Mall of America. Standing just out of reach, Ray laughed derisively. *Ripping off the Greeks? Really?* He had nothing to say about the man.

I didn't understand why, after I'd been recognized by *The New York Times* as one of the top ten most promising young playwrights in New York City (I was now Lizzie Stark) and had two serious boyfriends, one who'd proposed, Ray was still there, inexplicably there, to trouble my confidence.

I'd tried to exorcise him. For seven years, I attempted to write about Ray, and anything but Ray. Either way I failed. I couldn't bring him back to life, couldn't make him move, or hear his voice. I couldn't keep him out. It was impossible to control him. He'd bust in, put his feet up on the table, and run everybody else out of the room.

Desperate, I pressed drafts on my old workshop teacher. She'd been so helpful with my first play.

"It's just not on par with your other work," she said. "Something is missing."

The problem wasn't the idea. The flaw was in the execution. Yet, what was I if not an executioner? A serial killer of ideas? Any story dumb enough to climb into my car was a goner. I gave up. I stuck the play under my bed like a corpse in an iron drum.

Something was missing.

Then I forgot about it. I rarely ever dreamed about Ray. When I did, the dreams felt like gifts. I wasn't sad or angry anymore; what I felt was tenderness for the girl I'd been in the dream, the first self I'd ever really liked.

The fifth of November was the sort of fall day that makes New Yorkers feel superior to everyone else on the planet. I was standing on the sidewalk outside my corner market when Ray passed me. I didn't see him so much as feel him. The air changed. Molecules rearranged. There he was stooped in a yellow rain slicker, khakis, and white sneakers, his dark hair long to his shoulders, detailed with gray, his chin shaved clean. After all these years, it was like he was taunting me. *Look at how close I can pass by you without stopping.* I reached for his arm—the way I had hundreds of times before, because I could—and touched him.

"Ray." I said. "It's you, right?"

He turned. "B," he said, a calm statement of fact.

B. I hadn't been B for so long.

"Is it you?" I asked, thinking, *What has happened to you?* I knew. Like Burroughs and Basquiat, Ray was living the life of the doomed artist, and he'd become a junkie.

"What can I say?" Ray said, his voice hoarse like his throat was full of sand. "Nice, huh? Sounds pretty scary, don't it?"

"No, not scary, but telemarketing is probably out of the question."

"Nah. I look like shit." He grinned. "It's my heart," he whispered. "It's enlarged and pressing on my windpipe."

"Your heart?"

He nodded. "It makes it a little hard to communicate."

Of course, I thought, *your heart is making it hard to communicate.* I said, "You're going to be okay, though, right?"

Then he said it. He said it plain as anything. He said, "I'm dying. I'm on the donor list, but you never know." Not a trace of emotion.

He cleared his throat; it was obviously painful to talk. "So how is the writing going? I've seen your name in the paper. *Lizzie Stark,*" he said, half smiling. "I'm sorry I haven't seen anything, but, you know . . ." *I'm dying.*

"Of course," I said, "and you"—there was no tape on his fingers, no paint or charcoal smudges on his jeans, no coffee stains on the cuffs of his shirt—"are you—?"

"Yeah, I am. I do get tired real easy these days, though," he said, gathering his raincoat around him. I knew I'd offended him.

"I'm sure," I said, then, "I just know it's going to work out," like Pollyanna on the *Hindenburg.*

Ray shrugged. Like hope was this thing he'd grown tired of. Something he could take or leave. We stood there awkwardly, looking at each other—neither of us, it seemed, wanting to move. As if everyone on the street, in the stores, the people on the buses, everyone was watching us—it felt illicit. We shouldn't have been talking, but we were.

Exchanging addresses was like swapping fortunes. Ray was in Brooklyn, in Greenpoint. His handwriting was the same— all capitals, strong, block letters. I was living in the neighborhood we always used to call the Yuppie Ghetto. My script was jagged, the way my pulse would look if it were being graphed.

There was this moment when we might have hugged, but we didn't. We waved.

The list. People in hospital dramas on television were always on the list, and always got a heart/a brain/some courage right at the last moment. That didn't happen, though, not in real life.

I couldn't sleep. I got up, wrapped myself in a blanket, and went into the bathroom. I locked the door, lit a candle, and got into the tub, the way people do when they're bracing for a tornado. I wrote Ray. The kind of letter you can only write once, maybe twice in your life.

I wrote: *You broke my heart. You left me.* I left out how I'd hated him, how I'd wished him dead, how I'd cursed him.

The day he received my letter, this letter from him appeared in my mailbox.

He wrote: *I'd been restless a long time. Much to do, and miles to go. I fucked up. I lost it. I know that. I'm sorry. I should have said it to your face, but there it is. I'm sorry.*

I'm sorry. I read his apology over, and over. The old Ray wouldn't have done that. Dying had sweetened him. After that we wrote, in a fever—*Do you remember when, do you remember how, and which, and that time . . .*

Nostalgia is a narcotic.

Enjoy these last few months, I told myself. *Ray is dying.*

• • •

I bought myself this new journal. Like the one Ray had given me but bigger. Inside on the flyleaf I wrote the year, 2000. *How strange*, I thought, *to know Ray will die within this year, and yet have no idea when exactly, or how.*

Everything was different now that I knew Ray was dying. It was like it was in the beginning. Everything took on new meaning. Every cup of coffee seemed like the best coffee I'd ever had, the salsa music blaring from a car being washed below my bedroom window at eight on Saturday morning was lively, I was grateful for living in such a colorful neighborhood. Instead of pissing me off, it had sounded like a call to life. So what if you haven't had breakfast, come out into the street and dance! After work, when I was walking home past the addicts lined up outside the methadone clinic, the pink in the evening sky was so gorgeous, so celestially girlie—Mother Nature lifting her skirt—it stopped me in my tracks.

I vowed that when Ray started to fail I'd see him through to the end. That's what you do, right? You hang in there until the person is run through with so many tubes connected to so many parts he's more marionette than man. A solid tug on an oxygen tube and he raises his head, one yank on the IV and he waves. Wiggle that tube in his gut all you want, but you can't get him to hula.

In a month's time, I'd filled three journals with notes for the draft of a new play. I was more excited than I had ever been about anything I'd written. I wondered though about the heart. Could I really use a heart in a story like this? It seemed trite. I'd have to give Ray a rare blood disease, some disorder whose lesions take the form of shooting stars.

I pinned the postcards he sent me—Kerouac reciting poetry, a galaxy in a coffee cup, a dolphin jumping through a flaming hoop—on the wall over my desk like specimens. *I live in the moment now*, he wrote. *You gotta live every day like it's stolen.*

A month into our correspondence, a picture of *Apollo 2* taking off appeared in my mailbox. Ray wrote me: *Snail mail is bullshit. I ain't got the time. Here's my e-mail address.*

I'd miss the letters written in his own hand. The cards I'd collect from my mailbox and hang on my wall. I'd miss the rhythm and space between letters. Every time I turned on my computer, there he was, waiting, wanting. *Ding*, you have a new message, *ding, ding*, like an impatient customer hitting the front-desk bell. When I turned the sound off, I couldn't concentrate. What if I missed something? I turned it down as low as I could, so the sound was a distant chime.

He'd written: *Did I already send this? Did you get it? I have trouble remembering shit sometimes. It's too damn hot. My air conditioner is fucked. A friend brought—*

Why did this put my teeth on edge?

—a fan, but it sucks. I can't breathe. You know what I realized the other day. Even with a new heart, I'll always be an old man.

Ray's hope made me anxious. I didn't want Ray to die; it was the opposite. You know how it is when people are sick: All that exists is past suffering, present suffering, and future suffering. Imagining the person dead isn't wishing him dead; it's an act of self-preservation, preparation. You can't help it if those empty words of comfort—he's in a better place now, he's no longer suffering—begin to run through your head, unbidden, taking the shape of a song you hum to the tune of "Yankee Doodle Dandy."

On August 20, the hottest day of the year, kids at a summer camp in the Bronx fried eggs on the sidewalk to feed the homeless, and Ray left a message on my answering machine. He never did that. He hated leaving messages.

"Hey, B." His voice was wispy, barely audible above the hum of my air conditioner. "Guess where I am? They took me to the ER last night. Not good." He paused. "I thought my time was up."

I sat at my kitchen table and tried to breathe. Ray was at the Sisters of Mercy hospital. He was alive. However, if he had died, I told myself, at least it was sunny out, and he hadn't suffered, for long, and we'd come back together. That was what mattered most. The end.

With shaking hands I dialed the phone, and with each transfer—to front desk, to intensive care, to hold, to his room—my pulse picked up, raced.

He answered: "Ray here."

"Ray?" I said gently. "Is this Ray of *The Damned*?"

He chuckled. "B," he whispered in my ear. He might have been beside me, two heads on one pillow. Then he began to sing, *"Welcome to the Hotel Intensive Care, such a lovely place."* He stopped to catch his breath. "No pink champagne on ice, buts I've got air-conditioning and they've got to feed me, and here's the kicker: I'm on Medicaid, so it's a free ride."

"Must be nice," I said, walking over to my desk. I sat down. Switched on my computer.

"Can't complain—we've got your twenty channels, your pretty nurses, although Sisters of Mercy they ain't . . ."

I began to type: *He's singing the Eagles, a free ride—slow ride. No more sticking it to the man. Happy for the handout. He never paid his taxes, but now happy to sponge off govt.*

"I keep calling and calling for Sister Morphine—"

I typed: *Sisters of Mercy they ain't . . . Sister Morphine.* That was good.

"—to come and ease my pain, and they keep . . ." He stopped.

"Wait. You aren't typing, are you?"

"No."

No—I typed, pressing the keys more gently—I was *writing*.

"I'm sorry, Ray."

"I've come to the conclusion that I don't want to die."

"Of course you don't."

He said, "The end of my story has yet to be written."

"I know," I said.

After I hung up, I turned off the ringer. I pictured Ray reclining on his bed by a sunny window like he was on the deck of a yacht, a refreshing drink in his hand, cool wind in his hair.

I'd written from dusk to dark to dawn. Until I could no longer sit, or hold my head up, until the joints in my arms and legs hummed with pain and the tips of my fingers went numb. Then I put my head down on my desk and slept.

It took me a few seconds to get my bearings when I woke. I had a message. The red light on my answering machine was staring at me like a Cyclops. I pressed Play.

"Was that the beep? Is this thing on? Where are you, B, out slugging margaritas? Tripping the light fandango with the beautiful people? Okay, call me when you get back. Ciao for now."

Slowly I started to reach for the phone.

"*Hola*," Ray said, his voice filling the room. "Yeah, it's me."

I didn't dare move. It was like he was right there in the room. He could see me. He could hear me if I moved.

"You *still* out? It's late. Bad girl. Okay. Later."

Then: "Hey, it's Ray. Again. This is, what—the third message I've left? I don't know. Call me. Doesn't matter what time
it is, B. I'll be up, you know, just *killing time*."

Then: "I don't know if this is on, or if you got the, what,
four messages I left earlier, or hell, maybe you're just *busy*. Is
that it? You're busy?" Silence. "Are you there? Shit, if you're
there, B, I need you to pick up the goddamn phone." Long
silence. "Fuck," he said, as though it had just dawned on him,
"is someone there?"

I was holding my breath. What if there was someone here?

He hung up.

I had to get out of there. I walked up to Central Park and
around it. It was early. Just me and the dog people and the
people with babies, and those people without a hangover to
sleep off, or anyone to make love to, or a friend to meet for
breakfast, or a book to read, or schoolwork to get a jump on.
There were hundreds of people, but no one saw me, no one
touched me.

When I came back two hours later, the light was blinking
again. *Red alert, red alert, danger, danger, red alert.* I'd been a
coward. I'd said I'd stay and I'd run.

"This is my final message," Ray said. "I'm supposed to be
conserving my strength. Not that it's of any interest to you, or
you care, but I thought you should know I got a heart."

Hit Rewind, and Play again.

"I got a heart," Ray repeated. Hit Rewind, and Play again.
Over and over.

I told myself, *There is still the risk of infection.*

The ending wouldn't come. I'd written death scenes. Me at
Ray's bedside, stroking his hair, him apologizing, saying, *I was*

so stupid, you know I never loved anyone but you, mumbling about the next road trip while the heart monitor became a horizon line, and me, stricken with grief, pulling out the IVs and climbing into his bed. Me lying beside his dead body, waiting for someone to come discover me.

I'd written endings that became beginnings—I am married with two children you can hear playing offstage, and a letter arrives from his mother telling me Ray has died—and ended with Ray at twenty-three slipping offstage, a shoplifted tube of cadmium red in his pocket.

I hadn't written this ending.

The day after Ray's surgery I went to see him. I had to see him. Whacked out on pain meds, in and out of consciousness. I sat by his bed. I took his hand. How many times had I held his hand? I didn't stay long. Long enough. I stared at Ray, and around the room, memorizing details until I was full. Before I left, because I could, because I wanted to, I kissed him on the mouth. I don't know why I'd expected him to be cold. I don't remember the feel of the kiss as much as the warmth of his breath. I'd breathed him in.

Later, when he'd say he hadn't been sure if I had really come, or if he'd dreamed it, I wished I'd told him I'd spent the night at his bedside.

A few weeks after Ray came home from the hospital, he invited me to visit.

He e-mailed: *Every day I'm getting stronger. I'm not my old self yet. No coffee, booze is strictly verboten. I can however offer you an array of teas, lemonade, soda. I mainly want to show you my most recent work. You were very important to me at the time I was coming into being as an artist.*

I'd reread that last line until it no longer made me flinch.

I'm sorry, I wrote. *Wish I could come by, but I can't right now. I'm just at the end of something.*

Come whenever, he said.

Soon, I said.

The second time he called me. I couldn't say no.

"No pressure," he said, sounding like the old Ray. "Come when you want. It's not like I am doing anything. I've made a hundred paintings in my head. My best work, but most of the time it's friends stopping by, and visits from a Caribbean home-duty nurse who comes to take my blood. Other than that, I play way too many computer games. Eat lots of steak. Sleep. Cash my disability check."

"Sounds rough," I said.

"It has its moments."

We sat in his living room drinking organic lemonade out of striped highball glasses that in the old days we'd used for wine. I recognized parts—the blue Navajo blanket, the giant flying horse from an old gas station sign—but it was all different. Outside the kitchen, covering one wall, was this painting of a life-size deer frozen in the road, an eighteen-wheeler bearing down on it. It was so large it felt like I could walk right into that world.

"Yeah. That's a good one," Ray said when he noticed me looking at it. "People fall into two camps here, those who think the deer gets creamed, and those who think it escapes."

I waited for him to ask, *What do you think happens?* I'd say, *Depends on who is driving.*

"I'm still looking for the perfect title," he said. "I don't usually have any problem with titles, but this one . . ."

"I-Ninety-five." How many times had we driven that corridor?

"Maybe," he said.

"So," I asked, "is this driving you crazy, or what?"

Ray shrugged. "What can I do? I am taking hundreds of dollars' worth of pills every day just to keep my body from rejecting the heart."

I repeated in my head, *rejecting the heart.*

"Do you know whose heart it is?"

"It's not like I want to think about it," he said, moving away a little and crossing his legs.

"Right. Sorry."

"All I know is it was from an eighteen-year-old kid, from the Midwest."

I didn't like the way Ray spoke of his new heart as being *from* a kid, the heart had *belonged* to that kid.

"A boy."

"It had to be."

Eighteen years old. How untested that boy's heart must have been. Had he even gotten to fall in love?

"It was a motorcycle accident," Ray said. "You know, that could easily have been me."

But it hadn't been.

"Are you going to have a great scar, or what?"

"Best on the beach."

"Can I see it?"

Suddenly shy, Ray answered, "Don't worry. You'll see it sometime."

I don't remember what else we talked about. Trips he had taken with his friends. *Great people.* Friends I never knew and would never know. His work. Paintings I never saw or would ever see.

I told him I was finishing a new play. It was, I felt—and I used his word—"the most important work I've made to date."

I told him it was set in the late eighties and early nineties. It was a coming-of-age story. He didn't ask.

I told him I was going to this artists' colony, for six weeks maybe two months, in the hope of finishing it.

"You know, they give you your own cabin with a fireplace, and every day, at lunchtime, they leave a picnic basket on your doorstep.

"Hot soup, homemade muffins, tea. They really take care of you. It's the only way to go."

"Sounds nice," he said.

"It's like having a wife," I said. "What's not to like?"

Then I told him I had to leave. I didn't want to, but I should. He looked tired anyway. At the door, he fumbled self-consciously over a series of locks—there was a bolt and a chain. Who needed so many locks? What was there to steal?

"You know you can always stop by," he said. "Drop in."

"Soon," I promised. Knowing he would call me and he would write me, and each time I would take longer and longer to get back to him, until I didn't at all. I knew that I'd finish my play, and regardless of how it was received, it would be done. Maybe I wouldn't understand what happened with Ray any better, but R and B were finished.

The last time Ray wrote me he said, *I know you'll understand this, B. For the first time in my life, I'm experiencing a total lack of inspiration. I've got nothing. Nada. All I've been able to come up with is a blue rectangle. Just blue. I need something. I need to drive all night to nowhere. I need a punch in the face. I need the sound of waves on a beach. I need to lie on a pier and stare at the moon. I need to get stinking drunk. I need a kiss. I need something. Something is missing.*

Out of the Blue
and into the Black

I woke up in my own bed. Alone. Fully dressed, including underwear. *Thank you very much.* Lucky me because the ballet flats and pink polo shirt weren't mine, only the jean mini. I like to call it my Houdini skirt because it makes your butt disappear and you can slip out of it even in handcuffs. That's a joke.

I was feeling pretty good about myself. *What a good girl I am,* I thought, tucking my comforter up under my chin. You know, who cares if I was so hungover my head felt like a big old pumpkin someone had smacked with a baseball bat. Then, out of habit, I felt for my pearls, before remembering I'd lost them weeks ago. Crap. How long would it take before I stopped doing that?

Why do camels drink?
To forget.

I could hear Butter in our bathroom singing along to the Beach Boys, *I wish they all could be California girls,* and washing her face with Noxzema, which kills me. I mean, only little kids and old ladies use that stuff. My mom used to put it on my shoulders when I got sunburned. Which was nice because you know it's not the same if you do it yourself.

I'd never known anybody with a name like Butter until I got to college. My mother asks me, "What kind of people name their child after a dairy product?" I tell her, *rich people,* and she has to take my word for it.

When I explain it's a nickname Butter's brothers came up with because when she was a baby her hair was yellow, my mom says, "And the Butter just stuck?" My mother is constantly saying stuff she doesn't know is hilarious. She and my dad are both from small towns in the Midwest. My grandfather was a dairy farmer, and his dad was a dairy farmer, and so on and so on. I wouldn't tell anybody that. No reason. I'd told Butter once, I think, but she's my best friend.

Anyway, Butter's hair isn't yellow now. It's that white-blond color you only see on little kids, which goes with her eyes, which are this sort of unreal swimming pool blue. She says she misses the ocean. Which maybe explains why she only wears sailor suit pajamas.

My mom also wants to know why, if Butter is from California, she has a British accent. I can't really explain except to say, You know how some people go abroad and come home with a tapeworm or yellow fever? Well, Butter spent last semester in London and came home with a British accent. Our friend Deb (who spent the semester in Italy but didn't come back rolling her *r*'s, just twenty pounds heavier) keeps telling her to please, just drop it. She probably wishes she had an Italian accent.

Behind Butter's back, Deb accuses her of being a poser. To her face she says, "It's not you," but Butter says she can't help it. I believe her because I know it's contagious. One beer now and I get all cockney. Bugger this, and blimey that. It makes Deb bonkers. She says, "Are you trying to drive me out of my mind? Jesus H. Christ, listen to yourself, you sound ridiculous." She's wrong, though. You know how glasses make you seem smarter; it's the same thing with a British accent.

"Butter," I moaned, as loudly as I could. I thought she should know I hadn't gone all Karen Ann Quinlan on her. It wasn't even noon and I was totally awake. I wanted the points. She didn't need to know I woke up in Blackout City.

"Is that you?" Butter says. Like who else would it be?

"I think so," I say, sort of annoyed. I mean I hadn't had a scandal in my bed (and, for the record, she was conked out the whole time) in months because last time, she'd thrown such a fit you'd think I fucked Charlie Manson with the lights on. I mean, she was so mad she was practically in tears.

"Did you ring your mum?" she yells, but I can barely hear her over the roar of the faucet. "I don't want her to think I'm not giving you her messages, love. Please."

Fuck. Just kill me now, I think.

"Come again, ducks? Pipe up."

Double fuck.

The minute Butter got out of the bathroom, I'd tell her I called my mom back. I'd say, she didn't sound *worried* to me—had she actually said *that*? That she was *worried* about me? Because all she said to *me* was that she just wanted to hear my voice and tell me my dad's back had gone out but was fine now, and that my grandmother was in the hospital, which wasn't good, of course, and oh, she wanted to know how would I feel about taking a trip to Europe this summer—sort of like a college graduation present.

No, kill that—Butter would know I was lying.

I roll on my side and try to rock myself back to sleep. Rocking usually helps, except my arms and legs ache like I've been dragged through the streets by wild dogs.

What I needed was to see Andy. Andy. My Andy. I've never known anybody like Andy before. I've never had someone who liked me no matter what I did. I mean, really liked me. I knew, no matter what, I could always go to Andy, and curl up in his lap like a kitten and bury my face in his neck, and say, "Go ahead, tell me how horrible I was. Give me the bad news first, so by the end I won't feel so much like shooting myself in the head."

I knew that Andy, unlike Butter, wouldn't judge me. He'd never leave some stupid magazine quiz like "Are You a Raging Alcoholic?" on my pillow. No, he'd say, "You were cute. Don't worry about anything."

And I'd say, "Are you sure? Don't protect me, Andy. I'm a big girl, I can take it," I'd say, eyes screwed shut, arms covering my head, like the bad news is going to come in the form of a storm of rotten eggs and rocks.

And he'd say, "Belinda"—he was the only person at school who called me by my real name. "Why would I do that, Belinda?" Three years of college, and he was the first, and he said my name so prettily. *Bell-linda*, not *Bull-linda*. *Bell-lindahh*, with a sigh at the end.

And I'd say, "Okay, then why am I so sore today?"

And he'd say, "We danced a lot." (Andy was not a big dancer.)

And I'd say, "Okay, Fred Astaire, how did I get home?"

And he'd say, "I carried you."

And I'd say, "You did? You carried me all the way home?"

And he'd say, "Of course I did."

I love that *of course I did*. Of course I took care of you.

How often do you find someone like that? Someone you feel safe with? Like never.

It would be swell if I could call Charlotte, but she's probably sleeping, or watching *South Pacific* for the hundredth time. Until I got to be friends with Charlotte, I thought only blue-hairs and fairies watched musicals.

You know what, maybe I wouldn't even get out of bed today. Maybe I am really sick. I have to say there are days when I think I'd actually like to have something seriously wrong with me, I mean totally curable, you know, but real. Because you know when people have big stuff like that happen to them everybody sees them in a different way. Everybody forgets who they used to be, and they become better people, even though inside they're exactly the same person.

Or maybe not so curable.

Unless it's something like what happened to Charlotte. Nobody knew what to do with that. Butter says I'm thinking about Charlotte too much. I think no one is thinking about her enough. Even Andy, who after we told them what happened to her, said he wanted to go up to his frat and pulverize the motherfucker. Now anytime Charlotte's name came up everybody acted funny.

It wasn't like I meant *not* to call my mom. I just knew what she was going to ask me, because that woman is like a broken record. *I haven't heard from you. What have you been up to? Are you having fun? Oh, did you meet anyone special?*

And I would have to tell her, two weeks ago I went to an Around the World party at ATO with Butter. In the Mexico room I sat back in this barber's chair and did a mix-in-your-mouth margarita—which is a shot of tequila, some triple sec, then you shoot up, bite the lime out of some guy's mouth, and lick the salt off his stomach, or his arm. No, I don't think that really happens in Mexican barbershops. Then we skipped off to Ireland and I pounded a Guinness, after that, in Switzerland I snorted a shot of peppermint schnapps—yes, snorted; no, I don't think that's an authentic Swiss custom. In Jamaica I smoked some ganja. In Jonestown a guy in aviator sunglasses and a button-down shirt, with a Bible under his arm, served Kool-Aid punch out of a trash can, which probably had a jockstrap at the bottom. Why? I don't know. Flavor? No, it doesn't seem very hygienic. Or funny. No, I don't think it was grain; yes, I've heard it could blind you. I still have the newspaper clipping—clippings—you sent me freshman year. Finally, Mom, I trekked up to the very tippy top of the fraternity house, and visited Bolivia, snowy, snowy Bolivia, and danced all night.

I mean I could tell her that, but she'd have a heart attack.

I could tell her that guys expect tit for tat, or *dis for dat*, when they give you lines. Not that it matters.

I could tell her that every time you visited a "country" you got a rubber stamp, like you get on your passport when you go through customs. And that it would take me three days to get the Brazil off my ass. I tried soap, baby oil, rubbing alcohol. It was fingernail polish remover that finally did the trick.

When I'd showed Butter, she howled. "You're too much, ducks." Butter would never let anybody rubber-stamp her butt. Then again, Butter isn't as much fun as I am. Especially now that she's officially one of the top-ranked girl golfers in the country. She still smokes, but only one a day. Otherwise, she says, her body would go into shock. It's heartbreaking to watch her take that last drag, it's like the way a man who crawled across the Sahara sucks on a canteen.

I could tell my mom that before that I'd gone to a beach

party with my friend Charlotte. Yes, Charlotte, the one with the nice car. I told Charlotte before we went that there was this Around the World party I wanted to go to later. She knew. If you want to know the truth, I didn't even think to tell her I was leaving because she was dancing with this guy, and like I'd tell my mother, *She looked like she was having a blast.*

And my mom would ask (wishing it was me we were talking about, not my friend), *Who is this boy?*

And I'd say, *The guy that will rape her.*

Thinking, *And while that was happening I was letting some dude stamp "Brazil" on my ass.*

And for once my mother wouldn't say, *Maybe he has a friend?*

She would be speechless.

I could also remind her that I'm still reeling from my breakup with Stanley. Stanley, my imaginary boyfriend. I made him up so she'd quit worrying and get off my back. My mother was nuts about Stanley, she could yak about him for days. I'd tell her about how Stanley was always squiring me around town, buying me ice cream cones, and escorting me home from the library after dark. You can't imagine how disappointed my mother was when, over parents' weekend, Stanley's eczema was so bad he was confined to his bed, making it impossible for them to meet. Finally, it just got to be too much. I did my best to prepare her. After that, he started acting all distant, and moody, and stopped returning my calls. Oh ho. She'd seen it coming. She said she understood why I needed to be alone, and why the mere mention of Stanley's name was painful, and yes, that I'd be too fragile to even entertain the idea of dating for a long while. My reprieve lasted less than a month.

I could have told her about Andy, but I wouldn't because

it would just confuse her and she'd get the wrong idea and ask me all these questions I had no answers to.

What I knew was that right now, I really needed to talk to him. I'd throw my arms around him, and standing on my tip-toes, pressed tight against him, I'd whisper in his ear. Maybe he'd tell me that he loved me. He'd already done it once, just a month ago. No one, outside of my family, ever said that to me, but Andy had. He'd been hammered, sure—but you know what they say, when you're drunk, you speak the truth. He probably didn't even remember saying it. Which was for the best anyway, right? But he had said it. *I love you, Belinda. I love you.*

I was waiting for him to say, *I love you, Belinda*, again. He could be drunk. I didn't care. You know, it was better that way anyhow. I just wanted him to say it again. Just to be sure.

Butter didn't get it. She tells me that she's told Andy to give it up, but men are idiots. Anytime she saw Andy giving me a piggyback ride, or carrying my books, or saw me sitting in-nocently in his lap, she shot me the stink eye. She didn't even have to say it anymore. *Leave him alone. Stop playing with him. Why are you doing this? It's just cruel. You don't love him.*

Yes I do.

Not like that.

But I do. I've felt it. Around midnight, in a certain light, when he shakes his bangs into his face, then pushes them back so I can see his eyes, the way he looks at me—like he's letting me in—I love him so much it hurts.

Did you ever wish someone would just be mean to you? Even a little?

It's weird, but I started doing this thing in high school, of making up playlists for my funeral. Some songs have stayed the same. "Here Comes the Sun," because my dad taught me to play it on the piano. "Amazing Grace," because my mom would want a hymn and it would make everybody, even people I barely know, cry. You want crying. But mostly they change. Freshman year I was crazy about "Dust in the Wind" by Kansas, depressing but true. Senior year it was all about the Rolling Stones, "You Can't Always Get What You Want" — because that line *you just might find, you get what you need* slays me. And, of course, last, "Stairway to Heaven." By the time I'd get to *And she's buying a stairway to heaven*, I'd have freaked myself out totally and be sobbing so hard, like practically to the point of throwing up, it was ridiculous.

As of now, though, I end with Neil Young's "Like a Hurricane," because it's Andy's and my song. You know, *You are just a dreamer, and I am just a dream.* That kills me. He'd get it.

I'd only seen Charlotte twice in the last week. She hadn't been going to class. Not that she felt like talking anyway, she just wanted to watch *South Pacific.* I took her a bag of cookies last time I was there. These iced circus animals, pink camels, lions, and giraffes, they looked so darn cheerful. That was it, *cheerful.* I was feeling so good about them, you know, then I started to worry. What if the frosting was wrong and the animals looked like they had mange or a skin disease? What if their legs were all broken off? Who knew how many of them had been decapitated?

Good thing I thought to check, because when I opened the bag it looked like a mass grave in there. Half of them were in pieces or only partially frosted. I salvaged what I could. Anyway, luckily, she didn't seem to notice the bag had been opened.

I asked Charlotte if she needed anything. If she needed me to go anywhere with her. I meant, like, mental health services. Teddy says all you have to do is cry and flash them a copy of *The Bell Jar*, and they'll pony up some Valium. I practically begged her to let me take her. I did.

Last thing I was sure of from last night was the toga party. I was over toga parties—they were strictly JV. Like New Year's Eve parties that exist just so you can make out with a stranger at midnight. You have to. That's the theme. I'd only stopped to grab a beer—who can resist pledges playing eunuchs, fanning you with palm fronds while you wait for the keg?

So I was standing there when this girl in a sorry-looking toga appears. It's all pilled, but she's got her hair braided and pinned up on top of her head like a crown, and she's dragging along her friend, who's twice as big as her and totally wasted. You could tell the big girl's sheet, all pink roses and lace rickrack, was brand-new, like she'd bought it just for this party.

An ant and an elephant meet in a bar and go home together. The next morning the ant wakes up and the elephant is dead. "Damn," the ant says, "one night of passion and I spend the rest of my life digging a grave!"

You could tell the big girl was from Minnesota, or the South—she sure wasn't an East Coast girl, she was too big and smiley-looking. Anybody else with those big, doughy, freckled arms would have been wearing a cardigan. I kind of respected the fact that the big girl wasn't wearing a bra, when she really should have. How much do I hate those lame skinny girls who always wear bras with their togas, their straps plain as day?

The little one is upset. She goes, "We seem to keep losing ours. Some asshole in there keeps pulling her sheet off."

And the big girl goes, "Ah, don't get your panties in a wad," her voice all slurry. "It's just a jokey." And the little girl goes, "It's not funny," so mad she starts to shake. "They're taking pictures."

Here's what bugged me. I knew tomorrow there was going to be some picture of this poor, dumb, big-boobed girl floating around school, her face the bull's-eye on a dartboard in the fraternity basement (*extra point if you hit her in the jugs!*). They'd black out her eyes and a couple teeth, and everybody would be pointing and laughing at how fat she was, how her tits were bigger than her head. *Aw, be a sport*, they'd tell her. *It's just a joke. You can't take it personally. Don't get so broken up over this—next week it will be someone else. Everything blows over.*

But you know what, she'd never forget it. Ever. You know it would come to her in the middle of the night, like a hand over her mouth so she can't breathe, and she'd cry, and she'd pray, *Oh, please, God, please if I can erase just one thing in my life, erase that thing. Someday I want to have kids.*

I mean that was just my guess.

So, I fixed her toga. I'm good at that. It helped that I had a safety pin on the inside of my skirt. It had been there seriously for years. To be safe, my mom says, you should always have a safety pin and a quarter for a phone call. Still, even with the damn pin, it wasn't easy because The Go-Gos "We Got the Beat" was blaring and the fat girl kept bouncing up and down, a big mistake in her case. Girls with big honkers should never pogo braless, unless they want a black eye. You know, I felt sorry for the fat girl, but I wanted to slap her too, pinch her arm until a bruise came up. I mean, would she even remember I'd helped her?

The whole time her friend stood there, waiting and looking miserable like she was witnessing the fall of Rome. All she wanted was to be back home in her dorm making popcorn and watching TV. She didn't care if it turned out to be the party of the century, or worry that if she left she might miss meeting *the one*. She just wanted to get the hell out of there, but she wasn't leaving her friend behind.

Back in the days when we used to all go out together, we'd say, "Leave a trail of crumbs, sugar," which meant don't disappear without telling someone.

The second I was done fixing the big girl's toga she broke away, stumbling back into the party crowd, waving her arms like she thought everybody was just waiting for her to return. It was just sad.

Now when *I* show up at a party, people really are happy. It's not a party without Bender. People cheer. "Yay, Bender is here, now the real fun can begin!" You don't know what that's like. To be special like that. To have all those people know you, have you in common. The fat girl was deluded if she thought anybody cared whether she was at that party, or passed out under a bush, or got chopped up and thrown in a cornfield.

I bet she felt like someone poured kitty litter in her mouth while she slept. She probably wet the bed. I wonder if she noticed those safety pins in her toga and wondered who did that for her. It was me.

I got the nickname Bender because I bend every which way but never break. Freshman year I jumped out of a third-story window, and rolled right out of it. Not a scratch on me. Just like a cat.

I used to be a gymnast, so I know I can take a lot. I can't tell you how many times I cracked my head on the beam, slammed my chest into the vault, fell off the bars flat on my back, got the wind knocked out of me, saw stars, blacked out. My gymnastics coach used to tell my teammates, *Belinda may not be as skilled technically as you are. She may not have your strength or flexibility, or grace, but she's not afraid to throw the trick. If you don't have the guts to go for it . . .*

And he'd stare them down like they were a bunch of pussies. He was right. I wasn't as good as my teammates, but I was fearless. I wasn't afraid to throw the trick. Sometimes I wish that what happened to Charlotte happened to me, because I could take it. I'm brave.

I always say: *I can do anything for ten minutes.*

When Butter comes into the room, she stands over the bed in her sailor suit pajamas and looks down at me. Watching me. I catch her looking at me now all the time. I think to myself, *I'm dead, I'm dead, I'm dead,* which is supposed to trick your body into acting dead.

"You're daft. I can see you, you know." Then just when I think it's safe, she rips off my covers. I scream. She screams.

"Bloody hell, Bender, what have you done? Gone and got yourself a black eye? Seriously? Have you looked at yourself?"

"I know. I walked smack into the door last night. I can't believe you didn't hear me. I wailed like a banshee."

She crosses her arms and drops her head like I've done something wrong to her personally. It bugs me when she acts like this.

"You might have helped me. I was practically knocked unconscious," I say, but she doesn't look guilty like I hoped. She is too busy putting on her sneakers, white Keds.

Butter is one of those people whose sneakers always look brand-new even when they're not. "You really didn't hear me?" I'm waiting for any sign in her face, of when I came home, if it was Andy who put me to bed.

"No, mercifully," she says in this sort of brusque, matter-of-fact way and bends down to retie her shoelaces.

"Didn't you see Andy?"

"No." She says this like it's good news, like he's been spared some terrible fate seeing me lit up, like he hasn't a hundred times already. He isn't like her.

"So, you're leaving right now?" Golly, I can sound pitiful.

"I am. Unless you're feeling a bit peckish and want to dash into town for some breaky?" she says, looking at me with that sad you-never-want-to-hang-out-with-me-anymore expression that I can't stand.

Every Saturday morning somebody has a Wake and Bake. Who doesn't love eating Trix-is-for-kids! and doing bong hits while watching Bugs Bunny cartoons? You'd have to be dead inside.

How lucky that this Saturday it is at Andy's, and I was going there anyway.

I say, "Breakfast? That's exactly what I was thinking."

"That's brilliant," she says, smiling so you can see every tooth.

"Listen, I'm going on the wagon," I say, struggling to get out of bed and upright without my head falling off and rolling under the bed. "You'll see, I'll be the one in the bonnet riding in the back of the covered wagon. Seriously, me and Laura Ingalls Wilder."

"Cool beans," she says. We used to say that all the time.

It's hard to look at her when she is smiling so hard it's like looking into the sun. Then she looks at my skirt, and frowns. "What in the devil did you get into?"

My hands fly to cover the spot.

I remembered leaving the toga party, and thinking I'd go drop in on Andy at his frat house, but Aerosmith's "Walk This Way" was coming out of the Beta house, and it seemed like a sign, and maybe Butter and Teddy and Deb were there? I wasn't going to stay, just check in. I wanted to dance.

I remembered the line for the ladies' room being long, and a girl choosing to pee in the sink instead of wait, and thinking, *I've got a skirt on, I could do that too*, and then being in the upstairs hall, feeling dizzy and so sleepy, I thought, *I'll just lie down for ten minutes—just like Goldilocks—a short nap to get me back on my feet.* I'd gone into an empty room, it was dark, the lights on the stereo were flickering like lightning bugs. I lay down on the couch and fell asleep . . . how long? When I woke up, I remembered seeing people standing around me, three or more bears. In the story Goldilocks takes a shortcut out the window; I just jumped up and ran.

Had I gone to Josh's room last night? But his room was downstairs, not upstairs. Would I have done that? Did Andy know? Andy wouldn't know. Still, even without knowing about me and Josh, Andy hated him. Andy, who never swears, calls Josh "the fucking fascist," because he's a member of the Young Republicans. Apparently, Andy is more passionate about politics than I realized. You'd never know from looking at Josh that he's a dealer. Not the hang-around-the-playground-selling-Quaaludes-to-schoolkids creepy dealer, just dime bags, hash, that sort of thing. Coke. Definitely coke. *Coke Adds Life.*

He's a great businessman. He writes down every sale in a spiral notebook, but he never makes me pay for anything.

He was the only boy I'd do it with with the lights on because he said, "I want to look at you. I want to see your face when you come." That just floored me. So every time I was supposed to come I'd try to make my face look sexy.

I used to practice that in the mirror when I was in high school.

Afterward he'd turn out the light and fall asleep, and I'd lie there up in his loft and stare at this poster of Van Gogh's *Starry Night* over his desk. You'd be surprised what you can see once your eyes get accustomed to the dark. Once I told him that staring at that painting made me feel high, and he said, "Van Gogh cut off his ear for a woman. She was a whore." What kind of man would do that? A crazy man.

I'm sorry, but after a man cuts off his ear for you, declarations of love like candy or flowers, even diamonds, seem cheap.

Over winter break he'd gone home to D.C. and come back dating this dimwit sophomore who was working on Reagan's Just Say No campaign. Yes, really. And if there's one thing that makes me crazy, it's a hypocrite! You know I couldn't have cared less, but PDA—the way they were always hanging on each other was just disgusting. I'd never have been caught dead holding hands or kissing in public. It was so typical. So lame.

You'd never know by the way Josh looked at me now that I was once special. We'd see each other in the student union and he'd smile, maybe wave, maybe if I was close murmur *Hey*, like he was such a champ to acknowledge my presence.

Not that I wanted anything more. But I was curious. So

once or twice I'd cruised by his room just to see. I didn't knock or anything, I just listened. I never heard anything, so I bet she was holding out on him. What a waste.

The last time she sensed it, poor little bunny. Animals low on the food chain need sharp instincts if they want to survive. *Josh,* she said, *Joshy, there's someone at the door. Get up. There's someone there. Go check. I don't like it.*

I might have been a customer, right? The second that door opened I was a ghost. Maybe he saw the back of my head. If so, let him think I'd been partying in one of his fraternity brothers' rooms. Yeah, that's right, deal with that.

Had I gone to Josh's last night? Would I? No way. Okay, maybe, yes. Okay, *honestly*? Yes. And, maybe I knocked. Maybe he came out, carefully shut the door behind him, and whispered, "What are you doing here? What do you want?" Maybe he suggested that I should go home. And when I said I didn't want to, he said, "Then come back later."

"When?"

"After she leaves."

Maybe then I tried to kiss him and he turned away, and said didn't I know what *later* meant? I touched the pillow of bruise around my eye socket, the most tender place, and pressed on it. It hurt. It still hurt. I couldn't stop, though. It hurt.

Maybe I had gone back later. Maybe I had taken off all my clothes, and climbed naked up the ladder to his loft. Maybe I had crawled into bed beside him and started kissing the back of his neck. Maybe he'd pushed my head down and said, "Jesus, can't you just suck my cock and go?"

Or, I don't know, maybe that was another night, maybe none of that happened at all.

I shut the bathroom door behind me and take a deep

breath. *Have a sense of humor about this, Bender,* I say to my-self as I start to get undressed. *Worse things happen at sea.* I look down at the spatter of stains on the front of my skirt. Like glue. The largest was in the shape of Florida. I start to see if it would come off with my fingernail, then stop. I'd never get it clean. I knew that right away, so I buried the skirt in the trash.

Then I look in the mirror. There's a puffy ring of dark blu-ish purple around my entire left socket, my eyelid swollen and spongy like the time I got stung on the eye by a wasp in kin-dergarten. It brought tears to my eyes, but goddamn there was no reason to cry. I just felt sorry for it. Poor baby.

I turn the water up as high as I can stand it and sit down on the floor of the shower, pretending it is rain. When I get up my skin is pink and there is steam rising off me, like my superpower is the ability to bring things to a boil. Butter gave Charlotte a hard time for taking a shower that night. She said, "You didn't! Don't you know you're not supposed to do that? That's the first thing they tell you." Butter says in America a woman is raped every six minutes, and that she didn't mean to yell, didn't mean to make it worse, but she'd destroyed evidence, and if Charlotte didn't report it, he'd just do it again to another girl. I thought, *What in the world did you expect her to do?*

Actually, what they say is don't try to memorize everything about him, just focus on remembering one detail. Something he can't change—like a birthmark, or a scar. Which doesn't really matter if you already know the person.

I chase three Tylenol with water right out of the faucet, put Visine in my eyes, get into my clean blue-and-white flowered Lanz nightgown—Butter let me stick it in with her wash, so it smells like Ocean Breeze fabric softener. I instantly feel one hundred times better.

If somebody asked what happened to my face, I'd say, It was really dumb. My friend hasn't been feeling good, so she asked if I'd get her some books out of the library, which I was happy to do. I couldn't really see over the top of the stack and misjudged her stairs and—you can see what happened. I went down like a *ton of books*.

When I come out of the bathroom, Butter has made my bed. She's turned down the top the way my mom used to do for me at bedtime. I'd forgotten that. I barely ever make my bed.

Butter is waiting. I open my underwear drawer and take out the Ray-Bans I'd lifted off Andy's face a few weeks ago. I had put them on and he'd said, "Those look good on you," and he never asked for them back, so I figure he meant me to have them. That would be just like him.

"Just give me two shakes of a lamb's tail and I'll be ready to roll," I say, weakly passing a brush over my hair, which is thick and long. Nebraska Corn Queen hair, my mother, a former Nebraska Corn Queen, calls it, even though I was born in New Jersey—our hair is capable of annihilating ordinary brushes. "Oh, you know what?" I say like I just remembered it. "I seem to recall that there's a Cartoon Keg at the lads' house this morning. We should at least stop by."

Butter bites her lip. "Blessed hell, give it here," she says, snapping the brush out of my hand. "Though why I bother— why I arse around with this I don't know."

Butter has four brothers and short hair, so brushing my hair is fun for her. Sometimes she'll brush my hair while we watch a movie. To tell you the truth, half the time, I don't even want to watch a movie, but if Butter's going to brush my hair, I will. It's funny how much more you relax and enjoy something if you know the other person doesn't expect you to do anything. I mean, you'd never ask a boy to brush your hair, would you?

Hey, want to lose fifteen ugly pounds?
I'd love to!
Cut off your head.

You'd think by the way my eyes burn when we step outside that they've caught on fire. At the far end of our block a tour group of prospective students is disappearing around the corner, which is too bad because usually we flash them from the porch and scream, "This is not a party school!" Still, I can't imagine the tour guide is much happier that they're being followed by this burnout dog that lives at the fraternities, a perpetually stoned yellow Lab with *Don't Paint on Me* painted on its side in safety orange.

I generally like it when Butter takes my arm. I'm not like Deb, who acts like this means she's a lesbo. I don't know, this morning it just bugs me. When we start to cross the street, I pretend to sneeze just so I can pull my arm away to cover my mouth.

Andy's house is a white two-story, with a wide porch, and has one of those granny swings, which is where he is supposed to be, stretched out on the sofa in his madras shorts and white button-down, black loafers, porkpie hat, looking like a man from the fifties trapped in the eighties, playing the harmonica to Jimmy's guitar. Even when he's got his shades on, he closes his eyes when he plays. He's shy, and without them you can read whatever he's thinking in his big brown eyes. The time I can most imagine kissing him is when he has them on. He should never take them off.

Did you ever notice everybody throws their panties at the guitar player or the lead singer, but nobody ever throws their panties at the harmonica player? Why is that? Why didn't any other girls want Andy?

There are about a dozen people on the porch—mostly seniors, though there are a few underclassmen. On the steps Jimmy is playing Dylan's "Like a Rolling Stone" on his guitar, and Deb is out there in her long blue Lanz nightgown and duck boots pumping the keg, her jaw set like that of a pioneer girl working a butter churn. She's big-boned and strong—she rowed crew in high school for god's sake—but she'll pretend to get tired, or sometimes ask a guy to do it for her, just to seem more girlie. She's sensitive. You can barely hug her without her freaking out and jerking away and accusing you of feeling her baby back fat. That's when she turns.

Deb couldn't look happier to see me, which is never good. "Heeeere's Bender," she says, staring at the sunglasses. Knowing they're Andy's makes her insane. It's not my fault he likes me and not her. "Well, hello, Betty," she says. "And how are we feeling this morning? Looks like someone's got a wicked case of the cocktail flu."

"I'm just peachy," I say. "You look well rested."

The move for the pitcher of Bloody Marys on the porch railing is pure instinct, reflex. Tomatoes are packed with vitamins. Next, I'll duck into the loo. Deb always hides a box of Munchkins in the bathroom, because she hates to eat in front of boys.

"Now, now," Butter says jokingly. "Play nice, ladies." The look on her face as she watches me pour myself a Bloody is increasingly pissy.

Oh, shove it. You're not my goddamn mother, I think.

"I promise, Butter my love, just one."

Butter sighs. "Half an hour," she says, tapping her finger on the face of her watch for emphasis. *Just kill me now*, I think, watching her sit down beside our other housemate, Teddy.

Teddy grew up in Manhattan. For a while, her grandfather owned the Empire State Building. She was in rehab when she was seventeen, so she doesn't drink. Instead, she rolls these skinny joints, which she smokes like cigarettes. Deb sometimes says, "What do you think this is, an opium den?"

I watch Butter bum a smoke, one of the robin's egg blue cigarettes Teddy smokes. Ha. I swear it's Butter's second.

"So," Deb bellows, circling me like a ringmaster about to call out, *In the center ring* . . . "What . . . the . . . fuck, Bender? Look at your face." She gasps in mock horror. "What did you do? What did she do?"

"You should see the other guy . . . ," Teddy says, in this laconic tone that matches her black kimono. She takes a drag on a joint, barely glancing up from the crossword, which she always does in pen.

"Aw, you look foxy as ever," Jimmy says and winks at me— which is sweet—then starts strumming on his guitar and singing, "*Wild thing, you make my heart sing* . . ."

I take the joint from Teddy.

"Oh my god, don't encourage her," Deb says and, pretending she is talking into a microphone, goes, "Tragedy strikes *again* as another coed falls prey to battered party girl syndrome. Film at eleven."

Everybody laughs.

"Ha, ha. You're such a hoot," I say. "A real comedian. You oughta take this show on the road, Deb. Really."

Where the heck is Andy when I need him?

"Hey," I say, leaning back on the porch railing, letting the pot smoke drift out my nose the way Teddy did, "did anybody call Charlotte?"

The question just lays there in front of us, like a body. I don't know why I asked. I mean, I knew the answer already, but I asked it anyway. I knew what would happen. I couldn't help it. There is a silence, big, wide, like someone has turned off all the sound—except there is music coming from the stereo in the living room. Teddy and Butter look like I've punched them in the stomach. Deb stands up. "I have to pee," she says and leaves the porch.

"Sure, go pee," I say. "Why not? Go."

Jimmy doesn't look up, but his face and neck turn red. "Andy has Spanish with her, I'm sure he told her. He would tell her. I mean, she knows anyway—it's a tradition now."

It is tradition, but Charlotte didn't come last week, or the week before.

I knew the boys still loved Charlotte—that hadn't changed—but none of them had any idea what to say to her anymore. I mean, they were boys. It wasn't their fault or anything. But the thing that was their fault was they didn't go up to that frat house and beat the living shit out of that guy the way they said they were going to. They should have done that. They said they would, but they didn't.

Maybe if we hadn't told them that someone had returned her shoes the next morning. Just left them outside the door of her apartment. Maybe finding out other people knew what had happened let them think they were off the hook.

Andy said the fraternity had a moral obligation to punish him. He said he was friends with the president of the house, and he'd talk to him. He'd tell him what his *brother* had done. He promised he'd do it. He'd make it right.

He had to know I'd ask. He might have just lied. I didn't say I was disappointed when he told me he hadn't found the right time yet. It was a private matter. That's what he said, *a private matter*. I'd given him three days. Then I had to ask. I'd never seen anybody struck dumb with shame before. He stood there and flapped his hands, like what, he was a bird? A magician? What was he trying to make disappear?

I've learned that you shouldn't ask questions you don't want the answers to. Because it's nearly impossible to unknow something you know. Even if your brain forgets it, your body remembers.

All I knew was the guy was still at school.

I kept wondering, who brought her goddamn shoes back? And did he return them because he was a friend of hers and felt bad, or was he covering up for his brother—you know, getting rid of evidence she'd even been there. Been there and been so freaked out she'd run home without her shoes on. Or both? Was it possible that there could be someone who felt for both of them?

No way.

She was a virgin, you know. Not that it mattered, but it mattered.

After I say the thing about where is Charlotte, Butter says she thinks it is time to go, and I say I'm not ready to go yet. That I'm not even hungry yet; she says she is, and I suggest that she round up some of those yummy and nutritious celery sticks not being used to garnish to Blood Marys, or have some Cap'n Crunch. There are also donuts in the bathroom.

I wish Andy was here because whiny old Neil Young is

singing our song, "Like a Hurricane." It's not like we officially said, "Oh this is our song," it just is.

Then just as I am about to give up hope and go back to bed, I see Andy coming down the block. He has this slouchy walk, like he doesn't want you to see how tall he is. He stops and picks up one of the neighbors' trash cans that had fallen in the street. Who does that?

"You're here!" I hug him so hard, I knock his hat off.

"Whoa, careful, little girl," he says, catching it in midair, the way tap dancers do. I'm not sure, but I think he seems a little nervous.

"Where were you?"

Jimmy starts coughing.

"Nowhere," he says, his face red. He shakes his bangs into his face, then pushes them back. "Lemme see," he says, turning my chin to him, although I don't think he can see a thing behind the shades. I hope Deb is watching this. I am glad Butter isn't.

I follow him into the kitchen and sit on the counter watching him make toast with strawberry jam. He always cuts the bread on the diagonal. Why does everything taste better in a triangle?

"Oh no, it's a Towering Toast Inferno. Save yourself," I say, stealing a piece off the top. I'm waiting for him to say something like *Wow, who knew you were such a card shark, we made a hundred bucks last night.* You know, just a hint, when he goes, "So hey, Belinda, Cutty Sark tonight . . ."

It takes me a second. I'd sort of halfway forgotten he'd even invited me, because he'd stopped just short of actually asking, "Will you be my date?" Because that would sound too serious, just too freaky.

"I can't wait. It was the first thing on my mind when I woke up this morning."

"Really? Great. That's great. I was like, afraid with all that's going on, you might forget."

"Oh, come on. No way. I'm psyched."

"I think it'll be a good time. I mean it."

"Always," I say. "I'll have a great time. When have I ever not? We not?"

We both laugh, sort of nervously. Out of habit I reach up to fool with my pearls, but they aren't there, of course.

"I thought, maybe, you know, it would be fun before-hand . . . We could go out for dinner, before. Nothing, you know— Just eat real food for a change, nothing out of a can, or a box, no sauce you just add water to and stir. Wine."

Andy smiles, his hand reflexively covering his mouth, be-cause he's self-conscious about how crooked his bottom teeth are. Because he was the youngest of six, there wasn't money for braces. I wish he'd just smile normally. "I could swing by and pick you up—that would make the most sense, right?"

"Or, we could meet there," I say.

He looks pained. "What?"

"No, it's just . . . I was thinking I'd go check in on Char-lotte, but I don't have to—you know. Or"—I wait—"you could come with me?"

It had just come to me—it wasn't a lie—I'd just forgotten I wanted to do that. I could swing by, just for a few minutes even. Say hi. It was a good plan.

He looks flustered, I knew he would be, he'd understand. It was the sort of thing he'd do if he could. I knew he'd never say yes.

"No, you, you should go alone. That'd be better. I know she'd like that—to see you. Whatever. I can meet you there."

"Really? Only if you're sure," I say "She's expecting me at six. So, give or take, I'll be at the house at, what, seven?"

"Seven, seven thirty, whatever is cool. Party opens up at eleven."

It's always a bad idea to set an exact time to meet because you never know what might come up. But nothing is going to come up. Nothing could come up.

Then I have this brilliant idea. "Why don't you let me pierce your ear? You need an earring. You're supposed to be a pirate, right? It's about authenticity."

He laughs, like he thinks I am kidding around, but even so he reaches up and covers his ears. "I don't think so."

"Why not? It'll be fun," I say. "Live a little."

"Forget it. No way. I'm not going to become another one of your victims."

"You're not scared, are you? If you don't like it, you know, you can always take it out." I reach up and push the hair back away from his ear, and my fingers brush his neck. "I've done it a million times. So many times—do you know how many guys I've done, for Cutty Sark even—"

His fingers find his earlobe, like he's considering it. Why not?

Then for some reason, I don't know, I suddenly don't want to do it, don't want him to say yes.

"How can you call them victims? They come to me. I don't go looking for them."

Toby had heard I did ears, and I was good. He'd shown up at my door sophomore year with a six-pack, as payment. He was so cute I'd have done it for free, but he didn't have an earring with him. Anyway, I had this tiny silver and turquoise stud I'd gotten at a gift shop at the Grand Canyon; I hadn't worn it since I was like ten. I numbed his ear—two ice cubes for just a couple minutes. It wasn't nearly as good when it was frozen like steak.

Maybe it was the way the metal post looked as I started to push it against his earlobe, the way he winced when it went in, the pop of the piercing, the way the end came through the other side, but it was such a high. For a second, I couldn't even breathe. You know that saying *Better than sex*? It was way better. Way better than sex.

"So, I've just got to go into town real fast," Andy says. "I'll be back."

I suspect he'd gotten me a corsage.

"Come back, soon?"

"Will do," he says and tips his hat—that slays me.

I don't know how tired I am until I lay down on the sofa. It smells funny, like dog. I wonder how much pot that painted dog has had blown into his face over the years. How many tabs of acid have been dropped in his water bowl? How old was he anyway?

On the TV, Mighty Mouse is snorting the pollen out of a magic flower for energy. That is what I need if I am going to make it. Does anyone have any blow? Maybe Josh. Ha, that is funny.

Using the last of my strength, I reach over the arm of the sofa and drag some ugly gold blanket that looks like a curtain over me. It is a curtain, but who cares. It is brocade. Nobody seems to notice I'm not around. Which is fine. *Damage is getting done*, I think. It feels peaceful, and safe, on the sofa, under the curtain, falling asleep in front of the TV just like I did at home. I touch my eye, it hurts. I touch it again, it still hurts. One time, though, I know I'll touch it and it won't hurt as much, and I'll know it is getting better and soon I'll even forget it ever happened.

• • •

It hadn't been my idea to go to the farm bar last week. It was Deb's. She said we deserved it. It was one thirty in the morning and we'd been studying all night. I just didn't feel like going, but how would it look if Bender said no? No, it's a school night and my stomach hurts; *no,* I have a paper due on famous poisoners throughout history; and you know what, *no,* I don't feel like it because I keep thinking about what happened to Charlotte last week at that beach party.

Even if I'd said no, no one would have believed I was serious.

I didn't used to feel this way, but unless you're blotto, the best part of going to the farm is being able to say, *I went to the farm bar last night.* People look at you differently. It's sure not the sort of place you go on a date. It doesn't open until 3:00, and depending on how wasted you are it takes an hour or more to get there. There's no jukebox, no music at all, just a black-and-white TV behind the bar, and a radio set on the Weather Channel or the station that plays Bible sermons. No reason to go there except that it's the only place open at four in the morning that serves booze. No Johnnie Walker Black or Famous Grouse, just their poor relations Jack Daniel's and Rebel Yell.

The only bad thing was the floor. It had a rotten, sweet-sour smell like they'd never wiped up anything that spilled, just let it sink into the wood. The floor felt weirdly spongy when you walked on it. Otherwise, it was a perfect bar.

It was the middle of the goddamn night, so of course we were in our pajamas—but Deb called, nobody changes, not that anybody wanted to anyway. On the weekends we always go out in our nightgowns, into town for brunch, shopping. Our nightgowns, with the lace and the neck and wrists, were nicer than the dresses half the women in the state wore, and with pearls, we looked ready for church. My pearls were passed down from my grandmother to my mother to me. I was only supposed to wear them on special occasions, but because none of the girls at my school ever took theirs off, I didn't either.

Even though Charlotte wasn't feeling so social, it would have been weird for us not to invite her. We couldn't not ask her; if she found out it would hurt her feelings. And she wouldn't have to drive either like she usually did. Deb was going to drive. For once, Charlotte could get as hammered as she wanted—if she wanted. She could sit in the back with Butter and me. The thing is we all assumed someone else had called her. Nobody said a word when we drove past her house. It wasn't until we were literally there that we figured it out.

Deb said it was my job to call Charlotte. One simple job, she said. Butter didn't call because she said Charlotte had no business going out to bars. Teddy didn't bother because even if Charlotte were awake, she wouldn't answer the phone. Not only that a late-night phone call could set off a panic attack. Deb was driving. That left just me. They could pretend to be mad at me, but none of us wanted her to come.

A piece of string walks into a bar and asks for a beer. The bartender says, "Sorry, we don't serve string." So the string leaves, then comes back and again asks for a beer. The bartender says, "I told you we don't serve string." So the string leaves. Out in the alley the string rubs its body against the brick wall, then walks back into the bar and asks for a beer. And the bartender says, "Hey, weren't you the string that was just in here trying to order a beer?" And the string says, "No. I'm a frayed knot."

I couldn't even see the farm bar until we were almost on top of it because the black cinder blocks blend into the dark and there are no windows. It's like if you didn't know the bar was there, you'd never see it. But if you needed it, you'd spot it low down, sort of hunkering in the weeds.

The sky was that weird grayish color that tricks you into thinking dawn is right around the corner, but it's not. It's the time when all the animals that hunt at night, like owls and foxes, start crawling, or flying, or whatever—creeping back to their holes. You know, *Last call for field mice! You don't have to go home, but you can't eat 'em here!*

It wasn't a time you'd think of people being awake, and drinking, but the parking lot was jammed with rusty cars and hay wagons and tractors, pickup trucks with gun racks. I always wonder when a guy tells me I have a nice rack if that's like a gun rack, like deadly—or a rack of antlers, like a trophy you'd hang on the wall over your fireplace. Either way it's a compliment.

"You know this county has the highest incest rate in the entire country?" Deb said.

"Ah." Teddy sighed, making a frame with her fingers as she squinted at the bar. "I do adore early American bomb shelter architecture, don't you? When the big blast comes, the only survivors will be drunken farmhands and cockroaches."

The echo of our laughter bouncing back at us, across the fields, was a little creepy, like there was another set of us out there in the dark and we were throwing our laughter back and forth. Playing catch. Which made us laugh harder, and longer.

"You go first, Bender," Deb said, stopping right in front of the door to the bar. She rubbed my shoulders. She was practically daring me, so of course I opened it. It was heavier than you'd think. Like a test. If you can't open the door with one hand, you aren't man enough to get in. I'm stronger than I look.

When we walked into that bar in our gowns and matching pearls, the way those farmers turned and looked at us, we must have seemed like something out of a movie. A fantasy.

Men sat lumped shoulder to shoulder at the bar, or crowded around the tables. In their blue jeans and overalls, plaid work shirts and baseball caps, you could hardly tell the farmers apart, their faces as blank as cattle. Staring down into their beers, like the meaning of life was at the bottom. Even the ones in the safety orange caps and hunting vests only stood out because of the color.

As usual, I got elected to get the drinks. I didn't mind. I was the best one to go anyway. I mean, Butter looked like a toy in her sailor suit jammies and Deb was a chicken, and Teddy smoked blue cigarettes, for god's sake. Like my coach said, *Bender's not afraid to throw the trick.* It was a little weird to be there and not be wasted. Up at the bar there was a bowl of hard-boiled eggs. I wondered what my grandfather and dad would say if they saw me now, out here rubbing shoulders with the common man. There were probably some dairy farmers here.

I'd practically thrown my shoulder out trying to wave down the damn bartender when this guy in a red shirt and mustache sat down next to me with a cup of coffee.

"Well, hey there," he said, pushing his John Deere cap back. Maybe this was some form of tipping your hat. Maybe he'd take pity on me and wave down the bartender. "What's your name?" he said in that voice grown-ups use on children who insist on formally introducing them to their stuffed animals.

"Belinda," I said, without thinking. I never tell anybody I

meet in a bar my real name, or give him my real number. A girl needs to protect herself.

Maybe I forgot because he was a grown-up and I was raised to be polite to grown-ups and have good manners. Maybe I forgot because I'd never seen a man with brown hair but a red mustache, or a person who could smile with just his mouth and not his eyes.

He asked me, "Where you from, Belinda? Not around here."

"You're spot-on. I'm from England," I said in a British accent so thick you could roll me up in it like a rug. "London, actually." I could talk to anybody with this accent.

"London, huh. Never been," he said, picking up a hard-boiled egg and rolling it between his hands. "Been to Asia, though—you ever been to Asia, Belinda?"

He tapped the egg against his teeth until it cracked, then started peeling it and dropping the bits on the floor. Without its shell the egg looked wet and shiny in his hand. I swear it was the whitest thing I've ever seen.

"You're pretty far from home, aren't you?"

"Quite right. I'm at university in Wallingford."

He slipped the egg into his mouth whole. You could hear little bits of the shell crunching between his teeth.

Just kill me now, I thought.

"Yeah, I thought maybe. What're you doing here?" Then he said, "You sleepwalking?" Shaking me by the shoulder like he was trying to wake me up, and I realized, *Oh my god. I'm not wearing a bra. I should've worn a bra. What was I thinking?* I didn't think. I never think.

"Hey there, jumpy, jumpy," he said, massaging my shoulder. "Little jumpy." I tried to move away, but he had a hold on me. *Calm down,* I told myself. *At least you have underwear on, right?* Could he tell I didn't have a bra on? Sure he could. That's why he picked me.

Then he said, "That's a nice necklace you've got on there, *Belinda,*" hooking his pinkie under my pearls. I told myself, *Be a good sport, Belinda.* Then he gave it a tug, pulling me closer. Tug. *Worse things happen at sea.* Tug.

I told him to be careful.

"Be careful," he said, tugging on my pearls. Then he said, "I know why you're here." I realized he was looking at the hickey under my chin. He let go. *I can do anything for ten minutes.*

Then he said, "I know your type. You like it a little rough, *Belinda,* huh? Or," he said, a grin cracking across his face, "did you try to get smart with somebody, bad girl?"

He put his arm around me, his hand moving slow as a spider over my shoulder, down my collarbone, hanging there over my tits, then like by accident he touched my nipple, then again not by accident at all.

The sound came out by accident. It wasn't that loud either, but Deb and Butter must've heard because they froze like rabbits. The bartender heard it too, and came walking over to us. He'd make the asshole apologize to me. Give us drinks on the house. And that's when I'd kiss him. At the very least I'd kiss him.

The bartender stopped in front of us. He folded up his rag and put it down on the counter. *Now,* I thought. *Now you're going to get what you deserve, motherfucker,* I thought, *in front of all these people.*

"Thank you," I said to the bartender in my regular voice. I wanted him to know I was like him.

"Look at you," the bartender said, disgusted. "You ought

to be ashamed of yourself. What are you thinking coming in here like this?" It wasn't until he said, "It's indecent," that I knew he was talking to me.

"We just wanted a cocktail," I said, wanting to explain. "A nightcap." A pair of white-haired old men playing checkers, shots of whiskey set beside their cups of coffee, stared at me.

"I think it's time you and your girlfriends left. Now."

All those men in their baseball caps and overalls, their old Carhartt jackets and windbreakers with FORD or CHEVY on the pocket—all of them, brothers, fathers, grandfathers—they were looking at me with nothing but contempt. I thought, *Couldn't I be one of your daughters?*

Deb and Butter were waiting for me at the door. As we were leaving Deb pulled open the door, turned to face the room, and said loudly, "Fucking hicks."

And then we ran for it. I was halfway across the parking lot before I felt the first pearls spill down inside my nightgown, across my stomach, and out under the hem. I tried to grab the broken string but couldn't; the pearls were shooting through my fingers, bouncing and rolling across the parking lot, under cars and trucks, leaving a trail.

Ahead of me Butter and Deb, holding hands, bolted toward the car. "Bender, come on!" Deb screamed. Butter saw what happened and dared to slow down. "Your pearls, your pearls," she yelled, reaching down and grabbing at the gravel.

"Just go," I yelled, "it doesn't matter."

I wanted to stop. I wanted to stop. I wanted to stop and get down on my knees and rescue as many of my pearls as possible, but I couldn't. Why did I even have them on? They were the best things I had.

We jumped in the car. Deb gunned the engine, and we took off like a rocket, gravel shooting out from under our tires.

Deb cranked up the radio—and music came blaring out of the speakers. "Woo-hoo!" she screamed, pumping her fist.

Butter, who'd jumped in the front, reached back between the seats and said, "Hold out your hand." And then she handed me a pearl. "I'm sorry it's only one, ducks," she said, like it was breaking her heart.

In the rearview mirror you could see the cloud of dust we'd raised still hanging there. I should have been happy, right? But I didn't even want the pearl. It would just remind me that I'd lost the rest.

"Thanks," I said, wondering if I should maybe just drop it out the car window. Maybe some farm kid walking down the street would find it and think, *Wow, look at this.* And then they'd think that maybe the world wasn't as ugly as they thought it was. Maybe there was magic in it, after all.

When I wake up it's one o'clock in the afternoon, the Wake and Bake is over, and I'm in Andy's bed. Not on top, but under the sheets, tucked in, under an afghan you know somebody made him, still wearing his sunglasses. Being in my nightgown, like that, like I'd put it on last night to get into bed with him—I don't know, it wigs me out. And did I crawl into his bed—just snuggled right in—or had he put me in it?

Balanced on top of his bookcase are some artsy-looking black-and-white photographs of trees. There is a guitar in the corner, and a pile of library books. I didn't even know he had a guitar.

"Hey, sleepyhead," Andy says. He is sitting at his desk like he's been studying, but I don't think he has been. "I was getting worried about you. You were dreaming."

"How did I get up here?"

"I carried you, of course. You fell asleep on the couch in front of the TV." He doesn't say *passed out*. He says *fell asleep*. This is why I loved him.

I could see a life with Andy, a fun, wonderful life. The two of us traveling around the world, me speaking French, him speaking Spanish, cocktailing in all the most fashionable bars, me getting drunk and dancing on tables, and him carrying me out in his arms, my high-heeled shoes dangling from his fingers.

My angel, he'd say, looking down at me.

My hero, I'd say, looking up at him.

Strangers would look at us and think how glamorous we were. They'd look at us and think, *There is a perfect couple.*

He says, "Deb was threatening to give you a mustache. You know, so you'd look like a pirate—for Cutty Sark."

"What a sweetheart. She worries about my inability to accessorize." I sit up in bed. "Did Charlotte ever show up?"

"Don't know but I've been up here studying for Econ. I haven't seen her." He looks embarrassed.

"I need to call her." I keep forgetting. "How did I get up here?"

"I carried you. You fell asleep on the sofa."

"No, no, no. What is going to become of me?" I groan. Without thinking I touch my eye. It still hurts.

He blushes. "It's my pleasure. I'm sure you'd look real cute with a mustache too, but . . ."

"No, really, Andy. What would I do without you?"

He picks up an autographed baseball he is using as a paperweight off his desk. Downstairs someone put Neil Young's *Rust Never Sleeps* back on; everyone was singing along to *"Hey Hey, My My."*

"When I was a kid, my friends and I used to sing, *Hey, hey, my, my, none of us will never die.* Isn't that stupid?" I say. Actually, no one but me had sung that.

"Not stupid," Andy said. "Just immature, you were a kid. I can see the point. I like your way better too." Sometimes he seems so much older than me.

"Me too," I say, thinking, *I could wake up every day in this bed. That'd be good, wouldn't it?* "What would I ever do without you?" I tell him. "I'd be lost."

Andy gets up from his desk like something is about to happen, but then he just walks over and looks out the window. "I guess when school is over, this is all over too?" he says in a faraway voice. "We'll go to different cities, get jobs . . ."

"Don't say that," I say. "What about Paris? I want to go to Paris."

"City of lights, city of love," he says. "You'd do great there. You could be an actress, or something else creative."

"I think I would." Why not Paris?

"You would too," I say. He'd get used to it.

He sort of laughs, and comes over to sit on the edge of the bed. Then without warning he reaches over and starts to take his sunglasses off my face. "Let me see," he says. "Up close. Someone should look at it."

I curl up into a ball. "No, no, no. Trust me. You don't want to."

"They're mine, aren't they?"

He knows they are. I wouldn't lie and say they were some other guy's. So, I let him do it. He studies my eye, like it's a problem he's pretty sure he can fix. He very gently examines the swelling, the bruising on my eyebrow, without ever looking into my eye.

"Don't worry, you can't hurt me."

When he pulls down my lid with his thumb, I automatically shut the other one. I feel his breath, then the pressure of his lips against my eyelid.

He stays like that for just a second, then sits up. When he does, he has the look, his eyes sort of dreamy and half closed; he is staring at my mouth, he is tilting his head—

His sheets are tucked in so tight around me. I can feel the stubble on my legs.

"Hey, Belinda," he says leaning in and I panic. I turn my head and yawn, like I have no idea he was about to really kiss me, but he knows and I know. It's impossible to un-know something. The way he recovers by pretending he's reaching past me, across the bed to adjust the afghan. I hate myself. Just kill me now, I think.

"Okay, so, yeah, since the patient seems to be resting comfortably, I'm going to go and grab a cold one," he says heading for the door. "You stay here. I'll be right back. Can I get you anything?" His voice has like ice in it.

"Surprise me." In a minute I'll be gone.

Before I leave I pull the covers so you'd never even know I'd been there.

There's this other Neil Young song that should be on my funeral playlist, but I can't have two and I can never remember the title anyway, but the line that always gets stuck in my head is: *And once you're gone you can't come back. When you're out of the blue and into the black . . .* It's like the saddest song in the world. You can't stand it.

Back home I chug the last half of a bottle of NyQuil and climb into my turned-down bed. When I wake up it is dark, and Butter, Deb, and Teddy are all gone. There is a note from Butter on the floor by my bed.

Charlotte's gone. Her parents came and got her.

I have to read it a couple of times. Then I get up and start digging through my drawers, pulling books off my shelves. *Frankenstein, The Bell Jar, Now We Are Six,* but goddamnit—I got *nada.* I have this thing where I like to hide drugs from myself. That way when I find them it's like this nice surprise. I'm happy. Finding a snow seal of cocaine is better than Christmas. On the plane ride home at Easter, I had one of those Bic pens in my mouth, and suddenly my tongue went numb. I guess I'd taken it apart so I could do lines in the library bathroom during midterms. That was sweet.

Only I can't find anything, nothing except for two NoDoz, which I chop up on my dresser with my school ID and halfheartedly try to snort. But it's real sticky, so mostly, I have to jam it up there with my finger. Hey, *if you got 'em, snort 'em.*

It occurs to me that I could call Andy—Charlotte is gone—and we could go to his party together, but then it seems like more trouble than it's worth.

My next imaginary boyfriend is going to be named Tex, he's going to have a gold tooth and a motorcycle and carry lots of cash.

In the hall I check my wench costume—the low-cut blousy white shirt pulled off the shoulder, a tight red-and-black skirt that laces up the back—in the full-length mirror, admiring the great job I've done masking my black eye with foundation and lots of liner (I only look a little bit like a battered wife), and then—hope springs eternal—I lift the mirror off the wall, lay it on the floor, and on my hands and knees lick around the edges.

● ● ●

I arrive at the party at 8:00. I've had two beers and hope that Andy has had twice that many. The NoDoz has done nothing but make me jittery. Even though I'm fashionably late, nothing seems to be happening yet. The lights are bright, and the music isn't loud enough, and everybody looks about thirteen. All I can see are these dorky little sailor boys and Captain Hooks, paired up with their perky wenches, all of them drinking punch. I feel like I'm spying on Peter Pan's bar mitzvah. I can't be sure Andy's even there.

Across the street, I spy that stupid painted dog from town, staggering back up the hill toward the fraternities. The *Don't Paint on Me* is wearing off. Now it says, *Don't Pain on Me*. That's pretty funny. I whistle for it to come, but it ignores me. No one else even notices this dog, or cares. That bloody dog slept with guys who fed it mushrooms, and laughed when it peed on itself. And it couldn't stop for me? Here I was feeling all sad for it, and maybe it liked being painted on.

Down the street on the lawn outside of his fraternity is Josh, along with the rest of the rugby team in their black-and-yellow striped jerseys, like a bunch of bees, hovering around the keg. I know what I need to do. One last time, just say good-bye. Make it official.

I go in through the back. Downstairs, the hall smells of dirty shorts, spilled beer, hash, and peanut butter. It makes me sort of sad to think that after college I'll never smell this boy-smell again. I sit down at Josh's desk and stick one of his paper clips in my pocket.

Then I'm up in his loft bed. When he comes in and locks the door, I am pulling off my blouse.

"I have a girlfriend. A serious girlfriend."

I wait.

"You can't keep coming here like this."

"Like this? When was the last time I was here?" I say, trying to sound lighthearted, and teasing, but I want to know. I
wait for him to say something, anything. Just one clue about
whether I'd been with him last night.

"You've got to go," he says. I can hear his resolve slipping
away. After all, we have a thing. I know he wants me.

"This is the last time—" I say.

He sighs.

"Uh-huh," he says, turning off the lights so it is totally dark
except for the ones on the stereo, and they don't look like
stars, just bright yellow holes.

He climbs up into the loft and pulls off his shirt and shorts.
He smells like sweat and beer. He turns me over, lays me
facedown, stretches my arms and legs into an X, lifts my butt,
and pushes in. "You're going to take this?" he says, his voice
shaking, going farther. He collapses behind me. He doesn't lie
beside me and fall asleep. Nothing normal.

I don't get a chance to ask him if he has any coke.

Then groggily he says, "I gotta go. Don't fall asleep." He
runs his hand over my head, not unkindly, like I am a doll.

I wake up with a start, the party in full thunder over my
head, and unable to breathe. It is almost midnight. Outside
I take off like I'm running for my life and I will press charges
against whoever is chasing me. I would. I would do it.

The fraternity house looks like it is on fire inside. All
the lights are on, blazing. Two guys in bandannas, striped
shirts, and raggedy cut-up pants are up on the wall outside
the house, beers in hand, waving plastic swords and screaming, "Shiver me timbers!" Fun. The front hall is just a mass
of people. Smoky and hot. As soon as I walk through the
door I'm swallowed up, sucked into the center, spun around,
squeezed, and then forced out the back door. Someone hands

me a cup of rum punch and I pound it. I can't stop shaking, my arms and legs all loose in their sockets. I don't see Andy anywhere. Not on the dance floor, or by the bar in the other room. I need a minute to think. Maybe he just didn't feel like dancing since I wasn't there. That would be like him, not to dance with another girl even though his date hadn't shown up yet. How could I have made him wait? Made him worry. I hear someone say I've just missed seeing a guy who had tried to throw an empty keg off the back porch sail over the wall still holding on to it, and fall two stories. He'd gotten up, perfectly fine. I take this as a sign that this is a lucky night.

I hope Andy is drunk. Maybe he won't know what time it is. Maybe he's been drowning his sorrows, afraid I wasn't going to show up. I ask a guy I think is his little brother if he's seen him. "Last I saw he was serving punch," he says.

Thinking of Andy standing there alone by the punch, sober, a ladle in his hand, bandanna on his head, and a plastic eye patch, serving people, breaks my heart. Is is possible that he just left? He's mad at me, no, worse, worse, disappointed. Maybe he is at home watching TV in the dark and finishing off the keg. I'd do another circuit, ask around, then I'd call. No. I'd just run to his house. I'd surprise him. I'd show up with something—some ice cream, some wine, a twelve-pack. We'd get a little wasted and I'd let him kiss me, and I'd like it. A few more and one thing would lead another, and I'd want him. I know I could do it.

That would make everything all right, wouldn't it? I wondered what he thought I would be like. He must have wondered.

I am on my way out, pushing my way through the crowd, when I feel it. An idiot girl, not even in costume, has doused me with punch. My hand flies to my throat. No pearls.

I stand there dripping wet, my white shirt soaked red, stuck to my skin and stained beyond repair.

"Oops," she giggles, and covers her mouth, which seems to be all gum. "Ouchy, you have a black eye." Another time I'd have returned the favor, and thrown my drink back at her, but I don't. *Don't let her know you felt it,* I say to myself. I'm not supposed to be alone. I am supposed to be with Andy. I am his date. They should all know that. I'm not alone. Are that girl and her friend laughing at me? *See, Andy . . . what did we tell you?* I'm sure I heard my name. I don't recognize any of them.

I don't know where the voice comes from, but I hear it clear as day. "Andy's gone. He left."

With who?

"Hours ago."

I have to push people away to keep moving, saying to myself. *Keep going. You're doing great. You can do anything for ten minutes. Just get outside.* But there are people on the lawn too; I can't tell where the party starts and where it ends.

I'm going to run home. I'm going to run to Andy. I'm going to as soon as I catch my breath. I notice someone has left a full beer on the wall behind me. A gift. I sit down and lean against the wall.

But what if Andy didn't go home? Had he gone after Charlotte's guy? What if I went home and he wasn't there? Then, there I'd be, all alone. He might be looking for me. I should just wait. He had to come back.

And when Andy comes back, he is going to say, "I'm sorry I left."

And I am going to say, "Oh, it doesn't matter now. We found each other."

And he'll say, "You're right."

And I'll kiss him and say, "I guess it's destiny."

And he'll say, "I always knew it was."

And we'll both be thinking—I don't ever want to forget how happy I am right now.

So, I wait and I wait. Once, I see a shadow of a boy that looks like Andy, walks like Andy, coming up the hill but that boy's holding someone's hand, so it can't be him. When the real Andy finally shows up it's almost dawn.

"It's done," Andy says staring at his shoes, his mouth looks pink and puffy. He doesn't have to tell me. I already knew. I know.

I say, "Better late than never."

I want to tell Andy that Charlotte's already gone home, but what's the point? I pick my cuticle till it bleeds. Andy looks up, studies the empty sky hard, like he's afraid it's going to storm.

I say, "Here is a good one. A cat and a dog are sitting next to each other on a plane . . ."

He gives me a tired smile. I know he has low expectations.

"However, it is a short flight and they do not talk to each other."

He says, "Is that supposed to be funny?"

"No," I say. "It's sad."

I'm Only Going to Tell
You This Once

"M om," Sam calls from the den. "I need to talk to you about
something."

I know what is coming.

"Mom?" he tries again, louder and deeper. "Mom."

"Okay," I say.

I'm still not used to how my son's voice has changed. I miss
the days when it went in and out of tune. When I could pass
off a pubic hair in the laundry as an eyelash.

I sit down at the kitchen table and fold my hands—then
unfold them. I don't care. I won't call her his *girlfriend*. I
won't. She's *Candy*, and I hate her.

Roger, looking bemused, doesn't lift his eyes from the old
copy of *The New Yorker* he's been flipping through for the past
half hour.

"He's eighteen, Heather."

"He's seventeen. What twenty-one-year-old woman wants
to be with a seventeen-year-old boy?"

"I was older than you when we met."

"Don't be an ass, Roger," I snap. "That's different. He's

barely shaving. She doesn't wear a bra." Candy was curvy and bronzed and wore loose Indian-print blouses cut low so you could see her beautiful, honey brown tits. No tan lines.

"Neither did you when we met."

"This is different. Her name is Candy."

"I miss those days, dearly."

"Candy!"

"I think it's sweet."

"Laugh. Make jokes," I say. "You do that. You only like her because she flirts with you, and makes you feel like you're not an old man." She'd gushed over Roger's collection of original Dylan bootlegs like they were the Dead Sea Scrolls, while Sam and I rolled our eyes.

"Is that so wrong?" Roger says.

"She's a barracuda. She's got an overbite, her eyes are too close together—she looks like a cigar with teeth."

"Come now, Heather. You can't deny she's an attractive girl."

"She's slow."

I'd never seen anyone move at such an exaggeratedly leisurely pace, every step flaunting her lack of interest in or concern for others. Candy knew she didn't have to hurry, because she knew and you knew, you'd wait. I hated watching Sam standing at the door waiting for her, like a dog waiting to be taken for a walk.

"Stop it. She's not slow. She's rather bright, I think."

I'm sure when Roger's whacking off in the shower, it's to Candy. Candy slinking barefoot across our kitchen floor with Freud balanced on her head.

"Oh well, bright, attractive, braless. Perhaps you'd like to date her, Roger?" I give him a look. No doubt he suspects that I'd prefer he was the one sleeping with Candy.

I pour myself more coffee, then for Roger, although why I'm

waiting on him is beyond me. "You know he sneaks her into the house, don't you? I'm not an idiot. She's hardly discreet. You can hear the bells on that stupid silver anklet all the way down the hall. I suppose that's so she can't creep up on birds."

Sam's sheets reek of patchouli. *Patchouli to mask the stink of sex on her skin.* I wonder if he knows I'm onto them, if he even cares.

I hear the toilet flush. Lately Sam has started shutting the door when he pees, but sometimes he still forgets. I hear him coming down the hall.

For many years, like clockwork, it was the sound of Sam's footfalls padding quickly down the hall toward our bedroom in the morning that woke me up. When he woke in the night with a fever, or a bad dream, the moment his toes touched the ground I was awake. Roger never heard him. It was a mother thing. I just knew.

"I told him she's not allowed to spend the night. It's not acceptable . . ."

Roger looks at me like who am I to lecture anyone.

He downs the coffee I just poured him. I've always wondered at his ability to withstand heat. Depending on my mood, I attribute this to a sort of dumb insensitivity, other times it's strength.

Either way it's a metaphor for our marriage.

A week after graduating from college I left the East Coast for a job at an environmental organization, S.O.S., or Save Our Seas, in Seattle. The pay amounted to a handful of shiny shells, but I was young and idealistic. I imagined being part of a human chain of activists protecting the ocean and her inhabitants from extinction by any means necessary. One day it would be hand-to-hand combat with the crew of a Japanese whaling boat, the next rescuing near-death pelicans and sea turtles Exxoned in the gulf. I pondered getting a tattoo of waves around one of my ankles. *I've got one foot on land, one foot in the sea.*

The reality was I spent the day on the phone soliciting money from people who considered the ocean little more than a wave machine, an exotic fish toilet. I licked stamps, picked up laundry, and made copies. The reality was I was as far away from home as I could be without leaving the country, and that was all that mattered.

I'd become a regular at a bar that for months played a loop of raceway crashes during happy hour. Cars spinning out of control, smashing into the wall, erupting in smoke and flames. I knew to the second the moment the car was going to flip. When it would break in two. Whether the driver would get out or not. Some people complained that it was upsetting, tasteless. Even if the driver got out alive, who knew if he lived, or how disfigured he'd be. It was an auto-erotic snuff film. Foreplay at two hundred miles an hour.

Then one day they stopped playing it. The bartender said he wasn't sure if they'd lost the tape, or if the owner got sick of customers bitching that it was either too violent or not violent enough. Even so, I kept going back, hoping to see it one more time.

In that bar and other bars like it, places that don't cultivate regulars, I met men. When they approached me, I'd tell them, "The last man who loved me killed himself. I want to warn you. I'd expect no less devotion from you." After that either they'd run, thinking I was going to pour out my heart to them, or they'd lean closer and say, "He killed himself, huh? You're that good?"

And I'd say, "No. That bad," and flash them my new man-eating grin.

I told Roger this on our first date. "I'm trouble," I said over roast beef en croûte, and a red wine he'd ordered ahead of time so it could breathe.

"Trouble?" He speared a piece of meat on his fork. "Excellent."

Roger was ten years older than me, and in the middle of an amiable divorce; his wife, also a psychologist, was, he said, *a great mind, a wonderful mother,* and—as if I needed the fact that they no longer had sex spelled out—*a Scrabble champion.*

I told him that in my early twenties I'd sought out men who avoided tenderness like a flesh-eating virus. Men who would rather have the clap for a lifetime than a girlfriend for a year; men whose names I never asked and, if they'd ever told me, I'd forgotten.

Roger passed off my wild past as a stage. Normal. On the pathology scale it fell somewhere after shoplifting and before arson. He would fault my parents—classic narcissists, who had flirted with the swinger lifestyle in the seventies—for not paying better attention to me.

Over a second round of after-dinner drinks, I told Roger I had a reputation in high school. He responded with an intentionally comical leer. "Why Heather Chase, you were a bad girl?" he said, the brandy slurring the *l* in *girl,* so it sounded like *grrrr.* I should have been amused, but I wasn't.

"No. I was a good girl with a bad reputation."

"Ah." He steepled his fingers and nodded in that way shrinks do. "The kind of girl you don't take home to meet your mother?"

"The kind of girl who *doesn't want* to meet your mother."

"That's fortunate. My mother is dead."

"The kind of girl who *doesn't want* to be a mother."

"Ah." He nodded again.

"The kind of girl who'd forget her kid's birthday."

Roger looked at me expressionless as the Sphinx.

"The kind of girl who'd leave her kid in a bus station with a Free to a Good Home sign around their neck."

"First," he said gently, "you're *not* a girl, you're a *woman*. Second, people change." He discreetly signaled the waiter for the check. "They grow up."

Months later, we got engaged and he named his new boat *The Troublemaker*, after me. A year later, I was pregnant.

I don't think Roger imagined I'd turn into Mother of the Year overnight, but when after three months I was still calling our son "the baby" instead of his name, Sam, I know it concerned him.

This time, he said, he was going to do fatherhood right. He wanted to be around more, and more involved in his son's life than he had been with his girls, despite the fact each had graduated from an Ivy League college and appeared to be a model citizen. This meant being home from work by 6:30. Shelving Sibelius for Baby Mozart, scooting around on the floor in sweats. This meant me coming home to find him lying beached on the living room rug surrounded by toys and the butts of teething biscuits, the baby crawling over him like a fly. I'd just as soon have fucked Barney.

He wouldn't admit it, but I think my husband also wanted to keep an eye on me.

Roger had noticed the scar on the inside of my arm the third time we had sex.

"What happened here?" he'd asked afterward, running his fingers over the letters *Willjay* like he was reading Braille. He looked younger without his glasses on.

"Where?" I turned my arm over so he could see it better. It had faded a lot in ten years. "Oh, there's a story to that," I said.

"I imagine so," he said.

"The summer between my junior and senior years of college the boy I loved died."

"I'm sorry to hear that," Roger said, laying his hand on my stomach.

"So I carved his name into the inside of my arm with a paper clip."

I had never experienced that level of pain or that much blood. My arm wet with it like paint. It made me feel better. For months I'd picked at the letters, peeling up the scabs like tape. It had taken a long time for the pink to fade to white.

"I didn't want to forget," I said.

"Hmm," Roger said. "But some things you're supposed to forget, little bunny. One has to forget. Not completely, of course, but memories have to fade. Otherwise one can't get on with the business of living."

I put my hand over the scar. Writing the word on my body in pen hadn't been enough.

"Well, it's barely visible now," he said in a misguided attempt to make me feel better. "You can hardly see it. I'd never noticed it before. It healed nicely."

"Put your glasses on," I said. "It's very noticeable when I tan."

I shouldn't have expected him to understand.

The only person who had ever understood was a girl I'd worked with briefly at S.O.S. By all accounts, we had nothing in common. I doubted her conviction, certain that Emily, despite her professed love for all sea creatures, would be perfectly happy if the oceans were turned into a gated community for just dolphins, sea turtles, and clownfish. She reminded me of the girls I'd grown up with. Spoiled, undeniably pretty girls who tirelessly solicited compliments by claiming to be disgusted by their looks (too fat, too thin), who'd beg you to order nachos or fries *to share!* and then, claiming loss of appetite, sit and stare at you while you ate like they were watching porn. Who one day are your best friends and the next the agents of your destruction.

So, I was taken aback when, as we stood washing our hands in the bathroom at the same time, she asked me about my scar. I'd told her the story without hesitation, expecting, hoping to shock and horrify her. I'd done neither. In fact, she thought carving Jay's name into my arm was terribly romantic. Jay and I were so like Tristan and Isolde—deeply in love and tragically fated to die, both of a broken heart. She was jealous, she said, and she envied my passion.

A few weeks later, she quit. She'd broken up with her boyfriend, and her mother had sent her a plane ticket. After hearing my story, she realized the man she loved could never possibly cherish her enough to do what I had done for Jay.

We'd hardly known each other, and yet here I was, all these years later, remembering her. It's funny how that works.

I told Roger, "It hurt." I had really wanted him to understand.

"We'll have to make sure that never happens again," he said cheerily, as though, if I stuck with him, he could ensure this. Then he sighed. "I wish I'd known you then."

"No you don't," I said roughly. "You see, there were two boys, not one. One was my boyfriend; the other was his best friend. Will and Jay. They were like brothers. So close their mothers called them in to dinner by one name: Will-jay." *Will Jay? Yes he will.* "Have you ever heard anything like that?"

Roger listened, nodding almost imperceptibly, just enough to encourage the patient to continue.

"I know it's hard to believe, but in my glory days, men fought over me." I was aware of how ridiculous I sounded, pathetic even, but I couldn't help it. It was true.

"I'm sure," he said evenly.

I got out of bed. "I still feel guilty," I said, pulling on my jeans. "I couldn't love one boy enough, and I couldn't love the other less."

"Well," he said, "what could you have done differently?"

Under my breath I say, "He's not taking the car tonight, Roger. He's not. I mean it."

"He respects his curfew," my husband says, as though logic has any place in the discussion. "He's a good kid."

He was a good kid. His teachers always pointed out how kind he was to the other kids—the bird-with-a-broken-wing type—a peacemaker. Everybody wanted their kid to be friends with Sam. It was a testament to Sam's charm. I never made friends with those women. They had no interest in having coffee with me.

"Be reasonable, Heather. Come now. Let him live a little." Roger sways his hips like he's doing the samba. "Have some fun."

"Fun?"

Roger's attention snaps back to his magazine.

"Did somebody say *fun*?" Sam is standing in the doorway

in jeans worn white through at the knees and an ancient, now too small green T-shirt that says LOVE YOUR MOTHER EARTH.

Here is what it feels like when Sam walks into a room: It's as though a party is about to start, the light changes, and the air thrums with expectation that at any moment music is going to come on. "I heard the word *fun*," he says, loping into the kitchen, all arms and legs. "You talkin' about me?" Even his bad De Niro imitation is charming. "I don't see anybody else here." He checks over both shoulders. "So, I know you must be talking about me."

"Who else?" Roger smiles with bemusement and closes his magazine in expectation of what comes next.

"Yeah, I thought so," Sam says, half falling, or half diving, into the chair beside me. He's still getting used to driving his new, man-size body. He kisses me on the cheek. "Hey, Mom," he says and scoots his chair closer to the table. My boy smells like cut grass and bike grease and . . . what? Christ. Is that sandalwood? Has that bitch got him wearing sandalwood?

"Hello," I pause, "you," and brush his shaggy blond hair away from his face. He's been growing it out. It's now almost to his shoulders. In a few months my son's hair will be bleached white and he'll be wearing his puka shell necklace, although I've told him, for his own good, it's a fashion faux pas. Even in the seventies, they were only cool for fifteen minutes. Then he'll remind me that in Hawaii sailors and surfers wear puka shells for good luck, to ensure a safe voyage home. What can I say? I can imagine living without Roger but never Sam. In a few months, as ever, he'll have a cold sore on his lip from the sun. I'll be the only one in the world who'll let him kiss me. I'm sure that he's never noticed that the place where he always gets his cold sore is the mirror image of where I always get mine.

When Sam was little I called him *my most beautiful*

boy, and he would call me *my most beautiful mommy*. Even though it's silly, I still address his birthday cards *To my most beautiful boy*.

Last summer, standing in line at the snack shack on the beach, I saw a young man five or six people ahead of me, tan, shirtless, purple boxers riding up over the top of his board shorts—bright, flashy plumage—and just as I was thinking *Would you look at that gorgeous ass*, he turned around to take out his wallet and said, "Hey there, Mom . . ."

I was stunned.

"Can I get you anything?"

"No. I'm covered," I stammered, waving my ten-dollar bill at him. He was such a good son. "Do you want anything else?"

"Nah. I'm cool," he said, raising his iced tea, extra lemon, to me.

It took days to get over that.

"Soooooo," Sam says. "Are you guys talking about me borrowing the car?" He drums his fingers on the edge of the table, looking at me hopefully. He's started plucking the hairs between his eyebrows.

"Ah, that's my cue," Roger says, straightening up. "I'm late." As he walks past Sam, he puts his hand on his shoulder and whispers loudly, so I can hear: "Good luck, son." Then he winks at him. He winks.

"Thanks," Sam says, patting his dad's hand.

Roger has coached him. Is he joking? Does he seriously believe teaming up against me will work? Roger may be Sam's father, but Roger has daughters. Sam belongs to me.

He knows I want Sam to be happy. I want him to fall in love.

I'm just praying that it will be with a man, not a woman. Women are nothing but trouble.

• • •

Will was the first boy I ever loved. I was twenty, and after dating him for nearly nine months—a personal best—spending a day apart, let alone an entire summer, had been unthinkable.

I'd never really been a girlfriend before. I wasn't that kind of girl. It had never appealed to me, but Will wanted that. He wanted to hold hands and carry my books and be seen holding my hand and carrying my books. "I want the whole world to know you're mine," he'd say. "My girlfriend," he'd say, then kiss me like that made it official. He was like that, always filled with purpose and energy; it was how he moved, as though he was on the way to a podium to give a speech or accept an award.

He bought me flowers, and little gifts—gold knot earrings, pearl button mittens and a matching pink scarf—for no reason at all except he said he liked seeing them on me.

Until Will, my longest relationship, if you can call it that, was in high school with a wrestler, and it was secret. We never went out, we just hid out in his room having sex with the TV on. It wasn't healthy.

Will was everything I was not. He was popular and likable. He managed to seem both familiar and special at the same time. Will wasn't the sort of person you whispered about. He wasn't the subject of rumors. No matter how loud or rowdy he became, bartenders never cut him off. Any run-ins with authority all ended in warnings. Boys will be boys. Everyone knew he'd grow out of it and into the kind of man they could one day brag they'd known when he was just a kid. In part, it was his confidence. A quiet confidence that sprang from being told every day of his life how special he was; it made him appealing to women while being nonthreatening to men.

I hadn't asked my parents if I could live with Will and

his parents for the summer, I'd told them. If I'd expected any sort of resistance, I'd have been disappointed. My mother was thrilled. The fact that the suburb where Will's family lived was famed for having been home to more senators than any other town in America would alone have been good enough for her.

My father at least had the decency to ask if I had a job yet. He'd asked me three times, in fact. The third time I realized that calling my parents any time after eight in the evening— the cocktail bell went off at six, or after three on the weekends—was a waste of time.

I told him that Will, who already had an internship lined up working as a clerk for a very influential judge on Capitol Hill, had been confident that I'd get one of the highly coveted internships at the National Aquarium on my own merits, but just to be sure, he'd gotten his father, a lawyer who had a client on the board, to make a call.

Three days a week, I'd work in the touch pool, the aquarium's answer to a petting zoo. Urging the squeamish to just pet the sea anemone while keeping the enthusiasts from peeling the starfish off the rocks and the sadists from violating the sea cucumbers quickly became tedious. The best part of the job was when a kid, the one kid who, even if they had a buddy, was alone in the group, would come up to the water, and I could get them to stroke the wing of the mantra ray. *Look, it feels like wet velvet.*

From the very beginning, Will had talked about Jay. He was the costar of all Will's best stories. Stolen golf carts driven into the water hazard on the eighteenth hole, a summer spent breaking into each and every one of their neighbors' swimming pools, M-80s set off in a graveyard behind a church.

Even if I hadn't known all about Jay before I met him, I'd still have known him the moment I saw him.

• • •

Sam sits up straight, and laces his fingers together, ready to argue his case. "Listen, Mom, about the car. I know, I know, I know how you feel, I get it—I swear—and I promise in, like, two months I will never bug you about borrowing the car again. Okay?" He crosses his heart. "Cross my heart and hope—"

"You know I hate that saying."

He holds up three fingers in the Boy Scout salute.

"Okay, swear to god."

Sam had fortunately lost interest in scouting when he discovered it wasn't all sleeping under the stars, starting fires, and whittling. Perhaps I should have encouraged him to continue. He might have found a love interest who knew how to use a compass.

"Really, why is that?"

"Well, see, I've been thinking. I know what a hassle me needing the car all the time is, right? Bugging you and Dad. I'm sorry about that. And I have a solution, I think. What if I was living at the beach this summer? That would solve a lot of problems, right? You know, I could get a job at the marina, sail. I wouldn't need wheels there. I can bike or board everywhere." He leans back in his chair, full of confidence.

"The beach?" I ask, straining to contain my incredulity. "Alone? You're seventeen, Sam."

"I'll be eighteen in a month, Mom," he reminds me. "And I won't be alone. You'll come visit whenever you want. The ocean's your thing, swimming in the waves, collecting shells. Some of our greatest times have been at the beach. It'd be so chill. We could take the boat out, do some waterskiing, you and me."

He thinks that is the key, *You and me.* He tips back farther

in his chair, balancing on two legs. He's not that much different than he was when he was ten years old.

I pretend to ponder this, then ask, "What do you do if
you're out in the water and you get attacked by a shark?" How
many times have we done this? From the time he was three
until about ten or eleven, it was like a comedy routine we per-
formed for guests.

What to do if you're attacked? We'd started with bears—
play dead; killer bees—*run through tall grass;* and ended with
sharks.

Sam sighs but delivers his line perfectly: "When attacked
by a shark, punch or kick him in the nose." He used to act out
the punching and kicking—that was a crowd pleaser—but he
doesn't do that now.

"Why do sharks attack people on surfboards?"

"Because they look like seals . . . Mom," he says, exasperated, and rocking forward brings the front legs of the chair
banging back down on the floor. "Can we please get back to—"

"What do you do if you're out in open water and you en-
counter a full-size Portuguese man-of-war? Tentacles fifty feet
long."

He looks flummoxed, annoyed.

"Here, I'll help you. There's nothing you can do but hope
you're washed ashore so your body isn't lost at sea."

"Um, okay . . . Mom, but what does this have to do—"

"Can you tell me how is it that a translucent blue bubble
resembling a lady's hat, that doesn't even attack but just drifts
with the wind, can kill you with a touch but a bloodthirsty,
two-ton killing machine with a double row of razor-sharp
teeth can be beat off with a kick in the head?"

"I don't know, Mom. How?"

"I don't know either."

Why isn't it called a Portuguese woman-of-war?

I ought to know this. I used to know everything.

When Sam was maybe five, he'd asked me what the scar was on the inside of my arm. It had faded so you could only make out the swirl of letters. I told him I'd accidentally swum into some stinging coral. "Probably fire coral," he'd said with great authority.

"I bet you're right," I'd told him. "I wish it was a better story. I could make one up for you, if you want?"

After that, I started putting vitamin E on it.

Sam pushes away from the table, chair scraping across the floor, and heads for the fridge. "Here's the deal, Mom. Candy and some of her friends are renting a place at the beach this summer, a huge house, like ten rooms," he says, putting the kitchen island between the two of us, as though he's lit the fuse on a firecracker and is now taking cover. "Dad already said he was cool with it."

"He did, did he?"

Over the last few years, I'd come to think of Roger's and my marriage as a glacier. A beautiful block of ice which one day, beaten by sunlight and time, despite appearing blindingly solid and virtually unmoving, became two. There was nothing wrong with that. We were still in the same waters, still touching.

"This thing with Candy is real, Mom," Sam says defensively. "I know you can't understand it—"

"I understand." He can't imagine that I know what it's like to be in love at his age. "I understand better than you think."

He rolls his eyes. "Okay then, so, what's the problem?"

He takes a club soda out of the fridge and pops the top. When it starts to fizz he presses his mouth to the top to stop it from frothing over. Club soda is more grown-up than Mountain Dew.

"I thought she had a boyfriend, Sam."

"Used to. Used to have a boyfriend. It's over—which is why I need the car. To help her get the rest of her stuff out of his place. You know, CDs, clothes—"

"It's over, you say, but is it official?"

"Official? Is there paperwork?"

"Candy broke up with him? She told him she was leaving him for you?"

Sam groans. "They've been growing apart for a long time," he says, blissfully unaware of how clichéd this all is. "I know the dude, Mom. He knows it's over. Trust me."

"Did Candy tell him she was in love with you?"

Sam walks over and places his hands on my shoulders. Then, looking me square in the face, he says, "You don't know her like I know her, Mom."

"Is that so?" I have looked into Candy's eyes, and the girl looking back is very familiar. I don't trust her.

I wasn't excited about meeting Jay. I'd never liked Will's friends, and they never liked me. It's true I wasn't the type of girl Will usually had on his arm. He had only ever dated petite girls with noses like gumdrops and pink cheeks as if they'd just come in from sailing or playing tennis, their hair purposefully swept away from their faces in headbands and ponytails, advertising the fact they had nothing to hide.

In his company, Will's friends were polite, cordial. *Nice to see you. How was your summer? Can I get you some eggnog?* He was, fortunately, oblivious to the chill that followed me, the way fires of conversation went out and, one by one, his fraternity brothers excused themselves. He cared what they thought, and what I thought of them too. He was loyal.

It bothered him that I thought his friends got off on fucking the same handful of girls. *I'll have sloppy seconds, and thirds, and fourths . . .* That I thought the reason they fucked the same girls was that it was as close to fucking each other as they could get.

It bothered him that I got upset hearing them talk about the ways they'd dominated and mastered these girls as though they were mountains they'd all skied, or waters they'd rafted together. What was their degree of difficulty, skill level, how loud each boy made them scream. In the stories, the girls always begged for more.

Will insisted they really were good guys. That he only laughed at the jokes—*I don't trust anything that bleeds for eight days and doesn't die*—because they were his brothers, and not to would seem weird.

Then, by way of assuring me he wasn't like his brothers, he'd tell me, "You'll like Jay. I swear. He's like a brother to me."

If I didn't like Jay or Jay didn't like me, it would break Will's heart.

"How do Candy's parents feel about this arrangement?"

"I don't know, Mom. There are going to be other people living there too. It's not like a love nest. I know there's at least one other guy."

"How many girls?"

"I don't know," Sam says, sounding frustrated. "I just know—"

"I'd think Candy's parents, if they knew, wouldn't be comfortable—"

"No, they're cool—and it's not guys. It's me, Mom."

"And another guy? Who is this guy?"

"God, what are you so worried about anyway? It's not like she's your daughter. Anyway, it's safer for her to have a couple guys around, you know, for protection."

"For her protection?" I can't help myself. "That's the stupidest thing I've ever heard."

He takes a step back and crosses his arms against his chest, sliding his fists under his biceps to make them look bigger.

Sam says, "I love her, and she loves me."

I can't sit and have this conversation with him anymore. I get up from the table slowly, casually, walk over to the cabinet, and take out a plate.

"You know, Sam, Candy reminds me of a friend of mine from college." I've learned that if I appear busy with something else, and never look Sam in the eye, he'll talk. "She was pretty too, like Candy—but different, of course." I open the refrigerator door and stand there, staring at the lightbulb. "She was a lot of fun. The two of us used to double-date a lot."

When Sam rolls his eyes, something claws at my heart. "I know you find it impossible to believe I was ever young or pretty or had boyfriends—"

"Ah, jeez, Mom . . . ," he says, sounding vaguely disgusted.

"Shut up, Sam."

"Whoa," he says, surprised. "Don't let me stop you."

It takes a remarkably short amount of time for the bulb to heat up when you have the door open.

"Are you hungry? Can I make you a sandwich?"

"Sure," he says like he's doing me a favor.

"So sit," I say. "This friend of mine, she was, let's say, a free spirit."

"I just told you, Mom," Sam says, sitting down hard in his chair. "Candy is breaking up with her boyfriend."

"Just listen," I say. "I'm only going to tell you this once. This friend of mine, she was a free spirit. She didn't care what anyone thought of her. She did what she wanted when she wanted. No one owned her. No man could hold her down. I admired her for that. Until one day, she meets this boy and like that—" I snap my fingers.

"This boy, he's sweet, good looking, rich. Nobody can believe it. Candy . . . no, I'm sorry, not *Candy*—of course—*Jane*, that was her name, was in love. You could see it."

"Jane?" Sam raises an eyebrow.

"Yes. *Jane*, Sam. This was back in the Stone Age, when people had simple one-syllable names you could grunt."

"Ha ha," he says. "Whatever."

"He was good for her. She stopped running around and partying. So summer rolls around, and Jane and this boy are still dating. This is a record for her.

"Neither of them can stand the idea of not being together, so he invites her to come live with him and his family. If I remember right, Jane's home life was pretty screwy . . ."

"You must have bonded on that," Sam says.

He knows about my father's drinking, my mother's depression, my sister Cecile's desire to live on nothing but air and prayer, until she discovered acid.

"Let's just say no one was going to miss her."

Will had said his house was big. I couldn't be in the way if I tried. He assured me his parents would love me like he loved me. Every night we'd fall asleep together and wake up in each other's arms.

Will had told the truth; his family's house was like a mansion. White with pillars and bay windows, and a roof steep
enough that when it rained, fallen leaves and branches were
washed away with the power of a waterfall. A team of garden-
ers, none of whom spoke English, kept the grass trimmed
short and perfect as a golf course, the bushes properly shaped.
Will's mother's garden was full of flowers grown to be cut, and
artfully arranged. There was a pool in the backyard, and a
high fence.

Will's house bore no resemblance to my own. In comparison, my family's modest ranch house, with the flat roof
and the black trim, might as well have been a boxcar. It was a
starter house, my father always said; they'd never intended to
raise a family there, but they were slow starters.

Will's father was a workaholic. He was a lawyer. When he
was in the middle of a case, which was often, he'd sleep on
the couch in his office. It was a nice couch, he said. He got a
better night's sleep on that couch than in his own bed. When
he was around, not in the office, or playing golf, or at the
club, he was kind to me. I'd arrived the day Will's little sister,
Jenny, was leaving for tennis camp for the summer. Will had
wanted us to meet. When we pulled up, she and Will's father
were waiting outside by the packed-up station wagon. Will's
mother, having already said her good-byes, was inside preparing for our arrival.

Jenny wasn't what I expected. Her blond hair was thin and
scraped back into a ponytail her mother had braided so tightly
it stood out like a pencil, and even though she was sixteen she
looked closer to twelve. She reminded me of my own sister in
that way. Cecile was a freshman at Notre Dame and, through
force of will, biology, or God's will, still hadn't gotten her period, a fact she'd hidden from my mother. I couldn't imagine

Jenny swinging a racquet, forget chasing down balls, but she'd run to meet the car. I was shocked when we shook hands at how tight her grip was, the way she held on like she was trying to catch her breath.

When I asked Will later if Jenny had always been so thin, he looked surprised. She wasn't that thin. He thought she looked great.

I know Will's father missed her. He'd look embarrassed when I caught him looking at me that way, sort of sad and full of longing. I didn't care. I was no replacement for her. He told me he envied me doing what I wanted. He wished he'd taken time off to explore the world before he settled down.

Will's mother hated me on sight.

Not only would Will and I never sleep in the same room but we were forbidden from even sleeping on the same level. His mother put me up on the third floor. Banished to what the family jokingly called the tower. An all-white room, empty but for a high canopy bed with a lace spread, an antique desk with a chair too delicate to sit in, and an old sewing machine, which was set up in front of the bay window, from which you could see for miles.

In the middle of the staircase leading to the top floor was a step that squeaked, like a rat.

Will and his mother were close. Oddly close, it seemed to me. Although he assured me, they had their problems. Mostly she was overprotective. Sometimes he forgot to call when he was going to be late. She couldn't stand it when he locked his door. *What if there's a fire?* Every year since he was twelve she'd given him a photograph of her taken at whatever age he was at that time to remind him that she'd been his age once too, and could understand his problems. She'd paired up their pictures in a series of frames that opened like books, or an accordion. A picture of him at camp holding up a fish faced a shot of his mother in tennis whites holding a ball and racquet; a picture of him lying out wet beside their pool was coupled with one of her looking tan in a two-piece bathing suit sunning on a dock. Will posed in front of the fireplace in a dark blue suit and tie, his hair slicked back like that of a boy from the fifties, was coupled with a portrait of his mother in a dark velvet dress with a sweetheart neckline, sitting in a chair, a book in her lap, as though she's waiting to be picked up for a date.

"Jane takes one look at this house—it's huge, like a mansion, there's a pool and gardens . . . It's just as he promised."

"Mom . . . ," Sam groans. "I wanna take a shower, and if you're not going to let me take the car, I need to leave, for real, in fifteen minutes, or I'm going to be late. Plus, I have to shave."

I try not to smile. Sam barely has a beard. Roger shaved his off after Sam was born because, he said, he didn't want his rough whiskers scratching Sam's skin, but really it was to make him look younger. His beard was starting to gray. He didn't want anyone mistaking him for Sam's grandfather.

"However, his parents, who he promised would love her as he did? Well, the dad, he likes her—he would. But the mother is another story." Sam flashes me a sarcastic smile. "However, he assures Jane she will warm up. After a few days his best friend—who he'd been talking up to Jane ever since they met—"

"What was his name?"

"Which one?"

"The boyfriend."

"Will."

"What about the friend?"

"The best friend was . . . I can't remember his name."

Jay had come in over the back fence. As was his custom. I was lying in the shade in one of the chaises with my eyes closed waiting for Will to get back from playing tennis with his mom. I thought I'd just heard the car pull into the drive.

He'd stood silently by my chair, blocking out the sun, throwing his shadow over me. I thought it was Will. When I reached for him, he stepped just out of my reach. That was when I opened my eyes. He was in a pair of madras trunks, a faded blue Hawaiian shirt, and a Panama hat, all of which I'd guess belonged to some long dead uncle. He wasn't wearing shoes. His hair was dark and needed cutting; it flipped up at the ends in a way that I figured would make a boy crazy.

"Don't tell me," he said. "Let me guess—no, not a word. You can't fool me. You're the new maid. Good old Marcy is on course for a record here. No? Wait"—he grinned—"you're a pool-hopping grifter, here to rob these nice people blind."

I sat up. "I'm Heather," I said, glad I'd kept my clothes on over my bathing suit.

"Jay," he said, as though I couldn't have guessed this. "I was just joking. I'd know you anywhere. Even if I hadn't seen your picture, no wait, *pictures*, a veritable photo spread, I'd recognize the *girlfriend*."

I'd gotten used to Will calling me his girlfriend. I liked it.

I liked being able to call up Cecile to tell her that I was moving in with my *boyfriend*, Will, even though I knew she wouldn't approve. I liked leaving phone messages for him with the secretary in the clerks' office. *Please tell him his girl-friend called.* This was different, though.

"You surprised me," I said. "You shouldn't sneak up on people like that."

"I'm from a long line of ninjas," he said, trying to keep a straight face.

Jay always looked about to make some crack, or slip an ice cube down the back of your dress. Even without the thin scar that made his smile crooked, it seemed everything that came out of his mouth was a joke, like even against his will his mouth seemed to say, *You can't take me seriously.* I saw myself in Jay.

Where was Will? Will should have been there for the introduction. I stuck out my hand for him to shake. I don't know who didn't let go first, but it seemed we stood there shaking hands for a long time, as though we were each daring the other one to let go. It was the sound of Will's voice that ended the contest.

"Brother, my brother—I didn't know you were here!" He was elated.

"William! Where else would I be?"

I watched Will bounding across the expanse of lawn toward us to hug Jay—not one of those one-arm, we're-not-gay hugs he gave his friends at school but a big thumping hug—and then he embraced me.

"So?" he said, picking me up and holding me aloft like I was the prize he'd come to claim. "So, what do you think, Jay? Isn't she great?"

"Put me down," I asked, suddenly uncomfortable.

"Isn't she the greatest? Have you ever seen a prettier girl? Ever?"

"You were right," Jay said.

It was clear that, unlike Will's mother, no matter how Jay had felt about me, he would have told Will whatever he wanted to hear.

"I knew it," Will crowed finally, putting me down. "I knew you'd like each other," he said, grabbing on to each of our shoulders. "It's awesome. I've got my best girlfriend, and my best friend." *Best friend* sounding suspiciously like *best man.* "Together, all summer."

The occasion called for drinks. I'd never been a drinker before that summer. It started with the screwdrivers. All summer long the three of us sat around that pool tossing back orange juice and vodka as though we were deathly afraid of scurvy.

"You two kids get to know each other!" Will said, as he headed for the house.

"Will do. See what old Marcy's got in the fridge to eat! She must be knocking herself out with the company here, right? Standing rib roasts, pineapple upside-down cake, leg o' lamb . . ." Jay winked at me.

"Fuck you, bro," Will called back happily. "And no fighting! I mean it, you two!"

I answered, "You don't have to worry about me!"

Will flashed me the thumbs-up.

"So," Jay said, "how are you and old Marcy getting along?"

"She hates me."

"No, she can't hate you. Hate you? No." He paused. "Of course she hates you. How could she not? You've stolen her precious treasure."

"No, I haven't."

"Just try to cut her some slack. I've known her my whole life. She'll come around. She's a good lady. Did Will tell you our moms used to call us by one name?"

"He did."

"It's true." Jay pulled the neck of his T-shirt up to cover his mouth, like he was cold.

"He doesn't lie."

"No, you won't find a better man than our boy Will. He's a real catch, as they say."

More than once a friend of Will's, his tongue loosened by booze, would take me aside at a party to remind me how great Will was and warn me, *You better not hurt him.* Never considering that Will might be the one to hurt me.

I waited for Jay to do the same.

"I'm a lucky girl." It was true too. How handsome Will looked standing on the diving board, his hair slicked back, gleaming like a golden helmet. How smart he was, captain of the debate team. He never lost an argument. His internship clerking this summer, all this was leading to something big. He was going places. Everyone said so.

I stared at Jay's mouth, the thin white scar bisecting his upper lip. Was that why he was pulling the neck of his T-shirt up over his mouth? Was he self-conscious? Could you feel it when you kissed him? How many girls had Jay kissed? I didn't want him to kiss any other girls.

I can't explain it other than to say it was as though I recognized my kind.

"Hey," Jay said, pushing back his straw hat to better see into my eyes. "What's going on?" He waved his hand in front of my face. He smelled like cut grass and oranges, and faintly of cigarettes. "Seriously? Don't do this to me, girlfriend. Not on my watch. If you so much as stub your pinkie toe, he'll never forgive me. Seriously."

"Mmmm," I said, staring at the scar on his lip.

"Wait, are you faking? Seriously? Are you playing? I don't mind." I believed him. "Do you need to be thrown in the pool?"

It was then, when he playfully grabbed me by my arm, that I bit him.

He might have yelled, or flinched, or tried to pull his arm away, but he didn't. He didn't even seem surprised, more curious; amused, like it was the best thing to happen to him all day. So I held on, bit down harder, testing him. I felt awake for the first time in my life. How long would it be before he stopped me? Then it occurred to me, *He isn't going to stop you,* and I immediately let go.

"I'm sorry," I mumbled and wiped my mouth on the back of my hand. It was terrible and glorious, to feel, for the first time ever, perfectly understood.

"Don't apologize," Jay said, calmly examining the deep pink imprint my teeth had left behind like they were something miraculous.

"I didn't mean it."

"C'mon now, don't say that," he said, an edge of seriousness in his voice. "That just cheapens the whole thing, doesn't it?"

"No, really. That was just weird . . . just weird." I laughed nervously. What was wrong with me? What if he needed a tetanus shot? How would he explain that? *My best friend's girlfriend bit me? No, she wasn't foaming at the mouth, or not that I could see.* "Please don't tell Will?"

"Never. Not even torture," Jay said. "Not a word."

"He would never—"

"Your secret is safe with me," he said, and I trusted him.

"Thank you."

"Don't thank me." He looked uncomfortable then.

He looked at me, and I looked at him, and in that way, it was decided.

I can't believe that Will didn't know. He didn't want to recognize it, but on a cellular level, he had to. How could he not see how, despite the fact that Jay and I barely knew each other, we finished each other's sentences; we told each other's jokes, our words sliding on top of each other, clicking together. We were always accidentally touching each other, bumping elbows and hips, stepping on the backs of each other's shoes, as though we had trouble gauging distances or were always a little drunk. We could sit and not talk.

I had wanted to sleep with Jay. I had pushed it. I wanted to keep him.

"Why," he said, "can't you believe anyone could ever really love you?"

Sam is running his hand over his cheeks and chin, feeling for whiskers. "So, did Will know what was going on?"

"No—he was blind to it. She was his first love. He'd had girl-friends, Jane wasn't his first girlfriend, but she was his first"—I hesitate—"and he mistook—the way people often do—the intensity of that, those, first physical relationships for—"

Sam makes a face, blushes. "Mom."

I have found condoms in his room under the mattress; found lube in his sock drawer. I'd thought about throwing them out but stopped myself. What a hypocrite I've become in my old age.

"But the mother, Jane thought, had an inkling. Mother's intuition. She didn't like the way Will's mother looked at her." *It's a mother's blessing and burden to see things her children can't.*

"Jane never said it, she might not even have been conscious of it, but I think she hoped Will's mother would embrace her. Be the kind of mother Jane never had.

"That was not the case, however. Jane said she tried. She'd offer to cook, clean, do the grocery shopping, the laundry, but Will's mother wouldn't let her. She acted like it was a hardship for Jane, and after all, Jane was their guest. Of course, Jane felt the reason she wouldn't let her help was because she felt she wasn't even fit to be their maid."

"I can't believe she wouldn't let her take out the trash."

"Will assured her time and again that his mother enjoyed waiting on him and his father, and that Jane should just enjoy it. So she did."

I'd been staying at Will's for almost a month when I finally got up the courage to make a BLT for Will and myself. I knew there was bacon left over from breakfast, and a tomato in the fridge. I thought the house was empty. I don't know what alerted her, maybe the rustling of the bread wrapper.

"What are you doing?" she said with alarm, as though she'd caught me going through her purse. She elbowed me aside and picked up the knife. She said, "You sit down, or go outside. I'll take over. I've been doing this for years. I know how Will likes his sandwiches." She hummed.

She wouldn't even let me make her beloved son a sandwich.

Before I could think I said, "I'm *intimately* aware of how

Will likes his *sandwiches.*" I might as well have said, *I'm aware of how your son likes to fuck.*

"What about the dad?"

"He sounded nice, a bit retiring. Beaten down by that wife, I'd think. Jane said the two of them watched golf together on Sundays. I don't know how close he and Will were. It seemed clear that Will was more like his mother than his father. Jane said he liked her. Which I'm sure was true. She was, as I said, pretty, and she could be very *charming.* Maybe he liked her just to spite Will's mother."

"Hmmm," Sam says with interest, as though this concept has never occurred to him before.

"It would turn out, of course, that Will's mother's instincts about Jane were right. But what could she do? It was a fool's errand to tell her son his girlfriend was cheating on him with his best friend. He wouldn't believe her anyway. Worse, he might turn on her."

"I can see that." Sam raises an eyebrow, giving me a meaningful glance.

What did he love about Candy? I'd heard the murmurings coming from under his door, been awoken in the middle of the night by her laughter, which floated down the hall and into my room like gas. What could there possibly be beyond the physical attraction?

"Wait, I was going to make you a sandwich, wasn't I? I got distracted."

"Do we have any roast beef or turkey left? One of those big rolls?"

"Of course." I get out the roast beef, cheese, lettuce, mustard, pickles, and an onion. They are his favorites.

"No onion," Sam says. "Breath." This is new.

I take out a knife and split the roll.

"Jane said she and the best friend tried to ignore their feelings, but it was impossible, especially since Will was always working late, she was only part-time at the aquarium, and Jay was working at a local radio station and cutting lawns. His family didn't have the sort of money Will's family had. Any time Will had free, he wanted to spend with his best friend and his girlfriend, so he was always unwittingly throwing them together."

"That was pretty stupid."

"She said they fought it, but they couldn't keep their hands off each other. Even in public, they found excuses to touch each other. That magnetism thing may be a cliché, but that's what it was. Or it sounds like."

He considers this.

"You don't believe me?"

"I'm just saying, how could he be so blind? You know . . ."

"Before long Jane is having sex with both the boyfriend and the best friend. Sometimes both in the same day."

Sam's jaw drops. "No fricking way. You're joking. What a *slut*," he says, and in that moment, he's so ugly to me, I don't recognize him. I can't speak. If he knew the names I'd been called, the things people had said about me. I can't look at him. I focus on the sandwich, split the roll.

I say, "I don't like that word, Sam."

He rolls his eyes. "Jeez, Mom, chill out, everybody says it."

"I don't care. It's wrong."

"She was," he says more softly. He turns to look at the clock, to make a point. He can leave whenever he wants.

"Put yourself in her place. In her mind, she had no choice. If she suddenly stopped sleeping with Will, he'd suspect something was wrong. Of course, she told Jay she wasn't sleeping with Will. She was lying to both of them."

"Who knew you had such wild friends?"

"I think Jane really just loved the way they loved her. All of them—her boyfriend, the best friend, even the father."

"The dad?" He shudders. "Ah, jeez, that's gross, man."

"See, even older men can confuse beauty with goodness."

I fold the roast beef inside and cover it with slices of yellow American cheese. Neither Roger nor I will touch the stuff, but Sam loves it.

"Put some turkey in there too, why don't you?"

"I remember she used to tell stories about the mother," I say, laying down turkey and shredding lettuce over it. "Splitting her sides over how she'd torture that poor woman. She'd opened up her house to her, she'd even lent her a bathrobe and—"

"And don't forget the mayo," Sam says, as though I haven't been making his sandwiches for a lifetime, as though I don't know what he likes.

"She wore this tea rose perfume that made his mother sneeze; she'd sit by the pool for hours, knowing his mother wouldn't come out if she was there," I say. "Lying out in the sun like she meant to soak every ray, every ounce of light out of it. She'd come down to breakfast in nothing but panties and one of Will's old football jerseys. She was"—I pause—"*loud.*"

I blush. Me, who doesn't blush, I blush. "It was all a joke to her."

"Wow—and you called this chick your friend? Seriously?"

Sam is a smart boy, I think. *He'll be fine.* He leans back in his chair and rubs his stomach.

"I'm making her sound terrible. She wasn't, she was just young and selfish. She wanted what she wanted. I don't think she knew how much power she had. Not really. She could see what was happening, of course. The way the two boys, who'd never fought before, began arguing over inconsequential things—a broken bike chain, whose turn it was to buy beer. Will accusing Jay of cheating in a swimming race."

"The best friend's name was Jay?"

"Yes." I hesitate. "I guess I just remembered. Jay. It's amazing how it's suddenly all so clear to me—like it just happened yesterday."

Sam doesn't seem one bit suspicious. Why would his mother tell him a story?

I take a deep breath. Cutting slices of onion so thin you can barely see them hidden under the layers of cheese. "Eventually she managed, intentionally or unintentionally, to alienate Will from everyone who mattered to him. I don't think the people he worked with much cared for her, except for his lecherous boss."

"What about the dad?"

"It didn't matter if the father liked her, he didn't call the shots. The mother tried to talk to him—"

"Nobody wants to hear their girlfriend being slagged, Mom." He gives me a look.

"Of course not." I put the overstuffed sandwich in front of him. It looks like a zeppelin flying into his mouth.

"Umm, good," he says, wiping mustard from his chin.

I slide into the seat across from Sam.

"Anyway, Jane had pretty much managed to convince Will that his mother hated her because she loved Will so much, and she wasn't from a good family. She convinced him that it was his mother's fear that one day they'd get married and she'd be stuck with her for a daughter-in-law that made her paranoid."

How many nights had I sat here just like this helping him with his math and science homework? Roger was hopeless.

"Cut to Labor Day weekend. Will's parents are throwing a big end-of-summer party. Later, the three of them are supposed to meet up with some people from Will's work at a bar. It's a big party. The parents' friends, kids' friends, neighbors, everybody is drinking. Will is in his element, so Jane and Jay figure it's safe for them to sneak off and none will be the wiser."

Sam stops chewing.

"What they don't know is that Will's mother is onto them. She's been watching them all night and follows them, hoping to catch them in the act, and she does."

Sam recoils in disgust. "That's just sick."

"No, no. It's not like that. No mother wants— For god's sake, Sam."

"What a bitch," Sam says.

I flinch. I've never heard Sam call anyone a bitch before. And the mother? He's calling *her* the bitch?

"How could she even be sure what she saw was right?"

"No, his mother *saw* them having sex. She *heard* everything. They were *laughing*."

"You just said it was dark. And it was loud—music and people. Your ears can play tricks on you too. Maybe she heard what she wanted to hear. Maybe she was drunk."

"No. The mother sees them, she knows the score, she says, 'I hope you're proud of yourselves. This will kill him, you know,' and leaves. Jane and Jay are panicked. They don't know what to do. There's no way she's not going to tell Will.

"For the rest of the night Jane clings to Will's side, so his mother can't get to him. All Jane can think about is talking to Jay. They'll pick him up, they'll go to the bar, and they can talk then.

"They are almost out the door when his mother grabs Will and says, 'Can I talk to you, just for a moment?' Jane said she'd given her this smile like 'Your days are numbered.'"

Had Will's mother ever really looked at me like my days were numbered? Even if she had, I wouldn't have believed her.

"He, of course, suspects whatever his mother has to say to him has to do with Jane, and he doesn't want to hear it, so he tells her, 'Don't wait up.'"

I knew she would.

I now understand. Even if his mother didn't want to, she couldn't help it. She'd have been listening. It is impossible, even in sleep, to not be a mother.

"Was it weird when Jay got in the car?" Sam licks his finger and picks up the last crumbs.

"No. They left him behind."

His mother's voice had sliced through the dark and noise, as clean and bright as a guillotine. "Why, Heather, what a surprise, and Jay."

We were back behind the fir trees that grew along the stretch of fence Jay used to climb over. We were going over our plan. Will couldn't know. Once Will and I got back to school, I'd get my own apartment. I'd say I needed space; we'd grow apart. Break up. Months later, while visiting some friends in D.C., Jay and I would run into each other somewhere. *It all happened so fast*, we'd say. No one can deny true love.

"If it isn't the hostess with the mostest," Jay said with remarkable calm. "Another top-notch shindig, Marcy. I've been meaning to congratulate you all night, but you've been swarmed by adoring guests. Outstanding canapés, by the way."

"I'm so glad you've enjoyed yourself," she murmured.

"As you can see"—Jay patted the fence—"I was just preparing to make my exit. So, I bid you fond farewell and thank you, for a lovely time. You're the best."

Then he turned and pulled himself up on top of the fence, as he always had, and she shook her head as she always had. Jay was Jay.

"Give me a call when you guys are ready to shove off," he said, then disappeared over the other side.

Will's mother and I stood there for a moment. "He'll never grow up," she said.

Back at the house, I heard the phone ring. Heard Will's mother call to him over Herb Alpert and the Tijuana Brass, "Jay is on the phone." Heard Will say, "I'll call him back." Fifteen minutes later, I heard the phone again. Heard Will's mother say, "Will, it's Jay, asking for Heather"—there was a long pause—then I heard Will say, "Tell him she doesn't want to talk to him right now."

Minutes later he came out with his keys and my coat and said, "Let's go."

He slowed down outside of Jay's house, looking in the windows, and then sped off.

"Wait," I said, "aren't we picking up Jay?"

"Not tonight."

"I heard he called," I said haltingly. "Did you call him back?"

"Why do you care?" he asked, not taking his eyes off the road.

Will tried parking right in front of the bar, but the space was tight. He kept jamming it in and out of reverse, swearing, like it was my fault. Finally, he gave up and we parked out back. His mood lifted the moment we got inside. The place was shoulder to shoulder with familiar faces, buddies from high school and work. He moved swiftly and purposefully through the crowd, introducing me to everyone like he was gathering a pool of witnesses, all of whom could be called on later to testify to his greatness.

When people asked, *Hey, where's Jay?* Will was the picture of cool. *I don't know,* he said. *He's not here?* Only I could see he was grinding his teeth.

"Okay, so they get to the bar," Sam says. He wants me to get to the good part, even though he's not sure what the good part is.

I look up at the clock. "It's getting late," I say. "Maybe you should go?"

"No, no, it's cool," he says. "We didn't pick a specific time or anything."

"Really?"

"Really. Keep going."

"So of course, Jay shows up at the bar. He's walked there. Jane can't believe it—he walked—they start talking. Jay wants to tell Will. If they don't, Marcy will. He has to know, he says. Jane convinces him that they have to wait. They can't tell him tonight—in a bar, like this. Will is drunk. But when he sees the two of them in the corner talking, he makes a beeline for them. He says to Jay, 'What the hell are you doing here? Are you following us?' Jay says, 'Why don't we take a walk?' And Will says, 'Why don't you stop hitting on my girlfriend?' And Jay says, 'We need to talk.' And Jane says, 'No, Jay, don't,' and without thinking grabs his arm. That's when Will knows. He says, 'Everybody told me you were a lying whore, but I didn't listen.' That's too much for Jay. Will is his best friend, but this is the woman he loves. He tells him, 'You can't talk to her like that. You better shut up before you say something else you're going to regret.' He tells him, 'Don't make me hurt you.' But

Will won't listen. He throws a punch, probably the first of his life, but it's a good one—all those years of being best friends and never a fistfight, until now. The crowd moves back, space opens up around them like a ring."

My heart is beating fast.

Sam looks at me expectantly. "And, and . . . ? C'mon, Mom, this is the good part. Jeez, finally we get some blood and guts. What happened? Did one of them pull a knife, or break a bottle and start wheeling around with it, or—"

"No. They just hit each other."

"Well, did Jane jump in and try to break it up?"

"No."

"Really? She must have been freaking out."

"No, not at all. She liked it. She said it was exciting having two boys fight over her."

"Wait—*exciting*? She liked it? That's sick."

"I don't think it's so hard to believe."

He rubs his chin like he's never considered this. How can he be so naïve? Is he imagining what might happen should he go to collect Candy's things from her boyfriend's apartment?

"C'mon, Sammy, who wouldn't like that? And best friends—what power. What girl wouldn't like that?"

I'm only allowed to call him Sammy at home.

"In the middle of all this, Will starts yelling at Jane, telling her she has to choose between the two of them. Right then. Choose. Which one of them does she love? How could it not be him? Right?"

"What did Jay say?"

"Jane said he didn't say anything, he just kept wiping the blood off his mouth, feeling his teeth. Grinning like he'd happily get punched in the face a hundred times for her."

"But he wasn't yelling at her to pick him, or anything?"

"He told her she didn't have to say anything."

"Okay . . . ," Sam says quizzically. "But did she?"

"She had to; otherwise, it would be like saying she chose him. So she said, 'I can't . . .' and at that, Jay takes off. He doesn't even wait for her to finish her sentence. He is devastated. Jane, who is anything but stupid, falls into Will's arms, sobbing. She lets him play the hero. Will, well, Will, what can he do? Even if he suspects she was going to say, *I can't lie to you, Will, I love him,* she's his girlfriend. She's chosen. He's won."

I didn't want a drink. I said I had a headache. Will wanted to know why I couldn't get into the spirit of things. What was wrong with me? Why couldn't I just, for once, relax and have a good time? Make any effort to impress these people? All I could think about was Jay. What was he thinking? Did he really believe I'd rejected him? Or, was he afraid we'd been found out? When Will insisted I get a drink, I ordered a screwdriver. I asked the bartender, "Do they call them screwdrivers because they fix you, or because they take you apart?"

He said, "Either way you're screwed."

Will and I were around back getting into the car when we saw Jay. The look on Will's face was one of disbelief. He'd walked to the bar. It was miles from home. What the fuck was he thinking?

I knew. He was coming for me. He loved me.

"He's here." I'm sure Will could hear it in my voice.

"Would you just get in the goddamn car," he said.

"That's it?" Sam says, exasperated. "That's it? She betrays him. She cries, he takes her back like that?"

"No. Will and Jane go home. They barely speak. They go to sleep. Then around four in the morning, Jane wakes up, and there is Will's mom standing by her bed. Jane said the moment she opened her eyes she knew."

"Knew what?"

"Jay was dead."

"Dead," Sam says, sounding surprised. How could he not have seen that coming?

"They found his body washed up on the rocks below a trestle bridge less than a mile from the bar."

"What? He killed himself?" Sam wasn't expecting that.

"It looked that way."

I'll bet Will's mother knew the moment the phone rang. She didn't even need to answer it. But she did. Even so, did she have to ask Jay's mother to repeat herself? It could so easily have been her Will. Her most beautiful boy. Did she scream? Did she make any noise at all?

I'd known by the way she was holding the neck of her robe closed. Her eyes half open, she looked as though she'd been choked and dragged up the stairs by her hair; she hadn't wanted to come.

She said, "There's been an accident. Jay's dead," then clapped both hands over her mouth, as though she could push the words down her throat. The news was obscene. It made no sense.

Of course, he was dead. What had I expected?

"He needs you," she said.

The way I'd slipped out of bed, and into the robe she held out to me, it all happened so smoothly it seemed rehearsed. As though we'd been anticipating this moment all along.

The way I'd followed her, focusing on how her robe was flowing out behind her as though she was a ship cutting through the water, with me in her wake. Both of us moving toward this terrible howling sound—my boyfriend's sobbing, which was getting louder and louder. When we reached the bathroom door, we stopped and she said to me, "Go to him. It's you he wants."

What had it taken for her to admit this to me? How she must have suffered, knowing that she couldn't give him what he needed. I wonder if in that moment, when she shut me in that room with Will, it was possible that she felt some pleasure.

.

"Jane said she knew she couldn't cry. Not then. She wasn't so selfish as not to realize that right now Will needed her, and she wouldn't give Will's mother the satisfaction of seeing her break down—but how could she not cry? This boy she was in love with—*or thought she was in love with*—was dead."

I sweep the bits of fallen lettuce and onion skin into my hand and dump them into the disposal.

"His mother told her she had to go to him. Jay was his best friend. He wouldn't come out of the bathroom. It was then, Jane said, she realized that in a sick way she'd just won. Will's mother had been forced to acknowledge the power that Jane had. Will had chosen her. Jane could comfort him in a way she never could."

"Whoa. I can't believe that. That's kinda sick, isn't it?"

"That's what she said." I pause. "It's complicated."

"How is it complicated? Whose side are you on?"

"I can't take sides. I knew these people. I mean, not the friend or the mother but . . . You know, love isn't always simple."

• • •

I got into the shower in my nightgown, curled up with him around the drain. He kissed my mouth so hard I thought our teeth would break off in each other's mouths. I thought, *That's right, knock out my teeth. Go ahead, make my mouth a hole, a grave.*

"It's my fault," he said, and he meant it. "It's my fault," he said, looking squarely at me. I was a monster. We all knew it. I couldn't even cry. That was when I lost it. I lost it and couldn't get it back for weeks. It was like I sank down below the surface of myself and just lay there. It wasn't supposed to be my tragedy. It was Will's tragedy. If I'd ever loved him at all, I had to know that.

Will hated me after that. He hated me so much it freaked him out. You could tell he'd never hated anybody before. I could see it. The best sex we ever had was in the days right after Jay killed himself. He'd grab me, and hold me down, fucking me like a machine gun.

He cried all the time. It never lifted. Sobbing, he'd reach for me as though he expected me to save him. I couldn't save him. He'd have had me go under too. I can hear his voice in my head, high and broken up into little pieces. *You can't do this.* I can still see his red, wet face, his mouth hanging open like a flap, something torn apart.

"So," Sam says, "did the mom tell Will that the two of them were fooling around behind his back?"

"I don't know."

Had Will's mother told him he was better off without me? Had she watched him cry, caught between feeling sad for him

and thankful I was gone? And after I was gone, had he, sobbing, let her hold him in her arms?

"C'mon, she must have told, right?" Sam says.

"She must have wanted to dearly, but I bet she didn't—
she'd want to save her son from further pain."

That's what mothers do.

"Even though it would have proved she was right, proved
all she'd been doing was trying to protect him." I pause. "But
again, I don't know . . . All I know is what Jane told me. Will
was destroyed. And then there was Jay's family—his mother
and father, his siblings, his friends. Can you imagine? One
girl. To have that kind of power . . ."

So much power.

Sam sighs, folds his arms on the table, and puts his head
down. Perhaps he is forming a mental image of Jane. I gave
him no physical description of her. What does he imagine? A
big-breasted succubus with hypnotic eyes and torrents of raven
hair that fell to her waist in waves.

"And she was no beauty queen, just a very ordinary girl."

With pale skin and gray eyes and red hair that was always
unruly.

Sam lifts his head and rests his chin in his hand. "So, what
about Jane?" he asks. "What happened to her? Was she okay?"

His question takes me by surprise. "I'm sorry?"

"I said, What about Jane? Was she okay?"

It never occurred to me that he'd wonder or care what happened to her. That he'd think of her having a life past the end
of the story, and I suddenly felt this pitiful sadness, I couldn't
explain. He was asking about me. Was I wrong to have told
the story this way?

"Mom?" Sam looks concerned. "Are you crying?"

"No— Didn't you see? I just threw out the onions from

your sandwich." I smile, feeling my mouth stretching like a rubber band. I get up and go over to the sink, and turn the water on.

"I'm not sure what happened after that. Jane and I had started growing apart by then."

"But she told you all this."

How many more times would I tell this story?

"She had to tell someone. Maybe she thought I wouldn't judge her. Anyway, I don't think she ever got over it. I don't know about Will. I only knew him from a distance."

"But they didn't get married or anything, did they?"

"No. They hung on a few months, but no. Neither could forget."

I'd brought so few things with me it hadn't taken long for me to pack. Will sat on the edge of the bed, staring out the window, crying. *You can't leave me. First him and now you.* He'd called me in Seattle, on the first anniversary of Jay's death, woken me up in the middle of the night, and cried. What had I done? After that, I got an unlisted phone number.

"What about Jane? Where did she go?"

"I'm not sure. She moved around a lot, place to place. Like I said, I lost track of her. She wasn't exactly the change-of-address-card sort of girl."

"So, when was the last time you talked to her, like thirty years ago or something?"

"Thirty years ago? Seriously, Sam? Is that what you think? Try twenty years ago. That's not so long ago."

"I know, I know. Chill. Calm down, Mom."

"No, really. How can you say that? Thirty fucking years, Sam?" I turn away so he can't see how upset I am.

"Jeez, Mom, I was joking." He gets up and comes over to the sink.

"I don't know where she is, but I'm sure she hasn't changed all that much. Why would I want to know a person like that? Trust me, people don't change that much, Sam. Remember that."

He gets up from the table, my golden son, in his seventies T-shirt and puka-bead necklace, his cutoffs and converse sneakers, comes over and puts his arm around me. He rests his chin on my head. He's late now, and he wants to ask me again for my keys.

"Hey," he says, "you're my most beautiful mother."

And I say, "My most beautiful son."

"So . . ."

"You knew it was going to end, but not like that," I say, pulling away.

"That's true," he says.

"I don't think I'll ever tell it again," I say. "Can you imagine if you had to carry that burden for your whole life?"

"Maybe she hasn't." He shrugs, without even considering the question of what he would do in the situation. "Maybe she just let go of it."

Let it go?

"You know," Sam says as though he's so wise, "it wasn't really her fault, Mom."

"How can you say that? Of course it was her fault."

"How could all that be her fault?"

"Weren't you listening to me?"

"C'mon, Mom," he says, "she was just a girl."

Had he not heard one word I said?

"Don't be a fool, there is no such thing as *just a girl*."

Acknowledgments

I am ever and deeply grateful to Jenny Offill, Helen Schulman, Rachel Urquhart, and Eddie Villepique for their boundless insights, guidance, and, moreover, their abiding friendship. I am greatly indebted to Aimee Bell and Joy Harris for their great wisdom and unflagging support, to Steve Rinehart for his killer instincts, to Sarah Hochman for her steady hand and sharp eye, to Michele Bové for her kind assistance, and Anjali Singh for her invaluable close critical attention and generosity in taking on more than she was obliged to, on and off the page. I should also like to thank Scott Adkins, Mandy Aftel, Susan Karwoska, and Vicki Sher for giving me spaces in which to write, and Matthew Miele, Dawn Raffel, Betsy Sussler, and Hannah Tinti for places in which to publish. To the Hyntersack family, and Big Red White—home is where you are. Isadora and Miles, you deserve more than I fear I can ever give you, including the words to express how much I value your intelligence, honesty, and humor. Nothing would happen, and little would matter were it not for Rob Spillman's enduring love, faith, and extraordinary cool.

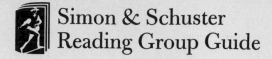

*Blueprints for Building
Better Girls*

Introduction

In eight darkly funny, linked stories, Elissa Schappell delves into the lives of an eclectic cast of archetypal female characters—from the high school slut to the good girl, the struggling artist to the college party girl, the wife who yearns for a child to the reluctant mother. Their struggles illuminate the common but rarely discussed experiences that build girls into women, and women into wives and mothers.

In "Monsters of the Deep," teenage Heather seeks real intimacy despite her reputation for being a slut; years later in "I'm Only Going to Tell You This Once," she must reconcile her troubling memories of youthful misadventure with her current role as the mother of a teenage boy who is falling in love for the first time. In "The Joy of Cooking," a mother struggles to support her adult daughter, Emily, a recovering anorexic; in "Elephant," we find Emily's sister, Paige, confiding her ambivalence about motherhood to her new best friend, Charlotte. In "Are You Comfortable?" we meet a twenty-one-year-old Charlotte cracking under the burden of a traumatic secret, which also sends her college friend Bender, a troubled party girl, nearly to the brink in "Out of the Blue and into the Black."

These women weave in and out of each other's lives, connected by blood, friendship, or necessity. As girlfriends, wives, new mothers, and empty nesters, they continually buck our expectations of how "better girls" should behave.

Topics & Questions for Discussion

1. In "Aren't You Dead Yet," Beth reads a 1963 etiquette book called *Blueprints for Building Better Girls:* "It was hilarious how clueless these women, teetering in heels, on the cusp of sexual revolution, were." (p. 165) In what ways are the girls and women in Schappell's book also clueless? How are they, too, teetering on the cusp of sexual revolution? What did you first think of when you read or heard this title? How does this title fit Schappell's book?

2. Consider how Heather and Ross of "Monsters of the Deep" fit particular stereotypes. How do they conform to these stereotypes? Both teenagers are saddled with labels: Ross is the "fat boy" and Heather has a reputation for being a "slut," although she isn't promiscuous. In "I'm Only Going to Tell You This Once," she tells her husband that she "was a good girl with a bad reputation." (p. 247) How do these labels influence the way the kids see themselves, and each other? What do you imagine are the lasting effects?

3. Discuss Kate and Douglas's marriage in "A Dog Story." How do the losses they share—the miscarriage and the death of their dog—bring them closer together? How do these tragedies drive them further apart? How does Kate's inability to conceive impact her friendships with women who have children?

4. In "Elephant," Charlotte wonders about Kate, the head of human resources at her old job: "What did a woman who didn't want children want? Or, what did she want more than children? It was creepy." (p. 112) Why does Charlotte find Kate "creepy," and what doesn't she realize about

Kate's desires? What does this say about what our culture at large, rightly or wrongly, values?

5. Charlotte reminds her ailing grandfather about a trick he used to play on her in the car. "We'd be going down a hill, and you'd suddenly take your hands off the wheel and say, 'Somebody steer, somebody steer, we're out of control!'" (p. 79). How does the metaphor of reckless driving apply to Charlotte and to her grandfather? How is Charlotte verging on a wreck? How is her grandfather, too, increasingly out of control?

6. Discuss how Charlotte and Paige, two mothers who frequent the same Brooklyn playground, slowly become friends. How do they test and impress each other? How does the friend-making process differ for adult women, as opposed to the teens and college students in Schappell's other stories? Did you recognize any of their rituals as your own?

7. Discuss how the women of *Blueprints for Building Better Girls* juggle career, romance, and family. Which characters seem to strike the best balance? Which women have the hardest time negotiating these responsibilities?

8. Charlotte's date rape can be considered the central trauma of the book. List which characters are affected by Charlotte's ordeal. Why does this tragedy radiate outward into other girls' lives, even years later?

9. The narrator in "The Joy of Cooking" thinks, "No one saw how much the mother hurt. No one knew, or cared, what she'd lost." (p. 151) Which of the stories in *Blueprints for*

Building Better Girls focus on daughters' pain, and which consider mothers' losses? The power dynamics between mothers and daughters are constantly changing in these stories. What is it like to see Heather, Charlotte, and Paige at different points in their lives—as daughters and as mothers? Did any of these stories make you think of your own relationships with parents or children?

10. What the culture considers proper and improper behavior for women shifts from generation to generation. How do the choices made by older generations of women, like the grandmother in "The Joy of Cooking," influence later generations? Can you point to the ways in which past generations of women in your family have shaped you?

11. Discuss the narrator's telephone conversation with her daughter Emily in "The Joy of Cooking." How do this mother and daughter depend on each other? The story closes, "I knew it the way I knew I'd always be hungry. Like Emily, only different." (p. 160) What is each of these women "hungry" for?

12. In "Aren't You Dead Yet," when Elizabeth writes her play Food Fight, she realizes, "I'd never written anything like that, nothing expressly female. Nothing that felt true like that. I mean, nobody cared about that stuff." (pp. 172–173) How would you define an "expressly female" subject? Why does Elizabeth assume that nobody cares about female subjects, and how is she proven wrong? Would you say that *Blueprints for Building Better Girls* is an "expressly female" book? Why or why not? What are the larger central human themes?

13. Bender says in "Out of the Blue and into the Black:" "You don't know what that's like. To be special like that. To have all those people know you, to have you in common." (p. 208) How many characters in *Blueprints for Building Better Girls* have Bender in common? Why does Bender think that makes her special, and in what ways might she be wrong?

14. If "Nostalgia is a narcotic" (p. 187), which of Schappell's characters are most under its influence? Who seems the most stuck in the past, and who is able to move on? What is lost or gained by moving on? Or choosing to stay the same?

15. In *The New York Times Book Review*, Jennifer B. McDonald calls Elissa Schappell "a diva of the encapsulating phrase, capable of conveying a Pandora's box of feeling in a single line." Read aloud a line from *Blueprints for Building Better Girls* that conveys a "Pandora's Box of feeling." Why does this particular passage speak to you? What feelings does it convey?

16. In the last line of the book, Heather tells her son, Sam, "Don't be a fool, there is no such thing as just a girl." (p. 288) What does Heather want to teach her son about girls? Why is she so upset that Sam doesn't blame Jane for Jay's death? How does the last line of the book resonate in terms of the rest of the stories in the book?

Enhance Your Book Club

1. Get inspired by Heather's body drawings, and treat your book club members to temporary tattoos. Pick up a package at your local party store, and let your guests decorate themselves during your book club meeting.

2. Toast your book club with ice-cold mint juleps, the drink Charlotte mixes for her grandfather. Find the recipe here: http://allrecipes.com/recipe/mint-juleps/

3. Kate and Douglas adopt their dog, Thelonious, from animal shelter volunteers in "A Dog Story." Visit http://www.petfinder.com/shelters.html to find an animal shelter in your area, and find out how you and your book club can volunteer, donate, or even adopt.

4. The women of *Blueprints for Building Better Girls* are connected in subtle and intricate ways over the course of their lives. Make a blueprint of your book club. When did the club start and when did each member join? How do you all know each other? Who do you have in common? Take it a little further: Have the kinds of books you've read over the years have changed? Have your interests shifted? If so, is this in reaction to something in particular?

5. Bender and her college friends spend weekends in their nightgowns, even when they leave campus. Turn your book club meeting into a pajama party, and ask members to attend in their coziest sleepwear. (Don't forget the cocktails, and mocktails too!)

A Conversation with Elissa Schappell

Your first book, *Use Me*, was also a collection of interconnected short stories. What draws you to this form? What are you able to do with interconnected stories that you wouldn't be able to do in a traditional novel or in a short story collection?

Frankly, at least right now, I have no interest in writing novels. I am a creative polygamist—the idea of being in a monogamous relationship with one set of characters and one landscape (oh god, like the Welsh countryside) for years—sounds wretched. Perhaps when I'm older. I like dipping in and out of people's lives. I want to be there in the moment when something transformative happens, some truth is revealed, if not in the mind of the character, then hopefully in the mind of the reader. You can't do that over and over again in a novel—all those epiphanies going off like flashbulbs.

As for the "traditional" short story form, it doesn't appeal to me in the same way as interconnected stories, which possess for me the pleasures of a novel in that they feature a reappearing cast of characters, narrative through lines, and as the book progresses, the deepening exploration of central themes. Unlike in a novel where you have a central narrative, stories each have their own drama and I like puzzling together the various connections between the stories, be they in the characters or the landscape or the theme.

While each story is told from the point of view of a single narrator, as the stories accumulate, we see the way these women's lives overlap and echo one another's, whether they are aware of it or not. We see how in some cases they live in each other's imaginations and memory, and when they do, how they affect each other, knowingly or unknowingly.

What compelled you to write this book? Did you have specific goal you wanted to accomplish with *Blueprints for Building Better Girls*?

As a writer, I feel it's my job to say the thing everyone knows is true, but no one wants to say, either because they can't articulate it, it's too dangerous, or, if you want to use the language of Emily Post, "it's simply not done." In the case of this book I wanted to tap into the vast collective experiences of a certain segment of women—white and upper-middle class—from the 1970s to today, present their stories singularly and in contrast to each other, and tell the truth about what it means to be a woman in our culture.

The theme and structure of the book are like that of an etiquette book, or anti-etiquette book. However unlike in those books, the stories don't start with a question—*What do I do if I'm seated next to a boor at a dinner party?*—but with an archetypal female character: the slut, the good mom, the bad wife, the party girl, the anorexic, and subvert the reader's expectations of who they are. How at odds the reality of these women's lives are versus the labels we give them. So, each story is a reflection or response to the image we have of these women, and the messages the culture has given us over the last thirty years, and how they have informed our ideas about female identity.

The various points of view and voices provide the reader with intimate knowledge of a character's life while also showing them and their various personas through the lens of those around them. I wanted to challenge the reader to consider as they formulate opinions about these women—who later they will see from another angle in another story—why they judged them in a particular way, to have readers confront their own biases and prejudices.

Although there is pain and trauma in *Blueprints for Building Better Girls*, plenty of humor and hope shines through these women's perspectives. How did you manage to balance heartbreak, humor, and human connection in these stories?

My aim is to write, as truthfully and authentically as I can, about how human beings solve the problem of being alive. Humor is often born in the dark. In my experience, in times of trauma and crisis we employ humor as a shield to deflect pain, diffuse awkwardness, and protect ourselves. Or we use it to as a sword, to strike back at the world, to deliver stinging truths. Oscar Wilde said, "If you want to tell people the truth, make them laugh, otherwise they'll kill you." It's easiest to run your blade through the side of someone who is laughing. That's what my characters do—it's their voices I hear cracking jokes.

Humor helps disarm the reader, enables them let down their guard, so they'll follow me into a dark place. If I make them laugh they trust that I'll protect them when things get intense. There are moments where I want the reader to laugh at something they think they shouldn't laugh at, but want to, need to. I want to give them that catharsis. There is release in that. There is hope in that. *I'm not done in yet.* Sometimes you have to laugh or you'll die. The ability to laugh in the face of terrible trauma and pain is empowering, and you know what, it's human. We all do it. Part of why I write is to make people feel like they aren't alone in their experience.

The characters are linked in complex and subtle ways. How did you keep track of their various acquaintances and interconnected lives?

In the beginning before I was completely solid on the ways in which the characters were interrelated, where they overlapped in reality and virtually, those places where a landscape or location reappeared, I did what I often do, which is to ascribe a color to each character, and then laid the pages out on the floor. This way, laid out almost like a tapestry I can see the designs, places where lives are woven together, where characters appear and disappear, spot the snags in space and time.

Do you remember which character you invented first? Can you tell us which character you relate to most?

Heather was the first. I'm fascinated by the mythologies that spring up around certain girls—the mystery that surrounds them, and how at odds this fantasy can be with their reality. No one can control the way in which others perceive them yet each of us creates our own personal cosmology, a script that dictates to some degree how we see ourselves. In Heather's case, she's taken on mythic proportions as the school "slut" and it completely shapes her sense of identity. It seems fitting that her stories open and close the book. Because a large theme here is how the culture we grow up in, the experiences we have in our youth, shape our identity and sexuality.

I don't know that there's one character I relate to most, perhaps B. in "Why Aren't You Dead Yet?" At least on paper because I came to New York, a little starry-eyed, to be a starving artist (I succeeded) and can relate to the pain that comes when a very intense friendship ends. It's like a death without a body to mourn.

However, the character that cracked the book open for me was Bender, the out-of-control party girl. Sometimes a story starts with an image, or an idea, or as with "Out of the Blue and into the Black," it's a character. It was the voice of this young woman, asking me over and over again, "Why don't you write about me? C'mon, why not? What's wrong with me?" And I'd think, "I don't want to. I don't want to write about you because you are a ridiculous person."

After a while it occurred to me what a hypocrite I was being. What was I doing? I was judging this girl, denying her experience, writing her off (as it were) as not worthy of my attention. Which is what everybody else in the world does. I thought if I didn't take her seriously, who would? That was when I realized that all the women I'd been writing about—because it was always a book populated by women—were those who the culture had labeled. The stories were about identity: how these women were struggling against the strait-jacket of stereotype, and the costs of labeling women, not only to the women themselves but to society as a whole.

How did you come up with the title _Blueprints for Building Better Girls_? Is there an actual 1960s etiquette book by that wonderfully alliterative name? If you could give these diverse, complex characters just one piece of advice, what would it be?

No, there is not an actual etiquette book with that title. But I do collect etiquette and female self-help books. My first was Betty Cornell's _Glamour Guide for Teens_. (I'd kill to have a copy of that book today.) I find them fascinating because they not only nakedly reveal what the culture values but clearly dictate the rules one must obey if they are to be considered cultured gentlefolk and not harlots and knuckle-dragging ingrates. For women, who pay a much larger price for not conforming to the rules society lays down, the stakes are high. In some cases, these books are survival manuals.

The title comes in part from a writing workshop I took years ago with an author of whom I was most enamored. The feeling, however, was not mutual. The problem with my work, the teacher began, was that my female characters weren't role models; the stories themselves weren't instructive in terms of teaching future generations of young women how to live their lives. She truly hated me, and my work. It was a huge blow for me. I'd thought this teacher was going to save me, make me a real writer, and I was wrong. I gave her way too much power, I shut down, I couldn't write. It took a long time to get myself straightened out.

As to advice, I'd say: Don't let anyone tell you who you are.

These stories are populated by women who are vulnerable yet dangerous to themselves and each other. What do you think is distinctive about female friendships?

I don't think being vulnerable and being dangerous are at odds with each other. I think sometimes we only become "dangerous," and by that I mean assert our power, when we are pushed to do so. In our culture women are rewarded for being "good," meaning nonthreatening, accommodating, playing nice, and are punished when they aren't, derided as sluts, bitches, hysterics, or flat-out crazy. In reality women are complicated creatures and so are our friendships.

From the very beginning we are told that we must have a best friend (and we will sign all our letters to each other, *Your BFF . . .*) or a bunch of best friends that we'll grow old with, racing our wheelchairs through the parking lot of IHOP. While lovers will come and go, your girlfriends are supposed to be forever, which is preposterous. Why the double standard? We are constantly evolving. It's only logical that friendships end; some die long slow deaths, others blow up in a shower of psychic sparks; some friendships by nature are destined to be fleeting. What is clear is that we forge new bonds in times of transition, especially during major life ones. Women bond over the ways we are alike, and intimacy is our currency. We get close by sharing our innermost thoughts and feelings. As such, we make ourselves vulnerable to being hurt in a way that a lover—with whom we sometimes don't share much more than a bed—can't.

That desire for intimacy and acceptance is what is at play in several stories, among them "Elephant," which focuses on the friendship between Paige and Charlotte. Because we possess so much personal, intimate knowledge about each other we are uniquely qualified to emotionally annihilate each other.

You dedicate *Blueprints for Building Better Girls* to your "adored mother and sister." What kinds of role models have they been to you? Were you "cursed with a happy childhood" like Beth in "Aren't You Dead Yet?" (p. 162)

I was in some ways cursed with a happy childhood in that I had stable happy parents who were more in love than any couple I've ever seen, and who tirelessly encouraged us in our vast pursuits, from trampoline to drawing to horseback riding to guitar.

My mother is a master of balancing her family life with her creative life, which when I was growing up included painting and cofounding and running a small catering business. My parents were very keen on traveling. That was how they chose to spend their money. Every other summer, when my sister and I were in school, we'd rent a car and drive around Europe for a month. Later they'd get into the hard stuff—Africa, Asia, South America. When they came back, they'd tell us what it was like hanging out with the bushmen in Papua New Guinea, taking school supplies to kids in Botswana, drinking chicha in a village in Peru. She taught me that we are citizens of the world and that no one is beneath you. Everyone has a story and a right to tell it.

My sister and I have always been very close. My first memory is of seeing her in her crib, which feels appropriate as I imagine she will be there at my end. She has always wanted to be a teacher. Her specialty is working with children with autism and severe developmental difficulties in the public school system. She is passionate about what she does. She finds ways of reaching kids that other people can't. She is dogged in her desire to educate these children. She is tireless and boundlessly patient, she possesses strengths I can only marvel at. It's a terribly difficult job, emotionally, physically, forget that she does it for very little money. Whenever anyone says, "How can you do it?" she says, "They didn't ask to be born this way."

So, yes. I'm spoiled. Growing up I always knew that no matter what happened to me, no matter what trouble I got into, my family was always there for me, and thus I'd always be okay. I'd never be alone.

You wear many hats in the literary world, as an editor, book columnist, and fiction writer. How do you think your work at *Tin House*, *Vanity Fair*, and *The Paris Review* has shaped your own fiction?

First, being in this world in the way that I am has given me a great appreciation for how hard it is to write, and write well. I have also been privileged to work alongside and learn from some of the best and most inspiring editors—like George Plimpton and Graydon Carter—and writers in the world.

I don't think being an editor or book columnist or nonfiction writer has shaped what I write about, but it certainly has shaped my feelings about when and how I release my work into the arena of critical opinion.

In the early stages of writing, I don't think about the end game. By that I mean I'm not thinking about how an editor, or anyone for that matter, is going to read my work. It isn't until much later, when I'm editing—full of the knowledge that if I don't do my job well—if the writing feels facile or sloppy, inauthentic or overly clever, not only will the reader/editor never engage with my world, they will reject it—and rightly so. Thus, I think, I tend to be very hard on myself. I am reluctant to send out stories unless I feel they are perfect, or as perfect as I can make them.

Many of the women in your fiction are juggling family and career at the same time. Do you think you've struck a balance between your writing and your home life?

A balance? Let's say a delicate balance. I'm extraordinarily lucky in that I have a partner who is wholly my partner. He carries as much of the domestic load—if not more sometimes—than I do.

I've tried to tailor my work life to fit the realities of my home life. I go to the studio when my kids go to school. I try to end my workday when they do. Unless I'm slammed by a terrible deadline, I try not to work on weekends. (You'll notice there is a lot of "trying" in there.) That said, if I'm completely honest, the reality is that when I can write, really write, on the occasion it's going well, it's all I want to do. And when I'm writing, and writing well, life is good, and I'm certainly nicer to be around.

The girls and women of these stories seem to fit some of the archetypes of femininity, though their lives turn out to be more complicated than they seem at first. Did you fit any stereotypes when you were in high school or college?

In my mind, no, although it's a given that there is no faster or efficient way to literally put a person in their place than to reduce them to a stereotype. As we're talking about high school, the Thunderdome of natural selection, I'm sure I was. Although going on appearance alone—a whirlwind of costume changes, hair colors and styles, and personas—I suppose it wasn't always easy to pin me down. I never fit in with just one crowd. I floated between cliques, perhaps because as a writer I was curious about people unlike me and could empathize with many different sorts. What has always been consistent though, and the short answer, I suppose, is that I've always been the short girl with smart mouth, drawing in her notebook and talking to her neighbor.

In the last story, "I'm Only Going to Tell You This Once," Heather tells the story of her past as "Jane," the center of a love triangle. What inspired you to have this character tell her own story to her son, as a lesson in love?

I believe everyone has a story or two that has informed our sense of self, which we see as defining who we are, or why we are the way we are. From the first story in which Heather is labeled a slut, we see how this experience has shaped her ability to trust and get close to people, and why she is the woman, wife, and mother she is in "I'm Only Going to Tell You This Once." Heather needs to be known. She loves her son and feels more bonded to him than she has ever felt to anyone. So when he falls in love with a girl—a girl she recognizes as not being unlike the girl she once was, a girl who in her mind was capable of destroying lives (something she has at once taken pride in, and been ashamed of)—she can't bear it. She is afraid for him. She doesn't want her son to know the "truth" but she needs to tell him. In part to protect him, but also because, on some level, she's proud of the power she felt she once had. She loves him so much—and trusts him more than she's ever trusted anyone—that she wants to give him what she feels is the truest part of her but is too ashamed to claim it as her own.

What can your readers look forward to next? Will you continue to write short stories, or strike out in a new form?

I'm listening for the voices; wherever they go I shall follow.